D1571784

The Sixth Realm

Part 1

MICHAEL CHATFIELD

Cover Art by Jan Becerikli Garrido
Jacket Design by Caitlin Greer
Interior Layout & Design by Caitlin Greer

Paperback ISBN: 978-1-989377-80-2-
Hardcover ISBN: 978-1-989377-82-6

Back to the Old Ways

Emmanuel Fayad stood outside Aditya's office. King's Hill Outpost was in various phases of construction. Walls and buildings rose from the ground almost daily; building with mages on hand was a simple task.

Aditya had drawn the outpost lords around Beast Mountain Range to his side, giving them positions suiting their abilities and placing their outposts under the control of King's Hill.

Emmanuel inspected the hem of his robe's cuff, glancing up as the rough wooden door groaned open.

Pan Kun, Lord Aditya's guard captain and leader of the newly formed Beast Mountain Range Army, walked out.

"Sorry for keeping you, Outpost Lord Fayad. We weren't expecting you. Lord Aditya will see you now."

Pan Kun stood aside, holding the door open for Fayad.

"Thank you." Fayad walked into the room.

Aditya stood up from his desk with the confidence of a man who controlled his own fate and the fate of others.

"Lord Aditya, thank you for agreeing to meet with me." Fayad cupped his hands to Aditya, making to bow.

"Lord Fayad, there is no need. You asked to meet with me, and I am happy to do so." Aditya smiled, stopping him from bowing.

"Please, tell me what worries you." Aditya gestured for him to take a seat next to the large windows overlooking King's Hill Outpost.

"It is growing fast." Fayad gazed outside.

"Things are much slower to build than destroy. We are just laying some hopeful groundwork," Aditya said.

Emmanuel sat on the couch opposite, watching Fayad's every move. "And what are your plans for the outpost moving forward?"

Aditya chuckled. "I'm not the leader of King's Hill. That will be voted on today. How should I know what the future will bring?"

Emmanuel sized up the man in front of him. Aditya might seem like a simple man on the surface, but he was a true outpost lord. Who knew just how far his reach spread?

"If the conditions are right, Shadowridge will pledge fealty to you."

"What would you want in return?" Aditya's words were sharp, his gaze unwavering.

"Equality."

"Oh?" Aditya rubbed his chin.

"While you are the interim council leader of the outpost lords right now and the figurehead of King's Hill Outpost, you need as many votes as possible at the meeting today to confirm you as the Beast Mountain Range's true leader. I am sure you could carry out your plans without the position, but it would be much harder. I would pledge an alliance if I thought you just wanted the leadership of Beast Mountain Range, but I pledge my fealty because I know that no matter what comes to pass, you will own the Beast Mountain Range completely."

Aditya raised his eyebrow.

Emmanuel took the silence as permission to continue. "You have alliances with all the major outpost leaders and have settled them into positions they enjoy. They have become pillars for the future Beast Mountain Range nation. Even if you get replaced as Lord of King's Hill, you control a powerful faction that listens and obeys. Possibly even an army that thinks the same."

"And what do you want to be equal?" Aditya asked, his words smooth.

Emmanuel smiled. Aditya hadn't denied his plans or acknowledged them either. He cleared his throat and met Aditya's gaze head on. "There is one path ahead—Beast Mountain Range. Unify or control the outpost lords. Control the outposts, and we control the range. A new nation would be a problem to the outside nations, but a trading conglomerate spread across a wide area, well, that is something they can live with. You have many lords, those who are skillful fighters and good administrators, but you have few who have powerful trade connections. I hope that I might offer my services to work under you to facilitate trade between the outposts and the surrounding kingdoms at large."

"In return?"

"Shadowridge is a trader clan and will take posts based on merit. We do not want people saying we bribed our way in." Emmanuel cut the air with his hand.

"Some will say you did."

"That is for them to worry about, so as long as the people who matter know the truth. I will place Shadowridge under King Hill's management, with the same conditions you gave to the other lords who have joined you."

"Joined me? They have given up their outpost positions for the benefit of all of us." A sly smile spread across Aditya's face, disappearing as soon as it had arrived. "And what brought this on?"

Aditya didn't seem shocked or surprised, merely interested.

"I could say many things: your wealth, your tools, your military. Your shining personality."

Aditya snorted.

"You have Beast Mountain Range in the palm of your hand. You are direct. Your plans might work in the shadows, but you are not one of those people who offer peace in one hand and hold a dagger in the other. You're smart and you have the strength to back it up. In the Ten Realms, does one need more than that?"

Aditya's expression was unreadable.

Finally, he pulled out a mana-imbued paper that had been written into a contract and put it on the table between them. The price of such a piece of paper would make many balk in the First Realm.

"Making sure I don't talk to others?" Emmanuel said as Aditya handed him a pen.

"One cannot be too careful."

Emmanuel nodded and signed the contract and Ten Realms binding him.

"Pan Kun tells me that your military is one of the most dedicated and well equipped. They will need to train with my recruits. We will treat your traders as our own—fifty percent less tax and security while on our lands. I will need your help to manage trade. You are possibly the best manager the Fayad family has seen in three generations. Also, the outposts you secretly control will need to join. Everything else will rely on a person's abilities."

Fayad smiled.

"Also, Lord Fayad, if I learn you wish to betray me or the Beast Mountain Range, trust me when I say not even ascending the realms will free you from my reach."

"I understand." Fayad opened his hands, his secrets had been laid bare.

There was a knock at the door, and it opened to reveal one of Aditya's guards, a woman.

"Lord Aditya, the meeting to elect the leader of King's Hill is beginning soon."

"Ah, Evernight. Yes, okay, well, I guess that we should head on over." Aditya rose and held out his hand to Fayad. "We'll get the contract written up and completed tonight."

"Understood." Emmanuel shook Aditya's hand. The guards closed the door as Emmanuel left the office and walked through to the grand reception area where his guards waited.

They moved with him, crossing the headquarters building. The lords, ladies or the envoys of outpost leaders moved aside as they strode past the main entrance and moved with the rest into the main hall.

There were two tables, creating a stretched D shape with the back of the D being higher than the curve. Behind the high table were three empty chairs.

A silent reminder of Aditya's ambition he will not be satisfied with just being a lord of the Beast Mountain Range, he'll command it all.

The main hall filled quickly, with people taking their positions at the U-shaped table. Emmanuel greeted some people he knew.

The doors closed, sealing them inside as Old Quan sitting at the head of the table rapped his knuckles on the dense wood, drawing silence and attention as he stood. "Well, I think I speak for all of us when I say that it is about time we figured out who will lead the King's Hill Outpost and the outposts under its command," Old Quan said. "First, nominations. You can only nominate someone other than yourself, and one cannot vote for themselves. With that in mind, I nominate Lord Aditya of Vermire."

The room grew quiet as people glanced around. Old Quan took his seat.

"I nominate Lord Gerroud," another lord said.

There were two other nominations. Emmanuel glanced at Aditya, who quietly sat in his seat in the middle of the table, gazing around the room with a simple smile.

Does he know the outcome already?

"Are those all the nominations?" Old Quan looked around the table. No one wanted to raise other names.

"Very well. Then we shall vote. Raise your hand for the person you want to be the ruler of the King's Hill Outpost. "For Lord Aditya."

Old Quan raised his hand. He scanned the room as others solemnly followed his lead.

Fayad gazed around. Raised hands were quickly joined by several more.

"Good! Over fifty percent agree. Lord Aditya, you are now the head of the King's Hill Outpost for three years."

Lord Aditya stood and bowed to the people at the table. "I thank you for your confidence in me."

Emmanuel peeked at the sour faces around the table. It seemed as if he had played his cards right; Lord Aditya had left nothing to chance. Now, the decision was plain to the other outpost lords. They would either join them or become potential threats of those who would wish to take Beast Mountain Range.

He failed to notice that Aditya made no move to sit in any of the three chairs behind him.

"Well, that went smoothly." Evernight shifted her scabbard away from her uniform to avoid sitting on it.

"Lord of King's Hill Outpost," Aditya said, his hands behind his back as he studied a wall map of the Beast Mountain Range.

"Ruler of the Beast Mountain Range," Pan Kun said.

Aditya chuckled and turned to face his two compatriots. "Pan Kun, tell Miss Evernight what you just told me."

"We had a windfall. The Gelabo Kingdom has had poor harvests and little coin for the last few years. The peasants will come to work the farms as long as they are safe, and we should get another two thousand mercenaries. Seems the Gelabo have not been paying their bills."

"Militaries in peacetime are an expense few kingdoms will support." Aditya shook his head. "Make sure there are no spies in their ranks or anyone who plans to use us as a steppingstone."

"You're as paranoid as me now. Taught you well." Evernight winked.

Pan Kun snorted as Aditya rolled his eyes.

"Just got elected leader, and I'm getting my balls busted by my *guard*. I think we should get a re-vote!"

"What did Emmanuel Fayad want?"

"Trading rights. A possible position dealing with the Range's trade. Said we'd get him a contract by tonight," Aditya said. "On the side of trading, we'll diversify the industries of the outposts under our direct control. If we can create and sell goods instead of acting as a transaction point for materials, our profits will increase. We gain crafters and coin, hand in hand."

"So, do you approve of Lord Fayad?" Evernight curled her elbow around the back of her chair.

"I think he's a smart man, and I have you to assure me and make sure he isn't smarter than me." Aditya raised an eyebrow.

"Don't worry, that's all part of the job. I might be able to get some crafting teachers to visit King's Hill and teach people a thing or two."

"Good. We need a market hub for the surrounding area. If we have crafters, then traders and buyers will rise in number. Traders have a lot of say in kingdoms and empires."

"Here is a survey." Evernight took out a map from her storage ring and threw it to Aditya. "Your army will never get lost with this. I marked locations with resources that could be mined or cultivated."

"I guess I should stop being stunned at this point."

"Ah, well, it is nice to see you all flustered." Evernight smiled and continued to read her reports.

"Anything from the kingdoms and other places along our border?" Aditya asked.

"They are waiting to see what happens. As you've said, the Beast Mountain Range will need a lot of funds and people to maintain it. Right now, you are loose sand. If you can entice the traders and pull the outpost leaders together, they will think twice about attacking."

Aditya bit the inside of his cheek. "I have a… proposal."

"What?"

"Build a sect." Before Evernight could cut him off, Aditya continued, "The outpost lords will work together, but the people of Beast Mountain Range don't know us. Most of the people who were forced to move lived in the outposts we were fighting. With a sect, we can teach people how to craft—and fight. We give them security and opportunity, and they'll give us their loyalty."

Evernight was quiet, mulling over the idea.

"I don't see an issue with it. Are there any other plans you want to pursue?"

"Self-reliance—raising crops and food in some of the safer outposts with farmable land so we don't need to deal with the fluctuating food prices. If we have enough crops, we can sell them to the different cities and kingdoms. They're always looking for more food. We also need to draw the traders back. They were scared off with all the fighting. Traders are Beast Mountain Range's lifeblood; we need them to ship our goods in and out."

"I can help on both counts. I know some farmers who should be able to help to teach the basics. I'll contact the Trader's Guild about increasing trade, but you best have some products or coin to entice them."

"Don't worry, I'm working to finish those roads and create camps near resource locations. It won't be long until a new Beast Mountain Range nation rises," Aditya said.

Evernight peeked at Pan Kun and Aditya. "I, and those above me, are pleased with what you have done here already."

She took out a book and four vials, putting them on the table. "This is a Body Cultivation manual and will teach you about Body Cultivation. Take the potions to the healing house, and they'll help you temper your bodies. I have a feeling you'll need Stamina in the coming days."

Pan Kun and Aditya stood, cupping their hands and bowing deeply. "Thank you, Miss Evernight."

"Only use the book between the two of you. In time, you'll gain access to much more."

Erik scratched the growing scruff on his face as he rode Gilly while Rugrat, who was still growing out his own facial hair, sat on George's back. Special Team One spread out around them, babysitting them as they rode. They were in the forests to the west of Vuzgal, traveling along the path they had taken from Aberdeen.

Erik checked over his stat sheet.

Name: Erik West		
Level: 59	Race: Human	
Titles:		
From the Grave II		
Blessed by Mana		
Dungeon Master III		
Reverse Alchemist		
Poison Body		
Fire Body		
City Lord		
Earth Soul		
Mana Reborn		
Strength: (Base 54) +41	950	
Agility: (Base 47) +72	654	
Stamina: (Base 57) +25	1230	
Mana: (Base 27) +79	1166	
Mana Regeneration: (Base 30) +61	73.80/s	
Stamina Regeneration: (Base 72) +59	27.20/s	

He had lost almost five stat points. The quests and Body Cultivation gave more stat increases than leveling up ten or even a hundred times. When he reached level fifty-nine, he had put all five points into Stamina Regeneration. If he were ever injured, he would need Stamina to survive. Still, the jump was so small.

Erik checked his latest quest to stave off boredom.

Quest: City Leader 2

You have unlocked the **City Leader Quest Line**. Grow your territory and your population, and protect what you have.

Requirements:

Have a permanent population of at least 100,000 for 3 months.

Rewards:

+10,000,000 EXP

Upgrades to defensive formation. Attackers stats decreased by 1%

Able to create (2) village cornerstones.

"A hundred thousand people for three months. Looks like it's a slow growing quest. Increased the defensive buffs for Vuzgal nicely. Just like the dungeon, we need to be within the city to get the updates."

Erik leaned forward and scratched Gilly's neck. She tilted her head so he could give her a good rub.

"Doesn't really affect us that much. Also, is your Healing Skill still increasing?"

"Yeah, slowly. You know, just need more time to work on it. Luckily, I have a lack of patients. I have dealt with combat wounds nearly this entire time, but there are a lot of things with healing that goes beyond being stabbed, shot, or hit with magic." Erik fell silent.

"What is it?" Rugrat asked.

"Skill levels—they're not simple or linear. In games, the more you do one thing, the higher it grows. Sometimes you have to create something powerful to grind out more experience. That relates to the Novice, Apprentice, and partly to the Journeyman—but not the Expert. It is not just about repeating and recreating. It's like the Ten Realms wants to test how much you know."

"The more you show what you can do and the higher your ability in different aspects of the same skill, the greater your skill level will be."

"Look at the brain on you." Erik grinned.

Rugrat flipped him the bird and shrugged. "You have a point. Figuring out these damn skill levels is a pain in the ass."

Niemm, the leader of Special Team One, rode his panther over to them. Erik and Rugrat sat up as George and Gilly's eyes opened completely, the four of them giving off a faint pressure.

"I think we've found it," Niemm said.

"Putting that Dungeon Hunter title to good use," Rugrat said.

"Might as well," Niemm said.

Rugrat had given him a Dungeon Hunter title, and Erik had passed one onto Gong Jin, the second in command of Special Team Two. Now, each team leader and second in command had the title. With the people on protection detail coming close to finishing their training, it wouldn't be long until there was some new blood on the special teams. When that happened, Storbon and Gong Jin would become special team leaders, like Niemm and Roska.

Erik and Rugrat had been cooped up, working on their crafting skills and fighting techniques, and had decided they should deal with the dungeon they had noticed when they were running from Aberdeen.

"Well, lead on. Let's see what we're dealing with," Erik said.

Niemm clicked his tongue, and took the lead with his mount.

"Nice to be doing something for once. I've read so many books on formations and smithing, I think my head might just pop," Rugrat said to Erik, his eyes almost glowing in the dim light as he studied the area with his rifle in hand.

"Yeah, I know how you feel. I've been stuck fighting to increase my Alchemy and was just able to get it to level seventy-three." Erik sighed, taking a glance at his skill.

Skill: Alchemy
Level: 73 (Journeyman)
Able to identify 1 effect of the ingredient.
Ingredients are 5% more potent.

"Two more and you'll be an Expert," Rugrat said.

"Yeah, learning Flame Puppeteer increased my control and speed. I found some Expert-level pills among the information we collected from Vuzgal—Masterful Healing and Ascendant. The Masterful Healing pill helps recover Stamina and health over a period of time. It can bring someone back from the brink without needing to look after them. The Ascendant pill is a training aid that can assist in Mana Cultivation."

"What about that Age Rejuvenation concoction for Elder Lu Ru?"

"I haven't been able to make it. My control is better with the Flame Puppeteer, but taking apart century-old Lidel leaves is hard. I'm just looking to hone my crafting. Maybe later I'll get inspiration." Erik shrugged.

"Well, shit, I'm just happy we're hunting a dungeon instead of being cooped up doing paperwork!"

"There it is." Niemm halted and pointed between trees to a dark space between boulders.

Tian Cui, another member of Special Team One and their resident assassin, appeared from the shadows. "We checked inside. It looks like the entrance is clear."

"Damn, sneaking out like that, nearly browned my undies," Rugrat said.

Tian Cui smiled.

Niemm pulled out his sound transmission device. "Deni, Yuli, and Lucinda, keep watch on things out here while we check out this dungeon. Don't want anyone creeping up on us."

Erik didn't hear the reply before Niemm started talking again.

"The rest of you meet up at the entrance to the dungeon. Yao Meng, you have point. Setsuko, right behind him."

They got off their mounts as it would be hard to fight with them in the tight quarters of the dungeon.

Gilly and George grew smaller and rested on their master's shoulders.

Erik absently scratched the back of Gilly's head as Rugrat threw a monster core. George raced off in his miniature form to chase after it with an excited look on his face.

Finding the monster core, his head returned to its normal size, and he threw the monster core down his throat with a pleased look.

Gilly bit Erik's fingers. With her own temperings on the Earth floor, she had increased her Strength. The browns of her body were almost as bright as the blues.

"Hey," Erik complained. He'd reached the Body Like Sky Iron stage, but her little teeth still bit into his skin.

She let out a shrill noise, not letting his finger go, a playful light in her eyes.

"Little Miss." Erik took out a monster core. She released his hand as he tossed it up. She moved, and her head grew larger to catch it and then became normal size again.

The change in weight barely registered for Erik. He hadn't seen the limits of his Strength since he had reached Body Like Sky Iron. He'd been restraining himself in his fights with Rugrat, not wanting to maim or kill him. They didn't go all out in training or they might critically injure the other.

Erik stroked the appeased Gilly, his heart and head troubled. He and Rugrat had always joked that they were fight junkies. *Are we?*

The rest of the special team appeared from the forest, still on their panthers. Each of their beasts showed different markings as part of their bloodline awakened or their masters had increased their Strength with feeding them attribute-aligned monster cores and ingredients.

Erik peeked at the people with them.

Storbon—a gravely wounded boy when they had met him in the First Realm, where there was no hope for him to recover—was now a man. Erik had worked hard to heal him, and he had followed Erik and Rugrat, becoming one of the strongest people in Alva.

Setsuko Ket's father, Fehim, was the leader of the farmers in Alva; he was one of the famed rangers-turned-sharpshooters and sported a repeating rifle. Yao Meng was a generalist and now the resident explosive Expert after spending his time with the alchemists and Han Wu of Special Team Two. Yawen was one of the quieter members, an ace with a rifle and bow. Niemm led them all, a sword and shield melee fighter and professional gunfighter.

Acting as a scouting screen was Deni, a sharpshooter; Yuli, an elementalist mage; and Lucinda, a beast tamer.

Yao Meng and Setsuko dismounted and moved toward the dungeon entrance, their weapons ready as they headed between the rocks and into the darkness.

Erik cast Night Vision on himself as the group followed them. They squeezed between the rocks, finding a path with tree roots, dirt, and rocks leading down. They entered a small room where there was one other doorway but no lights. All of them had their rifles out and ready.

Dirt and rocks made the floor uneven, and there was more of it around the entrance to the dungeon. It looked as if something had dug its way in or had clawed its way out.

They followed behind Setsuko and Yao Meng, came to an intersection, and turned right.

The dungeon was formed from damp stone with moss on the walls. The ceiling was high but unfinished with rough rocks.

They passed alcoves carved into the walls and found another intersection. Seeing a dead-end ahead, they turned right. Yao Meng stepped out, and Niemm yanked him backward.

"Tripwire." He pointed at the ground.

Tian Cui moved up, traced the tripwire, and disabled the trap.

"What kind of trap was it?" Niemm asked.

"Not sure, but probably mechanical."

"Keep a lookout," Niemm said for the benefit of those in front.

They pushed forward, taking different corridors. They didn't run into any creatures, just two dead-ends. Finally, they reached another room with doors wide enough for four people.

Yao Meng slammed through the doors. Setsuko, Niemm, and Storbon came in behind him. Erik saw three large, green-skinned humanoid creatures trudging around the room, sloshing through the ankle-deep dirty water, searching for food.

Swamp monsters were brainless and only cared about consuming and spreading their rot.

The group who entered fired, and it was over in just seconds. The swamp monsters had been surprised and hadn't had time to react.

Still, with their powerful bodies, they took several hits before they collapsed.

The team took the time to search the room and loot the swamp monsters' bodies.

Earth-grade iron ingot x3

Mace of Fortitude

Mortal mana stones x7

"Not a bad haul," Rugrat said.

"Bit lackluster compared to what we're used to," Erik said.

"It would be a pretty good haul for any other team or group in the Fourth Realm randomly exploring a dungeon."

"True. I guess my sense of scale is a little skewed."

"Well, the last dungeon we captured did come with a city attached to it."

Erik laughed and glanced over to Niemm. "So, where to next?"

Niemm used his Dungeon Sense to scan the area. "It should be in that direction." Niemm pointed to a wall with a door. "Tian Cui, you're on point. Form up. Let's get moving."

Yao Meng gave the door a swift kick, sending it flying off its hinges and crashing into the corridor ahead.

Tian Cui moved forward. Erik heard a noise coming from the hallway.

Humanoid creatures with skin hanging off them and eyes like hot coals charged toward Tian Cui.

She took a knee and shot her rifle. Yawen, who was behind her, fired over her. Erik watched, unable to shoot for fear of hitting his people.

The ghouls were dying, but there were a lot of them, and they were fast.

Niemm yelled and charged forward with a shield. Tian Cui and Yao Meng lowered their weapons as Niemm hit the creatures, tossing them back in a shockwave.

One avoided the attack and leaped, grabbing onto Niemm's shield as they clawed at him and tried to bite his hand.

"Pull back into the room. Create a firing line," Niemm yelled, his attack having made breathing room for the rest of the team.

The others retreated as Niemm pulled a sword out from his storage ring and stabbed it into the ghoul's eye, killing it. He backed up quickly as the other ghouls groaned and slumped over; they lethargically forced themselves to their feet.

Erik and Rugrat were part of the firing line with the rest of the team.

"Move!" Deni yelled.

Niemm turned and moved out of the way as Deni and the rest of the firing line shot into the hallway, bolts cutting down ghouls.

"Cease fire, cease fire!" Erik yelled. There was nothing left alive or even undead in the corridor—just a collection of tombstones.

Niemm sent Tian Cui and Yawen to scout the dungeon.

"Path ahead looks clear. No traps either," Tian Cui said.

"Let's move," Niemm said.

Erik looted the bodies, finding some Alchemy ingredients as well as mana stones and a pair of slippers. He was glad they had other alchemists now, and he didn't need to eat everything to understand the ingredients anymore. Erik shivered, thinking about the things he had eaten to identify their properties.

"Why the hell does a ghoul have a pair of slippers? Did it not want to get its footsie-wootsies dirty?"

"Footsie-wootsies?" Erik blinked at Rugrat.

"What?" He shrugged at the incredulous looks from everyone.

"Let's keep going," Niemm said.

They headed down the corridor and kicked open another door into a new room.

Storbon entered first. The floor started to split, and a dungeon core floated out of the ground.

"Check the room for traps first," Storbon said.

"Well, looks like we didn't need to do much," Rugrat said.

"Hmm," Erik said. It was a perfect dungeon raid, but he wanted to see more, do more, not just tag along.

"Got an arrow trap here." Yao Meng used a dagger to pull out the mechanism from between two rocks in the wall.

"Don't think we've got anything else in here," Storbon said after some minutes of searching.

"Well, then…" Rugrat walked up to the dungeon core, whistling as he input some commands. The dungeon core dropped into his hand as the dungeon shook and collapsed around them.

In a flash, they appeared at the entrance of the dungeon.

The ground changed as they peeked at where the dungeon had been.

Everyone stared at Rugrat, who was tossing up and catching the dungeon core.

"What did we get for loot?" Erik asked.

"Mechanical traps, scythes, arrow traps. We can create ghouls and swamp monsters and zombies and some creepy insects. Uh, we've got Mortal mana stones, about three hundred of them. And, uh-huh. Am I seeing this right?"

Master-level scribe's tools

With these tools, one will have an easier time creating Master-level prints.

Increased concentration

Effects are increased by 5% on Master-level items

20% on Expert-level items

60% on Journeyman-level items

Increases the chance of succeeding on one's project by 10%

"I'm sure the scribes will be pleased. Who would think that something like that would be out here?" Erik shrugged.

"What are you going to do with the dungeon core?" Storbon asked.

"Well, Alva is plenty strong; same with Vuzgal." Rugrat tossed it up in the air again and caught it.

"Why not the Adventurer's Guild?" Yao Meng asked.

"It'll give them somewhere to increase their people's Strength to take on the Willful Institute," Erik said.

"Niemm." Erik tossed the dungeon core.

Niemm grabbed it.

"Take this to Matt. He should have some training dungeon plans. Grab some mana-gathering and illusion formations to hide the dungeon. Am I missing anything?" Erik asked.

"What about weapons and armor at the low Journeyman level? A strike force?" Storbon asked.

"Recovery potions of different kinds," Tian Cui said.

"Spell scrolls for them to use when in dire need and support potions like Stealth, Detect Life, and Night Vision?" Yuli added.

"Books on fighting?" Setsuko said.

"Low grade defensive formations for the guild headquarters?" Deni asked.

"That should do it," Rugrat said.

"Niemm, once we get back, take half the team and run the core down to them," Erik said.

"Get to make my first dungeon." Niemm grinned.

"This fucking guy." Erik tilted his head at Niemm.

"Well, you know it *is* pretty fun to make a dungeon." Rugrat shrugged.

"Let's head back," Erik said.

They mounted up and headed back toward Alva. The roads to the west were dead; the fighting in Aberdeen was reaching its final stages, and refugees were fleeing to the east. It had worked out well for Vuzgal as the refugees stopped in the city, spending their coin before continuing or settling there to create a new home.

Along the eastern road, traders and other people were going to and from the Chaotic Lands stretched along the way, hoping to make their mark on Vuzgal.

As they rode, Erik patted Gilly, staring at the trees, the forest, and stars above. He felt stifled. He had been the one charging forward all the time; now he was protected and coddled. Fighting made him feel alive. Even with the dungeon, it was too easy.

The Fifth Realm was fun to watch, but everyone was competing to join academies. Erik didn't want to join some academy. He wanted to face challenges, fight beasts, and battle people who were as strong or stronger than him and win!

For the past several months, he had increased his Body and Mana Cultivation. He'd reached powerful heights, but his Alchemy had only inched up and his level progress was painfully slow.

Maybe it was time for himself and Rugrat to head off again on their own. A smile appeared at the corner of Erik's mouth and stretched across his face.

Rugrat breathed through his nose. He had sunk into a deep, almost meditative state as he looked through his scope on his old M40. He had loaned out the gun to the smiths so they could see how it worked and was put together to create the Mark One bolt-action rifles. They hadn't gone into mass production with the Mark One before the M2 semi-automatic rifle was created and then mass-produced.

A new M1A2, the second generation of the rifle, had since been created by the smiths. Using a larger round and sturdier materials, its power rivaled that of an anti-material rifle of Earth. They were passed out to sharpshooters and members of special teams.

Still, Rugrat had a special place in his heart for his M40.

Rugrat blinked slowly, everything under his control as he followed the movement that had caught his eye.

"Wind is picking up," Erik said beside Rugrat.

Rugrat clicked his tongue. His domain stretched over the barren mountain. He felt the slight change in the wind. His mind worked the calculations, adjusting for the variables.

"Movement, fourteen degrees," Erik said. "Range, fourteen hundred meters."

The wind rippled the camouflage tarp that hung over them.

The two men were like rocks as Erik checked the target area with his Ten Realms-modified ranging spotting scope.

Rugrat shifted his aim. "I have a brown tree, a small stream."

"Adjust upward. See that boulder with a chunk out of the side? To the left-hand side where the stream goes," Erik replied.

Rugrat made his scope create a "W" across the area, keeping his eyes fresh for any movement.

"Seen. Looks like a supersized bear," Rugrat said as he ran mental calculations. He changed the dials on his scope.

The bear cocked his head and sniffed the air, making sure there were no other beasts in the area. *Take your time, stay a while,* Rugrat coaxed the beast as he flicked off his safety. The wind changed, and Rugrat adjusted his point of aim. *That's a good mutated bear.*

It stopped shifting around and ducked its head to drink from the stream.

Rugrat cast a Piercing Shot on the custom round within the rifle's chamber. He breathed out as he squeezed the trigger.

The gun bucked and the round was sent flying, disturbing gravel and debris.

Rugrat worked the action, watching the target.

The bear stilled, tensed, and then collapsed with a spray of red on the ground.

"Good hit," Erik said, calm, emotionless.

Rugrat felt a tide of Experience rush over him as his notifications pinged.

"One kill." Erik pulled his eye away from the scope and glanced over to Rugrat, who was covered in the golden goodness of Experience.

"Damn. It is good to be a Master," Rugrat said.

"Shit, really?" Erik asked.

"Oh, hell yeah, buddy." Rugrat grinned as he raised his hand. Erik laughed, and the two of them High fived.

"Shit, if I can get Expert in marksman, I'll be happy. You'll get your Expert and Master-level reward in one. Looks like the information we got on crafting was right." Erik started to clean up his gear with his storage ring.

"Stupid, though. Even if we have the knowledge and abilities, we have to prove it to the Ten Realms. Shooting farther distances at smaller or tougher targets. The Ten Realms just needs us to demonstrate it. Have you figured out a way to do it for healing?"

"You think that it's annoying for your marksmen skills? Try healing. You can either grind out a lot of patients to prove your ability or take on a really bad case to heal them. It's twisted. You need to heal someone severely wounded to increase your skill, but, hell, you don't wish those kinds of injuries on anyone. Wish there was just a written test or questionnaire instead."

"Yeah, that's frustrating," Rugrat said as the duo walked back from their firing position.

"Done?" Niemm was waiting with the rest of the special team, watching over their two lords.

"Yup, send out the boys and girls. We got us a grizzly." Rugrat smiled.

"Well, did everything go well?" Niemm asked.

Rugrat grinned.

Erik sighed, checking his rifle. "He made it to Master-level marksman, with one damn shot. I'm up next. Let's see if I can't catch up."

It didn't take them long to get to the next firing position.

They set up their position, this time changing around who was shooter and who was spotter.

"All right, we'll do the left edge along that stream visible through the trees." Rugrat pointed.

"Got it."

"Right edge—that rock outcropping."

"Got it."

"Nice. From left to right. Cut down into sectors. Sector Alpha is from that stream to the hill, where that tree is."

"Across from where the stream bends?"

"Yeah."

"Tree on the hill. It looks like a dead evergreen?"

"You got it. From the brown evergreen, trace down the hill about four hundred meters out; there's some fallen trees piled up."

"Yeah, got an opening into the forest there. The roots are sticking up, and it's crushed some other trees," Erik said.

"Yeah, that's sector Bravo, and from there to the rock outcropping, that'll be sector Charlie. Rugrat moved to the side maneuvering rocks to get more comfortable. "You want me to break it down more?"

"No, should be okay. Remember, I'm not even a hundred percent on the right way to talk onto the target," Erik said.

"All right, we'll do this nice and easy. I'll do sector and range, then walk you closer to the target"

"Works with me," Erik said, lowering the rifle.

"Got any jerky?" Rugrat asked, tracing his binoculars right to left and then scanning up and down the other way to keep his eyes active.

"Should have." Erik checked his storage ring, pulling out jerky strips. "Here you are. Open up."

Rugrat opened his mouth, and Erik put the jerky between his teeth.

"Tanks," Rugrat said, chewing on it.

"No worries, man." Erik sipped from his drinking tube and chewed on his own jerky. He raised the rifle, checking his sectors and movement between them, and adjusted his rifle bag and position.

They laid in silence as several small creatures passed their field of fire.

"I got something a bit bigger. Left limit of sector Alpha, five hundred and-fifty meters. About ten mils to the right. Sector B, range five-fifty."

"Got it."

"Go to glass."

Erik looked through the scope. "Target is a gray, deer-looking creature. Opening in the trees. Heading to the stream's edge."

"Good. Check your parallax and mil."

Erik studied the creature, thinking of the other animals he knew the internal structure of. He picked out a perfect target and started taking up the slack in the trigger.

"Ready."

"Left, point six."

He fired, breaking the silence.

Erik kept his scope on the target.

The deer-like creature raised his head just as the round went through his ribs.

"Good hit."

Skill: Marksman

Level: 82 (Expert)

Long-range weapons are familiar in your hands. When aiming, you can zoom in x2.0. 15% increased chance for a critical hit. When aiming, your agility increases by 20%.

Upon advancing into the Expert level of marksman, you will be rewarded with one randomly selected item related to this skill.

You have received the *Eye of True Flight Technique* book
+10,000,000 EXP

Skill: Stealth

Level: 68 (Journeyman)

When in stealth, your senses are sharpened by 5%.

Movements are 15% quieter.

Upon advancing into the Journeyman level of Stealth, you will be rewarded with one randomly selected item related to this skill.

You have received the *Silent Breathing, Unheard Footsteps* book
+100,000 EXP

12,548,136/86,100,000 EXP till you reach Level 60

"Not even a single point of Experience from the actual kill. Creatures are too low level here," Erik said.

"But we can still use our skills on them. Nice hit, by the way. Should be good eating. Let's bag those kills and get back," Rugrat said.

Adventurer's Guild Mobilizes

The Adventurer's Guild boardroom was surprisingly full of all the branch heads sitting around the table.

"What is this about?" Derrick shifted his twin rapiers so they wouldn't get caught in the chair as he lazed back and rested his booted feet on the table, his cloth shirt falling open.

"Will you cover up!" Joan crossed her arms. She looked like a cute younger sister, if one disregarded her beast-hide armor, array of daggers—oh, and the large, black bow on her back. "Did your shirt just happen to lose all of its buttons?"

"To bring all the branch heads together, it must be something big," Kim Cheol spoke slowly. He was a larger man with a kind-looking face, wearing armor that covered his entire body. His helmet had tusks on it, making him look like a boar. He rested his hand on his helmet on the table.

"Still so noisy," Stephan said. The thin man looked like he belonged in a library or academy, not in a mercenary guild.

Derrick's gaze slid to Emilia, who wore her armor like Kim Cheol. But instead of looking like the iron war boar, she resembled a paladin.

"Pull those eyes back, Derrick," she said, her glare locking on him.

"Just wanting to see if you'd like to test your sword and shield against my blades." Derrick's smile widened as his lazy eyes seemed to show life.

"Wouldn't want to hurt that pretty face of yours," Emilia said.

"Oh, come on."

"I'd be interested." A woman appeared beside Derrick, testing her curved dagger. A scar ran down the side of her face, and she wore a leather mask that covered her nose and mouth. Her hair pulled back tightly, and black, flexible armor covered her form.

"Lin Lei," Stephan said as he flipped his page.

She rippled before appearing behind Stephan. Even wearing a mask, one could tell she was pouting.

Derrick made to open his mouth and then closed it.

"Even Derrick can't beat Lin Lei," Joan said and winked at her.

Lin Lei's cheeks lifted in a smile.

"There are plenty of others to fight out there," Kim Cheol said, calming Derrick's pride.

"Seems you're getting along well." The door opened as Blaze and Jasper entered the room. Blaze was middle-aged, which had only seemed to hone his Strength, adding an edge to him. Before being the leader of Alva, he was a knight for most of his life. Once Erik and Rugrat became the leaders, he had returned to the fight. The Adventurer's Guild had come under his care. He helped people develop from trainees into adventurers who were able to spread their name throughout the cities and routes they traveled, and they became the eclectic group of branch heads who filled the conference room now.

Jasper, on the other hand, was a younger man who always looked as if he had everything under control as he dealt with the madhouse that was the Adventurer's Guild.

All the branch heads stood and bowed, even Derrick.

Blaze and Jasper nodded and took their seats at the head of the long conference table. Jasper took out large tomes from his storage ring and tossed them to the branch heads.

Lin Lei sat in a seat already, attentive.

Emilia opened the large book. "Yes," she said.

The words on the pages seemed to burn through the book, turning into a stream of light that shot out from the book to between Emilia's brows. The book fell apart and turned to dust as the stream of light dimmed.

The others did the same, assimilating what was stored within.

Derrick blinked a few times after he had finished and rubbed his head, thinking on everything he had just received. *We're finally going to war?* His eyes snapped open.

Stephan spoke first. "Alva has agreed to support us against the Willful Institute?"

All of them had gone to Alva to hone their skills, accepting oaths that had made them people of Alva.

"Yes," Blaze said. "The Willful Institute has attacked us again and again, and they have impeded the plans of Alva. We were waiting for permission from higher up. Now we have it. We won't go for their throat—but for their arms and legs. With this information, we can cut off their major businesses. We can take over their contracts. We will bleed them dry by a thousand small cuts.

Derrick rapped his knuckles on the table. "They killed our people, attacked them without provocation, and when we asked them to punish those responsible, they treated us like sewer trash. Every person who joins this guild is our brother and sister. If they err, we deal with them harshly. If they have been the victim, then we need make sure they can rest easy in the next life."

"We have waited silently, and they think we have forgotten. We haven't. We were merely biding our time until they were relaxed and unaware," Blaze said.

Jasper's sound transmission device went off. He raised it, listening. "Come on up." He glanced at Blaze. "Sergeant Niemm."

Blaze's eyes widened.

It wasn't long until the door opened.

Derrick's blood chilled. Niemm looked younger than Blaze, but there was something about his eyes, as though they'd seen ten lifetimes already, and he moved as if ready to attack.

Niemm gave them a brief nod, but Derrick felt as if he had been assessed and categorized in a moment. Even though they were in Hersht in the middle of the desert, a cool breeze ran through the room.

"Blaze, Jasper." Niemm smiled as if seeing old friends.

"Sergeant." The two of them rose and hugged the man.

"What are you here for?" Blaze asked.

"Erik and Rugrat sent me. Is it okay to speak here?"

"They're sworn in," Blaze said.

"Good. I have a dungeon core for you. You can create a dungeon to train in—a simple survival dungeon. It has four different rooms of varying difficulties. Formations, spell scrolls, weapons and armor, supplies."

Derrick and the branch heads leaned forward, their eyes widening. *A dungeon? A damn dungeon?*

Niemm took off a storage ring, breaking his binding with it and passing it over to Jasper.

"Where do you want it located?" Niemm asked.

"Might as well have it here in the Second Realm, far enough away from prying eyes so we can control most things in this area," Blaze said.

Niemm nodded. "Are you taking part in Vuzgal's fighter's competition?"

"Yes. We've got some people who can make it into the Fourth Realm." Blaze's gaze moved across the room. "Another group is training in Alva right now."

"I've heard the rewards are pretty good—wouldn't want to miss out," Niemm said. "I've got to head back up. Can we get this dungeon set up now?"

"Jasper, help him with it," Blaze said.

"This way." Jasper headed out of the room.

The door closed behind them, and Joan couldn't contain herself anymore. "Is that the competition in Vuzgal?"

"Yes, and it's only two weeks away, so I hope you've all been training. If you place high enough, the rewards should increase your fighting Strength rapidly. You can also see how strong people are from the other realms. We'll need that Strength in the fight against the Willful Institute.

"You should all have your assignments. I want no less than three people recommended by all of you for additional training. We will strike out at the Willful Institute quietly, and, using the resources at our disposal. We will train and cultivate with Alva's help so we can compete with them directly."

Derrick looked at the other branch heads, seeing the same determination in their eyes. They cared for the guild deeply and were eager to strike out against those who dared to hurt their people.

Hiao Xen turned from Vuzgal's main arena to look at the two people beside him. "So, are we ready?"

"People are coming in from across the realms to participate in the fight. Registration is in the hundreds currently," Chonglu said.

"Our crafters are busy making and selling items for fighters and Body Cultivators. We had to open Wayside Inns in the unclaimed regions to host the influx of people," Elise said.

"The auctions are all set up on different days as well?" Hiao Xen asked.

"Yes. I checked with the Alchemist Association, the Fighter's Association, Crafter's Association, and Blue Lotus. All of them will have an auction on a different day. On the days they are not hosting an auction, we will host one. There will be auctions for items that we hold, and others for items that people put up. Our bartering services will be open to everyone," Elise said.

"With all of that going on, anyone who is interested in fighting should come over." Hiao Xen smiled.

"Good thing we built those Wayside Inns before anything else," Elise said.

"And for the competition—how will it run exactly?" Hiao Xen asked Chonglu.

"For the first week, we will check everyone's qualifications. Those who don't qualify won't be allowed in. Those who do will go through a series of fights, a round-robin to establish the top one hundred. The fights will take place on the main floor, and we purchased formations that can project these events at another location. People can watch the fights within bars and other places for a fee.

"Once we have our top hundred, they will compete based on points. A win is two points, a draw one point, a loss no points. The competition will last two-and-a-half weeks total."

"Should be good. As this is our first competition, we need to show that we can control everything in the city. I will talk to the military and see if they can spare some people to act as guards and assist in the running of the city, backing up the police force. I think that covers everything?"

"I think so. It should be good," Chonglu said.

Plans in the Dark

Esther Leblanc marched through the opulent halls. She wore a rapier on her hip, and an array of pistols adorned her chest and hips. Her midnight hair was pulled back in a braid, contrasting against her light tan. Standing out against the guards, ladies and gentlemen with their wigs and powdered faces.

Guards waited by the walls as her footsteps reverberated against the marble inlaid floors. The decorations of the hall were lavish.

Doors opened ahead of her, and she reached a sunroom. An attendant wearing an artful, white-haired wig waved her forward and bowed out of the way.

She walked to the door to see *him* sitting there. He tapped his pen as he wrote on the paper scroll.

Esther controlled her smile and kept a professional, cold demeanor as she walked up to the man. "Uncle," she said.

He wore a fine coat made from heaven-and-Earth treasures. His black hair was augmented with gray instead of fading into it.

She didn't miss the smile at the corner of his mouth as he continued to write.

"Little niece, it seems that as soon as you returned from your last mission, you're looking for another. Didn't I say you should rest?" His eyes flickered over to her and away again.

Esther thought of her last mission. "It was only a trade negotiation."

"Ah, but trade is the basis of trust and trust will lead to alliances, and we need more allies now." Her uncle's voice turned firm as he continued to write.

"The Black Phoenix sect continues to apply pressure on us from every direction. It is becoming hard to live with them eyeing our techniques and technology." Her hand touched the grip of one of the pistols.

The scratch of pen on paper continued.

Esther looked up at the manicured garden, the carved fountain, the hedges that had been turned into a maze, and the dozens of colorful flowers that were grown together. With the power of the Seventh Realm, they had turned into treasures that alchemists in the lower realms would fight over, even draw blood to get.

Here, they were just a background for her uncle. A man of great taste who had saved her mother and united the seven clans together against a sect that wanted to use them as training resources.

They kept the name Sha as a homage to where they had come from, but everything was controlled by her uncle. Many referred to him as the Marshal. Edmond Dujardin, the creator of the Sha weaponry, the leader of the Sha and the Iron Rifle, and the one who had led them to higher realms and turned them into a power within the Seventh Realm.

He put his pen down and checked the scroll. He held it out to the side, and an attendant came from the sunroom and took it from him.

Edmond stood and indicated for her to join him as he walked.

"I have heard rumors and noises from the Fourth Realm. A new city has been established called Vuzgal. The city doesn't interest me, but the residents do. They use what appear to be guns. Their tactics are quite different from our own, working in small groups instead of going head-to-head with their enemy in long firing lines. I want you to travel to the Fourth Realm as my envoy. You will have your closest compatriots. I want you to learn about Vuzgal, the people there. Find out if their weapons are indeed like ours. If they have copied our ideas, come back with images, and I will deal with it. If it looks like they are similar but they have been further modified or changed in some way, I want you to give this message to the leader of their people." Edmond pulled out a letter with his seal on it.

She took it and put it away. "Won't the clan leaders want you to deal with them?"

"Of course they will. They think if we kill everyone who is trying to copy our designs, we will stop the information from getting out. We have done so for some hundred years. But now, well, I don't think it is realistic. I also have a feeling about this one."

Edmond turned to Esther. "Will you take the mission?"

"Well, I already have the letter, don't I?" Esther smiled.

Colonel Yui, Rugrat, Erik, and Commander Glosil were all seated in the military's briefing room.

"While we prepare for war, we need to make sure we have a fallback plan," Erik said. "If we lose, if we're pushed back and Alva and Vuzgal are taken, then our people will be under threat. We need to build locations for them to retreat to."

"Then there is the Trader's Guild and the Adventurer's Guild that have locations in different cities, warehouses, and apartments. Though if we're exposed, they will be as well. Trying to hide in other cities could lead to complications, and the influx of people would lead to suspicion," Glosil said. "The most secure locations are dungeons."

Erik waved for him to keep going.

"If we have dungeon cores, we can replicate the Alva living floor, create a contained underground location for them to hide in and wait out whatever purge comes after the fall of Alva and Vuzgal."

"Add in teleportation formations to link them together and spread them across the ten realms, maintaining the network we have built already," Erik said.

"It would be a massive feat," Glosil said.

"I'm not sure it would. While Alva looks complicated on the surface, it isn't really. Egbert!" Rugrat lifted his chin and yelled.

"Yes?"

"Could you replicate the Alva living floor with a dungeon core of the Common Mortal Grade and an Earth-level mana cornerstone?"

Mana moved on the table, creating a mana stone. The rune-covered crystal directed attribute-heavy mana into the dungeon core and pure mana upward. Like the roots and branches of a tree, the mana-storing formation appeared above and the mana-gathering formation below.

A network of formations spread across the ceiling and the ground, with the dungeon core at the center.

"Beautiful. I never thought that the formations looked like that," Yui said.

"How many people could this fit? Taking into account supplying them with food and water," Glosil asked.

"Four hundred people," Egbert said.

"How quickly will the dungeon core upgrade?" Rugrat asked.

"Depends on the environment it is placed in. The harsher, the better. I would say if left alone, it would take a year to increase a grade. If you were to install mana-gathering formations in the surrounding area to increase the draw, that would decrease the time. Add in people, and it should decrease by one-third."

"Why so short?" Yui asked.

"Think of mana as clean and pristine. It is only when it goes through the realms that it becomes muddied with the attributes. When we temper our bodies with mana, we can handle more of it without falling apart. When we temper with the attributes, or body tempering, then we ingrain those attributes into our bodies. Instead of it being treated as an impurity within our body, it is something that increases our Strength," Rugrat said as he studied the floating blueprint. "I'm guessing that as there are more people, they're taking in the clean mana, muddying it up, and feeding it right into the dungeon core."

"Correct," Egbert said, his disembodied voice carrying through the room.

"It's like entropy, but in this case, it can be reversed. Instead of losing the energy, it is consumed by other things, creating a renewable cycle instead of one that has a limited lifespan?" Erik half-asked.

"From what limited things I know, I think so." Rugrat tilted his hands open and shrugged.

"Entropy?" Yui asked.

"Basically, everything becomes chaos, no matter how ordered it started. That energy is finite and will burn out. One good thing is is that it won't do it for a *really* long time," Erik said.

"We're getting a little off track." Glosil coughed.

"That's a lot of dungeon cores." Yui sighed.

"Well, the special teams are always looking for something to do," Rugrat said.

"We know the kinds of areas we're looking for. I'll check with the traders and Elan's people. That should slim down the search. Egbert find the best setup of cornerstones and grade of dungeon core, as well as mana-gathering formations," Glosil said.

"That should make it a lot faster." Erik nodded.

"We can connect the dungeon cores and separate them out into the different grades, so it won't matter which ones we get. Who will be in charge of this?" Yui asked

"Sounds like we have a volunteer." Glosil smiled at Yui.

Yui looked around the room. "Should've kept my mouth shut."

"Teleportation will be limited. The power required is massive. When we started Alva, we had to limit teleportation too. With these locations like this, they would need time to gain enough mana to start the teleportation formations or people would need to supply it with a lot of mana stones."

"To teleport in?" Glosil asked.

"The teleportation will only take power from the outgoing teleportation formation. Teleporting out is going to cost the dungeon power stores."

"Yui, coordinate with the other council leaders. Have a plan to install the Alva bank and shift the Alva medical staff, as well as the members of the academies and all our information books," Glosil said. "If shit hits the fan, we'll need a plan in place to carry it all out."

"Secrecy is our greatest weapon," Erik added.

"Yes, sir, I understand." Yui's face was grave.

Tying Up Loose Ends

E rik and Rugrat appeared in Alva with a flash of light.

Quest Completed: Ten Realms Dungeon

Created a Trial and Tribulation Dungeon, a place to reward those with Strength and to cull those without power.

Requirements:

Create traps and other tests for adventurers to pass through (Complete)

Randomly generate a Trial and Tribulation Dungeon (3,000 Mortal mana stones) (Complete)

Rewards:

+1,000,000 EXP

13,548,136/86,100,000 EXP till you reach Level 60

Looks like we need to be in the dungeon if we want to get dungeon-related rewards. One of us can't activate it for the other," Erik said.

"Uh-huh, and if someone else carries out quests for the dungeon or city for us, we just come in and get that sweet, sweet Experience," Rugrat said as he peeked at his stats. "Should reach Vapor Mana Core soon." He grinned at Erik. "See you later. I'm going to the library."

"Did you listen to anything I said?" Erik's voice rose as Rugrat walked away.

"Some of it!" Rugrat waved his hand in goodbye as he continued in the direction of the academy.

Erik shook his head and walked toward the dungeon headquarters.

Rugrat's words made him look at his ongoing quests and stat sheet.

Quest: Body Cultivation 4

The path cultivating one's body is not easy. To stand at the top, one must forge their own path forward.

Requirements:

Reach Body Like Diamond Level

Rewards:

+24 to Strength

+24 to Agility

+24 to Stamina

+40 to Stamina Regeneration

+100,000,000 EXP

Quest: Bloodline Cultivation 1

The path cultivating one's body is not easy. To stand at the top, one must forge their own path forward.

Requirements:

Unlock your bloodline

Rewards:

+48 to Strength

+48 to Agility

+48 to Stamina

+80 to Stamina Regeneration

+100,000,000 EXP

Quest: Dungeon Master

You have returned your dungeon to its former glory. Advancement quests are unlocked. Grow your dungeon's power!

Requirements:

Increase your dungeon core's grade to Sky Common

Increase the Strength of your minions (Complete)

Rewards

40,000,000 EXP

Dungeon Master Title IV

Quest: City Leader 3

You have unlocked the City Leader Quest. Grow your territory and your population, and protect what you have.

Requirements:

Have a permanent population of at least 1,000,000

Rewards:

+10,000,000 EXP

Upgrades to defensive formation. Attackers stats decreased by 3%

Able to create (4) village cornerstones.

Quest: Mana Cultivation 2

The path cultivating one's mana is not easy. To stand at the top, one must forge their own path forward.

Requirements:

Reach Vapor Mana Core

Rewards:

+20 to Mana

+20 to Mana Regeneration

+50,000,000 EXP

13,548,136/86,100,000 EXP till you reach Level 60

Name: Erik West

Level: 59   Race: Human

Titles:

From the Grave II

Blessed by Mana

Dungeon Master III

Reverse Alchemist

Poison Body

Fire Body

City Lord

Earth Soul

Mana Reborn

Strength: (Base 54) +41	950
Agility: (Base 47) +72	654
Stamina: (Base 57) +25	1230
Mana: (Base 27) +79	1166
Mana Regeneration: (Base 30) +61	73.80/s
Stamina Regeneration: (Base 72) +59	27.20/s

Erik had thought that a million was a lot of Experience not long ago. Now, he was getting a hundred million Experience with a few quests, but it wasn't enough to increase his overall level anymore.

He found Delilah working in her office, absorbing information books then using a scribe spell to control her pen and add her notes to a blank piece of paper. She checked the paper, rubbing her forehead as she heard a knock on her door.

Erik stood in the doorway, his knuckles against the wood with a smile on his face.

"Are you free?" he asked.

"I've got most of my reports done already. I've been meaning to give you something." Delilah checked her storage rings and then pulled out a pill bottle.

Erik's eyes twitched.

She walked around and passed it to Erik. "This is my own creation, the Heartflame Transformation pill. I know you have been worried about Rugrat. This should help him temper his body. Now, what did you need?"

Erik shook his head. "This is your first Expert-level pill."

"And pills are meant to be used," she said firmly.

Erik sighed. "Guess there are times when the teacher learns from the student. Thank you, Delilah." He smiled, feeling proud of Delilah and thankful for all her work. She could have made something for herself, but instead, she had put Erik's mind at ease by helping out Rugrat.

She blushed.

"Want to take a walk in the Alchemy gardens?" Erik asked.

"Okay." Delilah sounded relieved for something to break the tension.

They left the headquarters and went to the Alchemy garden it had remained while much of the farms had been turned into parks and moved to the lower floors of the dungeon. A few smaller farms and growing buildings had been erected on the living floor.

Alchemy gardens appeared on each floor, to create specialized ingredients, but the main Alchemy garden remained. A complex system of ingredients altering the mana and elements around them to support one another.

"So, what is happening with the Alchemy garden? It can't continue to expand," Erik asked.

"A secondary garden is being made on the Earth floor. It will have a special formation to take in the different affinities of mana going through the dungeon. Tertiary Alchemy gardens will be raised and maintained on separate floors for the plants with the same Affinity. We want to not only grow enough to keep the students supplied but have extra we can leave for a longer period of time, allowing them to increase their potency. I agreed to a plan that allows a greater mana density within certain growing areas: within the refineries of the smiths, curated forests of the woodworkers, and assorted plants the tailors use for their threads among tester fields of the farmers and the two main Alchemy gardens. This will decrease the growing time and increase the potency of the ingredients."

They walked in companionable silence.

"Alva has come really far under your leadership." He inspected the assorted plants. "I remember when this garden was newly planted. You could look clean across it and there were things spaced out all over the place that I thought would never fill up the space. Now, it's a veritable jungle in here."

Alchemists were working in the garden, tending to the plants or harvesting ingredients. A class of low grade alchemists walked through, as their teacher showed them assorted plants, combining what they had learned in the classroom with what they saw in front of them.

"Shall we go and see the other floors to see what's been happening with them?" Erik asked.

"Sure, we can. The varied groups were all brought together. We created a plan that would get us the greatest benefits from each floor. Nearly every floor has a compound on it for people to live in. There is a rifle squad in each floor's settlement to evacuate people if something happens. We control every floor except the Water floor."

They headed out of the Alchemy garden and toward the teleportation formation. "Metal floor." Erik stood on it and they disappeared in a flash of light, Egbert sending them off before the controller could.

The Metal floor appeared in front of them. While still barren, the light formations on the ceiling had been partly recovered. Lightning still struck the largest mountain, illuminating the rest of the floor as it underwent repairs and upgrades. A small mining and refining compound stood off to the side. Metal beasts pulled carts filled with raw materials into the compound; others were left empty.

"Miners and smiths are clearing up the floor and mining the metal. They haul it into the compound and separate out the different metals roughly. Then they take the sorted materials and take them to the Fire floor. There, smiths refine the metals into ingots. With the control formations, the beasts can work without needing beast tamers guiding them. It saves on manpower needs."

"What's that?" Erik pointed to a large fenced area away from the compound.

"The bestiary. Every floor has a group of beast tamers on it. They're learning more about the beasts, seeing how we can use them. Sure, we have panthers that can run through forests, but what about orokai that can run quickly in a straight line, has a hide as tough as Earth-grade metal, and run for days without resting? Or the fona birds, which are made of wind and carry only one rider, but can reach speeds that can make the air explode?"

"That certainly adds more options. We have a shortage of panthers, and breeding them in such numbers would be terrible for them. Diversifying our mounts could work well. Anyway, which floor next?"

"Down to the Earth floor," Delilah said.

The scenery changed, and Erik felt his mana gates open wider, relaxing as they drew in the Earth attribute mana as if it were a revitalizing tonic. Any fatigue he had washed away. He moved his neck around, hearing satisfying popping noises. He reached out with his hand, and the mana stopped moving; he collected and compressed it even more.

"What are you doing, teacher?" Delilah asked.

"Just exercising my domain. If I'm in areas rich with Earth mana, the Strength I can use increases."

The Earth floor was recovering rapidly now the doors between the floors were open, and with the dungeon core being moved between the floors to reorganize, rebuild, and upgrade them, the air on the separate floors was able to move once again.

The barren landscape was being flattened by beasts towing plows and levelers. Several fields had been created with different dungeon mobs walking around, leaking Earth-attribute mana to help the plants grow at an astounding rate.

"So, how many people are living on separate floors?"

"No more than one hundred, and everyone has to have at least Body Like Stone tempering. That way, the mana on the floors won't harm their bodies too much. Many people are going to the Fire floor to temper their bodies and work at the same time," Delilah said.

Massive grain silos had been erected. Farming was no longer a one-person job; several farmers worked in concert with one another, guiding their different beasts and working with various tools that had been purposely built for farming. They were clearing the floor and turning it into fields at a visible speed.

Erik couldn't help but smile. "Let's head to the Fire floor."

Delilah nodded, and they used the teleportation array once again. Heat, the kind that made you blink and cough, washed over them.

Erik breathed in the air, relaxing. Just like the Earth floor, his senses reached farther, meaning the Strength of his spells should increase.

The housing compound and the working areas were a little larger than the floors above.

"This floor has a great number of alchemists, smiths, miners, and people looking to temper their bodies," Delilah explained. "The formation masters came up with formations to control the flames; they're excellent for smithing and Alchemy. Their power can be adjusted, and renting them is less expensive than the Alchemy rooms at the academy. Also, they can be a great aid when someone is making concoctions that have ingredients with Fire-attributes. Most of the alchemists down here make Fire-tempering pills of different kinds and then sell them through the Mission Hall to the people here.

"Something I should have mentioned is that every floor has a group of healers, just in case there is an accident. There are people from each of the different crafts on the floors as well. The alchemists are studying ingredients and working to make tempering concoctions. The smiths are looking for diverse materials to work with, same as the tailors and the woodworkers. Someone made a bow with some wood from the Fire floor. Each of the arrows gained the Fire attribute when released. They're looking to see if it can be applied to the rifles, but the heat radiating from the wood is a worry as the rounds could possibly go off." Delilah shrugged.

"Alva has come a long way. There are new changes every day because of what people have figured out."

Delilah nodded, a proud look on her face as she surveyed the floor. She took it in for a moment before pointing at the working compound again.

"That raw ore we saw on the Metal floor is sent to those massive refineries. They save a lot in materials and mana stones by refining the metals down here. Once it's in ingot form, it is sold to the smiths of Alva. There are also jewelry workshops, and there are many precious gems on the Fire floor. People search for them and sell them to the jewelers, who sell them to the school, crafters, or traders. There are some formation masters located on the floor who will create formations powered or enhanced by gems."

"Makes sense. A lot of industry down here, well-suited for those working with flames." Erik noticed the larger medical building located near the entrance to the compound. He looked over to a small lava pond with formations laid over it, increasing the potency of Fire mana. There were medics nearby as people walked or crawled toward it, allowing the Fire mana to enter their bodies. Some medics walked around it, checking on them. All the medics had completed their Fire tempering and had achieved Fire Body in order to assist these Fire-tempering people.

"How is the Wood floor?" Erik asked.

"Complicated."

They went through the teleportation array and arrived in a tightly packed forest. Loggers were pushing through it while it grew back quickly. Farmers had carved out a section of land and planted different fruit-bearing trees.

"The Earth floor was filled with Fire mana, and it has taken some time to recover. The Wood floor was never tampered with. When the access tunnel to the higher floors was opened, the Wood-attribute mana only increased. The farmers love it, though, and can harvest in just weeks without growing spells." Delilah led Erik down a road to where a dungeon beast with scythe-like arms was cutting down trees at the side of the road. Another beast burned the stumps with acid, and a third leveled the ground as they moved.

They came to the end of the road. A compound rose from the ground that was not made from stone but from trees woven together to make homes.

"Makes me think about the elven homes I read about in books."

"Elves?"

"Don't worry about it." Erik waved.

"Many people come to live on the Wood floor for privacy and such. Same with the Earth floor. They're just not well-suited for towns."

"Well, they're not far away," Erik said.

"We should talk about when we will increase the size of the floors," Delilah said.

"I guess the dungeon core was bigger than when the gnomes controlled this place. What are you thinking?"

"We need to increase the size of the main floor—it is the smallest. With the dungeon core, doubling its current size shouldn't be a problem. Our population has exploded and we're nearing ten thousand people, and we have more joining Alva every week."

"Once Egbert is done with using the dungeon core to repair the separate floors and return their functionality, you have permission to increase the size of the floors," Erik said.

The two of them found a bench in the compound and sat down.

"Any other issues?" Erik asked.

"Vuzgal is getting ready for their competition, but you probably have a better idea of what is happening there than me. Lord Aditya took control over King's Hill Outpost. He is creating roads to link the other outposts at a furious speed. His guards are training the different outpost guards and turned them into a neutral army while he builds up King's Hill Outpost to attract traders. The Trader's Guild has been alerted, and those spread over the first three realms are heading toward King's Hill Outpost to check on the wares for sale there. It should show our support, and with several goods that are hard to find in the first two realms, the outpost will turn into one of the most visited cities in the First Realm. And it's close to Alva."

"Connecting the outposts of Beast Mountain Range, giving rise to a new nation of traders in one of the most hostile locations of the Ten Realms—he's become a lot bolder. What do you think of him?"

She didn't answer immediately.

"When we first knew him, he acted like most other outpost lords, but he's shown that he cares for his guards, his citizens, and those within his walls. Been some years now since he swore to us. He's about as close to an Alvan one can get without taking the oath."

"I feel like you're building toward something."

"He might have erred in the beginning, but he's an asset and a good person under his tough exterior. We should reward him. We should make him an Alvan." Delilah searched Erik's expression before continuing. "We should teach him Body Cultivation, Mana Cultivation, open his mana gates, and teach him crafting. He has done a lot for us. Give him a place on the council.

"There are many people in Alva who are grateful for him scouting them out and sending them this way. Whole families might have starved if they hadn't come inside our walls. We owe him at least this much."

"You keep surprising me." Erik smiled. "Okay, once he has stabilized the Beast Mountain Range, I'll personally take his oath."

"Thank you."

"You are right—he does deserve it. Now, we were talking about a competition between the crafters before. Is something happening there?"

"Kind of. With the fighters' competition going on, we didn't think it was advisable to hold a crafting competition right afterward. We don't want to compete with the fighters' competition, as there are people who would like to be part of both competitions. We're aiming to hold the competition in about six months. Word seems to have gotten out, though," Delilah said with a wry smile.

"Any problems I should know about?"

"Well, not really a problem. One could call it a blessing. The crafters are pushing themselves more than ever in their studies. We are planning to expand the Kanesh Academy workshops again because we don't have enough for everyone. It's part of the reason there are so many people on the other dungeon floors. I think that announcing the competition has made them excited."

"Most of them work on their craft behind closed doors, so people within their craft can show off their abilities, but others can't understand. With the competition, they can show off their skills to the public or to one another. And while they might succeed, it can drive them harder toward success, while seeing others may inspire them to change their ways and methods."

"Also, the rewards are pretty sweet," Delilah added.

"And the rewards are pretty sweet." Erik grinned. "What about the tier-four workshops and the crafter dungeon?"

"The crafter dungeon is in use, heavy use." Egbert's voice came from above.

"Matt passed along the plans through the blueprint department. Egbert took all but the Water floors of the secondary dungeon to create the crafter's dungeon. Its facilities have taken a lot of pressure off the academy. We have multiple Expert-level rooms, and, well, that kind of brings me to my point. The crafter dungeon shows signs of evolving and gaining higher-level facilities. Right now, the highest crafting room is Low Expert grade, but it could evolve and create a Mid Expert-grade crafting room. Our tier-four workshops at the academy hosts a Mid Expert-grade workshop. We can dump money into the workshops or let the crafter dungeon evolve. We have some Expert-level crafters, but it isn't at the point where we've run out of space for them in our workshops or dungeon," Egbert said.

"Okay, let's wait. If the dungeon does evolve, we can get the plans and create our own High level workshops," Erik said. "How many Expert crafters do we have who are from Alva?"

"Seven at this time: Tan Xue, Julilah, Qin, myself, Zhou Heng from tailoring and his student Helen Roth, and Shi Wanshu from woodworking."

"How many do you think will make a breakthrough in the next few months?"

Delilah pulled out a piece of paper. "In total, there are twenty-one people who are on the cusp of making a breakthrough, though there are other people who might make a surprise advancement. Expert isn't just a solid wall to break through. Some might have inspiration at Mid Journeyman level and accidentally create a technique that will allow them to break through or create an item of Expert grade with their own efforts."

Erik worked his jaw. *I'm falling behind now.* He sighed and then smiled. "Sometimes there are just people who are more capable."

"What was that? You're mumbling."

"Don't mind me," Erik said.

"So, Matt is in Vuzgal. He is working on plans with others to make higher-grade facilities, though most of them are busy with building Vuzgal."

"Keeps them out of trouble." Erik smiled.

Delilah rolled her eyes. "Doesn't seem to keep you and Rugrat out of trouble."

Erik scratched the back of his head awkwardly.

"So, when are you leaving?"

"Who said anything about leaving?" Erik asked.

"You took time off from tempering and crafting, and you're reviewing everything that has happened. You're also checking that everything is okay."

"You know me too well," Erik muttered.

Delilah smiled brightly.

Erik sighed and pulled out a piece of paper.

"Rugrat and I are fighters. We like being in the middle of it. If we aren't, we feel like we're losing our edge, losing a part of ourselves. We're looking at going to the Sixth Realm. There are academies all over the place, but there are dungeons too. We want to clear dungeons, fight something with a challenge, and experience the realms. We're not good with the building and managing of things. Punch that guy, kick that dude is much easier."

He passed the paper to Delilah. "Now, I made a promise to someone and I'm not able to complete it currently, so I wanted to ask you for a favor as well."

Delilah looked over the piece of paper. "This is an Age Rejuvenation pill?"

"Well, hopefully. I came up with this formula. I'm not sure how strong it will be, though my skill isn't high enough to make it. I've tried, and it ended in failure every time. I was wondering if you would be able to do it." Erik peeked at her, knowing full well that she could say no, considering how much she had to do already.

Instead, her eyes shone with excitement.

"I'll assist you as needed," Erik said. His words seemed to break her out of her thoughts.

"Yes, yes! Um, yeah, that should be fine."

Delilah kept studying the formula and closed her eyes.

Erik settled back on the bench and smiled. He contemplated their Wood floor, the birds and other creatures making noise. People were walking inside the compound while farmers sat out with their swamp monster hands, sharing lunch and laughing together.

Delilah finished reviewing the formula, pulled out a notepad, and made some notes before she stood up suddenly. "Okay, let's get started. Do you have the Lidel leaves?"

"Uh, yeah. You sure?"

"Well, if you've already made your decision, then you want to leave as soon as possible, no?"

"How did you get to know me so well?"

"I manage your dungeon, and you taught me Alchemy. I think I know you a bit too well for my own sanity."

"I remember when you became my student. You were all bows and 'yes, Master' that, 'yes, Master' this." Erik sighed ruefully.

"Are you coming or not, teacher?" Delilah asked, already walking toward the compound entrance.

"Hey!" Erik jogged over, missing the smile that appeared on Delilah's face. Still, his heart warmed at seeing how the young woman had become a confident, badass lady.

They returned to the alchemist workshop located on the first floor.

Erik watched from the side as Delilah worked. The Age Rejuvenation concoctions were some of the hardest to complete, as they required a high level of skill. The Blue Lotus and Alchemist Association, even with their resources and people, only produced enough to support their own associations.

If they had known how hard the concoctions were to make, the Blue Lotus wouldn't have let Erik sell his previous batches, snapping them up for themselves instead. They would need alchemists from a higher grade to complete them, which increased their market price by a steep margin.

When Erik had taught Delilah, he had started with the technically difficult concoctions and worked with her to increase the efficacy of her potions instead of the amount she could produce. It had set her up well. The flames in her hands moved with the slightest gesture. They felt alive, an extension of herself.

Erik sat beside her. He had readied the ingredients and partly prepared the Lidel leaves. They were time-consuming and demanded the alchemist's complete concentration. Delilah used her flames to refine the leaves while Erik sent in ingredients at different times, balancing the power of the Lidel leaves as more were prepared.

Erik waited as Delilah finished the final stages of refining the leaves. A powerful life force could be felt within the cauldron. Just smelling it, he felt revitalized. The beads of sweat on Delilah's face and the way she set her jaw told a different story as she focused entirely on what was happening within the cauldron.

Delilah and Erik knew each other's methods and tells; they worked as two parts of a whole. Erik introduced more ingredients into the cauldron, decreasing the growing pressure.

Delilah understood the changes, utilizing the ingredients and fusing them together. The tame Lidel leaves had revealed their Strength while the other ingredients were like wolves attacking a dragon, slowly overwhelming it, and then becoming fused with it. Its Strength was increased but also less violent.

There was a powerful suction as the haze was drawn into the spinning pill in the middle of the cauldron. A tornado of flames surrounded it.

The pill had reached the newborn stage and made a noise like a heartbeat. Delilah didn't seem satisfied and pushed on; her eyes filled with a competitive light.

Erik felt proud, silently cheering her on from the side as he watched her pushing past her boundaries, not accepting good enough.

She gasped as her control faltered, but she recovered. Her brows pinched together as she maintained the pill, ensuring her hard work didn't fall apart.

She sat back as the flames died down, a sardonic smile on her face. She opened the cauldron and tossed it into a pill bottle.

Letting out a satisfied sigh, she passed it to Erik.

"Low Expert-Concentrated pill," Erik confirmed after some moments. "Impressive. That must've been as hard as the best Low Expert-grade pills.

I wonder how high your skill will be by the time I come back." Erik laughed.

"All the way to Master!" Delilah declared and then laughed.

They had been inside the Alchemy workshop for several days, working on the pill. They had only left to sleep and eat. With their levels, they didn't require much.

"Thank you," Erik said.

"What are you saying?" Delilah pushed her hair behind her ear, blushing. "Isn't this what a student should do for her teacher?"

"You..." Erik felt his heart fill. He reached over and patted her head.

Delilah smiled as he pulled his hand back.

"You did well," Erik said in a deep, meaningful voice.

Delilah's blush increased, and she looked away again.

Trade

rik took a short rest and then headed to the Fourth Realm with the special team. The light dimmed as he looked around. He was in a massive city. All the buildings were white and blue, with lotuses worked into their architecture. There were ponds and bridges everywhere sporting blue lotuses.

It had been some time since he had visited the Blue Lotus headquarters. He walked over to the guards protecting the totem. It looked more like a reception than a security gate.

Niemm scanned the area as the special team moved around Erik.

The guard frowned and his eyes glanced over the special team before widening as Erik stepped up.

Erik wanted to be able to move by himself, but the special teams had their orders. If he were in their shoes, he would do the same thing.

"What is the purpose of your visit?"

"I am here to see Elder Lu Ru. I have something I promised him," Erik said.

The man seemed skeptical. "Name?"

"Erik West."

"Do you have an affiliation?"

"Vuzgal," Erik said simply.

The man's expression went through several changes. "I don't have any note of a meeting with Elder Lu Ru. Do you have some form of identification?"

"Uh…" Erik pulled out the honorary elder token.

"Thank you." The man received it with both hands and pressed it to a formation.

"Honorary Elder West, an escort will personally take you to Elder Lu. If you take a seat, your escort will arrive momentarily."

"Thanks." Erik took a seat and started chewing on an ingredient Delilah and the alchemists found and hadn't been able to categorize.

Dungeon lord, city lord, trained alchemist—and I'm still chewing on ingredients

He shivered at the flavor.

Crap. Forgot the tongue-numbing powder.

A woman appeared with a dominating air surrounding her. Behind her, there were several guards.

"City Lord West, I am General Lei Huo." The woman bowed.

Erik swallowed, his body shaking as if he had just swallowed chewing tobacco.

"Ah, yes. I remember you. You were at Vuzgal after that incident. Sorry I didn't get to thank you," Erik said.

"I am sorry. I was pulled away before I could express my gratitude. Thank you for looking after my people." She bowed from the waist again.

Lei Huo stood back up. "Elder Lu Ru is finishing a meeting or else he would've come personally. Could I escort you to his office?"

"Please." Erik walked forward with his group.

Lei Huo smiled and walked with them toward the main building in the middle of the city. "We have a carriage that can take us," Lei Huo said.

"Very well."

She pulled out two carriages from her storage ring and beasts from her beast storage. She signaled to her guards, and they got into the drivers' seats. Erik and his people filled the two carriages, and they set off.

Lei Huo couldn't help but cast a look back at the carriages as they headed for the headquarters.

Was he this strong when she had last seen him? His Strength was all over the place then, but now he seemed to have complete control over it and had even increased. It felt as though he had tempered his body to the Diamond stage—and not just to completion but beyond. Then there were the people around him. She recognized some of them. They were at Vuzgal as well, but their Strength was higher than what his was back then.

What had they been doing to increase their Strength so quickly and make it theirs? Most people who leveled up fast did it for the status and reached a point where they couldn't increase anymore as they had grown so quickly that their skills and abilities had fallen too far behind.

She shoved those thoughts to the back of her mind as they reached the headquarters. As the group got out of their carriages, she dismissed her guards and guided Erik forward. He left his guards at the door, showing his trust in the Blue Lotus. The guards didn't look pleased, but they obeyed.

A little yelp came from Erik's shoulder, and his tamed beast complained to Erik. The little lizard looked cute as she played around.

Lei Huo had noticed the shrunken beast but had been so surprised with the changes in Erik and his people that she hadn't paid much attention to it. Now, her hair stood on end. Her senses told her this was no simple beast.

She pulled her senses back as they reached the grand entrance and nodded to the guards. They opened the door, revealing a large office with windows that looked out over the Blue Lotus headquarters.

Elder Lu Ru had been standing near the door and moved over to them. He had a hot look in his eyes as he stared at Erik.

Erik laughed awkwardly. "I am sorry I took so long. I needed to get some help." He pulled out a pill bottle and passed it over to Elder Lu Ru.

Lei Huo glanced at it. *Expert-level pill, low level.* Being a person of the Blue Lotus, she had gained an eye toward appraising.

"Low Expert concentrated level?" Elder Lu Ru said with a glance.

"Your appraisal abilities are impressive." Erik nodded. "I hope this helps. I know you are a busy man."

"Honorary Elder West," Elder Lu said, taking a moment to form his words. "Do you not want anything?"

"I made an oath a long time ago. If I can help someone, I will. I said I would make you a pill. I'm guessing the person is close to you, and they need something to extend their lifespan. It is not my place to ask who or why. If I did, wouldn't you think I was trying to string you along and find a weakness?"

"In my position, good intentions are rare."

"You helped me and my people out. I hope this favor helps you and the person who needs it. There are no debts between us."

"I hear that healers from the academy heal anyone who comes to them for a low rate?" Elder Ru asked.

"That is part of it. People who have the power to heal shouldn't look at the coins they can make but at the lives they can save. Same with Alchemy."

Elder Ru fell silent.

"Anyway, I hope you have a good day." Erik smiled.

Elder Lu Ru put the pill away and performed a perfect bow. "Thank you for your hard work, Mister West."

Erik turned back and, seeing Elder Ru like that, gave an awkward bow. "Thank you for giving Vuzgal the time it needed to stabilize and grow."

Elder Lu straightened, his emotions hard to read.

"See you later." Erik flashed a smile and departed.

A man capable of getting a pill powerful enough to impress Elder Ru was a rare man indeed. Lei Huo hadn't paid a lot of attention to Vuzgal, other than the possible security issues for the branch there. Perhaps there were more secrets to Vuzgal than she had realized.

A Medic and a Marine Enter the Sixth Realm

Rugrat finished tying his boot, tapping it against the armory floor. It was laid out like a changing room. Rows of lockers stood on either side, and it had a bench running down the middle.

Storbon would be the squad leader on this op; Yao Meng was acting his second-in-command. Tian Cui, Yuli, and Lucinda rounded out the squad. They pulled on their combats and secured their fighting gear, checking one another as they did so.

"Good to go?" Erik pulled on his cocking handle. He pointed his rifle at the floor and checked the action.

"Yeah." Rugrat hit his plate carrier, which was frayed slightly at the edges, the stitching showing burn marks. The MOLLE was looser from repeated-use magazines lining the vest, and there was a medical tear-away pouch on Rugrat's lower left back, standard, so he could operate their rifle right-handed because they were always running *into* the enemy, not away. "Did you get the new armor plates?"

"Of course. Not going to let you have all the cool gear. What are you setting the formations on your rifle to?"

Rugrat picked up his rifle, slinging it, and checked the stats.

MK7 semi-automatic rifle (FAL)	
Damage:	Unknown
Weight:	4. 25 kg
Charge:	10,000/10,000
Durability:	100/100
Innate Effect:	Increase formation power by 12%
Socket One:	*Punch Through*—Penetration increased by 10%
Socket Two:	*Supercharged*—Increase bullet's velocity by 12%
Range:	Long range
Attachment:	Under-barrel Grenade Launcher
Requires:	7. 62 rounds
Requirements:	
Agility 53	
Strength 41	

"Increased bullet speed and piercing damage."

Rugrat cleared and worked the action of his rifle. "You?"

"Blunt instead of piercing."

Rugrat pulled a magazine from his storage ring, checked it, and loaded it, then flicked the weapon to safe.

"How am I?" Erik asked.

Rugrat pulled on magazine pouches and tugged on anything that hooked into his MOLLE.

Erik jumped.

"You're lopsided." Rugrat flipped up the front of his vest, pulling his sides in tighter.

"Again."

Erik jumped.

"Good to go."

Rugrat held the butt of his rifle, and Erik pulled and punched.

"Jump." Erik watched.

"Good to go. You ready for this?"

"Locked, loaded, and ready to rock." Rugrat gave Erik the devil horns and stuck out his tongue.

"You sure you don't need more backup? Dungeons can be dangerous." Niemm leaned against the end of the lockers.

"If we take too many of our people, others will ask. There won't be anything left for Erik or me."

"There will be four special teams soon, anyway, when the training is done," Rugrat said.

That slowed the preparations for a half-second. These people were like family and would be split apart, creating two more special teams. New people would fill the empty spots, with veterans teaching the newer members the ropes.

They all knew it was coming; it just wasn't something they were looking forward to.

"Just be safe," Niemm said.

"We'll do our best, but there are always risks," Erik said.

Niemm nodded. They were two sides of the same coin, but Erik and Rugrat had been caged for too long. They needed to be out in the world, alive. Staying back and resting had made them restless.

Storbon and his half-team finished their preparations.

"Okay, let's head out," Storbon said after a quick check of everyone.

They secured their loaded weapons in their storage rings and pulled cloaks over their armor and features.

The rest of Special Team One was waiting for them outside the armory, ribbing them and catcalling as they exchanged middle fingers, laughs, and embraces.

"All right, come on, love birds." Erik broke it up. The teams separated, and the half of the team staying behind headed into the armory.

Storbon led them through Vuzgal's under-city, a series of tunnels and caverns connected to the surface through carefully selected passages. They heard the mad rush of people yelling, the clinking of cutlery, and the sizzle of flames as they entered a sky-reaching restaurant's kitchen.

They met with the agent Elan had organized, who would take them to their guide.

The guide wasn't much of a talker. He took the fee with a grunt and escorted them to the totem in silence.

Rugrat rolled his shoulders, anticipating the change in scenery. George stretched on his shoulder, ready to jump off and return to his regular size in a moment.

All of them were alert and ready, the tang of adrenaline making them feel alive again.

They disappeared in a flash of light. A different city stood before them, just on the other side of the totem's defenses. Instead of being early morning, it was late afternoon.

"Ah, a time change," Yao Meng said.

"Like you sleep anymore," Tian Cui said.

Storbon paid the totem guide the other half of his fee, then watched him leave their group and walk up to the city gates to get his next client.

"Talkative type," Rugrat said.

"Welcome to the Sixth Realm, boys, girls, and redneck," Erik said.

Nothing in the Fourth Realm looked this old. The stone here was weathered uniformly, not a mixture of old and new. The design reminded Rugrat of ancient Chinese architecture.

"Five Earth-grade mana stones per person," the guard said.

Erik paid the fee for everyone.

"Welcome to Acal," the guard said.

Once outside of the defensive works around the totem, the city opened up. It sprawled over several square kilometers and had multiple totems in operation. Massive towers dominated the city, each with a different crafter, guild, and sect emblem. Each building had its own flavor and heritage. The academies looked like they had weathered centuries, an ancient inviolable air hanging around their worn stone-and-wood features.

"A city of academies," Yuli said.

"And an underground full of dungeons." Erik chuckled.

"Someone's excited." Rugrat tapped shoulders with Erik, sharing a grin. "Feels good to breathe free air again."

"Sign over here," Yao Meng said, pointing.

Erik gestured to another. "Dungeon entrance."

Rugrat looked around. "There isn't a single dungeon underneath Acal. but tens of smaller dungeons all linking together to create different environments and beasts. And there are smaller outpost cities located within the dungeon to support those who head deeper."

"To build a city on top of a dungeon—they have to be pretty ballsy," Storbon said.

"Remember, they've scouted the best people they can find from the Fifth Realm to fill their ranks. Everyone here is an elite," Rugrat said.

"So, don't get into a fight," Erik said.

"Unless you have to," Rugrat added.

"Unless you have to," Erik agreed.

They passed merchants selling supplies and books the students of the different academies might need. The larger markets sold all kinds of goods, from tools for students to weapons and armor for adventurers. There were traders hawking maps and other aids. They strolled through the crowds, and Rugrat saw people placing orders for custom weapons and armor, and alchemists negotiating with clients.

Mid Journeyman-level gear was the norm; Earth mana stones and Earth mana cornerstones exchanged hands freely. Here and there, Experts with a large entourage moved through. Most people vacated the path ahead of them.

There were main streets with carts picking up and dropping off people. Walkways were filled with stalls and vibrant fabrics. There was constant background noise. The city had various levels, with bridges crossing between different buildings.

New buildings forced their way between the old ones or built upon them. Everything seemed to sit on one another, built on top of the other in some places and open to the air in others to accommodate markets and fountains. Nature crawled between buildings and up the sides of walls.

"It's like New York; there's no end in sight." Rugrat glanced at Erik, who was taking it in, watching the people working the stalls—how the varied groups interacted, the customs and norms of the area that would help them blend in.

It had been some time since the special team had operated on their own, but they soon relaxed, falling into old rhythms.

While not their first time in an unfamiliar realm with just one another as support, they had more information this time and knew what they were walking into.

"Should we see what they've got for food?" Yao Meng said.

"Nice, sunny day like this, I could do with a beer or two. Should we find somewhere with food and drink, ask them about this place and the dungeon?" Erik asked.

"Sounds like a plan to me. I hate how the menus and food changes in each realm. Vegetables are the worst. Its like there's a different name in every city." Rugrat used his height to peer over people's heads down the stall-lined market street. He spotted a restaurant with smiling servers and patrons laughing and joking with them.

"Over there?" Rugrat glanced over to the rest of the special team.

"As long as it's not spicy," Tian Cui said.

"The more the spice, the more the love!"

They got a table and sat down. Each scanned the area, making a note of people, entrances, and exits.

"So, this is Acal." Rugrat elbowed Erik. "We should tell our city designer to add in some of this." He had to raise his voice over the merchants calling out to passersby, the clatter of carts, and the mounts pulling them.

People yelled to their friends, and children ran through the madness.

"It's like an ancient Chinese city mixed with a modern one," Erik said.

"Matt might have a fit. This shit definitely isn't up to code." He laughed.

"It is a *little* crazy." Rugrat smiled as the beers arrived, and everyone grabbed one. They cheered, tapping their bottles to the table in salute before drinking. Their tempered bodies made it hard for the alcohol to have any effect, but the taste was enough to relax them.

"Ask the server about the city when she comes back around," Erik said to Rugrat.

"Why don't you ask?"

"'Cause girls open up to you."

"Cause I'm irresistible, like a tattooed teddy bear."

"Sometimes I forget you're a marine, then you say something like that."

Rugrat opened his mouth to reply and then closed it.

"Why, thank you." Rugrat grinned, gave him a thumbs up, and chugged his beer, suds dripping on his carrier. He used the back of his hand to clear away the foam and burped. "Not bad."

Erik snorted, shaking his head, and threw the beer back as well.

The server came around and took their orders.

"What is the best way to get into the catacombs?" Rugrat asked.

Their server, a young woman, tapped her pencil against her chin and bit her lip. At her level, she could command a kingdom in the First Realm. Here in the Sixth Realm, she was a server.

"If you're not part of the academies, best to get maps of the dungeons first; otherwise, you might go into an area for wood when you're after ore. The academies have the best entrances and actually go down into outposts or camps. The city runs the other dungeon entrances. Some are close to outposts; others are in the middle of nowhere and still need to be mapped out. The better the dungeon area, the more you pay. Academies cost the most, then clan-owned or business-owned. City-owned and dungeons with little known about them are the least expensive. Could get a huge reward or could end up in the middle of a beast nest." She shivered

"Thank you. Do you know where we can get a map for the catacombs?"

"I have a cousin who knows some mapmakers. I can check with him and get back to you."

"That would be perfect." Rugrat smiled.

She blushed slightly. "Happy to do so. I'll put your orders in." Her eyes rested on him before she headed back into the restaurant.

"I love redheads," Rugrat said with a pleased smile on his face.

"Focus," Erik said. "Okay, so, map first, then down we go."

"Might be best to use the city entrances. The academies and businesses might pay more attention to us. City guards are just wasting their time," Tian Cui said.

"What about the cores?" Yuli asked.

"We should leave them be. There's no knowing if there are other people who have our skills. Let's not draw too much attention to ourselves," Erik said.

Their food was piled high when it arrived, steam coming off it still. Pieces of meat and vegetables were laid out in slices or cooked and covered in sauces.

Bowls of rice were served to everyone, and the dishes were placed in the middle.

"So, why are there cooks up here and not in the other realms?" Lucinda tossed some grilled pieces of meat into the different beast storage items on her belt.

"From Elan's information, at this realm and higher, all crafters are revered. In the Fifth Realm, people are competing to get accepted by a powerful academy. From them, the strongest crafters and fighters get accepted into academies in the Sixth Realm. Fighting isn't so big up here. Crafting is more important because beasts and people are a lot harder to kill. Crafting takes time and gives massive Experience bonuses. Competitions decide everything. Actual battles are rare, and the value of someone making it into the Sixth Realm is significant. People are seen more as the materials put in and performance out. The dungeons are the testing and training grounds of the academies," Erik said.

"The cooking craft is powerful. Even with these basic meals, we should be satisfied for at least a day. With High level cooking, you can gain passive boosts that could last several hours or even a day, instead of the seconds or minutes you get with spells. Some top-tier meals can supposedly change your body, like how Alchemy concoctions can increase your stats," Storbon said.

"You're learning to cook, aren't you?" Yao Meng asked.

"I want to eat something a little more edible than what you call food," Storbon said.

"You know, a man who cooks is really appealing," Yuli said.

"What happened with Shandra?" Tian Cui chimed in.

"Had to break it off—was getting into too many long-term plans." Storbon sighed.

They kept eating and talking, relaxing as they got used to Acal.

Once they finished their meal, they headed over to the server's cousin, who took them to a mapmaker.

The mapmaker's store smelled like musty, old paper and dust. Maps were on display in separate formation-covered glass cabinets on the wall and glass tables at hip height. A large map covered a central table in the middle of the shop, showing all of Acal segregated into squares.

There were students, fighters, and people eagerly talking to one another. Adventures and riches awaited them, and they shared their story of their time in the place.

Rugrat paid the cousin and walked to the front desk with Erik. The man at the counter had barely any hair remaining in a half-circle on his head. His face was lined and weathered, stuck in a permanent scowl, and he was hunched forward from a life spent working on documents.

"The maps, what information do they show?"

"Depends on what you want. I've got maps of the city, maps around the dungeon entrances, outposts, and the dungeons themselves."

"Do you have a map of the nearest city-owned dungeon entrances?"

"With or without information on the dungeon below?"

"With."

"Two hundred forty Earth mana stones," the man said.

Erik pulled out several boxes. The man checked them and then stored them away.

"You heard him, Darleen," he said, and a woman disappeared through a formation-covered door, returning some moments later with a beast skin map.

Erik took it and moved to the side. Rugrat looked over his shoulder as Erik took out his old map. He tapped the new map to it, the new map crumbled as if burned by an internal fire, and fell to the floor as ash. Lines and details appeared on the map in Erik's hands.

Once the transfer was complete, he touched his map to Rugrat's, sharing the information.

Erik checked the information on the map.

"Good doing business with you."

"Only sell the best maps here. Got maps on the different ores and resources you might find as well."

"No, thanks."

They headed out of the store. Storbon walked over and they tapped their maps to his, transferring the information. The others wandered around, watching the area.

"Okay, what about this entrance? There is supposed to be a group of beasts around level fifty-five, and their boss is level fifty-nine," Storbon said.

Erik and Rugrat studied the location on their own maps.

"Level fifty-nine, huh?" Rugrat said, checking the legend.

"Owned by a group. They'll take a share of our profits, and if we just pay them, they'll get suspicious. Think that we can get something we don't want to share and is worth more than the entrance fee. There was some information on dungeon entrances in a cabinet."

"I think we should try something a little lower. I just reached level fifty-nine. You and our beasts are higher, though it has been a long time since we've actually fought in a dungeon." Erik raised an eyebrow, looking between the two men.

"Lower level and city-owned." Storbon bent his head and went back to searching.

"What about this entrance here? Level fifty-three with roaming bosses of level fifty-five. That seems more manageable." Erik pointed to it on his map. Those checking their map examined it in greater depth and went through the maps of the dungeon underneath.

"Looks like caves underneath. Shouldn't be anything down there, and it's got an outpost nearby," Storbon said.

"Sounds like a plan to me," Rugrat said.

"I was just starting to work on my tan." The corner of Storbon's mouth lifted.

"Who needs a tan when you can work on your level?" Rugrat smacked Storbon's shoulder with a grin.

Crafter's Competition Preparation

"**L**ooks like construction is going well." Jia Feng walked up to Matt, who was busy working at a desk.

Matt greeted her with a wave of his hand before noting something on the massive set of plans in front of him.

The construction site took up a massive amount of space, right on the edge of Alva. The floor had expanded with the larger dungeon core, so they had a surplus of room now.

"Come to check on our progress, Academy Head?" Matt looked up from his hurriedly written note. "The dungeon core—its summoned creatures and the automatons—is the heart of it all. They do the heavy lifting. Us humans just make sure everything is properly bonded to one another."

"It is practically growing before our eyes," Jia Feng said.

"Seven stadiums for each crafting discipline: smithing, cooking, woodworking, tailoring, healing, Alchemy, and formation creation. Each arena supports floors that can be changed at will. The Alchemy arena can become a place to grow crops and Alchemy products. Or a square filled with Alchemy workshops for people to create concoctions. Healers can have practical simulation rooms or amphitheaters. When not being used for competitions, they can all be turned into classrooms or host lecturers to talk to students and the public on their own topics. It took a lot of work from the formation masters to create the plates to change the balance of mana and attributes within the overall stadium and the different arenas." There was a shine to Matt's eyes, seeing it all coming together.

"Will it be ready in time?"

"For the competition? Yes, it'll be ready in some weeks. The dungeon core can create walls in seconds, and the automatons can bring in supplies and formations that are too big or heavy for our people to move," Matt said.

Jia Feng peeked at the plans. She frowned, looking from the plans to the cleared space for the arena. "Won't it be too small if you're only work on it for a few weeks?"

Matt laughed. "You are underestimating the builders of Alva, Principal Jia Feng! The groundwork takes the longest as we have to make sure all the formations are in place. The walls, the seats, the stairs, and reinforcement—that will take no time. Each arena can hold around ten thousand people. The main arena in the center can host forty thousand people, with a total capacity of a hundred and ten thousand people."

Matt stood there, beaming

"Is it too big?" She blushed at the variety of her questions.

"Alva will grow with time. Think of this as a prototype. We are testing out everything here. We will see how things work, what needs to be changed, and so on. Then we will take this stadium and replicate it. Instead of there being one stadium for all the crafters, there becomes one for each of the disciplines and one for the fighters as well."

A tremor ran through Jia Feng's body at the thought of so many stadiums within Alva.

"I thought I was being ambitious, but it seems I am well behind you, Matt." Jia Feng smiled.

"I view things from a planning perspective. After all, if we continue to expand, we will need a greater number of facilities to support ourselves." Matt shrugged. "Is there anything else you require, Principal?"

"No, I just wanted to get away and see how things are. I have a meeting later today to go over the planned events and how we will organize everything," Jia Feng said. "Thank you for taking the time to talk to me. I'll let you get back to it."

"No problem. If it weren't for the academy, I wouldn't be able to do half the things I can. An education is more powerful than any cultivation manual."

"Seems like everyone is trying to learn more these days. Keep up your studies!"

Matt smiled and nodded.

Jia Feng walked around part of the stadium, taking in the different automatons and the builders who were using different spells or their own bodies to move massive pieces into place.

Jia Feng was the last to join the meeting. All the heads of the departments of the Alva academies, Kanesh, and Vuzgal were present.

"Look at how far we have come in just a few months!" Jia Feng said as she entered the room.

"We have added more Experts to our ranks in Vuzgal. Dozens of our own students and fellow teachers have become Experts, and they now share what they have learned and believe. It is just a matter of time until we can come up with lessons and methods for people to reach the Expert level of their craft!"

The people around the table clapped their hands.

Jia Feng raised a hand, calming them. They had reacted the same way when the city reached the Journeyman stage; now, they could tackle the

Expert realm and beyond. Working together, they could study all kinds of theories and ideas. There was no one path to reach the higher levels but hundreds.

"Forty-three crafters graduated the new teacher program. The best teachers are not the people who are the best in their given skill but those who can open their students' minds. Making what's difficult easy to understand. For every complete formation, potion, and meal, there are dozens that didn't work out. There are hundreds of prototypes and failures. Perseverance is the basis of our teachings. Eighty percent of Alvans have attended our academy, though I think the greatest accomplishment is how many children have completed the basic education courses. In Alva and Vuzgal, we have taught thousands of children, raising many them to the Novice level in different crafts and opening a world of possibilities to them."

The teachers and heads of departments shared expressions of fierce pride, sitting taller in their seats. They were more skilled than most adults in the lower realms—the future of Alva. What would happen when they entered the advanced courses, reaching Apprentice, Journeyman, and beyond? There was competition between one another, but little was for personal gain. Vuzgal's greatest pride came from helping others to become more powerful.

Jia Feng had altered the directions passed down by Erik and Rugrat. Teachers didn't have to be necessarily good at their craft, but they did need to watch out for their students. Some teachers didn't care for their students, creating an imbalance. They did the bare minimum and took all the resources possible to progress their own power. She had also added more assistants to help in the day-to-day management of the departments and more teachers to help meet the needs of their students. There would be more changes in the future, too, so they could help more people, but they were on the right path. Nothing was perfect. They would change and adapt instead of becoming rigid and unbendable like some sects, lest they snap in two.

"I just finished talking to Matt Richardson, who is working on our arena for the upcoming crafters' competition."

Her words sharpened the eyes of everyone.

"The stadium will soon be complete, as well as all seven arenas for each department. Have you figured out how the competition will be run in each of your departments?"

She contemplated their nods. "Okay, then we'll go department by department." Jia Feng glanced toward Taran first.

"For smithing, our main competition will have two phases. In the first, people will need to create an item. Their ability with picking materials, refining the materials, and turning them into products will be graded. In the second part, they will be given a broken item to repair and some random materials."

There were senior and junior department heads. The members in Alva were the senior department heads. Most of their abilities were on par or higher than those in Vuzgal, and their advances were faster too.

Senior Alchemist Department Head Fehim spoke next. "We intend to have some different competitions. A general growing competition will be hosted with alchemists and farmers in mind, as well as grading harvesting methods. The main competitions will involve crafting powders, potions, and pills. They will work with our standard ingredients and Alchemy equipment. It will test how well they can adjust. Points will be given based on time and quality. The next trial, they will have to grow and harvest their own alchemical plants from supplies we provide and create whatever powerful concoction they desire."

Jia Feng nodded to Nida Saldyte, the leader of the cooking department in Alva.

"With cooking, we will have trials for people to pick out ingredients and then use them to create different foods. We will have whole meals to just desserts, first creating one plate and then enough servings for thirty people." Nida bobbed her head.

"Select materials and create different kinds of clothing, from armors and specialty materials to regular shirts and pants. We will also have popularity contests afterward to decide the current styles and interests in Alva," Zhou Heng said lightly.

Zhou Heng made it sound so easy, but the tailors were one of the hardest working departments. They had the most Experts as well, creating the carriers and different gear the military needed to hold their armor to add in stealth formations to hide in the forest or to keep them warm in the winter and dry in the rain. Even boots, socks, and underwear were made by them!

Shi Wanshu cleared his throat before he spoke. "Again, picking out the best materials to create different items. Also, we will be having a growing competition based on tree-modification methods that have appeared within the woodworkers."

"Tree modification?" Taran asked.

"It happened after some of the wood crafters, farmers, and Alchemy plant cultivators started talking. It is based on the idea that we can use the tree as the building material, not just the planks. That way, we grow the trees to create different items; they could grow to create a house or building, say."

"And all it would require is the right nutrition. It could even grow buds that give off light in the night. If it is damaged, a little growing spell would repair it. If you want to expand, you just grow the tree more into the new shape," Fehim added. "We wondered which department to put it under. It is a new field of study, but we felt that it would be best under the woodworking."

"Interesting." Taran stroked his beard furiously, an excited light in his eyes.

It could open a whole new way to build things.

Fehim and Shi Wanshu smiled at each other.

"I look forward to seeing the results!" She glanced over to Qin Silaz.

"We will have two competitions: formation fighting—having formations fight against one another—and formation building. Based on materials they are given, the formation masters must create a powerful formation."

She glanced over to Jen, who radiated a confidence as deep as an ocean. She didn't spend much time in Alva or Vuzgal academies; most of her time was spent in the different healing houses, teaching people hands-on skills. She had dealt with all kinds of situations, day in and out. Her confidence came from her ability, which was unmatched by anyone other than Erik, and even Erik saw her as someone on the same level or higher. She'd dedicated everything to healing, and she had written many books on the subjects of anatomy and healing principles, expanding upon the information Erik had come up with and adding greater depth related to the Ten Realms.

"Testing for healing will be hard. There is a written portion to test competitors' general knowledge. A medical trial will examine different cases, ranging from easy to hard. They will have to show on a dummy what they would do and explain their actions."

Healing competitions in the Ten Realms were some of the worst. They would wound people and beasts, using them as unwilling patients to show off their abilities. They didn't care for the patient, worrying more about their performance. If things went well, they would look good in front of their peers. For the patient, their lives were on the line. No one in the healing department would dare to do that, though. They had all sworn the Hippocratic Oath to the Ten Realms.

Tan Xue raised her hand.

Jia Feng indicated for her to speak.

"There are Alvans in Vuzgal who want to compete. We talked about it before, but it will be hard to hide their participation. I think that the only way to do this is to shorten the competition time."

The other department heads grimaced.

"Keeping Alva's secret is our biggest shield," Jia Feng said, stopping the dissatisfied noises. "This competition will last four days. Make sure everything is prepared. In the future, we will run our own internal competitions on a craft-by-craft basis. We also plan to run an open competition in Vuzgal where everyone can compete openly. This is to satisfy our people's want for competition. In a year's time, we will host the largest competition the Fourth Realm has ever seen, and all our people can compete. Let us use this as a test of our own abilities and show the people of Alva the strength of our crafters!"

In the sky beyond the balcony, great airships with Blue Lotus markings were landing and taking off. Throughout the valley, city workshops were everywhere. In the distance, one could see a Blue Lotus, the massive flower that was actually a building—the headquarters of the Seventh Realm.

Elder Lu Ru's eyes focused on the pill bottle in his hands.

He felt an arm slip within his, and a smile rose as he covered the hand with his own and glanced up.

"What is distracting you for you to miss my creeping up on you? Does the Fourth Realm not need its elder?" Qiao Zhi smiled.

She wore beautiful, not flashy, embroidered clothes, and her black-and-silver hair was pulled back in a bun with jade pins. Her face had gained lines, showing maturity and laughter over age.

"That will be all, Hao Su," she said to her head guard who stood behind her wheelchair.

"Yes, my lady, my lord." She bowed and quickly left.

Lu Ru raised his wife's hand and kissed it.

"Can a man not just come and see his wife?"

"All these centuries, and you're still a flirt." Qiao Zhi's eyes thinned as she pressed her lips together.

"Seeing you makes me feel like a young man again!" Lu Ru sat up.

"You old fool, you." She rolled her eyes.

"A fool for you." Lu Ru's voice softened.

He paused, staring at her and pulled out the pill bottle.

"What is it?"

Lu Ru silently heard "this time" as he held the bottle.

"This is an age rejuvenation pill. Expert grade."

"I thought they only went up to the Journeyman?"

"I met with the man who made the first pills and powders."

"You met him?" Qiao Zhi sat forward.

"Yes, he's not what you'd expect from an alchemist." Lu Ru raised his brow and smiled before holding out the pill bottle.

Qiao Zhi stared at the pill and nodded.

Lu Ru quickly opened it. Mana from the surrounding area was drawn into the bottle and into the pill as a faint mist appeared on its surface.

"Strong pill," Qiao Zhi said as Lu Ru dropped it into her hand.

She rolled it around and then put it in her mouth, swallowing it.

Her face became flushed as her body warmed to the touch. Sweat appeared on her face, but she moved against her wheelchair like a cat.

She groaned as something popped, followed by another crack. Her free hand came to rest on her lower abdomen.

Lu Ru winced at her gasp. "What is it? Is something wrong?"

"No, no, the damage to my body… I think it's reversing."

"Your core?"

"It is still ruptured, but—" Qiao Zhi fell into silence for some time. The sun dimmed as the chilling breeze of night arrived.

Qiao Zhi let go of a heavy breath that distorted the air with heat.

"Dear?" Lu Ru asked.

"I… I, uh—" Qiao Zhi looked down and moved her robe.

"Your foot." Lu Ru moved the hem of her robe to see her sock-covered feet.

"Your toes! They're moving!" He laughed, grabbing her and kissing her directly.

She moved her foot as well.

Lu Ru laughed in victory.

"I can move some toes and my foot, you old goat! Calm down." Qiao Zhi batted at him, but she had a wide smile on her face.

"Aren't you my wife? If you can move your toes, you'll be running before I can stop you!"

She had no words and batted him again before staring at her toes once again.

Into the Acal Catacombs

The group stood outside a large building. It looked like a castle that had been inverted and had walkways on the outside facing in.

There wasn't much traffic in the area and the structures appeared rough, with signs of fighting around the defensive building.

"Just like totem security," Yuli said.

"Everyone good?" Storbon asked.

Everyone checked their gear and their storage rings. Storbon glanced over to Erik and Rugrat then followed them to the large gate.

"Forty Earth mana stones a person," the guard said.

They paid the fee, and he waved to another team who raised the second gate.

Beyond the outer defense, the cracked stone floor took them to a set of stairs that led into the ground, looking like some beast's maw, ready to eat those who entered.

They kept their cloaks on and pulled on their open-faced helmets as they studied the hole.

Each of them took out their mounts. George and Gilly wore full body-covering armor, as did all the beasts of the special team. Everyone but Erik pulled out a heavy dual repeater and secured it on the back of their mount, checking the weapon worked.

Gilly was like a T-Rex; if he put a repeater on her back, he would shoot her in the neck.

The guards finished their preparations, pointing at different things, unfazed. People used all kinds of different gear on their dungeon dives. It was a way for them to pass the time.

Erik and Rugrat grinned at each other.

Erik checked back at the rest of the group. Yao Meng was the last to mount up and grab his reins.

"Move out!"

Gilly let out a screech, rearing back before she charged forward. George ran after her, and the special team cursed as they followed their charges into the dungeon.

Once they were away from the surface, they pulled off their cloaks, revealing their carriers and weapons.

Erik used Night Vision on himself, but Gilly could see through the dark just fine.

Gilly sniffed the air.

They slowed their pace as the end of the stairs came into sight. Gilly entered the room at a slow gait, observing and snuffling the air. George did the same as Rugrat cradled his rifle with one arm and held onto his handholds with the other.

The rest of the group joined them. The opening looked like nothing more than a rough cave worn away by nature. Creatures living in the different nooks and crannies took off, too small to be a problem.

There were some glowing plants here and there, as well as shattered pillars and items that looked as if they belonged to the buildings above.

"Looks like there are roving bands of creatures around here." Rugrat studied worn paths in the dirt and stone.

"Gilly thinks the same thing. Should we head in the direction of Kuldir Outpost?" Erik asked.

Rugrat checked his map marker for the outpost and the paths to it. "Looks like that way—a few twists and turns." He pointed at one of the three tunnels before them.

Each of the tunnels was large enough for four carts to pass through easily.

"I'll take point," Storbon said.

They moved forward and into the tunnel, and Rugrat guided them through.

Gilly came up short after some time and sniffed the air. Her tongue shot out to touch it. An alarm seemed to go off in her head.

"Watch out!" Erik said through the communication net. Everyone moved apart, ready to react.

A roar came from up ahead. It seemed the enemy had smelled them too.

Two tunnels connected to theirs: one that went left and snaked around, and another right ahead that rose up and then back down, making it impossible to see beyond.

"Straight ahead," Erik said, trusting in Gilly's senses.

"Hold off on the grenades—too close quarters." Storbon got down low and primed his dual repeater.

The others staggered their positions, aiming their repeaters at the rising tunnel. Erik grabbed his rifle and Gilly lowered herself, shaking her body as the mana around her increased in density.

The heat around George was retracted as his fur showed blue lights at their base. Blue flames danced in his eyes and his mouth.

The ground shook as their enemy was revealed.

Orcs! The large humanoid creatures could use simple tools, and some could even cast limited magic. They ran at Erik and those close to him, their eyes shining red as their speed increased.

"Fire!" Storbon said.

Gilly fired out a stream of water that cut through the air. The ground underneath shot up in the attackers' path like jagged teeth. The water cut through several orcs as the "teeth" stabbed them from below and created a natural barrier.

Erik fired his rifle from his place on Gilly's back. He only stopped shooting when his target went down, and he aimed at the next orc.

At the same time, everyone but Erik fired their repeaters. Each of them controlled an area of the tunnel. Their bolts pierced through the orcs' armor and into their bodies. A red glow covered the orcs as they seemed to ignore their wounds and pushed forward even as more arrows pierced them. George stomped, and blue flames shot through the ground and exploded underneath the orcs.

Some of the orcs caught fire; others were killed directly. Tombstones appeared in the tunnels.

The orc group, numbering around fifteen, was reduced to nothing in a few minutes.

Erik paid attention to Gilly, even as he heard the sweet arrival of notifications.

"There are more bands coming toward us."

"All right. Yao Meng, Tian Cui, in the rear. Lucinda, Yuli, up front with me."

They quickly stored the loot.

Storbon lead the way as they charged forward. It seemed that every warband in the entire catacomb was chasing after them.

Erik checked behind as he heard the bark of a rifle.

Yao Meng and Tian Cui were firing their rifles, and Lucinda's eyes glowed. Rats and other small creatures hiding in the area poured out and leaped to attack the charging orcs.

There had to be about twenty orcs charging from behind. They were able to thin their numbers, but more charged out the tunnels and picked up speed.

"We need to get stuck in or else they'll tear through us," Erik said.

"Take a left at the next intersection. There is a cavern in that direction. Looks like it has a water source running through it."

Storbon led them forward and turned at the intersection.

The group followed him. Yao Meng fired his underbarrel grenade launcher, killing a group of orcs and making the tunnel shake violently, dislodging rocks and dust from the ceiling.

A spike of stone dropped. Erik threw out his fist, crushing the stone before it reached him.

They charged, streaming dust. Groups of orcs gathered behind them, moving across the rough ground tripping and stumbling.

Storbon entered the cavern first, scanning and looking for opponents. There, a waterfall descended on their right creating a stream that bisected the cavern. The roar of the waterfall drowned out all but sound transmissions.

Two tunnels were on the other side of the water, the three behind the team showed light from oncoming orc torches.

"We need to cross," Storbon yelled. The sound from the transmission devices blocked out the waterfall's roar.

Gilly seemed to understand and stepped forward as Yuli looked to be starting a spell. Gilly tapped the ground and roared, Erik felt the wave of noise in his chest and the rumble of stone under his feet. The water bubbled, spraying Erik as stone pillars rose from the depths and spread out, connecting to one another to form a bridge. Water rained down from the sides into the swirling water below.

Rugrat grabbed Erik's armor. "I'm going up high!" He pointed to an overhang in the cavern with vines hanging off it.

Erik nodded and gave him the all okay.

George jumped into the air with Rugrat. The ceiling was nearly two hundred meters high, giving Rugrat a great vantage point over the battlefield.

Everyone crossed the bridge as Erik jumped down from Gilly and pulled out his grenade launcher.

Gilly stomped her leg. A low wall of stone appeared from the shore of the river but ran parallel with it.

The others stored their mounts and grabbed their weapon systems, getting behind the short wall.

Gilly cried out to Erik, getting him to focus on her.

He nodded and ran over to Storbon, grabbing him and yelling in his ear. "We need to hit them and keep running. There are more orcs coming from those tunnels and looking to loop around to our rear."

Storbon had a thoughtful expression as he glanced at Erik's grenade launcher. "Grenades then?"

"Might as well. Blunt impact."

Storbon signaled he had heard.

As special team members, they had the best gear Alva could produce, and all of them had grenade launchers.

They adjusted their aim and readied themselves.

The orcs charged dust-filled tunnel, more rushed from side tunnels.

A spell formation snapped into existence around Gilly. A pillar of Water shot out from her and slammed into the orcs charging toward them. It tore up the ground, blasted the rock walls, and reformed it. The pillar of Water and tunnel debris cut down the orcs forcing the survivors back.

Rugrat fired his rifle killing an orc. A black spell formation appeared on the ground under them, and chains shot out, holding the orcs hit from behind by their charging compatriots before grenades landed among the group. The pause was enough to group them together nicely.

George swooped down, leaving Rugrat on his perch as he released blue flames into the remaining tunnel, and Gilly's attack ended. Erik and Lucinda fired on the tunnel, using their grenades to kill the recovering orcs and bring down the tunnel.

"Reloading!" Erik snapped the grenade launcher open and dropped the smoking shells before lowering it. He looked over the short wall and saw both the right tunnel was closed off and the central tunnel he had fired on was broken as well. George headed back to his perch. The tunnel had turned into magma in places. The last group fired their grenades, the molten stone hitting any remaining orcs.

Erik dragged his hand around the cylinder of the grenade launcher, dropping rounds out of his storage ring and directly into the weapon. He snapped it together and glanced over to Storbon, who was sending them all signals. They quickly mounted back up. Rugrat, riding George, dropped to the ground and took the lead. They exited the cavern and kept going. If they got bogged down in fighting, more orcs could flank around them and kill them. In unknown territory, they needed to keep going.

Once they were far enough away from the cavern, they could hear once again without needing to use the sound transmission devices.

"We're about a ten-minute ride from the outpost. We just need to break out of this orc area. I wanted to take the other tunnel, but that wasn't an option. This one leads to an orc camp. We'll need to rush past it, and then we'll be free of the orc's lands, I think," Rugrat said, getting everyone else up to speed.

"Anyone injured?" Yao Meng called out.

Storbon spoke. "If Gilly can cover them with Water and Yuli casts a lightning-based spell, it should have a greater effect."

"George can instant boil some of them and give us cover," Rugrat said.

Erik communicated with Gilly; she looked him in the eye before letting out a proud screech.

Mist covered the cavern. It shifted and distorted, the smell of ozone filling the air. Mana twisted in Yuli's hands as she cast Lightning Bolt. It struck the mist and spread. Like the roots of a tree, it arced through the mist, tearing up the ground and leaving blackened marks, striking the orcs with enough force to send them flying back.

As soon as it started, it was over.

"Clear." Yuli's voice was hoarse and drained.

Storbon blinked his eyes open against the light spots, scanning the area.

Blackened impact craters covered the ground, and tens of orcs lay dead and smoking, tombstones floating above them

George breathed in and exhaled flames.

The mist turned into a fog. Orcs yelled from the superheated steam.

"Move it!" Storbon yelled, urging everyone into action.

The steam condensed, covering the cavern in a wet sheen. They reloaded their weapons as they rode through the tunnels.

"Camp is just ahead!" Rugrat said.

Gilly keened in agreement while George growled and gnashed his teeth. The other panthers joined in.

The thrill of the hunt—the fight was on.

A faint haze shimmered around Gilly as she gathered her power, ready to carry out the Water spell.

The tunnel opened ahead. Flickering lights from fires inside the camp played on the rough, rocky roof and surroundings.

Erik studied the camp. Walls made of stones piled atop one another. Crude design. Sentries wandering around. Spikes with heads on the wall—mostly orc, others beast, some human.

High pitched yips and yaps from inside and outside the camp revealed scrawny, diseased, and crazed-looking dogs scavenging around the camp.

Orcs leaning on the wall raised their gaze, seeing the group. They started growling and grunting, waving their hands, and other orcs appeared on the wall.

A yowl went up, and some of the dogs moved forward.

"Looks like we have company." Rugrat raised his voice as he fired the repeater on George's back.

The magically enhanced arrows from the special team's repeaters acted as tracers as they reached out to meet the growing horde of scavenger dogs.

"Ready!" Yuli yelled.

"Do it, girl," Erik said to Gilly. His legs were clamped around her midriff, allowing him the freedom to fire his grenades into the large groups of dogs turning and chasing after their rear.

Gilly turned her head toward the camp. Her body glowed with power. Runes appeared on her skin as the air around her became heavy and cold. A rumble echoed through the area, and a blue line appeared above the camp. From the line, runes, and other parts, a magical circle appeared almost organically, as if it were being written in the sky with someone not taking their pen off the sky's canvas.

The spell formation drew in the surrounding mana, multiplying its power.

Gilly was drawing external mana, casting on instinct. *No wonder people are terrified of beasts in the Ten Realms.*

Mana surged out of Gilly, and the spell formation grew in Strength. Clouds formed above the camp and rain fell. It quickly turned from a shower into a tropical downpour so strong it created a visual barrier.

Yuli's eyes glowed as another spell formation appeared among the clouds.

The clouds rumbled as orc guards reached the walls and fired arrows at the group. With the rain falling on them and the changing direction of the group, they missed their targets. Orcs were used to using blunt weapons instead of short and simple bows.

"Shaman!" Lucinda yelled.

An old orc, a full head higher than its already tall brethren used its staff of black cracked wood to move its hunchbacked form, forward, wearing an extravagant headdress of carved bone hide and random feathers. The crack's in his staff glowed green, a necklace of small heads hung from the shaman's neck. He chanted, the heads on his necklace glowed as the light from his staff increased gathering mana.

Erik ducked in surprise. Was this the power of Sixth Realm dungeon mobs?

"Not today," Yuli said, her voice infused with mana. Her lightning fell upon Gilly's conjured rain. Thick, blinding arcs of lightning descended, weaving through the rain. The noise rolled through the camp and the tunnels, shaking the ceiling and foundation.

They looked away from the camp as lightning bolts crashed, one after another. Gilly's spell drew external mana, having a much greater effect than her spell would have had by itself. The high mana concentration fueled the spell that Yuli cast, the two of them working in synergy.

The dogs turned and fled, allowing the group to use all their speed to escape.

The shaman changed his spell, raising a mana barrier over the camp. Rugrat led them down a well-trodden trail down a small rise that led them around the camp and gave them cover.

Erik scanned the area and checked behind the camp. Lightning hit the side of the mana barrier and struck the ground. Earth exploded outward from the impact, and then, like someone pulling string out of dirt, it tore up the ground, scattering rocks and clumps of mud.

Erik glanced up as his notification symbol flashed.

The group reloaded again as they left the stone-and-dirt lands of the orcs behind. Slowly, trees, bushes, and other plants came into view. Everything had a sickly look to it. There was little light down here, but water fell from the ceiling in different places, making ponds that were covered in plants where different creatures gathered to drink.

A beast hiding in the trees jumped out at them. It had the body of a lizard with long limbs and barbed suckers on the end of them. Its maw opened, revealing three jaws all lined with teeth. Its mouth was big enough to fit a human.

Lucinda fired her repeater into the beast. She had blunt and increased speed sockets on the repeater, and the creature was tossed back and away from the group. The impacts rocked it, but its scaled body took the damage well.

Rugrat's chains rose from the ground and clamped onto the creature as Storbon fired his rifle. He used a piercing formation in the socket, and the round went right through the creature's head, deep into its body.

It slumped, and a tombstone appeared above it.

"Must be a lone hunter. Keep an eye out. Yao Meng, loot it," Storbon said.

Yao Meng rode over to the tombstone, his rifle pointed at the beast.

His mount started toward it, ready to attack.

He accessed the tombstone, and it disappeared. The next second, the beast dissipated.

"Let's get going," Storbon said.

They headed off again and didn't encounter anything else for a while.

"So, what kind of loot did you get from that thing? What is it?" Yuli asked.

"It's called a deep snapper. I got acid poison sacks, a small dagger, poison barbs, and monster core, greater Earth grade. Then a section of its hide—damaged, though," Yao Meng said.

"Deep snapper? What is it—a lost football player? Maybe an engineer? Those bastards could drink. Looks better than some of them did after a night out. Hey, there's light up ahead," Rugrat said.

"I'm surprised and scared by just how much useless information you store in there," Erik said.

"For a second, I forgot we were using Night Vision spells," Lucinda said.

"Night Vision spells make it a lot easier," Tian Cui said.

"Night creeper," Yao Meng said.

"What I do best." Tian Cui grinned.

Erik moved up toward Rugrat. "What does it look like to you?"

"That Tian Cui is a lot scarier than I thought. Can you hold me tonight? I'm scared. She could out-stealth a chameleon."

Erik held his face, talking into his palm. "Why did it have to be *him* who came to the Ten Realms with me? Couldn't I have someone normal?"

"Ah, you love it." Rugrat grabbed his shoulder and shook him. "Looks like more light. With my mana sense, I can pick out a lot of people with magical capabilities moving around. Based on the mana, I would say that they're humans." Rugrat checked the map.

"And that lines up with the map I have." He showed it to Erik, who compared the area around them to the map.

"Should be coming up on an outpost soon. Stay alert," Erik said.

They continued forward as a group, each scanning the area.

"These roads are more like a trail," Storbon said.

"The people in the camp must not go out and fight the orcs that much. Either they ignore them or don't know about them. If they're dungeon creatures, they will most likely keep to themselves unless someone enters their territory."

"They give a lot of Experience because they're intelligent creatures, albeit savages," Lucinda said.

"Look who's already trying to grind out Experience." Storbon laughed.

"That's why people probably don't engage them. You can learn how a beast will react. But sentient creatures? You can try to predict, but they can do something completely unexpected and take everyone out," Rugrat said.

"You sound like you've done it before."

"I hunted and was hunted by humans for most of my life. It was our job."

Erik grunted, and everyone else fell silent.

They kept scanning the area but relaxed as the outpost came into sight.

"Well, 'outpost' doesn't really cover that. Doesn't look anything like the outposts in Beast Mountain Range. More like a small city," Rugrat said.

"Just how much did the academies build? These outposts are all over the dungeon," Yuli said.

The outpost had reinforced walls made from formation-covered stone that reached fifty meters tall. Behind the wall was a bustling town, but there were some clearly separated compounds with towers embossed with the crest of the varied groups commanding them.

At the center, there was a lone tower with a book and sword crossing each other.

"Managing all this has to be a nightmare," Rugrat said.

"Yeah. Everyone fighting to get a better position," Erik said.

"All managed by a council. Like, I know we have a council for Alva, but it's slimmed down, and Egbert keeps things moving ahead so they don't get bogged down. Here..." Rugrat whistled. "Councils for research, councils for the varied groups, and then councils to deal with the needs of citizens. One to negotiate between varied groups, another to control it all."

"Yeah, that has to be one hell of a headache," Erik said.

"Why does it matter—all of the councils?" Storbon asked.

Erik and Rugrat exchanged a glance.

"Councils can come to a decision once in a while, but it is fucking painful. Everyone wants to be heard. They negotiate behind closed doors, but in the end, whatever the damn thing they were supposed to be staring at might be the last thing on their minds. With so many councils doing that and overlapping one another"—Rugrat shook his head—"nothing gets done."

"Sometimes you just need to act. If you're in a fight and you have to get all the sergeants together and have them talk about the plan of attack then pass that through the ranks up to the major and when the people higher don't agree, then return it to the people at the bottom." Erik grimaced.

"Everyone fucking dies." Storbon shrugged.

"Right." Rugrat sighed. "Well, I guess we know why it is so stable. Everything is a damn mess and connected to one another. It's hard to piece things together, so everything kind of just keeps on rolling."

"As long as it's stable, people aren't going to care, and it won't matter to us. We just have to remember to not piss off anyone who's in a high position or has a high standing. Keep it low key."

Storbon smirked.

"What?" Rugrat asked.

"You two? Low key? *Right*," Yao Meng said from behind.

"Hey! I'm super low key!" Rugrat said.

"In your short shorts and cowboy hat?" Yuli said.

"*That* is called *style*, Miss Yuli!"

"I'm really low key," Erik argued.

"Yeah, until you go around and start teaching arrogant scions and masters and start beating the hell out of them. Didn't you get chased across the entire Third Realm, a *peaceful* realm, by someone who wanted to kill you?" Storbon asked.

"That was *one* time!"

"What about how we are all now Honorary Elders of the Blue Lotus *and* the Crafter's Association? We own a *city*," Lucinda asked.

"Don't forget how you farted the other day and ripped your pants because of your Body Like Sky Iron," Rugrat chimed in.

"And wasn't it flammable in your room after you had Jia Feng's super spicy chili?"

"That was George!"

George howled with a look of pure puppy innocence.

"It wasn't George. Poor guy couldn't breathe, or else he might ignite it and turn your room into a methane-powered air bomb!"

"Kinda funny, though, wasn't it?" Rugrat grinned.

The others on the special team were working to try to not laugh. Erik pressed his lips against his teeth, seeing Rugrat observing for agreement.

"Let's just get to the outpost. And low key!" Erik said.

"Yes, boss!" Yao Meng turned to Tian Cui. "So, should I go with my glow in-the-dark, pink suit or my lightning trousers and flashing T-shirt? I think that would let me blend in."

Tian Cui snorted as they rode toward the gates.

Once inside, Erik finally took the time to look at his notifications.

9

Vuzgal Fighter's Competition Begins

Roska peeked at the applicants for the special teams. They were inside one of the tier-three training rooms located under the Battle Arena. There were medics on hand to put people back together. Broken bones and bruises sucked, but the applicants got used to it.

Knowing the limits of their body allowed them to know what would happen in a fight if they took a certain action. Applying their power into their actions meant they could push past their mental limits.

"They're looking good," Gong Jin, her second-in-command, said as they looked over the recruits.

"They've been quick to learn fighting techniques. The competition begins tomorrow. It will be a good way for them to deal with life-and-death situations," Roska said.

"Be good to see what they've learned. They've got the basics down. Just have to wait and see what they do with it." Gong Jin's eyes flashed as his smile deepened. "Just the first step."

Roska peeked at him.

"Even we have to work our asses off to stay ahead of everyone else to do our jobs, learn fighting techniques and increase our cultivation."

"We cannot be over-confident. There is always someone who is stronger," Gong Jin agreed.

They continued to look over the special team recruits. They had worked up to fighting with their full armor and weapons. The area was broken up into fighting squares. Their eyes were clear as the dense mana kept them alert and energetic.

The location was hooked up to the mana-storing formation under Vuzgal. They were practically burning mana stones as they trained. Still, the mana density wasn't as high as the general sparring areas in Alva.

As they fought, the recruits' fighting styles underwent massive changes in just a few hours of sparring. They only stopped when they were injured, closing their eyes and drinking healing and Stamina potions and concentrating on what they had learned before they clashed again.

The members of the special team jumped into the training as well, going up against the recruits, taking the opportunity to learn and point out issues or weaknesses that they saw in the recruits' fighting styles.

All of them were battle crazy. Wounds didn't matter to them as long as they got stronger.

Seeing them fighting day in and out and by working with them, Roska was able to see through to the person and understand who they were and what motivated them.

Each of them had transformed. While fighting, they were focused. Their reactions honed; they stopped being a person and became an operative, leaving their personal lives and everything else behind. All that mattered was the mission.

They had lost seven people through different trials, and she fully expected they might lose more as time went on.

She received a message from Domonos.

"Hey, Roska, I wanted to let you know that I've entered your people into the competition as you asked."

"Thanks."

"How is it going?"

"Good. They're doing well," Roska said.

"All right. Don't be a stranger." Domonos cut the channel.

Roska smiled. Since she had become the leader of Special Team Two, she hadn't really done anything other than practice, train, and go on missions to increase her Strength or deal with issues.

She wasn't upset with how her life had gone, but a part of her wondered what it would've been like if she had followed another path. She shook her head. *This is what my life is, and, well, it's not bad at all.*

She hid the smile that threatened to appear on her face. As the leader of Special Team Two, she didn't want to be anywhere else. Memories appeared in her mind: Erik, his face etched with concentration, and the tears that had appeared on her face back then—not from the pain as he helped to heal her, but the ones filled with thanks for this powerful man who took the time to care for her. Not caring about his position but caring about her.

She would follow those two idiots to the Tenth Realm and watch their backs. Someone needed to keep them out of trouble or save them when they fell into it.

Blaze stepped off the totem's pad. Behind him, there were nearly forty people openly wearing their weapons and armor. At the front were the six branch heads, and behind them were their personal selection of fighters to represent the guild. They were an eccentric-looking bunch from various classes. They had visited Alva and trained against the beasts in the battlefield dungeon and endless dungeons. They had attended classes held by the military and academy. Some had picked up skills in crafting; others had joined the army. No matter what their path, they had all grown. They had proved their loyalty and their drive, and they changed from simple mercenaries to members of the Adventurer's Guild.

Blaze wore his armor of peak Journeyman grade, his cloak covering most of it. He reached the guard.

"Ah, a good group of fighters you have there, sir," the guard said.

Blaze worked his jaw as he looked at the Alvan guard, feeling the rising smile fighting his cheek muscles.

He had never imagined they could make it this far. Seeing the Alvan sitting there with a smile on his face, Blaze straightened in pride at being part of something that was greater than himself, with the joy of being on the inside of the joke.

He paid the fee, sharing a nod with the Alvan before heading into Vuzgal. They left the defensive works around the totem and entered the city proper. Towering restaurants that kissed the sky dotted the city. His eyes were captivated by the main tower that stood over Vuzgal's castle from across the city. The streets were widened to move people through quickly. There was room for eight carts abreast on the main streets, but the stalls, storefronts, and pedestrians took up the sides.

Mounts could be seen everywhere, moving along the carriage roads.

Even with all that space, people were pressed tightly against one another. People wore all kinds of weapons and armor with crests showing which power they were from. Guards of the associations patrolled the streets. The Vuzgal Defense Force was out in strength, with police officers maintaining the peace.

A fight broke out as fire came from a store. People screamed and scattered as two people fought against each other.

An undead beast dropped from the sky, depositing guards and a police officer.

Somebody used a spell scroll, isolating the two and pressing them flat to the ground. A medic healed those who were injured while the police officer talked to the people in the store and then to the two who were fighting.

"What did they expect? This is Vuzgal. Nothing is missed by the guards and police here," one of the merchants said proudly.

"Too right. I could leave my wares out all night without fear of them being stolen. Thieves and pickpockets are banned from the city in quick order!"

"That has to be a lie," someone said.

"Dear customer, this is Vuzgal. It's not like other cities. The only fighting that happens here is in the arena, the barracks, and the dungeons."

"Come on, there have to be loopholes. The powerful can get out of everything," someone scoffed.

"Everyone is equal here. The city lord didn't hesitate to throw out those Expert-level crafters who were raising hell."

"I should look at getting housing in Vuzgal," another person said.

"Good luck. I heard that only large traders, sects, and High level crafters could afford the last houses put up for auction. Best bet is to get a room at a Wayside Inn."

The two who were fighting had their weapons stripped and armor taken off to be sold. The funds would be used to fix the damage they had caused and pay those who were wounded or affected.

Then the guards and police officer banned the two from Vuzgal. Enforced with the power of the city lord, the Ten Realms forced them to run for the totem to leave as fast as possible.

Blaze led his guild members forward. He checked his map and the marker on it.

They left the busier streets and headed toward the areas where the guild residences were located. These were larger, multi-story buildings. Very few of the buildings had been sold off as they went for astronomical prices, and although there was a great demand for them, most people didn't have the funds.

Blaze reached a gated area, and they entered. A full beast stable stood to one side and a large seven-story building on the other. A tavern took up most of the first floor, and there was a courtyard in the middle of the building. In the back left, there were mission boards and a counter where guild members could talk to administrators. The back right had a storefront and crafting workshops so people could get items made, altered, and repaired in the guild. Sparring and training rooms were in the basement. On the floors above, there were apartments.

Formations had been laid across the guild hall. The mana density was nearly two times as dense as the mana across Vuzgal.

"This is really ours?" Emilia asked, turning around and waving her arms at the hall.

"Yeah, I guess so." Blaze sat at the tavern bar. Kim Cheol was behind the bar, pouring drinks as people wandered their new headquarters.

"The beast stables will not only help our mounts recover from any injuries they sustain, but they'll be well rested and can increase in Strength the longer they remain there. If one pays the mana stones, then the stall their mount is in can have its mana density increased," Joan said, coming in from outside.

"Did you see the sparring rooms below? The combat puppets reach up to level fifty! And you can pay for mana stones to increase the mana density in there." Derrick came out from the rear of the hall, his hand opening and closing next to his rapier.

Mana stones were useful to increase one's Mana Cultivation when using them to increase the density of an area; although, some of them would be lost. Through the increased concentration and how their bodies would naturally draw in the mana, they could train on a higher level for longer, which would leave them constantly looking to increase their fighting skills to meet that level.

"Have you seen those smithing facilities? Even a peak Journeyman smith would be interested. If we can hire a smith like that…well, damn."

"You're forgetting some key things," Stephan said. "We are in Vuzgal now, a city that a lot of people are trying to enter but few are able to do so. If we can make a name for ourselves in the fights, we can advertise we are recruiting freelance fighters, people who want to join just for the location and benefits. As long as we vet them, we could get Fourth and Fifth Realm Experts."

"First, we need to register for the fight. Stephan is right. We need to prove ourselves and show the power of our guild. We are among the heavy hitters now. We need to show we're worthy of staying here."

Chonglu rubbed his face, feeling tired. He didn't remember when he had last been this excited, nervous, and tired all at once.

"Dad, are you okay?" Feng asked.

"Yes, I'm fine. Just a lot of work." Chonglu smiled at his son and gazed at Felicity. She stopped her chewing; she had noodles in her chopsticks, and her cheeks were puffed out. "Eat slowly or you'll get indigestion. And you don't need to stuff it all in your cheeks."

She dropped her head as she had to chew to even be able to speak.

I thought I raised her to be a lady! He hid his smile behind his bowl as he drank some soup.

The door opened. Mira stood there, a hesitant look on her face.

Chonglu stopped eating and smiled up at her.

Feng turned around at the noise, with noodles still hanging out of his mouth. "Murm!"

He ran over, and Felicity turned as well. The two tackled Mira's legs.

"Feng, you still have noodles hanging out! Felicity, remember to chew or you'll choke! Chonglu, what have you been teaching these two?"

"That they should sit down and finish dinner first." Chonglu frowned at the twins.

With sheepish looks, they rushed back to the table.

Chonglu sighed and served Mira a bowl. She leaned between Feng and Felicity, kissing both their cheeks, not minding their sauce-covered cheeks or the stain Feng left on her dress.

She went around the table and kissed Chonglu. "Thank you, dear."

"You always forget to eat! Tell me, what have you had to eat the past week?" Chonglu made sure to put an extra helping in her bowl.

Mira coughed, blushing. She quickly changed the subject. "What have you two been up to?"

"We learned about inscriptions!" Feng said. Felicity bobbed her head.

Mira frowned.

I'm innocent! Chonglu chewed furiously to try and defend himself.

"Come on, I want to hear all about your time in the academy. Show me your cultivation."

Chonglu grumpily swallowed, knowing his opportunity was gone.

They proudly released the power of their cultivation.

"You've improved quickly," Mira said, stunned. "It won't be long until you can compress your mana into drops!"

She reached out her hand to Felicity, who put her arm in her mother's hand.

The room chilled as Mira exerted the power of her constitution.

Slowly, a frost formed on Felicity's arm.

"How is it, Mom? Am I stronger than Feng?" Felicity beamed.

"No, *I'm* stronger!" Feng complained.

"You've done well. Have you used all the pills I gave you?" Mira asked Felicity.

"One every morning for a week and then two every day—one in the morning and one at night—until I have had them all," Felicity said, rattling off the instructions proudly.

"You did well." She smiled and completed the test on Feng.

"I'm stronger, right, Mom?"

"You're both strong. You two need to work together instead of fighting each other all the time," Mira said.

As she had tested her children, Chonglu had filled up her bowl with different things she liked.

"How has it been for you?" he asked as he put her bowl down.

She smiled as he kissed her.

"Training, training, and more training. They found a new dungeon in the Sixth Realm, and we've been asked to go and explore. It will be a long campaign, though it should raise our levels quick."

"You might be able to hide how excited you are from others," Chonglu murmured.

She pressed her lips together, but her eyes were shining. "It should be good. It has been too long since I went on a dungeon dive. What about you? Have you been in the dungeons? You feel stronger."

"Well, I should be. I've been training with the military and learning techniques. And I might've gone in the dungeon once or twice, undercover." Chonglu smiled. "I heard that the ones in the Sixth Realm are massive."

"Depends. Some are just large dungeons, while others are interconnected with dungeons that could fit multiple cities from the Third Realm inside them."

"Can we go?" Feng asked.

"Not until you're older," Chonglu said.

"You get to go." Feng stabbed his chopsticks into his food.

"You can when you're older. Now, how about that healing course? I heard you're doing well?" Chonglu said.

He caught Mira staring at him from the corner of his eye.

Felicity and Feng spilled everything the two had been up to in school, and their conversations turned more to what they had done with their friends than their studies.

"By the time you two leave, you might be Apprentices in all the major crafts," Mira said with approval.

"Plenty of people will want to hire you right away. Don't sign anything without your mother or I," Chonglu said.

"Can we go to the games?" Felicity asked in a rush.

Feng leaned forward, ready for the reply.

The two of them looked between their parents.

Little devils. They were trying to get them to fold and let them off school for two weeks!

"We can go this weekend. If you do well in your tests next week, then I'll take you to the arena. If not, you will have to watch from home."

They both groaned, staring at their mother for aid. She shook her head at their pleading eyes.

"Will Uncle Erik and Rugrat be there?" Feng asked.

"They're away right now, but there are some other people you can meet," Chonglu said.

Their faces dimmed. They were at the age when it was awkward to talk to older people. They had their favorites, but they didn't like being around those they didn't know unless they made a connection first. Then they would be enthralled with them, forgetting about the awkwardness from before.

"Can we just train in fighting?" Felicity said.

"No, you need to learn more than just fighting to succeed," Chonglu said firmly, seeing Mira hesitate.

"It's not a kind world out there; there are people who will want to hurt you. You will learn to fight with time. For now, learn what could help you with if you do choose to fight. Or you might find something even more fun to do." Chonglu's voice turned excited. "You could create formations that could stand against the strongest of monsters, create a flame pillar that reaches into the heavens, make clothes that will stop arrows and swords, or craft shields that will stop a charging rhino. Swords that can cut through a forest with one cut. Healing concoctions that could cure a person in a second or give you massive Strength. Spell scrolls that will allow anyone to wield the power of a mage grandmaster—even stronger. Tasty food."

Chonglu had a wry smile on his face as he looked over to Felicity, who lowered her head.

"When you finish school, I will train you to fight. Your bodies will be tempered. You will run day and night, do push-ups and pull-ups until your muscles burn, and then you will do more. To be fighters, you must suffer, sweat, and do hard work to save you from spilling blood. Training to fight comes with sacrifices. With your education from the academy, you will know how to repair your shield, set your bones, wrap your wounds, and use healing concoctions. You'll know where to strike a person's armor, and you'll recognize when someone is wearing well-made clothing and when they are wearing well-crafted armor. These are small items, but that knowledge, even at the Novice and Apprentice level, can save your life."

They fell quiet, and Chonglu smiled. He was their father, and they knew he had been an adventurer with their mother. He had many scars on his body that had been removed from when he had been badly wounded by assassins.

"There are always people stronger who can send one to death's door."

His words made them think of the condition they had seen him in. Their faces were haunted. Chonglu wished they never had to see something like that, but it was also a lesson for them. The Ten Realms was a savage place. They needed to be ready for anything.

They finished dinner, and the two showed their parents what they had learned. They had a building all to themselves within the Castle District. They had been given three mounts, special panthers raised in Alva. Chonglu received an older panther named Lola. She was Erik's older mount. She was a leader among the panthers and incredibly strong.

With Chonglu's companion and longtime mount killed and Lola without a rider, Erik had passed her into Chonglu's care.

Lola padded over to Chonglu, and he patted her and scratched her neck. She pushed into him, her body rumbling as she purred. She needed to get stronger, then he could hold his position confidently, riding without being conscious of how powerful she was and how weak he was.

A rule that Chonglu hadn't paid attention to had now become his mantra.

How powerful an individual or group was was the only thing that mattered in the Ten Realms. The stronger a person was, the less people would be inclined to attack the things they love. He would get stronger, and no one would dare harm his children or take his wife from him again. No one would kill those he cared about. His thoughts trailed off. Thankfully,

Domonos was more than willing to help him.

He felt stronger already, having completed his foundational temperings. Now, he needed to temper his body. He was waiting until after the competition and would then seclude himself to the Fire floor in Alva Dungeon.

The night quickly came, and the family went to bed. Feng and Felicity had laid down, and Chonglu went back with Mira to bed.

With it being so long that they were apart, they were nervous around each other at first but soon fell into their old ways as she held his hand and rested her head on his shoulder.

Chonglu heard noises from her.

He turned her around, seeing wet lines on her face as she tried to hide her tears.

"What are you crying for?" Chonglu asked, holding her to his chest.

"I'm so happy to be here with you all, but sometimes I remember all that you've been through. I missed seeing them grow from babies, taking their first steps, and becoming who they are today. I missed seeing you going from an adventure captain and new city lord to a father who can navigate the pitfalls of being an adult. Who was there for our children when they were happy or sad, picked them up when they were hurt, and saw them grow?" Mira said, looking away as she tensed.

Chonglu hugged her. He kissed her head and smelled her hair. "They are still young. There are plenty of memories to be made with them. You're their mother, and they want you in their lives."

"Maybe I shouldn't go on that campaign," Mira said.

"Being a fighter is part of who you are. If you don't go, you'll regret it. Just know that we're here and waiting for you to come back. Don't make snap decisions because of your emotions. Think them through," Chonglu said.

They fell quiet, and she relaxed against his chest.

"Plus, well, you know…not saying we couldn't have more children," he said with a wide grin.

She smacked his chest and smiled.

Chonglu cradled her neck and pulled her lips to his.

10

Land of Experts

"D amn"—a hammer slammed into a formation with every word—"power-freaking-runes!"

"Sooo, things going well in here?" Julilah asked from her workbench.

"The damn runes weren't able to handle the power. Burnt out the entire thing I was working on for…" Qin's tirade came to a pause. "What day is it?"

"I dunno." Julilah looked through her formation-enhanced glasses at the piece being held in a vise. Even with her fellow's tirade, her hands didn't falter.

"Urgh!" She hit the formation again with a hammer.

"You could get Tan Xue to hammer it back down."

"Days wasted!"

"You're guessing now," Julilah pointed out, lifting her fine mana tool and checking on her work. With a satisfied nod, she moved down the table and studied another band of metal that was clamped down.

"It must've been days with how hungry I am! Look at my skin; people are going to think I'm a witch." Qin sunk into her chair with a groan. She picked up a formation and dropped it into the socket. They snapped together as if magnetized. She pulled it out and then let it drop again; it lit up and then died as she pulled it out, and she repeated the practice several times. The simple actions calmed her.

A vein appeared on Julilah's forehead. "Will you go do that somewhere else?"

"Oh." Qin released the formation, and it snapped into place. She had a sheepish look on her face. "I didn't mean to do that one. Um, I'm going to take a walk."

Julilah turned back to her work.

Qin quickly left the formation workshop. With the drop in mana, she felt tired. She rubbed her face as she watched the sun set. Her eyes stung from staring at natural light. She wandered through the halls of Vuzgal's academy. The people around her wore medallions that showed off their profession and the level they had reached.

Seeing her medallion, most people would bow and make room. She saw many other Experts and nodded to them.

Since they gained access to the technique books from the higher realms, people have been using the information to enter the Expert level of crafting, while a smaller number have been making their own techniques to make it into the Expert realm. Now that she was an Expert, it was nothing more than just knowing she knew *something* to get a hint of an idea that worked. A theory that showed some promise. Now, all she had to do was remove all the extras, remove her assumptions, and find the truths contained within that theory. The closer she got to finding that truth about formations, the stronger she could make her formations.

Qin was surprised by the number of Experts in the halls. They had been hiring Experts not that long ago, and now they were hiring Low Expert-level teachers as general staff. Mid Expert-level teachers were also growing in number.

With the external Experts helping them, they should be able to produce more of their own.

Thinking on it, she got excited, wondering just how strong the different Experts' knowledge was in practical applications.

As a department head, she needed to show how strong she was. If she lost her position? She would lose access to the workshop, the alchemical aids, and the resources. She had already run out of her allotment for the month.

"So expensive!" She grumbled, heading homeward and thinking of projects to increase her skill level and retain her position.

Roska was looking over the measures the security forces in Vuzgal had taken to mitigate risks and issues around the Battle Arena.

Special Team Two rested in the lounge area. Gong Jin was studying the quickly filling stadiums. Each stadium was layered on top of the other. They had hundreds of stages, and people could see multiple fights from any of the stages.

"Must be making a killing off binoculars," Simms said as he looked from the couch.

"Don't forget the Sky Reaching Restaurant is making food and drinks," Tully said as she stretched.

"Come on!" Imani complained as Han Wu revealed his cards.

"Either you are the Ten Realm's best cheater or the luckiest bastard out there." Davos pushed his cards forward.

"Who you betting on for the fighting contests?" Yang Zan moved closer to Han Wu, as if he were getting the inside scoop.

"Xi knows better than me," Han Wu said.

Roska glanced up to Xi, who was passed out on the couch, snoring lightly.

She checked the report once more and put it away. "Well, it looks like we've covered nearly everything that could go wrong. Let us know if you need help in any way," she said to Chonglu, who stood beside her.

He looked a little nervous seeing them all. "Thank you." He sounded relieved.

"How many applicants are there for the competition?"

"Around two thousand people as of last night. There were some last-minute check-ins, but the number shouldn't have changed much," Chonglu said.

"And two weeks will be enough time for the competition?" Gong Jin asked.

"It should be. I talked to the Fighter's Association, and they reviewed my plan."

"Should be a good competition," Roska said.

"It's a lot of damn people. Not all the seats are filled, but there are a lot of freaking seats." Han Wu dealt the cards again.

"Are you sure you want to remain in here?" Chonglu asked.

"Best if we keep a low profile. We can use these viewers here to watch the different fights our people are in and see how they do," Roska said.

"Very well. Let me know if you need anything," Chonglu said.

He headed out of the room to carry out his other tasks. There was plenty to be done in the two hours before the first fights began.

Blaze looked over the members of the Adventurer's Guild. There was little conversation, some jokes here and there, but they were focused on preparing themselves for the fight ahead. Some of them had spent the night with the combat puppets to hone their skills; others had been cultivating to clear their minds.

They didn't seem to give off a pressure, showing that they had complete control over their strength.

"All right." Blaze whistled, and his mount, a large lizard, walked out of the beast stables.

She flared her neck and hissed as she stretched away her sleep. Mana seemed to ripple around her as her claws dug into the ground. Other beasts came out of the stables, greeting the branch heads.

Blaze got onto the lizard's back, patting her side. "Show-off."

She sent a tongue out toward him trying to give him kisses.

"Cut that out will you!" He laughed, dodging the tongue and giving her scratches. Appeased her leg started bouncing with his scratching.

The rest of the guild members competing, mounted up, making quite the sight with their powerful beast's custom armor and focused looks on their faces.

Blaze led them out of the guild hall as passersby talked amongst themselves.

"Do you know what guild that is?"

"Maybe they're new?"

"A new guild was able to buy a hall like that? Do you know how much those things cost and the upkeep on them? Not just any guild can buy them!"

They rode past, two columns following Blaze. They headed toward the arena.

A group of scalpers stood at the front of the Battle Arena. They had seen all kinds of people entering. A long line of fighters disappeared into the lower sections of the Battle Arena, and VIPs headed into several entrances that led to the different levels and booths.

"You were able to get some seats for the third arena? How were you able to do that?" one of the scalpers asked his friend who was showing off the tickets.

"I've got connections. You know, High class clientele!" the other bragged.

His friend rolled his eyes as people walked up to them, and they got to work selling them tickets.

A large group of over thirty people approached, riding on powerful mounts and wearing mix-matched gear and armor.

The scalpers looked up and then away, focusing on selling their tickets. There had been plenty of different kinds of groups and people joining the line of fighters.

They saw a leader talking to them and sending them over to the admission for the fighters.

The scalpers finished their business and sent on their customers.

"Tickets for the first elimination rounds of the competition! Get to see hundreds of fighters with just one ticket. Tickets up to the third arena!" they called out.

The scalper without the third arena tickets tapped his friend, pointing at the leader who had sent his group down to the lower levels. "Looks like a paper tiger. Brought his people here to compete, but he can't get a ticket."

"Why don't you try selling him one?" the younger scalper said and carried on calling out to people. Soon, another group came over to him.

"How much are the tickets to the third arena?" a young man, with a girl on his arm, asked.

"A man with a discerning eye! I have the best deal for you, and these are some of the only tickets left!"

The older scalper shook his head and walked over to the man sitting on a bench. "Looking for tickets?" he asked the man, feeling sorry for him.

"No. Thank you for offering. I'm just waiting on someone." The man smiled.

The old scalper shrugged and called out to people, looking to sell his tickets. He walked over to his friend. "How did it go?"

"Acted high and mighty, but he was too cheap," the younger scalper complained. "What about that guy?"

"He has the look of someone important, but he's not willing to pay for even a low level ticket to see his people fight."

"Some people are too proud for their own good, huh?" The younger scalper looked behind the older scalper, making him turn around.

A set of doors opened from the inside, the entrance for the VIPs visiting the Battle Arena. An official wearing a badge of a Battle Arena manager walked out and bowed deeply to Blaze.

Blaze nodded at the man and smiled, patting him on the shoulder. The higher-ups of the Battle Arena were all hard and exact, known to be emotionless in their dealings, but this man laughed and smiled as he ushered in Blaze as if they were long-lost friends.

"What?" the older scalper said.

"Looks like a *real* tiger," the younger man muttered.

"My eyes must be getting bad in my old age." The older man sighed, secretly thankful that the man had been so graceful when he approached.

He shuddered, thinking what might have happened if he had approached some of the other High profile people he had seen go through that entrance.

"I've never seen that group he was with," the younger man said.

"Maybe they're a new group," the older man said. "I wonder if the bookies know that."

The two men stared at each other.

"Once we sell these off, we should put down some bets." The younger man smiled. "I'm feeling lucky all of a sudden!"

Fighting in Vuzgal

Chonglu made it to the VVIP booth. Here, there were representatives from the associations, as well as High powered traders. Hiao Xen was among the group and so were Blaze and Elise, who were over in the corner. He'd only met Blaze briefly while setting up the competition, but he had worked closely with Elise, though.

He walked over to them.

"Blaze, I've heard a lot about you." Chonglu held out his hand.

"Lord Chonglu." Blaze shook his hand.

"Just Chonglu now. The only lords are Erik and Rugrat." Chonglu smiled.

"Yeah, like they'll let that title stick for more than ten seconds. They're more comfortable with their military ranks," Elise muttered. "How are things on your side?"

"Everything is running smoothly; although, some people are messing with one another down in the waiting areas. There has been an increased presence of guards. How are the stores?"

"Busy. Seems a lot of people came just to buy items after they heard the deals we have on fighting-related gear. The Sky Reaching Restaurants are full, and we had to open Wayside Inns in areas where we're still building. Just so many people. With all the fighters here, there is an influx of traders selling their wares and taking advantage of our bartering system. We had to open five more locations as the first three had too many people. You should talk to the Blue Lotus. They have so many people trying to buy tickets to the auction, but they don't have the capacity. They might want to rent out the stadium." She laughed.

"My builders and cleaners are going to have their work cut out for them."

"Aren't you using the undead as cleaners?" Elise asked.

"Well, yeah. Saves on wages. Give them a storage ring, and they can clean up everything while working through the night."

"Well, I never thought of that," Blaze said.

"Niemm told me about it when they were clearing out Vuzgal when they first arrived."

"Ah, makes sense."

"How are your fighters doing? Are they ready?"

"As ready as they're going to get. There are plenty of people in this competition. And who knows what talents are hidden among them?" Blaze's eyes focused as he scanned the people in the booth and those in other booths near them.

"I am hoping for it. Most of the other cities and groups in the Fourth Realm haven't sent people to compete. With the competition, it's the perfect scouting ground," Chonglu said.

"Boys and their competitions." Elise sighed.

"You want to talk about competitions, you should talk to my wife." Chonglu grinned. "Anyway, I should greet other people. Good to meet you, Blaze, and I hope your guild does well."

"That makes two of us." Blaze smiled.

Chonglu went over to the other important figures. He greeted Hiao

Xen. "You were able to get the day off work? Won't Vuzgal collapse?" he joked.

"It shouldn't, but my desk might with all the paperwork stacked on top of it. Please, let me introduce you to the head of the Blue Lotus, Nadia Shriver, and, well, you already know—"

"Klaus." Chonglu nodded to the head of the Fighter's Association.

"Where did those two get off to now?" Klaus asked.

"Who knows." Chonglu shrugged with a smile. He clasped Nadia's outreached hand, shaking it.

"It is sure to be a great competition. I hear that you are keeping the majority of the rewards hidden," Nadia said.

"Ah, well, to those willing to take a risk comes a reward," Chonglu said.

"Couldn't have said it better," Richard Emile, the head of the Crafter's Association, said. He was a shorter man with bushy, white eyebrows, deeply tanned skin, and a head that was so smooth it looked polished. "Do you know if Tan Xue and representatives from the academy will be attending?"

"They should be, but you know how it is with crafting—easy enough to get wrapped up in one's projects."

The two men shared a smile.

Chonglu waved Blaze over.

"Blaze, this is Klaus, the leader of the Fighter's Association here. Blaze is the leader of the Adventurer's Guild. He has some people participating the upcoming matches." Chonglu said.

Gu Chen frowned as Chonglu introduced Blaze to Klaus.

"Who is that?" Gu Chen asked some of the other mercenary representatives.

Gu Chen was a manager from the Silver Dragons adventure group.

Even though it was a group, with their connections and their fighters, they were equal to medium-sized guilds in the Fourth Realm.

"The one with Chonglu? I've never seen him before."

He and the other Silver Dragons managers had agreed that Vuzgal would be a good place to develop. With another powerful, established fighting guild in the city, it could only increase the competition for merchant caravan protection contracts. Vuzgal had thousands of caravans and traders visiting every month.

"I haven't seen him before, and I don't know that symbol." Gu Chen glanced over to his assistant. As if reading his mind, the assistant moved away and used his sound transmission device.

The Fighter's Association regularly hired people away from the Silver Dragons. It was one of the reasons that few of the guilds attacked them. Nobody threatened the Fighter's Association or their members.

Blaze and Chonglu moved away from Klaus to greet others, and he saw his opportunity. He excused himself and went over to Branch Head Klaus.

"Ah, Gu Chen, I have heard some good things about your Silver Dragons. Didn't four of your members join the Fighter's Association some months back? How are you training them to become so strong? The Fighter's Association will have to rope you all in, in the future." Klaus smiled.

"Head Klaus, you're too kind." Gu Chen bowed. His eyes showed a hint of pride.

Klaus nodded as Gu Chen rose.

"I wanted to ask…I have never seen that man you were talking to. Do you know who he is?"

"Oh, that? I'm not sure." Klaus looked pleased. "His name is Blaze."

Gu Chen frowned and looked over, extending his senses fully. He locked onto Blaze. Although he was staring at him, he couldn't sense him. Gu Chen was a level fifty-one and had accomplished a great feat reaching Body Like Iron. *Just how strong is this Blaze?*

Blaze was talking to Elise, a trading powerhouse in Vuzgal. She ran several trading houses and had close ties to Vuzgal's leadership. Her past was a mystery, though; few knew where she had come from.

Gu Chen had talked to her before, gaining information on trade routes and merchants to establish the Silver Dragons in Vuzgal. He had never used his senses to study her. Doing so took concentration, and it was rude to do so publicly.

Now, though, he felt some of the power rolling off her.

The hairs on the back of his neck raised. His eyes shifted to Chonglu. It was as if he were throwing a stone into the night. He could sense his power but not its complete depth or breadth.

"Vuzgal has many hidden Experts," Klaus said.

"That is high praise," Gu Chen said.

Klaus just smiled and glanced in the direction of the Castle District as he looked down into the arena.

Gu Chen felt Klaus wasn't telling him half of what he knew.

Not a Simple Fighting Competition

"Hey, Elan, you heading up for the games?" Matt asked as Elan and his guards walked along one of the secret passages into the Battle Arena.

"You coming as well? Aren't you scared you'll get mobbed by the various sects to make their buildings?"

"Ah, you know, it is a hard thing being that desired." Matt sighed in suffering before he laughed it off. "So, who are you cheering for?"

"Us, of course."

"'Course. Though all our people in the special teams are using different identities."

"Well, Roska is up in Chonglu's office."

"Sounds like an idea to me."

They boarded an elevator and it shot upward, passing through the Battle Arena. Its doors opened to reveal a lobby.

"So how have things been for you?" Matt asked.

"Busy. Gathering information on that Willful Institute, starting with the events happening in the First Realm around the new King's Hill Outpost. It also looks like some people are in Vuzgal as well—and not in a good way."

"Anything we need to worry about?"

"I'm not sure right now. This competition will be a good way to show our foundations aren't weak," Elan said.

"We're just hosting it, so why do you think that?"

"The referees are from our military. They will be breaking up the fights or using the undead to do that. We are keeping Vuzgal clear of crime, and with the dungeon's ability to detect anything in its sphere of influence, we can react to crimes immediately. With the organization of all this and the ties we will make with new groups—from sects and associations to guilds and adventurer groups—all these factors should reinforce Vuzgal's image and power."

"I didn't think about that," Matt said.

"It's the small things that have the greatest impact," Elan said.

His guards opened the doors. Special Team Two looked up from their positions around the room—playing cards, eating, napping.

"Matt!" Han Wu raised his hand to get the man's attention. "Up for a game of cards?"

"Jones, Qui, I wondered what you were doing." Gong Jin hailed the guards.

"Director Elan, I see you're staying in the shadows as always," Roska said.

"And you're hiding in lounges with gamblers," Elan said as he greeted her.

The groups intermingled, greeting one another in a relaxed atmosphere.

Tan Xue banged on the door again, but there was no reply.

"Weren't they the ones bugging me about going to these damn games?" She pulled out a punch and her hammer.

She used Simple Inorganic Scan on the lock and positioned her punch. She gave it two hits, breaking something inside the lock. She pulled it out, shook the handle, and opened the door to find a snoring Julilah asleep between her formations.

Tan Xue pulled out a vial of crushed-up herbs and, holding it at arm's reach, she pulled off the stopper and put it under Julilah's nose.

"Eugh!" Julilah about nearly reached the ceiling in a parabolic arch of flailing arms, legs, and wide, all-too awake, and watering eyes. Her face contorted to shake away the foul smells that had assaulted her olfactory senses.

Tan Xue reached out with her other hand, catching Julilah by the scruff of her robes.

Julilah coughed and looked around wildly. "Tan Xue—" Julilah spluttered as Tan Xue tossed a bucket of water from her storage ring at her. "Hey!"

Julilah struggled, but she was useless in Tan Xue's iron grip as she cast her Clean spell on Julilah.

Water and grime splashed onto the floor, and Tan Xue looked around the room. "Where is Qin?"

"She went to get some sleep, I think. Why are you putting things in my nose and throwing water on me?"

"The competition begins today, and we're late already!"

"It's today?" Julilah asked.

Tan Xue put her down outside of the puddle of water. "Yes. Get a Stamina drink in you. We've got to go and get her."

They ran across the academy grounds and reached Qin's home.

"What happened to the door of the workshop?"

"I had to get it open, and *someone* was asleep." Tan Xue shrugged as she knocked on Qin's door. She did it a few more times then used a key.

"Hey, you broke into our workshop, but you have her keys?"

"I made spare keys of both your apartments." Tan Xue walked in. She followed the trail of clothes to the shower and then the wet marks to the bedroom. Qin was facedown on the bed, the sheets in disarray around her.

Julilah threw a bucket of water on her friend.

"Ahh!" Qin jumped up and out of bed, tripping on the sheets and tumbling onto the floor.

"What was that for?" Tan Xue asked.

"You did it to me!"

"That was because you hadn't had a shower!"

"Well…" Julilah shrugged.

"Julilah!" Qin complained as she got up, her shirt and shorts soaked.

Tan Xue used her Clean spell again. "Competition is today. Get some clothes on," Tan Xue said. "Also, you might want to fix your hair."

It was currently bedhead central.

Qin looked between them and groaned. "You just said I had a shower this morning!"

"Doesn't mean you're still clean."

Qin dropped her head to the pillow and grumbled.

"You coming?!"

"Yes, just give me a minute, and get out of my room!" Qin threw a pillow that Julilah caught and tossed to the side.

Tan Xue and Julilah shared amused expressions and retreated as Qin rose from the bed, rubbing away sleep as she stumbled to her closet.

Tan Xue sat on the couch while Julilah rummaged through the storage crate in the kitchen, finding food and tea before sitting down and drinking the hot liquid. Her eyes fluttered as the stimulant touched her very soul.

Qin came out some minutes later, eyeing Julilah.

"There's more in there. I poured a cup."

Qin grumbled but went into the storage crate with a warm cup.

Tan Xue stood, staring at the two sipping tea. She felt that they were undergoing a transformation, using the black magic of their drinks to transform from demons into humans.

She didn't dare to disturb their ritual before they put down their cups.

"Well, let's get going," Qin said.

"The streets are filled. We'll take one of the undead." Tan Xue led the way out of the apartment.

"How did you get in here?" Qin peeked at the door.

"She has our keys," Julilah said.

They went to the roof, and Tan Xue waved in the air. A flying undead dropped toward the roof, throwing up wind.

"Take us to the Battle Arena," Tan Xue said.

The undead beast screeched and lowered itself.

They got on top; the beast scampered to the edge of the building and jumped. Spreading its wings, it flew over Vuzgal, and people looked up toward them.

"Where are the other crafters?" Qin asked.

"Those who wanted to have headed over already. Others are working on their crafts. They have their own booth."

"What booth are we going to?"

"The main one right at the top," Tan Xue said.

They saw other undead beasts flying around with groups of soldiers and police officers on them, keeping the peace.

The undead beast landed on the aerial platform. They quickly dismounted and headed inside.

13

First Round

Olivia Gray, head of the Blue Lotus guards, scanned everything from the upper booth of the arena. She had people out in the streets patrolling and assisting the Vuzgal forces. All the associations with contracts had to lend a part of their power to maintaining order within Vuzgal.

She looked over the crowds in the lower levels of the arena that were filled with powerful figures. Each controlled at least one city in the Fourth Realm or held the equivalent power. Some were leaders in trade; others were powerful fighters or crafters with renown.

Her eyes drifted to the managers of Vuzgal.

Hiao Xen was aptly dealing with the people who came over to him, and Elise was holding court with the different traders. People with trade routes that spanned across the Fourth Realm continents listened attentively and spoke to her as equals.

Chonglu introduced Blaze, a new member, to the Fighter's Association head. Other guilds and adventurer groups that were able to shake the Fourth

Realm looked over in jealousy at the attention Blaze was getting.

Her eyes moved to the lower levels where several booths were occupied by people from Vuzgal Academy. There were so many Journeyman-level students, and several had made the transition to Expert in the past few months. Was this the Fourth Realm or one of the admission academies in the Fifth Realm? No, this would be more like the student body of an academy in the Sixth Realm. If Olivia were a crafter, she would have lined up to take classes there too. The Blue Lotus was already looking to recruit people at the yearly graduation. They always needed more Experts, and if they had already passed through Vuzgal, they would have a firm foundation before heading to a Blue Lotus academy.

There was a commotion as the doors opened to the booth. Guards bowed to the three women who walked in. Tan Xue, the head of Vuzgal Academy, wore simple clothes of Low Expert grade. Qin wore a dress that complemented her fair complexion, and Julilah wore simple clothes like Tan Xue that highlighted her slightly tanned complexion.

They didn't look like Expert crafters, but their control over their powers was impressive. Olivia couldn't sense any of it. It looked as though they cared little about anything that wasn't related to crafting.

The trio talked amongst themselves until Elise disengaged from the merchants and walked over. They hugged and greeted one another with genuine smiles. Olivia didn't miss how they smiled and nodded to Blaze, Chonglu, and Hiao Xen.

Blaze intrigued her. Who was he, and how did he know them?

Olivia kept her observations to herself. A gong rang across the city. People moved to their seats, and Chonglu stepped up to the front of the booth.

Fighters across arenas and stages walked out to their assigned areas. Vuzgal soldiers walked out wearing their armor. They might be today's referees, but even a glancing blow could kill.

Qin and Julilah found seats near Olivia.

"The new personal mana barriers should protect us against Sixth Realm fighter's attacks, right?" Qin asked.

"They might be small, but we tested against your formations. Are you not confident? What about your arrays on the stages?" Julilah fussed.

"They'll protect the crowd just fine. They lasted longer than the portable mana barriers at least. Guess I'm just nervous. We had to make so many of them in a short period of time, and the last models we put out were nearly twice as strong as the ones we had started with."

"Yeah, they're going to use them for the later matches where people are throwing around a lot of power. Stop worrying." Julilah sat back and pulled out a cup from her storage ring.

Chonglu cleared his throat, and the venue went quiet. "Welcome to the First Annual Fighter's Competition of Vuzgal. Let us begin!"

People cheered as fighters stepped up to the stages. Hundreds of people were participating, just to slim down the number of fighters.

"Look, isn't that Yi Yin of the Silver Dragons?" a young woman spectator asked the man beside her.

"Sword of the East and Shield of the West, Zuyev Adreevich. He's the strongest sword-and-shield wielder of the Silver Dragons. With him here, the Silver Dragons aren't giving others any chances! Look—there's Cui Yang," her date said.

Their friend, sitting behind them, pointed at the screen showing another stage. "The Woman of a Thousand Fists! She's from the Stone Fist sect, right?"

"Bit bold of them to show up here, isn't it? I heard the leader of the Battle Arena is the Ice Empress's old husband," the man on the date asked.

"The Ice Empress is the one who ran off to join the Fighter's Association?" his date chimed in.

"Yeah. I heard she is now one of their leaders in a large campaign group," their friend said.

"I heard she married her old husband again," his date said to his friend.

"There was an uproar in the Stone Fist sect, but she cut off all ties with them," the man argued.

"If I could get a wife like that…" his friend butted in.

"You think you'd be able to handle a wife that strong?" The man on the date raised an eyebrow.

"Look, there's Amarann Rogarsson." The friend behind him ignored his words and pointed to another fighter.

"Just how fast are your eyes?" the man on a date muttered.

"The Lightning Hammer from the Crimson Wolves sect?" his date asked.

"Their people compete in the Fifth Realm regularly and are accepted into academies in the Sixth constantly. They're a group of mages who focus on combining their weapon skills with their attacks. All of them have learned at least one technique. As strong as he is, he must have learned three or four techniques by now," the friend said.

"You know a lot!" the man's date said excitedly.

"I need to change my bets. All three of them must know techniques by now. They'll be competing at the end for the championships. Ah, this is frustrating. I was hoping there would be more of a challenge!" an older man nearby said. "And will you quiet down! You're ruining the fight!"

The group smiled sheepishly and bowed their heads.

"There could be some people hiding their strength." The man quickly laughed to reassure his date.

"This is going to be so much fun!" his friend said from behind.

Gu Chen, leader of the Silver Dragons, took the papers his assistant offered him and looked over the information. There were thirty-six names, all with descriptions. "Is this correct?"

"Yes, sir," his assistant said.

It was no wonder he hadn't heard of the Adventurer's Guild before. They were all from the lower realms. *Must be putting all their money into that guild hall.*

"They shouldn't be a problem. Our people can deal with them easily." He passed the papers back. The assistant put them away and then stepped away.

Gu Chen's assistant pulled out his sound transmission device. "If you meet with anyone from the Adventurer's Guild, make sure they aren't able to fight afterward." His words were passed to the ears of the Silver Dragons. Eighteen of them were part of the competition. Not all were on the same level as Yi Yin, but they were not far behind. Most of them were new Experts who had joined their guild recently, and this was a way for them to test their fighting abilities against others and grow their Experience.

Gu Chen's assistant wrongly interpreted his words and sent out a command to eliminate the guild, serving to hurt rather than aid.

The atmosphere of the private lounge in the Battle Arena was relaxed. Screens showed all the major fights with the ability to switch them on demand.

Elan glanced between the different screens as the elevator doors opened. Niemm and half of Special Team One walked out.

"They let you out of the dungeon?" Niemm laughed.

"Hell, they had to kick you out as soon as possible with you just uglying up the place," Roska said with a grin. The two special teams laughed and greeted one another in their own way.

"Sir." Niemm gave a casual salute to Elan.

"Just here watching the game." Elan smiled and nodded.

"We're only here for the beer." Gong Jin grinned. "And I guess the recruits."

Elan smiled and turned away from the teams as the elevator doors opened a second time.

"This is where you're all hiding," Domonos said as he entered the lounge.

Elan brightened upon hearing his son's voice. He stood the other members of the room calling out their greeting as Domonos passed.

Elan hugged his son and patted his shoulders.

"You're getting bigger!"

"So are you," Domonos said.

"Ah, just some gifts from the job."

"How is Wren?"

"He's doing well. It seems he got my hints and is moving the center of the trading house to King's Hill Outpost. I am hoping we can bring him over, though there are so many things that could go wrong. I'd like to set him up with Alvan traders," Elan said.

"Eventually," Domonos said. "You think Qin made the right move?"

"Yes. I'm still embarrassed with how your brother tagged along like some puppy."

"He couldn't let her go away on her own."

"You kids." Elan smiled.

"Looks like they're walking out," Roska said loudly, sitting next to Niemm.

"There are twenty-five recruits in there for the special teams and thirty-six members of the Adventurer's Guild," Roska said.

"How do you think they'll do?" Domonos asked.

"I'm not sure. I haven't seen any of them fight yet. You?" Niemm said.

"I think our recruits will place high," Roska said. "And the Adventurer's Guild as well. They might not get as many resources, but they have more combat experience. They have their own techniques and what they have learned from others. They probably have higher levels, though fewer open mana gates. Mana and Body Cultivation should be close or lower. Some of them should get into the top one hundred, and all of them should get into the top five hundred, I hope."

Elan nodded and focused on the screen that showed a petite woman wearing black armor and a mask that covered half her face walking to the stage; opposite her, a beast of a man held a cudgel and a shield as big as him.

"Lin Lei—she's one of the branch heads, right?" Setsuko asked.

"Yeah, assassin type," Roska said.

"Who is she facing?" Setsuko asked.

"That looks like Gert Westerbeek, a general from the Purple Cloud sect. They say he has an animal bloodline and is called the Iron Shield. He's famed for his ability to tank powerful beasts and hold a line together in the battlefield. He has fought in plenty of wars to get to his current position. His reaction speed is impressive, and he has learned many techniques. Combined with his physique, he's much faster than he looks," Elan said.

"How strong is he?" Domonos asked.

"He's as strong as he looks."

Lin Lei could tell the man standing opposite her was a veteran. There was a chill in his eyes that gave it away. She looked up and to the side. She was on the second-floor arena; there were two more arenas above her where the guildmaster was sitting.

"Do I need to beat you off this stage?" Gert Westerbeek grabbed his cudgel, locking eyes with her.

She tightened her grip on her daggers.

He sneered.

Just how strong was he? Lin Lei hadn't exerted her full Strength yet. She wasn't even sure how strong she had become since she had only fought against beasts and hunting bandits, which took planning. The more planning, the easier it was to accomplish. She hadn't fought anyone other than the branch heads since training in the beast dungeon. *I can't make the guild look bad. I need to win.*

Fighting spirit filled her eyes, and she set her jaw.

The referee blew a whistle, starting the match.

Gert's size had nothing on his speed. He crossed the distance between them in an instant, and he aimed his cudgel at her head to end the fight quickly.

She moved her head, and wind washed over the stage with the blow. Gert jumped backward, his shield coming up, and he prepared to defend against a counterattack.

Lin Lei circled. He jumped backward, creating more room.

"Look, he's playing with her!" someone in the audience yelled out.

"Ha! It would be boring if it finished so quickly."

"Don't you think he looks weird jumping back like that? Ah, minus two points for style."

"Too scared to attack? Don't worry. I'll come to you!" He charged again, this time with his shield out.

She dodged his shield just as he brought his cudgel down.

Lin Lei flowed around the attack, and he swung to his side widely, changing the direction of his cudgel.

She ducked under his blow, causing his feet to shift and lift. He lost his balance as he was pulled forward with his attacks.

Her eyes were clear and without panic as she danced around him, her daggers lashing out at the back of his neck and knees, the barrier flashing into existence.

She put her daggers away and glanced to the referee.

"Match goes to Lin Lei of the Adventurer's Guild!" he called out.

She cupped her hands to the referee, and he returned the gesture.

She was about to walk off the stage when the referee pointed two fingers down on his left hand and tapped his forefinger against it, creating an "A."

Her cold expression turned into a smile, and she gave him an imperceptible nod.

"Ahh, Iron Shield of the Purple Clouds sect. It seems the Purple Cloud sect has just been talking up their members, bah!"

"I have a new favorite! Lin Lei of the Adventurer's Guild. How cool is she?"

"An assassin type—they're the coolest with their getups."

"Why are you talking about what someone is wearing? This is a fighting competition!"

"She's already strong. Didn't you see that move? *Pow!* One hit!"

Gu Chen watched the fights closely. Most of the Silver Dragon fighters had passed the first rounds, finishing their fights in just a handful of moves. One fight took just seven exchanges before the enemy fell.

"Impressive," Klaus said from his seat.

Gu Chen glanced at the screen showing the result of an assassin and a shield warrior.

Wait, isn't that the Iron Shield from the Purple Cloud sect?

Healers moved to him as the woman accepted her win.

The image changed to another fight.

He looked down at the stages. Motion blurred the stages as people fought with everything they had.

Lin Lei. Is she one of the people under Blaze? From the lower realms?

Lin Lei walked off the stage and to the waiting area. The first rounds of fighting were still ongoing. A few unlucky people had already lost, but there were plenty of undetermined fights across the different arenas. Two new contestants stepped onto the stage she had left, but she didn't notice as she replayed her fight in her mind.

At first, she'd been apprehensive. She had trained and leveled up aggressively, throwing herself into it completely.

The dungeons the branch heads had trained in were filled with humanoid creatures—those that were fast and agile, those that were slower but stronger, as well as variants of them both. They had pushed the branch heads to their limits. Under those pressures, they had improved their skills.

Lin Lei had thought the other contestants would be stronger. Maybe he was just weaker than others.

Still, even after all her training, the Alvan trainers could defeat her with ease. *Did I really get that much stronger?*

Blaze didn't know how well his guild would do in the competition. He believed they would place well; though seeing Lin Lei go up against Iron Shield, a man with considerable fame and prowess, he had expected Lin Lei to lose.

Once the fight had started, knowing how strong Lin Lei was and using her as a measure, he could see that they weren't on the same stage.

He couldn't get too cocky, though. After all, Iron Shield used to fight as part of a unit, not on a stage. His actions were exaggerated since that was how he had been trained. He had never needed to hide those motions in his fights as he used his overwhelming attributes to win.

Blaze continued to watch the other fights throughout the day.

The first round of fighting continued through the afternoon. Even with hundreds of stages, there were a thousand matches in the first round alone.

Four out of the five of the Purple Cloud sect's people had pushed on.

The Crimson Wolves, led by Amarann, had crushed their opponents, with all three people passing to the second round. The three from the Stone Fist sect had similarly defeated their opponents in one or two moves.

The Adventurer's Guild lost two people who had run into Experts. The rest had all been able to advance.

"Ah, this is frustrating. I thought more of the sects would participate. Are they looking down on Vuzgal?" one of the spectators snarled.

"It is the first competition, and we don't know what the rewards are yet. To put their people on the line for unknown prizes is asking a lot," another said.

"Hopefully, they'll show up in the next tournament. I want to see how the adventure groups from Vuzgal stack up against them!"

One of the last matches had Kim Cheol matched with one of the fighters from the Silver Dragons.

Kim walked up to the stage, his helmet under his arm. His opponent was a dazzling woman with wickedly curved blades on her hips.

The two of them, staring at each other, appeared really mismatched.

Kim Cheol extended his hand to greet his opponent, as was good practice.

Diana scoffed and slapped his hand away. "Don't think that you and your simple guild can stand in the way of the Silver Dragons. I don't know what you did to anger my branch head, but don't worry, I'll make your punishment quick. If you fight too much, then who knows…you might just die. These spars can have so many accidents," she sneered.

"What are you talking about?"

"The weak need to be culled."

Kim Cheol's expression turned dull, his eyes lifeless. He pulled on his helmet as if a machine in a man's body.

Until joining the Adventurer's Guild, he had been a miner in the First Realm, working to support the orphanage he had grown up in—his family. When a beast horde had descended on his town, the soldiers who were meant to protect the townsfolk had fled and run, leaving Kim Cheol and the miners to defend the town with their tools.

A group of fighters who were in the area hunting down beasts charged over. They fought alongside the miners and called their guild over to help. They weren't getting paid for it, but upon hearing that people were in danger, they had charged over. Leading them was their guildmaster, Blaze.

He didn't sit in the rear, but he coordinated the fight and they were able to blunt the attack and scatter the beast wave.

Kim Cheol was badly wounded, but the guild had helped with healing the injured people.

Blaze had offered Kim Cheol a job, a way to become stronger and to stand up for the people in the guild. To join a new family. A group of people willing to drop everything to stand up for others. It was the reason not doing anything against the Willful Institute had burned so badly.

Hearing someone threaten those he cared about, his easy smile washed away.

He hoisted his shield and rolled his shoulders, lowering himself.

The woman sneered and she met his eyes, looking down on him.

The referee waved his arms, starting the match.

She launched forward, her curved blades in both hands. Mana gathered on her blades as her speed reached its limit.

"So fast! That must be a technique—I can't even follow her shadow!" an audience member said, holding her face.

Kim Cheol kept looking into her eyes, feeling her murderous intent as the blades aimed for his vitals.

She lunged forward. A wind blade covered her blades, causing them to blur with speed.

Gu Chen looked over just as the two were closing in.

She's executing Wind Strike already? That's her sure-kill technique. Is she trying to kill him?!

He hoped Kim Cheol could dodge the attack somehow.

Kim Cheol shifted his foot and stepped forward.

"What is he doing? Why is he charging forward? Is he looking to die?"

With the aura of a boar meeting an intruder on his territory, Kim Cheol charged into the attack. His shield glowed with power, and his muscles bulged. His charge looked simple, but it effectively blunted the Wind Strike attack, broke Diana's stance, and launched her into the air.

He was some steps past her when he stomped the ground, launching himself into the air. He hit down and backward with his shield, and it rang out. She was slapped into the ground, creating a crack in the platform.

Her clothes were torn, and blood dribbled from her lips. She struggled to get up, staggering from the attacks.

The referee looked between them and stepped back while a medic rushed over to the stage.

Diana brandished her weapons, waving the medic back.

Kim Cheol touched the ground, taking the impact of his weight and armor with his legs. He walked over to Diana.

Kim Cheol undid the straps on his shield and tossed it off his arm and into his hands. His eyes were blank as he watched Diana getting up, her legs stuck out to either side to support her.

He charged, and she raised her weapons to defend herself, panic in her eyes. He appeared behind her, his shield raised in both his arms. He swung it like the hammers he had used in the mine. She half-turned, and his blow hit her.

She slammed into the ground again. Cheol's shield rang out as he struck her for a second time with three-quarters of his Strength. He didn't want to kill her.

The stage cracked around her as she was embedded into the stage's stone floor.

Cheol stopped hitting her; her weapons had fallen from her hands long ago. She coughed up blood.

A barrier appeared around her so she couldn't be hit again.

Kim Cheol sank to a knee. His cold eyes looked upon Diana.

"Back in your corner," the referee said with a hand on his armor.

There was no derision in her eyes anymore. Fear dominated now.

"Don't touch those who are precious to me."

Cheol stood and walked away.

The referee pulled out a healing potion and poured it on Diana's wounds as the medic arrived.

Cheol gave off the aura of a beast protecting what belonged to him. He put his shield away and walked toward the waiting rooms. Those waiting to go up on stage flinched as he walked down the stairs.

Blaze also felt something was wrong. As the matches had gone on, more of the people in the booth had come over to talk to him, discussing different deals and possible partnerships.

He told them he would meet them after the contest and host them in his guild hall.

As the last of the first round wrapped up, it was nearly dark. Some fighters' hopes had been crushed, while others reveled in passing the first round. All of Vuzgal was talking about the competition, and word spread through the totems and along the trading routes.

There were still one thousand contestants remaining. It was still early in the competition, and anything could happen.

Hidden Orders

Gu Chen returned to the Wayside Inn where the Silver Dragon adventure group rested.

"You did well," he said. All but Diana had passed the first round. "Make sure you rest. You have many fights ahead of you."

He headed to where Diana was resting. Her injuries were severe, and although the healers had worked on her, she needed to recover enough Stamina for them to heal the non-critical injuries.

She tried to get up as he walked in the room.

"Please, don't. You'll only make your wounds worse."

She gave him a look of gratitude and hissed in pain as she fell back to the bed. "I was too weak and underestimated him."

"Why were you trying to kill him?" Gu Chen asked.

"I got the order to eliminate the members of the Adventurer's Guild and make sure they know their place," Diana said, perplexed.

Anger built within him.

"Who told you to do that?"

"Your assistant," Diana said.

Gu Chen went silent. He looked away and took in a deep breath before letting it out slowly. "Fighting Kim Cheol. What was it like?"

Diana paled and broke into a cold sweat. "I thought he had lost where I was, but he saw through my attacks. He was playing with me. He could've sent me off the stage in the first attack. His eyes—" She froze before pushing forward. "They were dull, like it wasn't a man I was facing but a monster."

"What did you say to him?"

"I threatened him and his people. I wanted to throw him off mentally before the fight."

So, he knew Diana was aiming to take his life. Would he take it to Blaze? What would Blaze think if he heard they were looking to cripple and maim his people?

Gu Chen's anger grew, but he hid it from Diana. "Did anything else happen?"

"At the end, when he took a knee next to me..." Diana's hands trembled. "He warned me to not touch what was precious to him. He meant that guild. He would fight to the end for them."

Her eyes found his, and he felt the fear filling her mind.

Diana would need time to recover before fighting again. Until then, they had no idea how wounded she was, and there was a possibility that she might not be able to fight again.

"Rest up. It looks like someone passed along the wrong order. I'll see what I can do to smooth over the situation," Gu Chen said.

She nodded, and he left the room.

"Cordero!" he yelled as he stormed into the main courtyard.

A few moments later, his assistant appeared. "Branch head?" The man looked apprehensive.

"What order did you give to our fighters?"

Cordero shuffled forward. "I passed on your order to remove them from fighting."

"Why would I do that?"

"Well, Chonglu greeted him right away, Elise looked close with him, and even Klaus showed an interest. It is a new guild, and you should be getting that attention. If we can defeat them, then we can show those people we are stronger and that will give us more opportunities in the future to develop."

"So, you saw those things and thought I would want to step on them instead of taking my time to gather information?" Gu Chen's anger crept into his voice.

"They're just people from the lower realms," Cordero said.

"Just people from the lower realms who are currently blazing through this competition. Blaze must have a secondary relationship with Chonglu and Elise. Did you see how close he was with Elise? That is an intimate relationship. How he had talked to the guards and higher-ups of the Battle Arena? He was familiar with them, and they respect him."

Gu Chen took a step forward, his anger growing. "I wanted to know more about them. When have I ever issued an order to maim or kill someone? That's what guilds and sects do, not my Silver Dragons. If I am right, the Adventurer's Guild is not just some upstart but has deep links to Vuzgal and its mysterious leadership. They could be an arm of Vuzgal, and we have openly attacked them!"

Cordero had subconsciously walked backward, not willing to meet his eyes. The air around Gu Chen was thick with mana as his anger intensified.

"Get a carriage ready. We need to apologize for this misunderstanding and hope they are forgiving. Even if they are not a limb of Vuzgal, I do not want our adventurer group to earn a reputation for using nasty tactics to win fights."

On their way back to the guild hall, people cheered and yelled as the members of the Adventurer's Guild passed.

Blaze had sent a message through Alvan channels to the lower realms. While the competition was going on, more people from the lower realms were allowed to visit Vuzgal.

Jasper had sent up administrators to assist Blaze with any negotiations that happened.

When they reached the guild hall, the line of people out front brightened as the group entered and released their mounts to the stables.

Blaze hurried inside. An administrator approached him as he walked in the doors.

"There are three different people looking to talk to you personally. I checked our records, and I believe it would be worth your time talking to them."

"Very well." Kim Cheol caught Blaze's eye. The big man stood off to the side, waiting for him. "Make sure they are comfortable. I just have to talk to Cheol for a second. Once I'm done, have them sent up to my office."

"Yes, Guildmaster."

Blaze walked over to Kim Cheol. "I've been meaning to ask you about your fight." Blaze knew Cheol wouldn't get serious like that unless there was a good reason.

"Shall we talk somewhere more private?"

They headed up to Blaze's office and Kim told Blaze everything that happened.

"So, you beat her up to send a message and stop her from fighting our people for some time," Blaze said.

"Yes." Kim Cheol, who was larger than Blaze, looked like a kid who had done wrong.

"Good job." Blaze smacked him on the shoulder.

Cheol looked up.

"We stand up for one another. I would've done the same. You did well."

"Thank you, Guild Master." Kim Cheol relaxed. "What about the Silver Dragons, though?"

"With that—" Blaze was interrupted as his sound communication device went off.

"Guild Master, Branch Manager Gu Chen is here," Emilia informed him.

"All right, I'll be down in a minute." The air around Blaze chilled.

He had been forced to bear it when the Willful Institute attacked their people. He would not stand by this time.

"Cheol, it seems that Gu Chen has come here. Could you tell him I am too busy to meet with him? Tell him we will see one another at the arena tomorrow."

"Yes, Guild Master." Kim Cheol balled his hands into fists and left the room.

Gu Chen had a sinking sensation when he saw Kim Cheol step into the lobby. Everyone looked over as he locked eyes with Gu Chen. He was unaffected meeting the branch head, and he walked over.

Gu Chen and Cordero stood to greet him.

"I am sorry, but the guildmaster is too busy right now. He told me to tell you that he'll see you at the arena tomorrow." Kim Cheol, having finished what he had come to say, turned and left.

Gu Chen peeked at Cordero with murder in his eyes.

"Isn't that the Silver Dragons' branch head?" one of the mercenaries lined up outside the guild hall said

"Do they have a problem with the Adventurer's Guild?" another asked

"Didn't you see how their star was embedded in the stage? It looks like the Silver Dragons' ability is decreasing.

Gu Chen left the lobby, feeling ashamed, and got into the carriage. When Cordero made to get up, he pushed him, sending him sprawling in the dirt.

"Never appear before me again, and don't wear that crest again. I'm showing mercy by just kicking you out." Gu Chen looked down on his ex-assistant and slammed the door shut.

The carriage quickly disappeared, heading back in the direction it had come.

Rumors spread of the tensions between the Silver Dragons and the Adventurer's Guild.

Second Qualifying Round

The next day, even more spectators arrived from across the realms to watch the matches. Merchants had rushed over in the dead of night, not expecting Vuzgal's first competition to be so popular. Now, they could only kick themselves as they fought over even the worst stall positions.

The Fighter's Association, having heard about the competition, had sent more people down.

Through the streets, one could see people from various sects. Many of them were large powers where they came from, but the competition had quickly turned into one where Experts clashed. Even if they didn't have people in the competition, it was an opportunity to see the strength of their allies and enemies, and possibly scout some fighters for their own ranks.

Gu Chen and the Silver Dragons departed their residence, all of them wearing their guild symbol-embossed cloaks. They rode silver lizards that snapped at people who got too close to the procession.

People cheered and talked to one another as they passed.

"Is the Adventurer's Guild really that big of a threat?" Yi Yin asked Gu

Chen as they were riding.

Gu Chen sat up and looked around. "They have a lot of connections, and their base in Vuzgal is growing. If we want to develop here, we need to deal with them day in and out. If we need to watch our backs, our progress will be slower than if we have an amicable relationship. In that time, more people will enter Vuzgal, and we will lose some of our advantage."

"What shall we do?" Yi Yin asked.

"We must place well within the competition and show off our combat power. I will try to talk to Blaze again today and prove that this was an accident and not intentional."

"Lowering our head to a guild from the lower realms doesn't feel right."

"We are a small adventuring group. We have powerful members, but against the sea of people that sects can call up, we aren't much. It is not a loss of honor to bow one's head when we were in the wrong."

They reached the arena. The fighters headed down into the waiting area, and Gu Chen stored his mount before heading through the VVIP doors.

Chonglu stood to make his second announcement.

"Today is the last day of the qualifiers. All of you have shown your fighting ability to make it here. This round is based on points. The top one hundred people will qualify for the tournament. I know you have all been curious about what the rewards are—and have probably already heard that the person who places first will get a Sky-grade mana stone. The runner-up will receive five Earth-grade mana cornerstones, and the third will gain two Earth-grade mana cornerstones. Those remaining in the top ten will each receive one hundred Earth-grade mana stones.

"Everyone in the top ten will receive healing potions of at least the Low

Journeyman level, with those placing higher than fifth receiving Stamina and healing potions of the Low Journeyman level. The first-place participant will also receive Stamina and healing potions of the peak Journeyman level.

"The first-place participant will be allowed to use a tier-four training room in the Battle Arena for six months, with the ones in second and third place getting to use a tier-four facility for two months or a tier-three facility for six months. The fourth and fifth will get three months of time in a tier-three training room. Those from fifth to tenth will get access to a tier-two training room for six months. First place will get two pieces of Expert gear; second place, one piece; third place, peak Journeyman; fourth and fifth place, High Journeyman. Those to tenth place will receive a Mid Journeyman-level item."

The fighters' eyes glowed with intent. Although there were Expert-level items in the Fourth Realm, there were few ways to get them. They were tactical-level items that were held within guilds and deployed in the Great Wars across the Fourth Realm. Individual parties getting to see or earn them was unheard of. High Journeyman-level weapons were reserved for Experts whose levels were in the high fifties, and Low Journeyman and peak Apprentice weapons for those who were at least level forty. Although the weapons would make most of the fighters shake with excitement, the potions set their hearts on fire. The Stamina and healing potions might be a step lower than the straight healing potions, but they were much more effective. The mixed potions meant that someone could consume them right away, in whatever condition they were in. They didn't have to worry about how low their Stamina was before taking them.

It was a life-saving treasure.

While they were resting, they had stayed in tier-one rooms.

They all knew the effects of the rooms; with them, they could hone themselves and draw out more fighting power.

The people in the stands were all talking about the rich rewards.

"These kinds of items, aren't they enough to equip an army in the Fourth Realm?"

"I bet the larger sects are kicking themselves now. These rewards are just too rich! You know there were two sects who owned several cities that went to war with one another over a powerful Expert-level weapon. They were tied until one side got a hold of the weapon, and then they turned the battle around, crushing the other and taking over their cities."

"An Expert-level weapon has that much power?"

"Not by itself, but when paired with a powerful fighter, instead of simply adding to their fighting ability, it multiplies their combat power and gives them more options to deal with their enemy."

"I knew Vuzgal was rich, but isn't this just extravagant?"

Once again, the group hiding in the lounge reconvened. They had watched the matches from yesterday with some interest, taking time to review the different special team applicants and commenting on the fighters from the Adventurer's Guild and other talents who had revealed their true ability and caught their eyes.

On the other side of the glass window, people flooded into the arena and quickly filled the seats as they got ready for the upcoming match.

"I heard that there was some commotion at the guild last night?" Roska asked Niemm and Elan.

"Nothing serious. Blaze refused to see the leader of the Silver Dragons' team," Niemm said.

"About that fight?" Roska asked.

"Yes. It seems that someone took his orders the wrong way—most likely, his assistant. He was kicked out of his carriage and spotted leaving Vuzgal late last night. I am reviewing my information on the Silver Dragons before I take anything to Blaze, though," Elan said.

"Nothing happens in Vuzgal without you knowing," Roska said.

"And I aim to keep it that way." Elan smiled. "The recruits are looking good, but what if they're eliminated before the qualifiers are complete? Will that mean they can't advance?"

"Well, we might have hidden that from them. We haven't explicitly said what this counts for. We've seen them succeed so far, but what if they can't? We get to see how they react."

"So, what do they think right now?" Niemm asked.

"They think if they fail out too low, they will not be allowed to continue training or become a member of the special teams."

"So, it pushes them to surpass their limits and put it all on the line," Elan said.

"Yeah. There are plenty of powerful people in the Fourth Realm, Experts from all over. I don't think our people will be in the top twenty or even thirty, though we should have some people in the top one hundred," Roska said.

"That sounds realistic," Elan said.

"I wish we could rank higher, but there are people with a lot more combat experience. Trying to win against them all is unrealistic." Niemm sighed.

"In later competitions, our people should be stronger," Roska said.

"Yes, but once this gets out and the rewards are handed out, do you think the powerful sects will continue to look away?" Elan said.

Time passed quickly, and it wasn't long until fighters entered the different arenas and walked up to their assigned stages.

Referees checked on the fighters, and the first of the second-round fights began.

Those in the lounge talked to one another, commenting on the match.

"Look at Rajkovic—damn, he's quick." Tully pointed to one of the special team applicants.

Rajkovic moved around the stage with ease. He had a sword and shield, but he advanced at a run, dodging arrows as he moved.

"That kind of control is impressive. He needs to predict where the arrows will be, then cast a spell to hit them and make sure they don't deflect into him," Simms said.

"One only needs a sword and a shield. It is the mark of a true fighter," Davos said.

"You're just saying that because you prefer your sword and shield combo. A bit prejudiced," Tully said dryly.

Rajkovic reached his opponent, dodging a thrown bow. The bowman freed his sword and, carving out a fiery trail that lashed out across the stage.

Rajkovic's shield countered the fire blade attack, he stepped forward and thrust his shield forward striking the bowman, trapping his arm against his body as he stumbled. Rajkovic's foot snapped out, tripping the man. He hit him with his shield, smashing him into the ground. His blade darted out, stopping just inches away from the bowman's neck.

"Damn, for one of the first fights of the day, hah! My blood is boiling already!" Han Wu said.

"That doesn't sound healthy—should I heal you?" Yang Zan asked.

"Get away with your sobering hands!" Han Wu yelled in a panic.

"Come on, you can just drink more!" Yang Zan's smile was chilly as Han Wu drew the gourd filled with alcohol closer to himself.

"I'm fine, fine! Just a slip of the tongue!"

The others snorted or shook their heads at the two's antics.

"I swear, I spend more time healing you than Gong Jin, and he's our tanker," Yang Zan muttered loud enough for everyone to hear.

"That...isn't that Shadow Sword?" someone in the crowd asked.

"Isn't that the famous swordsman whose speed is on another level?"

"Yeah. It's said that before you see his shadow, his blade is already at your neck. He's got crazy speed. I heard that someone from the Purple

Cloud sect challenged him. They had just become an inner disciple and wanted to see their strength. Shadow Sword defeated them in two moves."

"Who are they fighting next?"

"Derrick? He's from that new group, the Adventurer's Guild."

Shadow Sword smiled underneath the mask that covered the lower part of his face.

A man wearing two thin swords on his hips stepped up to the stage.

Shadow Sword's eyes widened, and he smiled like a predator.

The two men eyed each other from across the stage and gripped their weapons, each sizing up their opponent.

They drew their weapons as the referee looked at them both.

"Begin!" he yelled and stepped backward.

Derrick charged toward Shadow Sword.

Shadow Sword was nearly twice as fast as Derrick. The two of them lifted the wind around them as they ran.

Just as they got into striking range, there was a change around Derrick as his speed increased again.

Shadow Sword was flustered, but he gritted his teeth. He had created his own techniques, using his incredible speed and naturally higher perception to strike faster than any opponent he faced. Others focused on Agility. As long as he had the power to move faster, he could defeat anyone's Agility.

This was his secret and how he could kill people in just a few strikes. He used his power to break their defenses, and when they were alarmed, he would drive his blade home.

His muscles bulged, and his veins traced against his skin as he attacked.

Derrick raised one sword to meet Shadow Sword, who was using both of his hands on his sword to increase the amount of power behind it.

The sound of metal striking metal rang out. Shadow Sword's unimpressed face turned to shock as Derrick deflected his sword, forcing him to take a step back. He had no time to be stunned as Derrick attacked with his other free rapier.

Shadow Sword's veins popped out as he just barely got his sword into the path of Derrick's rapier.

The force from the blow transmitted through his sword and arms, deep into his body, and he was forced to retreat two steps.

Shadow Sword lost the momentum of the fight as Derrick fired off attack after attack; each of them pushed Shadow Sword to the limit.

"Interesting." Derrick sent out another strike.

Shadow Sword made to receive it; the air around the sword distorted as its speed was greater than the previous strikes, but Derrick didn't show any signs of strain. He struck Shadow Sword, who was tossed off the stage and onto the ground below.

The referee announced Derrick as the winner as Shadow Sword groaned, taking his time to get to his feet as he massaged his forearm.

Seeing the man walk down from the stage, Shadow Sword smiled bitterly. He had become too comfortable with his power—and lazy. Once, people had heard of his feats; now, he realized they were just holding him back.

"That fight, it was too fast!"

"I couldn't follow them. Their swords moved so fast that I could only hear as they clashed!"

"He defeated Shadow Sword with speed. Just who is he?"

"He's one of those people from the Adventurer's Guild. That group that came out of nowhere the other day. They have a true guild hall in Vuzgal, you know? It was their assassin who defeated the Purple Cloud sect's Gert Westerbeek, only moving once. And another beat up a member of the Silver Dragons with just his shield."

"There are plenty of dark horses in this competition. Isn't that the best?"

Gu Chen shook his head as he watched the fights in the arenas. There really were a lot of talents. The people from the Adventurer's Guild and other independents were making a name for themselves.

The Silver Dragons were part of that talk, but they hadn't dominated the competition. So far, the biggest name, which was previously unknown, was the Adventurer's Guild.

Gu Chen looked over to Blaze, who had gone from an outsider yesterday to having a group of people swarming around him, discussing contracts and setting up meetings.

They were achieving what the Silver Dragons had wanted and using the competition to advertise their power and services.

The morning advanced into afternoon, and the third round started.

The fighters rested while different events happened within the city, including an auction held within the arena itself.

This genius ploy got people spending higher than they would normally, wrapped up in the competitive spirit of the day.

Gu Chen and others in the VVIP booths bid on items that caught their eyes.

The third round continued; although, there were a few upsets. The Adventurer's Guild lost four people from their roster, while the Silver Dragons lost two. Other groups were slimmed down as the true competitors revealed themselves.

As things wrapped up, Gu Chen braced himself. He walked over to Blaze and waited for him to be free to talk, but as the last matches finished, Elise extracted Blaze from the group. He told those around him to come and see him at his guild hall.

Gu Chen wanted to call out and clear things up with him, but with Elise there, he didn't want to bring up anything nasty. She guided the traders and merchants in Vuzgal, and if she had a bad impression of him or his adventure group, it could backfire, and the Silver Dragons would never establish a place in Vuzgal.

16

Round Four

During the day, Blaze talked to the higher-ups in attendance. At night, he met with them in his office to go over business dealings. At the same time, there was a line snaking down the road in front of the guild hall.

More of his people had arrived from the lower realms to ease the pressure, testing those who wished to join and dealing with the day-to-day running of the Adventurer's Guild's highest realm branch.

Blaze read through the reports that had been passed to him between meetings. One was from Jasper, who had remained in the lower realms to deal with the guild's other operations. He was also responsible for leading the attack on the Willful Institute.

The Adventurer's Guild had instigated a plan to undercut the Willful Institute in any way they could, offering cheaper rates to merchants who traded with them and allowing them to drop their prices and contend with the Willful Institute. They took on missions, protection contracts, and other tasks that would have gone to the Willful Institute and were in talks with other sects that associated with the Willful Institute, becoming trade partners or working out agreements with them.

On the surface, the guild was expanding, bringing opportunities to those who worked with them, while cutting off the Willful Institute from resources by doing what they couldn't or wouldn't do. The sect relied on others to sell their items and create the wealth they needed to nurture Experts. Now, they were slowly getting attacked from different sides.

The guild was pleased to be doing something, finally, and many had taken on lower paying jobs just to get back at the Willful Institute.

Blaze waved his hand. His storage ring cleared his desk of dust left behind by the information books, and he found the next report.

"Huh, so Shadow Sword joined the association after fighting Derrick." Blaze looked it over once again, curious. He wrote a message on the paper and pressed a formation on his desk. A moment later, an administrator walked in.

"Take this to Branch Head Derrick. I want him to make the final decision," Blaze said.

She took the paper and headed out of the office.

Behind closed doors, Blaze didn't care about courtesy, preferring to increase the speed he and others worked at.

He went through several more reports before there was a knock at his door. He checked the time and put the memos in his storage ring.

"Come in." He stood to greet his next guest.

The third day of the competition began as Chonglu stood, saying six simple words.

"Let us begin the fourth round!"

The fighters moved to their stages, staring at their opponents.

The fights began, and they were on another level compared to the fights over the last two days.

People who had been hiding their strength employed more of their power. Some fights ended in minutes, while others drew gazes as Experts attacked with all their power. The two on the stage were matched well as they had to dig deep, using their fighting techniques to compete.

Fighters who hadn't experienced any trouble before started to run into problems.

Here, the true powerhouses were revealed, surprising the crowd as contestants famed for their fighting ability were knocked off their stages or admitted defeat.

The fights had heated up, leading to more injuries. The healers made sure they didn't die, and the referees knew enough basic care to keep them alive.

Still, there were some close calls as blood discolored several stages.

Two fighters stepped onto a stage that had just been scrubbed clean. Each of them wore a full suit of armor and held a sword and a shield. Not only did they seem physically dominating, but the air was also thick with mana. The referee looked between the two knights with a frown.

"Isn't that Yi Yin and Emilia?" a woman called out.

"Who is Emilia?" a man asked.

"She's one of the people from the Adventurer's Guild!"

"Don't the Silver Dragons and the Adventurer's Guild have a disagreement?" The man turned over to look at the stage.

"Their branch head went to talk to Guildmaster Blaze, but he was chased out by Kim Cheol."

"This should be a good fight then!" The man chuckled.

"The top knight of the Silver Dragons and the top knight from the Adventurer's Guild. I didn't think such an exciting matchup would happen so soon!" the woman cheered.

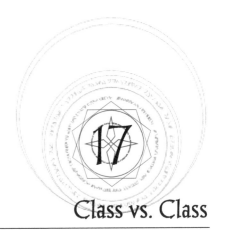

Class vs. Class

Yi Yin heard the cheers and felt the crowd's gaze upon him.

"Ready?" the referee asked.

Emilia lowered her stance, ready to fight.

"I want to say something first," Yi Yin said, remembering Gu Chen's order.

"You have one minute." The referee backed up, close enough to interfere if he needed to.

Emilia relaxed slightly.

"Branch Head Gu Chen apologizes for what Diana said and for her actions. There was a misunderstanding, and she was told the wrong thing. We do not want to fight against your association, and we seek an opportunity to make things right and even work together in the future, if possible. He wants to meet with your guildmaster to apologize and talk things over."

Emilia's face wasn't as grim as it had been. She nodded briskly. "Very well. I will pass your message to my guildmaster."

"Thank you," Yi Yin said and then got into his fighting stance. "Let us have a good fight!"

Emilia got into her stance again as the referee walked up.

"Begin!"

The two of them rushed forward. Yi Yin set his feet, raising his shield to meet Emilia's sword and angling it so her side would be open to him. She turned her hand and punched his shield and pushed her shield over to cover her side.

He took the hit on his shield. His brows pinched together, feeling the Strength she had displayed.

She took a step back and he charged, trying to force her off-balance.

Shield met shield as he attacked with his sword. She blocked him with her blade; they disengaged, using their sword and shield.

Emilia was stronger and regularly fought powerful opponents in life-and-death situations, but she was from the lower realms. The opponents were weaker, and although there was fighting in the lower realms, the Fourth Realm wasn't called the battlefield realm for nothing. Yi Yin's gear was better, and he had fought in the Fourth Realm for most of his life.

Being a member of the Silver Dragons, there were plenty of times Yi Yin had been contracted to fight bandits or hired as a mercenary. Yi Yin's combat experience allowed him to take more risks and accurately pin down Emilia.

He saw his opening.

He hit her arm to the side with his sword and attacked high with his shield; she covered her front with her shield, but it was a feint. He kicked out, and the sudden blow sent her backward.

He used his technique Sword Wall.

His sword turned into flashing lights. It howled, cutting through the air as it struck Emilia's shield again and again. Already off-balance, she threw out all her attacks to defend against Yi Yin's blows.

She roared as buffs appeared on her body, surging with power.

A technique? A buff?

He hit her shield with his sword, but she didn't fall back. She charged at him, and he dodged to the side, like a matador leading a bull.

He struck her armor, but she barely flinched. He felt his hits striking but doing no more damage, as if her skin had turned into armor.

Had she reached Body Like Iron already?

He didn't have time to worry; he continued to use his Sword Wall technique, but he was now slower as he had to defend himself as well. His own attacks landed, but she took them without pausing to attack.

Was she a knight or some kind of berserker?

His sword glowed as his speed picked up. His impacts made the ground under her feet crack.

Even under the attacks, he felt he was following her pace. His attacks became frantic, feeling the cold surety of death hang above him, setting his heartbeat racing. She came then, targeting his openings, he defended. But she floated away, her attacks light and playful feints. Her glowing eyes saw through every action.

How is she doing that?

He gritted his teeth, redoubling his efforts. Even as sweat coated his body he couldn't be free of the cold that pervaded him, that warned him he danced with death.

She backed off, pirouetting one attack and sending him stumbling. He jumped and rolled, turning around quickly. It was too slow, she had got the time she needed.

Her shield glowed with lightning that flashed over her body, and she charged forward.

He dodged her charge but didn't realize she had left behind a trail of lightning. It ran through his armor and he gritted his teeth, his nerves on fire as his muscles locked up.

She turned and charged again, aiming to launch him off the stage.

He was tossed up and backward, and he fought the lightning in his body, using his mana to suppress it.

He reached out with a spell and the ground shot up, creating pillars.

He slammed into them, arresting his movement and stopping before the edge of the stage.

She charged over, but her Strength was waning.

Yi Yin coughed, but he got up from the rubble.

He used his Fleet Foot technique and charged her. She increased her speed, and the two of them directed their shields to use the impact force to push them to the ground instead of into the air. The dust from the pillars drifted away, and they attacked each other as if they had gone mad. Some of the remaining pillars collapsed, and the attacks left dents, scratches, and scars on their armor.

Yi Yin could see the fatigue in Emilia's attacks. Her mana was starting to dwindle as they went all out with their techniques. Sweat trickled from under Yi Yin's helmet as they continued to come together. But he held back his trump card; the techniques he had employed already hadn't drawn too much energy from him.

He waited, getting her into a rhythm. She swung for an attack; he turned, taking the hit, and moved to her side. He kicked out, buckling her leg, hit the flat of his blade on her back, and used its enchantment. An explosion went off around his sword, tossing her forward and dropping her to the ground.

"Yi Yin as winner!" the referee said as he went over to Emilia.

Emilia groaned and picked herself up. She favored her sides, and it looked as though it were painful for her to hold her head up.

The referee used healing magic on her. "See a healer before you rest," he said.

Yi Yin had looked down on the people from the Adventurer's Guild when he had first heard of them. He didn't believe a group of people from the lower realms could reach the level of his Silver Dragons.

If they were able to get some fighting experience in the Fourth Realm, this fight could have turned out differently. She could have held back from using that lightning charge and conserved her attacks to go all out with her power.

He turned and left the stage, his blood pumping. It had been a close fight. If he had stepped wrong, he might have failed; she just had too many tricks. In terms of overall Strength, he had been able to keep some trump cards hidden to use in later fights.

The fights continued, but few reached the power between Yi Yin and Emilia.

At the end of the day, just one hundred contestants were left out of two thousand.

"Rest tonight and tomorrow. The day after, the real fights will start!" Chonglu's words got cheers from the crowd and made the fighters stand taller, staring at those around them. They would have to crawl over them if they wanted to win this competition.

"Eighteen people from the special team recruits and ten from the Adventurer's Guild made it into the top hundred," Roska said.

"That is more than I thought," Niemm said.

"Well, some had easier fights. In the next matches, they will have to rely on skill, not luck, to advance higher," Elan said as he got a message. He stepped away and listened to his sound transmission device.

He frowned slightly. The message ended, and Domonos walked over.

"Do you want to get a meal tonight?"

"I have to work. I might be free later. Will your sister be around?"

"I'm sure I can lure her out with some of the cooking academy's food." Domonos smiled.

Elan felt bad. He tried to spend as much time with his children as possible, but they were spread over other realms and all had their own tasks. Wren and Yui were in the First Realm while the rest of his family was here in the Fourth Realm.

"We should go down to the First Realm sometime and have a meal with your younger brother," Elan said, feeling sorry for Wren. His youngest was controlling his trading company in the First Realm.

"If we could get him to join Alva, that would be the best."

"I have asked the Alvan recruiters to look into it. Who knows what might happen?"

"Good. It'll be nice to have us all as Alvans." Domonos smiled as he received a sound transmission. "Got to go deal with this."

Elan nodded, and his son headed off while he thought of the message Blaze had sent him, asking him to look into Gu Chen and the Silver Dragons. He wanted to know if they could be trusted and whether they were looking to attack the Adventurer's Guild.

He quietly made his exit and headed down to his offices, toward the talking statue.

Kuldir

"Welcome to Kuldir Outpost. What's your business?" the guard at the gate asked the unfamiliar faces.

"We're just looking for somewhere to stay," Storbon said.

"Which outpost did you come from?"

"We didn't. We came from Acal."

"Acal, is it? That must've been a long walk."

"You could say that," Storbon said.

"You applying to any of the academies here or searching for work?"

"Neither really—just observing. Do you have a map store around here?"

"Check out Berk's Mappery. He has the best maps of the area." The guard looked them over once more. "There is no fighting inside these walls. Keep that for outside. The fee is three mana stones each."

Storbon paid the fee, and the guard moved to the side.

"Welcome to Kuldir, on the ass-end of the dungeon." He chuckled to himself, and the other guards grinned.

Storbon scanned their armor. It was pitted and scarred from use. Although it looked dirty, the joints were well cleaned and lubricated, and their weapons were in good condition. They were the type of men to look after their equipment first and themselves second.

They entered the outpost that was as large as some of the smaller cities in the First Realm. On the outskirts, there were simple homes. Everything here was made of stone, as it was an easier resource to find compared to wood.

People in the houses closest to the wall had lost limbs or had hidden wounds. Their eyes were dull; they dragged themselves onward, no longer looking forward to the next day. There was little moving wind this far out of the city.

The area got better the closer they got to the center of the outpost. There were large courtyards with several large job boards.

"Looking for a mining group, ten groups of ten. The greater your mining skill, the higher the payout. If you don't have the skill, this is your chance to learn! Danger pay included!"

"Looking for people to clean out Alchemy cauldrons. Long-term employment is a possibility!"

"Cleaning out cauldrons—that sounds pretty easy," Yao Meng said.

"It does. But who knows what kind of concoctions people are making or how your cleaning supplies will react with the bits left inside?" Erik asked.

"That doesn't sound too safe," Lucinda said.

"Well, money is money. People who come down here can strike it rich in a few years, buying rare resources and becoming strong enough to carve out a place in the realms. That is the hope, but reality is closer to the slums near the walls," Tian Cui said.

Things developed quickly as they reached the academy grounds. Here, people wore crests that denoted which academy they were from. Many wore weapons and armor.

Stores around this area held High quality goods.

The group reached Berk's Mappery and dismounted.

Storbon led the way into the store, and the door chimed. They looked around the room; some maps were on display along the walls.

An older man came out of the back of the map store with a large, amicable smile. "Hello, my name is Berk. Welcome to my store! What kind of maps are you looking for? High resource areas? Trade and travel routes to other outposts? Locations on beast sites to avoid or even dungeon raid entrances?" The man's smile didn't falter.

"Do you have a general map of the surrounding area?" Storbon asked.

"New to the area, looking for your bearings—that is always a good start!" Berk moved along his desk and checked something underneath it.

"I do have the map you're interested in. It covers a ten-kilometer area around the outpost. You will not find another of its quality! I can give it to you for sixty Earth-grade mana stones."

"Do you have a map that includes raid entrances, resources, and a larger area?" Storbon asked.

"We do! Always better to be prepared! Our best map covers one hundred kilometers in diameter and has information on the next three floors below us! It contains all recorded raid entrances and resource areas. It even tells you the time it will take the resources to recover if you harvest the materials."

"Price?" Storbon asked.

"Four Earth-grade mana cornerstones." Berk licked his lips.

Storbon looked over to those.

"Well, the more we know, the better," Rugrat said through his sound transmission device.

"Two Earth-grade mana cornerstones," Storbon said.

"People risked their lives to get these maps. Four!"

"Most I can do is three." Storbon pulled out Earth-grade mana stones, slowly piling them up. At five hundred regular mana stones to one cornerstone, it was quite the sight.

"Fine. Good doing business with you. I also have books on resources and valuable beasts you might find in the area."

Storbon poured out another two hundred Earth mana stones.

They disappeared into Berk's storage ring, and he held out the map.

"We should be good for now." Storbon grabbed the map.

Berk held it steady. "You might walk past a plant that could increase your Body Cultivation in one step! Or an ore that would make a master lose his mind."

"I'm sure," Storbon said.

Berk sighed and released the map. "Very well. Don't blame old Berk."

"So, what is the outpost like?" Erik asked.

"Kuldir is a gathering outpost. While there is a large group of orcs to the west of us, there are plenty of resource areas around us. Unfortunately, this area has a lot of monsters. The two fighting academies—the Golden Wolves and the Assorted Legacy Academies—use this area as a training ground and to make some money. They clear an area while herb collectors and miners work. The academies take their cut, and the rest is sold to the Kraxius Alchemy Academy or the Dreynas Smithing Academy. They refine the materials, turning some of them into items and ship the surface via academy carts that come once every month, dropping off supplies and taking away resources."

"A resource outpost," Tian Cui said.

"Yes, and a raid outpost. The fighters clear out raid dungeons and take along groups to gather loot, mine ores, and collect resources that the fighters would miss. There are several raid locations around us, and there are always orcs to kill. They're smart and difficult to fight, but you can get a lot of money for an orc body. The alchemists go crazy for them. Close to human, but not all the way there," Berk said.

"Are they affiliated with the Alchemist Association?" Erik asked.

"They wish! The Alchemist Association picks the best and grooms them over decades. The Kraxius Alchemy Academy has had many students joining the association and sells a lot of items to them, but they aren't associated. The associations are on another level compared to the academies. The true academies are in the Seventh Realm, the Sky Realm!"

"Where is a good place to stay?" Rugrat asked.

"You can try the Black Stalactite Tavern, or you can get a cheap place around here if you're staying longer. Most people come here for a few years to earn their prerequisites or to make some quick coin. The people who stay, well, they have a business or they can't keep up with the departing convoys and make it to the surface." Berk took out a large map from a storage item and put it on the desk. Instead of it being a rolled-up scroll, it was a massive tome.

"What do you mean 'can't keep up?'"

"Touch this to your maps, and it will transfer the information contained within. And, well, a lot of people get wounded, lose limbs, get lame, or get robbed. The merchants won't take freeloaders, and it's a premium to ride on a wagon."

Storbon took out his map and touched it to the large tome. The tome disintegrated. Ash and wisps of ink were absorbed into his map, filling it with information as their small path from before expanded greatly.

"Thank you for your help," Storbon said.

"If you get more information than is contained on that map, bring it back here. I'm always looking to expand the range of my maps and their accuracy."

Storbon nodded, and the group left the mappery and mounted up. He passed his map to the others, and they updated their own maps. The black area, other than the line that they had walked, started to fill in. The line from orc territory remained, as there wasn't any detailed map coverage over the orc area. A marker denoted it was an orc-controlled zone. There were several raid dungeons, resource points, and other areas of interest to them.

"I'm going to have a look around," Erik said. "Thinking about checking out those stalls I saw back a little bit."

"I'm gonna check out the smithing areas. You guys go and check out what you want," Rugrat said.

"We're meant to follow you two," Storbon said. "Yao Meng, go with Erik. I'll go with Rugrat. Where do the rest of you want to go?"

"I'll check out the stalls," Yuli said.

"I'll go to the smiths," Tian Cui said.

"Same here," Lucinda agreed.

The group split up, and Erik headed toward the stalls. Ever since they had passed the outer area, something had troubled Erik.

Erik looked around the places hidden between the stalls. He saw people working with old injuries that had healed wrong, leaving them with broken and twisted bodies, making every day a nightmare within the harsh outposts. In many cases, they were unable to do anything. The dungeon was a dangerous place and made these sorts of injuries and people common.

Erik was struck with an old memory. He came to a stop and chuckled. "Two copper coins," he muttered and smiled. "Excuse me, where can I rent a stall?" he asked.

The trader peered at him with a suspicious eye. "Go down that street and on the right. There's a place with a sign half-connected. Ask for Gerry. He'll get you your permit."

"Thanks." Erik found the building without issue and walked in to find Gerry. Yuli and Yao Meng gave one another a bewildered look, following him.

"Five Earth mana stones for the stall for three days, eight for a week."

"I'll take a week then." Erik put down the stones.

The man peeked at the stones and pulled out a piece of paper. He wrote on it before stamping it. "This is your writ. Present it to the inspectors if they come around."

"Thank you." Erik took the writ and headed back out.

His stall was closer to the outreaches of the city; it wasn't in the best condition, and there were many people there, all glassy-eyed, taking some kind of concoction to dull the pain of the day or trying to nap here and there to speed up time.

Yuli and Yao Meng watched as Erik pulled out a board.

"Healing, two cop—no, two Mortal mana stones can be paid after services rendered," Erik read the sign aloud and put it up on the side of the stall. Then, he took out a cot and laid it down in front of the stall, then took a seat and sat down.

"So, what are we doing?" Yuli asked.

"You both have your advanced medic courses, right?"

"Yes," Yuli and Yao Meng chorused.

"Well, we can put what you learned to some use." Erik looked over to one of the glassy-eyed people near the booth. He was a large man, but he had tired, sunken cheeks and a beard he had forgotten about.

"Hello. Would you like to be healed?" Erik asked.

"W-what?" The man scowled and covered his leg protectively.

"I ask for two mana stones, or you can swear an oath on the Ten Realms if you don't have them right now."

"Get away from me!"

Erik stood and repeated his words to others. Yuli went with him, and Yao Meng stood at the stall.

It took a dozen or so people before he found a mother with sunken eyes clutching a toddler.

"Please, look at my boy," she said.

Her son had a wet cough and a pale complexion. Erik extended his domain, undetected by the woman and her son.

Small cut on the feet, infection throughout the body, high temperature, brain swelling, liquid in the lungs, low Stamina from diet. Signs of growth issues from lacking nutrition.

"Let's go over to the stall," Erik said.

"I can carry him," Yuli said, seeing that she was struggling.

The woman shook her head, insisting that she carry her boy, and struggled over to the stall.

She laid the boy down in the cot.

"I'll need to see what's wrong with him first." Erik put two fingers on the boy's arm and used Simple Organic Scan to double-check the extent of the damage to the boy, which he had already figured out by using his domain.

Erik's expression was hard. "Okay, we're going to need a Stamina drip. Let's see if we can get a tube in to open his pathways. And we need to drain some of that liquid. Yuli, would you give her a physical and make sure she is okay?" Erik gave Yuli a look of "make sure she doesn't see what we're doing; we don't want to alarm her."

She nodded and turned to the mother.

"He is in the best hands. Come on, I need to check you over as well." Yuli took her to another section of the tent, separated by a thick cloth.

Yao Meng used a Clean spell on the boy.

"Take a big sniff of this, champ," Erik said.

The boy took some shaky breaths before he went slack.

"Okay, going to need a breathing tube, just in case," Erik said, putting the boy's arms on the cot and positioning his head.

Yao passed him a ventilator, and Erik inserted it with experienced hands.

His heartbeat was weak, and the infection was doing a number on him, focused on the lungs. *Nasty.*

"I'll need an empty needle. Give him a healing, Stamina mix." Erik put the boy in the recovery position and rolled up his shirt.

"Empty." Yao passed the needle over.

Erik used his fingers and his domain as he inserted the needle in the boy's lower back. He pulled on the plunger, filling the needle with a red-and-milky-like fluid.

Yao Meng found a vein and inserted the Stamina/healing potion needle with quick and sure actions before injecting the potion into the boy's body.

Erik finished draining the boy's lungs, and his breathing eased. He checked the boy's status, noting where the different infections had taken place.

Erik had a Cure Disease potion, but he wondered if he could instead use his knowledge on poisons to fight this.

A black thread left Erik's fingers and entered the boy's body. The poison potion attacked the infection and then circulated throughout the boy's bloodstream.

It didn't take as much Stamina. *Is that because it is attacking the infection instead of using the boy's reserves to repair him?*

Erik used the poison to attack different infections. They dwindled, allowed the boy's body to recover and fight back, showing that his immune system was learning and adapting from it.

He was scared that attacking it with poison would mean that he would still be susceptible to it. It looked like that wasn't the case. *Poison, if used right, can heal.*

Erik let the poison dissipate.

"Let's start with the healing spells," Erik said. "Without the infections, it should take less Stamina. Less stress on the patient's overall health."

"Is that why you fix the surrounding issues and then heal them afterward?" Yao Meng asked.

Erik didn't look up as he worked. "Healing is a fine balance; it can kill as surely as poison if done incorrectly. As a general rule, in battlefield medicine, stick someone with a Stamina and healing potion right away. That should give you both time. Then assess and deal with the most critical issues. The more you can patch up without using mana, the less Stamina the patient burns through. Healing spells are your mana plus their stamina."

"So, with Chonglu?"

"Removal of the limbs, less stress on the overall body—just sealed four wounds instead of managing tens of them, including internal bleeding and broken bones," Erik said.

Yao Meng healed the boy while Erik took out a towel and wet it, putting it on the boy's head. His temperature was coming back down to normal, and the swelling in his brain decreased.

The mother had finished her physical, so Yuli let her up, but the woman was tired from her ordeal.

Erik glanced over to Yuli.

"Minor infections, lack of sleep, malnourished. Nothing some good sleep and food couldn't fix," Yuli said.

"Is he all right?" the boy's mother asked.

"He had a small cut on his foot that allowed an infection to get into his body. It wreaked havoc, and then other infections piled on top of that. We've dealt with most of the issues. He just needs a little bit more healing, and he's good to go." Erik pulled out the breathing tube.

The boy's chest moved up and down, stronger than it had just some minutes ago.

The mother wrung her hands as she peeked at her son.

Yao Meng stopped using his healing spell.

Erik checked the boy once more and then pulled out a different vial and put it under his nose. The boy's nose twitched, and his eyes fluttered. Erik removed the towel, and the boy sat up, coughing and spluttering.

His mother rushed to his side and supported his back. Seeing his eyes wide and bright, she hugged her little boy. Tears rolled down her face as the anxiousness and fear she had bottled up was freed.

He hugged her back, not sure what was happening.

The group stepped back. A crowd had gathered as they had healed the boy.

Erik moved behind the stall and pulled out big sheets, creating a large sheet-covered area. Yuli helped him as Yao Meng turned to the people watching.

"If you or someone you know is suffering from an ailment, for just two Mortal mana stones, we will heal them to the best of our abilities. We accept payment upon a completed job. And if you do not have the funds now, you can say an oath on the Ten Realms to pay us when you are able to," Yao Meng said.

People glanced at one another. Some started to leave now that the spectacle was over.

The mother stood up with her boy and bowed to all three of them. "I cannot pay you now," she said in a worried voice.

"Children are free." Erik stepped forward and helped her back up. "Say this." Erik cleared his throat. "I will pay two mana stones to the health relief funds with money I do not require to care for myself and my dependents in order to have a roof over our heads, food, water, and simple clothes. I so swear on the Ten Realms."

She repeated the oath. Light covered her as the Ten Realms confirmed it. She bowed again. "Thank you, thank you!" Tears once again filled her eyes.

"Please tell those who you know who are injured to come to see us. We'll do our best," Erik said.

"I will," she said.

An older-looking man, hunched over and using a cane to stay upright, tilted his head to them.

"Lies! You think that you could fix someone like me?" He snorted.

"As long as you are willing to swear the oath with the stipulation that we must heal you," Erik said.

The man sneered. He looked as if he were going to walk away or spit on them before he sighed and raised his hand. "I swear that if you are able to heal my ailments that I will pay two mana stones to the health relief funds with money I do not require to care for myself and my dependents to have a roof over our heads, food, water, and simple clothes. I so swear on the Ten Realms."

The oath was completed. As Erik guided him forward, he used a Clean spell on the man, cleansing him and his clothes in a flash. He and Yuli took him behind the sheets.

"Yuli, please examine him. Tell me what you find." Erik moved to the side.

Yuli put her hands to the man's neck and used Simple Organic Scan.

"How do you feel?" Erik asked.

"How do I feel?" The man spat. "I have no feeling down my legs, I'm in pain all the time, and I can't straighten my damn back. I've been stuck like this for years."

"Okay," Erik said. "Yuli?"

"He isn't really injured, just things are in the wrong place," Yuli said, annoyed with how the man had talked to Erik.

"Right. For this, we need to adjust his body. We'll just use healing to get him to recover faster." Erik moved to the man. "Okay, I need you to lie down."

The man laid down with Erik's help.

"I'm going to use some salve, so this won't hurt," Erik said.

He put Wraith's Touch on the man's back, and the man sighed as his body relaxed.

Erik scanned again. "This looks like a muscle and bone placement issue. The muscles have pulled on the bones and joints, and they've stuck in place. Now, if I were a chiropractor, I would know how to work these joints and get everything re-aligned. I'm not, so we'll take the easier approach. We'll heal his body. That will re-align everything; although, he's lost considerable muscle mass." Erik faced the patient. "Sir, once we're done here, go and get some food, walk around and stretch, then come back so we can continue healing you. It should allow you to regain some Strength in your muscles. The more you do when walking around, the faster the recovery rate."

The man grunted.

Erik gathered mana around him, and the man's eyes widened as it condensed under Erik's command.

He used Simple Heal, and the man groaned as his body made satisfying pops and crunches. His grimace turned into a look of relief.

The small scratches and bruises on his body disappeared, and the man looked as if he were ready to take a nap as Erik finished after some short minutes.

His healing spells were a lot more powerful than when he was working on Chonglu as a healer.

The mana dissipated as Erik stepped back. "All right, get up and take a walk around the room."

The man put his feet under him as he sat on the corner of the cot. He was unsteady as he slowly raised his back with a grunt. He grimaced in expectation of the pain he had lived with for so long, waiting for it to return. He raised himself slowly, surprised as he went past his previous limits and continued to stand upright.

He grabbed his walking stick and took a hesitant step forward, followed by another. Then he moved across the room, widening his gait. His surprise turned into a smile, and he laughed as he walked back to Erik and Yuli.

"Okay, everything looks good." Erik waved Yuli forward.

She steadied the man with her hands. "Do your legs feel tight?"

"A little."

"Since you haven't used some of those muscles in a long time, it is normal that they are tighter than usual. When you walk around, they will loosen."

"Okay," the man said between labored breaths.

"All right, well, have a good day, and we'll see you later." Erik smiled.

"Thank you, thank you so much." The man dropped to his knees and bowed his head, unable to bend forward anymore. "What I said before, I was blind!"

"Ah, no worries. I'd be skeptical too." Erik reached down to help the man up.

The man took the offered hand. There were tears in his eyes.

"Look after yourself," Erik said. "I don't want to heal you for the same thing twice!"

"Understood." The man nodded sheepishly.

Erik and Yuli guided the man outside. People gasped when they saw him standing upright. The man bowed to Erik and Yuli before leaving.

Yao Meng had a list of people waiting and had categorized them based on their condition. "We have a patient who breathed in fumes from an alchemist's cauldron. She has burns across her face and neck, and it got into her lungs too. She's in bad shape." Yao Meng moved to the side, indicating the woman lying on a handmade stretcher, burns covering her as she wheezed and coughed.

"Bring her in right away. I'll deal with it personally."

"Yuli, your next is over here." Yao took her over to another patient.

"Frank…is there a Frank out there?"

"I'll deal with it." Yao Meng walked to the cots and waved two people forward. Both were coughing and looked ill. He put a mask and gloves on, using a Clean spell on them and then administered a needle with a Cure Disease potion in it.

The crowd grew as more people came over. They were in the worst part of town, so the people who lived here had been forgotten by others, and all they had to do was give an oath to pay two Mortal mana stones. How much was two Mortal mana stones? It was nothing at all.

Erik examined the girl with the burns. He could see the pain she was in, but he ignored it and got to work. He couldn't get emotional; it wouldn't help.

The girl's sister was there, holding her hand. He used a Clean spell on them both and then a vial filled with crushed-up ingredients. The pungent smell caused the person smelling it to fall into a slumber.

He stoppered the vial as he checked her vitals. With his domain, he was able to see the damage to the girl's body. It was a miracle she was still alive. If he were back on Earth, with the technologies there, he would have had a hard time saving her.

He pulled out a needle and filled it with some Stamina potion, checked the quantity, and then injected it into the girl's body. She had barely eaten in days, and it showed.

With that shot of Stamina recovery, he focused his healing on her lungs.

As her lungs were repaired, more of the air she inhaled entered her blood. He moved to the neck; it was cut up and mangled, obstructing her airways.

Once that was done, he applied Wraith's Touch to the woman's face and burns.

He put her in the recovery position and used a vial to wake her up. Her eyes opened, and she choked.

"Get it out," Erik said.

In the healing process, the old materials were left behind. She coughed violently, pushing out the objects trapped within her lungs and airways.

He patted her back as she coughed out black impurities. Erik used his healing spells on the girl's face, opening her melted nose and healing the wounded muscles around the jaw and the interior of her mouth. She focused on coughing up all the gunk.

Finally, she stopped coughing, breathing heavily and looking pale.

"Your lungs are nice and open. Your airways are clear, and you should be able to speak. You're in good hands," he said to the woman, patting her shoulder before looking to the sister. "Right now, I'll heal one of her eyes, and then you'll need to feed her—the more food the better— then let her rest. When she wakes up, bring her back to me. I'll heal her other eye and the cosmetic issues," Erik said.

He really didn't want to push her limits. This way, she would live, and the eye will allow her some relief.

Erik healed the woman's right eye and eyelid.

She opened her eye and curled into herself, her breathing quick and shallow.

She must have been living in darkness since this had happened. Scared, in constant pain, and unable to talk.

Erik gave her a reassuring smile and stepped back.

"Alina!" her sister cried out.

"Linda," Alina said. The two of them hugged, crying and shaking together. Linda studied Alina again and hugged her. Erik quietly excused himself from the ad-hoc privacy tent.

There was a much larger crowd now. Erik grabbed the clipboard. There were no immediate aid cases.

He went over to Yao Meng. "I'll create a Hallowed Ground. Get people to swear the oath and send them in, then I'll send them out when they're healed. We should get through the people with infections quickly and save some of our potions."

There was a loud *crack* from the tent. Yuli was seeing to a patient who had a broken leg that had set wrong; it sounded as if she had rebroken it.

Erik headed into the covered tent, just as Yuli sent the person out. He moved to the side, checking the area around him, and was about to cast his Hallowed Ground spell when he frowned. What if he combined Hallowed Ground with his knowledge of poisons that could heal and the combined healing practices?

Divine Ground

Expert

Someone who steps into the area of effect is healed rapidly

Cast: 500 Mana 200 Mana/minute – 20m radius

1500 Mana 500 Mana/minute – 40m radius

For teaching yourself an Expert-ranked spell, you gain: 5,000,000 EXP

"If I combine Stamina Regeneration?"

Divine Ground

Master

Someone who steps into the area of effect is healed and regains Stamina rapidly

Cast: 1000 Mana 400 Mana/minute – 20m radius

2000 Mana 700 Mana/minute – 40m radius

> For teaching yourself a Master-level spell, you gain: 50,000,000 EXP

A flood of Experience filled Erik's body. People peeked at the tent and then away, continuing their conversations. It wasn't that strange to see powerful people in the Sixth Realm leveling up.

Erik had totally forgotten about the notifications from the fight with the orcs.

Skill: Marksman

Level: 85 (Expert)

Long-range weapons are familiar in your hands. When aiming, you can zoom in x2.0. 15% increased chance for a critical hit. When aiming, your agility increases by 20%.

Skill: Riding

Level: 57 (Journeyman)

Melee attacks while riding are 10% stronger

Rider's Strength increases by 5% when fighting atop their mount

Upon advancing into the Journeyman level of Riding, you will be rewarded with one randomly selected item related to this skill.

> You have received the spell scroll: Knight's Saddle
> +100,000 EXP

He stopped reading as light flashed and two items appeared in front of him.

Knight's Saddle

Defense: 134

Weight:	7.3 kg
Health:	100/100
Charge:	100/100

Innate Effect:

Increase rider's stability by 3%

Increase speed by 9%

Enchantment:

Enhanced Charge

Mount's charging speed increases by 2x for 5 seconds

Requirements:

Agility 65

Strength 47

He would have to check these with Rugrat. The saddle could help him out, but Rugrat shot from his saddle all the time. The increased stability would be useful. Maybe George could use the charge enchantment to take off faster?

Erik stored it and peeked at his Experience bar.

69,087,321/86,100,000 EXP till you reach Level 60

Erik clicked his tongue.

He had earned fifty-five million Experience points from learning two spells and had received six hundred thousand from fighting the orcs. Most of them were level fifty-five, which had decreased the Experience he had earned by a large margin.

Yao Meng cleared his throat. "Are you ready to begin?"

"Yes, let's start," Erik said.

Erik cast his new Divine Ground. The mana from the surrounding area poured toward him. Golden threads rose from the ground, the threads of power weaved together, a tapestry of light, of lines and runes. The tent glowed with the spell formation. Staring at it, one would feel relaxed. There was none of the chilling aura that came with the original Hallowed Ground that would attack an enemy.

He stepped clear of the Divine Ground maintaining the spell's mana drain.

The next batch of patients entered.

"Stand in the glowing circle, please." Erik sent out Clean spells to them all. They stepped into the Divine Ground and let out surprised noises as they were healed. Erik watched them, seeing their injuries as he changed the Divine Ground, speeding up their recovery. At the same time, his healing skill was quietly but quickly increasing.

19

Mining Trip

Rugrat wandered into one of the smithing sectors dotted across the outpost. He was eating some skewer from a stall that he had found in passing.

Storbon surveyed the area while Tian Cui's hands were never far from her daggers. Lucinda petted the bird on her shoulder.

"Huh," Rugrat grunted, finding the scene amusing. "Most of these smiths are refineries. It's like that map guy said—this is just a refinery town. The enhancers are interesting, though," Rugrat commented to himself. He had become an Expert on the matter; he just needed the damn system to realize that as an Expert and give him the skill level.

"Have you been mining before?" He turned around, seeing their blank looks. "Me neither. Want to check it out?"

"Why?" Tian Cui asked.

"Well…" Rugrat thought back to the time when he had been standing at the top of Vuzgal's tower and had thought on smithing and weapons; it had opened a new path for him. "If I know more about the materials, it could help me with me smithing. If I want to make weapons that are the other half of the natural whole of a fighter, I should learn the basics, right?"

"I guess?" Tian Cui shrugged.

"Good!" Rugrat turned.

"Are we going to do it on our own?" Storbon asked.

"I was thinking so," Rugrat said.

"We're in a new realm. Who knows what we might run into? If we haven't mined before, shouldn't we learn from the people who have?"

Rugrat opened his mouth and then closed it. "Yeah, that makes sense." Rugrat spotted someone coming out of the smithy. "Hey, where can we sign up to go mining?"

"Mining?" The smith's tired expression turned to anger. "This place is for smiths, not miners. Go to the job boards and join a group. If I see you around here again, I'll get the guards to throw you out of the outpost!"

The man turned and headed back into the smithy.

"Someone has a stick up their ass." Rugrat kept eating his skewer. On the being-chewed-out scale, the man's rant barely registered.

It didn't take long to get to a courtyard.

"Looks like there is a team leaving in a few minutes. If we run, we can catch them," Lucinda said.

"Lead on! I smell gold!" Rugrat said.

"That's not that valuable up here, you know," Tian Cui said.

"It's a saying," Rugrat shot back.

"How do you smell gold, exactly? Is it a spell?" Storbon asked.

Rugrats shoulders slumped and he sighed, chewing on his skewer as he petted his support, George.

"Looking for ten miners! Keep forty percent of your haul!"

"Need four more guards for mining trip! You'll get paid based on your contribution. No less than one percent of entire haul!"

"People with mining-related spells, come right here! Everything is negotiable."

Lucinda found them a group and got them the position of miners.

The guards eyed them. Bandits weren't unheard of around these areas.

They got into carriages and headed out of the gates. After a short ride, they reached a mining plot that had been rented out to the foreman running the operation.

Several other groups were in the large, cavernous area. Great pillars of stone supported the ceiling above. There was a big pit in the middle, where indentured members were breaking stone apart and shoving the fragments into storage rings. The stone could be re-fused and create strong walls or floors.

Above and around the mining pit, different tunnels and openings led to other caverns. Miners in their group rushed into these tunnels to find their riches. The area was enclosed in a simple wooden barricade to fend off beasts.

People jumped out of the carriages. Groups of miners who were working together rushed out to different plots, setting up quickly. They were using all kinds of gear and spells to check the walls while the guards watched the area, blind to the miners' actions.

"Why do we need so many guards inside the walls?" Tian Cui asked.

"We're mining through the walls of the dungeon. There is no knowing if we won't open up another dungeon filled with all kinds of creatures," Lucinda said.

"Oh, that's terrifying," Tian Cui said.

"What's worse is if you hit a pocket of gas. It can kill you before you have time to get a second breath." Rugrat watched the miners working.

Rugrat moved along the walls and used his hand to see through the stone.

He pulled out a pickaxe and swung it at the wall. His powerful blows sent stone flying. Storbon raised walls on either side of Rugrat so he didn't hit others with chips.

Rugrat worked for a good half hour before he slowed his attack, opening the hole he had made. Then he used different tools and mana-created blades.

He pulled out a shimmering blue-and-silver metal with hints of pink deep within.

Rugrat frowned, putting down the metal.

"What is it?" Storbon asked

"It's called chrysantaline rock. Great with spell scrolls and explosives. Not so good with formations or anything you want to keep for a long time." Rugrat seemed distracted.

"Something wrong?" Storbon asked.

"Nothing is wrong. I thought there was something romantic about smashing rocks all day. Doing it, you can change the world. If you're a miner, harvesting all this rock, it is a thrill to think of how you might get a big score. I've spent weeks in libraries learning about all of these diverse materials. I know what temperature they need to reach to melt and what other enhancers they need to combine with before they can be used for spell-scroll ink. Mining isn't going to be the way to get to Expert."

Rugrat rolled his shoulders. "All of this jumping around, trying to figure out what I am missing—it is like I am chasing my tail. I need a new project."

"What kind of project?"

"Instead of aiming to make an Expert-level weapon right off the bat, let's make some gear that is useful. At some time, our normal gear will not work; our rifles won't be as powerful, nor will our gunpowder rounds. There is a limit. It's high, but it is there. On Earth, we were talking about rail guns, coil guns, and such. I know how weapons work; I'm familiar with them, and even if it doesn't reach Expert, we get new gear that could save a person's life. Maybe I won't make it through the barrier of Expert. Maybe I don't need to in order to make a weapon stronger than an Expert's. That could be cool. Use different information from different places from the start to make a better weapon instead of creating a weapon then adding a formation. Like with the repeater, the formation is a core part of the weapon. Combine Earth and realm knowledge completely."

"Well, what do we do with this?" Tian Cui nodded at the crystalline rock.

"Beer fund." Rugrat smiled, feeling as if a weight had lifted from his shoulders. He couldn't do everything, only keep working on the things he knew he could do and set a path forward. Maybe later he would see a clearer path.

"What our real target is, is this," He pointed at bands of gray-and-red rock.

"What's that?" Tian Cui asked

"*That* is a nice band of Earth-grade iron ore." Rugrat smiled.

"Give me a hand. We need to get as much of this as possible. Then we can get it back, melt it down, and refine it into iron ingots."

Renowned Competition

As the preliminary matches ended, the betting houses faced another wave of patrons coming in and placing their bets.

News had spread across the Fourth Realm, and more people had headed to Vuzgal to watch the competitions. Sects that had previously believed the competition beneath their standing could only watch. Their fighters, unable to join, wore fake smiles upon hearing the rewards the competitors would receive. Some sects planned to bring their people over for the next competition to get a chance at part of those rewards.

There were very few guilds in Vuzgal, but that was starting to change. Most of the guilds saw the crafter dungeon and the crafting that went on inside Vuzgal, and although they purchased items, they didn't think of making it their base of operations. They were fighting guilds and based themselves in dangerous locations where they would get the greatest payouts for their services and could fight to their heart's content.

It came as a shock when a rumor circulated that eighty of the top one hundred people in the competition had trained in Vuzgal's Battle Arena.

After testing out the training rooms, most guilds invested in Vuzgal, looking to buy land. Many were scraping together as much money as they could to get a guild hall after learning of the benefits one might earn.

They complained to the guilds that had already purchased a guild hall and silently kept the advantages to themselves. One could see how their people's fighting abilities had increased greatly.

Vuzgal was a holy land to crafters, and it appeared that it was becoming a holy land for fighters as well.

The military and the police of Vuzgal had the time they needed to mature and grow into their roles. With the military's formations and teamwork, even if some of the higher level visitors wanted to make trouble, they were unable to.

As this was unfolding, the first day of the true competition began. Blaze sat in his seat once again, and the area around him had more people than before. The guildmasters who resided in Vuzgal already were quickly snatching up contracts.

Blaze listened to the conversations around him as people settled into their seats in anticipation of the fights.

"I heard there was another fight last night between the Executor Guild and the Voidless Guild," one of the merchants said to his friend.

"Those two are like fire and water. Whenever they see one another, they're sure to break into a fight." His friend sighed.

"I thought they would tear up the whole district, but the Vuzgal guards, police they're called, came in on their mounts. The Executor guildmaster warned them to stay out of it. There were thirty police to, fifty Executors and fifty Voidless."

The second merchant let out a hiss, "No stopping that."

"Hah, you'd be surprised! The police waded right in, just ten of them, laid the Executors and Voidless out flat!"

"What? But those are both high level guilds."

"Don't matter, they pissed off the cops. They're spending the day in jail to cool off and with a hefty fine on both guilds."

"How is that possible? The Vuzgal army is just a bunch of fourth-realm recruits."

"Well these are police, they're different from the army apparently. I talked to some people I know from Vuzgal. It isn't strange for someone to join the army and reach Mid level forties after a few months of training."

"Are they hiring Experts? How can they level up so fast?"

"They're not hiring Experts, no. They don't care about previous record—just their loyalty, supposedly." The first merchant seemed a little shocked as well.

"A fighting force with Mid level forties as the main body of soldiers—isn't that a little too powerful?" the second merchant said.

"Well, makes me feel safer with all the guilds and fighters moving around here."

"Too right," the second merchant agreed.

Blaze smiled. The endless dungeon was closed off every night to the adventurers, and while that happened, a group from the Vuzgal army would head over to fight the beasts, increasing their levels and acquiring loot and gear. They kept the monster cores and sold the rest as training resources for the group. Groups cycled through the endless dungeon, one after another. After several weeks, their levels were bound to increase.

The creatures reached level forty-three at their peak. As the army reached that level, they used their saved monster cores to increase their levels again, leaving them at their current range. Still, they were looking for more ways to increase their power. What they couldn't do with levels, they did with training, honing their abilities. Add in learning skills and techniques, and some were able to gain a few extra levels.

Blaze had exchanged messages with Glosil about the operations against the Willful Institute and the dungeon core he was given by Niemm. From it, he had learned about the Alvan army's training regimen. He was excited to see how it would improve his own guild members' power.

Referees walked out to the stages; larger stages filled each level of the Battle Arena for the fighters. It reduced the number of fights happening, but each one would be a soul-stirring battle between Experts.

Those who weren't in their seats rushed to them, while others slowed their conversations to a stop as they looked out at the stages.

Cheering erupted from the stands. Fighters who had been well known or not known at all walked out. Some had grim expressions while others waved to their fans.

Blaze's attention turned to one of the screens in the booth and found Joan walking out of her tunnel.

She stepped up on the stage and studied her opponent. The woman had a tattoo down the side of her face and had more markings on her skin. She wore a mage robe and held a worn wooden staff with a yellow, glowing crystal in it.

"Silent Spring," Blaze said the woman's name.

"The Dark Horse," Elise said from beside him.

"Yeah, a summoner mage," Blaze muttered, his focus on the screen.

Joan assessed her opponent. Her senses were pushed to the max as she tried to learn more about her. Joan had made it through some easy fights in the beginning, but the difficulty had sharply increased as she had gone through more rounds.

She didn't walk into any of her matches lightly, and her expression turned frigid as she pushed her senses to assess the mage-type fighter standing across from her.

The two of them faced off from opposite sides of the stage. The mana around the mages thickened as they readied for the fight.

The referee brought them together. The two women shook hands and then went back into their own corners.

He waved his hand. "Begin!"

Joan drew out an arrow from her quiver. As she raised it, mana flowed into her opponent's spell circle, creating a bear's outline.

Joan released her arrow as the outline solidified. It stepped into the arrow's path, defending its caster.

Everything happened in a moment. Joan drew another arrow back on her bow string as fast as possible. It was a war of speed!

The beast stomped the ground and jumped forward. It had a bear's body, snake's tail, and a crow's face.

Joan fired at the woman. The beast's snake tail whipped out, shattering the arrow as Joan moved, shooting more arrows.

A second circle formed as the mage chanted and moved her hands.

Joan had to break the spell before her opponent had a chance to call in a second beast. Under her breath, she lay spells on the arrow as she moved around the beast to line up her shot. She drew and released in the same breath.

The arrow churned up air as it passed, humming before it struck the half-formed beast in the shoulder. Black and orange runes collapsed and spread out from the point of impact, fluctuating; the mage's face paled as she fought to keep the construct together.

The beast roared, attacking with its paw, and Joan dodged the attack. Grabbing a dagger on her waist, she stabbed it into the summon and jumped backward. She used the force to tear the blade through the beast's hide.

Its magical construction shuddered as the power that made up its body shifted to deal with the damage.

Joan drew an arrow. The damn mage had recovered and continued to summon a second beast, which would likely be stronger than the one she had insta-cast.

The mage raised her head and opened her hand, firing a blast of wind at her.

She dodged it, which put her in line with the tail of the first summon. *Shit!*

The snake tail released poison, and the construct turned to face her.

The poison hit her side, burning her skin where it touched it. She focused on drawing back her bow, her spells carved along the arrow.

The crow head opened its mouth to roar.

A beast is just a beast.

She fired into the crow's mouth. It stiffened as runes flashed across its body.

The construct came apart with a clink that sounded like breaking glass.

Joan turned and fired at the nearly formed second construct. It shimmered, but the backlash wasn't as great.

The mage released spells of Fire and Water created shimmering air attacks, cutting apart arrows that exploded with their released energies. Joan's spells took them on strange paths, making them hard to predict.

The mage's face was covered in sweat.

Joan moved around the stage. Her bow was as fast as a repeater and gave her opponent no chance to recover.

"This speed!" a man yelled out, sitting at the edge of his seat and grabbing his friend's sleeve.

"Isn't that instantaneous casting? I thought summoning spells took the longest to complete!" She smacked the bannister in front of her seat.

"She must have trained to use that spell! But look at the archer! She is firing arrows so fast I can't see them!"

"Look—there is another summon!"

"How large are her magical reserves?"

The mage tried to insta-cast her summoning spell again. A creature flashed into existence, only to be met with an arrow. A second arrow chased after the first and silenced the creature.

A massive, slime-covered worm shot out of the ground and wrapped itself around its caster protectively. Its aura made Joan shiver slightly before her face shone with excitement.

The worm beast opened its face, revealing eight folds covered in spikes and a mouth with long tentacles that lashed out at the air, making it crack with a simple flick.

As Joan fired an arrow at the creature, it released a breath tinged with black and green. The powerful poison covered the arrow and destroyed it before it reached its face.

Joan jumped and dodged to the side as the poison breath hit the area of the stage where she had been standing. The ground melted. Joan jumped away again, firing arrows at the same time. Two of her arrows struck, burying themselves deep in the creature's side; it cried out in pain. The third was smacked out of the air with one of its tentacles.

A powerful force grabbed Joan and tossed her backward.

Telekinesis? It's a magical summon?

Joan was under threat of being thrown off the stage.

The air around her became thick and hazy as she grabbed three arrows. The mana around her turned chaotic. She grinned and pulled back on her bowstring.

The arrows released, howling as spells revolved around them. They grew in size with every passing meter. When they hit the big worm, they were the size of spears, without losing any of their momentum. The spear-arrows struck and exploded.

The power holding Joan loosened, and she fell onto the edge of the stage. She rolled forward, panicked.

She landed, and the smoke on the other side of the stage lifted. The worm was in bad condition but looked pissed. Another creature stepped forward, a half-sized, mean-looking humanoid. He had a cruel look on his face, held two scythes, and wore boots made of metal.

With a cackling yell, he stomped forward with a speed that didn't match his size.

Joan advanced as well; she needed to get away from the edge of the stage. She fired arrows as she moved. The little creature deflected the first. The second hit him in the leg, making him stumble. He cut off the arrow with his scythe as Joan fired two arrows into the worm. The worm hit one out of the air and sent out a poison breath to stop the other.

The worm's breath destroyed the arrow, but it also caught the other summon, coating him in poison. He cried out in pain. Joan was there, waiting, her eyes cold. The little beast peeked at her with wide eyes and opened its arms in shock and pain.

An arrow shot out.

There was no wind or sound as the arrow passed through the beast's eye. Runes appeared over the little man, and he exploded with the sound of breaking ice.

Joan ran into the poison breath, strung a new arrow, and fired. Five others appeared around it, and the arrows stabbed into the worm.

"She's running into its poison! That's suicide!"

"Is the poison not working?"

"Look at her armor!"

Joan's armor and clothing—all peak Journeyman level—showed signs of collapse as they lost durability.

The spells she had laid on the arrows activated, and the worm cried out. The arrows burned through the creature, depleting its last remaining mana reserves.

It cracked like those before, and the powerful, magical runes collapsed with the creature, falling into nothing but motes of mana that dispersed through the area.

Joan passed through them, an arrow on her bow.

The mana cleared enough to show the caster. Her face was pale and strained; there was a cold sweat on her brow, and she looked as if she were about to throw up or pass out.

"I have lost," she said to Joan.

The referee stepped forward and tossed out a powder to diffuse the drifting poison gas before announcing the winner.

"I was wondering if I could apply to the Adventurer's Guild," the woman said as Joan put her arrow away.

"You want to join the guild?"

"I wanted to show how strong I was before I started, but now you should have a good idea of my strength." Silent Spring smiled.

Joan didn't know how to react and laughed.

"Come 'round to the guild hall. You'll have to answer some questions, but it shouldn't be too much of a problem." Joan extended her hand.

Silent Spring reached out and the two of them shook, smiles on their faces.

"Good fight," Joan said.

"You were hit with poison. I have a potion to cure you."

"Ah, no worries. I'll be fine." When she had tempered her foundation, instead of using the easier route that would temper her body without much difficulty, she had tempered her body with poison. It had allowed her to get the Poison Body title, but it had been a pain, literally, to do. It had cost a lot more as she had needed someone around her to make sure she survived the tempering.

"Looks like I'll need to get my gear fixed, though," she complained as she picked at the frayed material.

Creating Bridges

Blaze watched the end of the fight with interest as he wondered what the two women were talking about. Silent Spring and Joan walked off the stage together, as if they had not been fighting seconds ago.

He had a good feeling, seeing that, and smiled.

Someone cleared their throat behind him.

He checked behind to see Klaus, the leader of the Fighter's Association.

Blaze's eyes widened as he realized that he hadn't sensed the man. Klaus's control over his skills and abilities had reached a stage that Blaze hadn't even touched on yet.

Klaus grinned. "We met on the first day."

"Mister Klaus of the Fighter's Association." Blaze stood and greeted him, cupping his fist to the other.

"You have raised some interesting people and good fighters. I wondered if you would like to have a talk?"

"Please," Blaze said.

Klaus coughed lightly, and the people around Blaze moved to leave them alone. Most were merchants; their eyes glowed as they eagerly made way for the Fighter's Association branch head.

Elise excused herself as well and the area was left to Blaze and Klaus. Blaze waited for the other to sit before he did so.

"I believe the Fighter's Association would be interested in talking to some of your members. We are always looking to raise new talent. Is this something that you would be interested in?"

"Of course. I can only offer them so much."

"Good, good! We do not like to poach people or cut them off from where they came from. When someone joins the Fighter's Association, they have options of advancing into the higher realms to join fights they might not have been able to participate in in the past. They would still be your half-member as you helped them get to that stage. We would not stop you from talking to them, and they are free to do as they want as long as they meet the requirements of the association," Klaus said.

"I understand. You can take them to a bigger stage."

"Exactly." Klaus smiled. "We hold recruiting events every year. I think this year, we might hold one in the Battle Arena here. There are a limited number of spots, but I can give you ten. If your people show their ability, they can join the association or apply later."

Ten spots—the best of the internal competitors joining the Fighter's Association. It was also a form of protection, few people wanted to piss off a guild that had connections to the fighter's association. There was a good chance that their old members would return from the higher realms if their old guild was attacked.

More people would join the guild, seeing there was a clear path of progression.

"What if they have learned secret arts or secrets from our guild?"

"We do not need to know everyone's secrets. What they have learned in the past is their information. We might ask them about it, but it is up to them if they reveal it or not. The oath they take when joining means that their actions cannot hurt or harm the Fighter's Association members. As long as nothing circumvents this, they will be fine."

Blaze nodded. Some of his people had secrets they wanted to keep to themselves. To the Fighter's Association, some of these might be interesting, but for most part, they weren't interested as they had more advanced techniques and methods compared to the groups they recruited from.

"I'll let you get back to watching the competition." Klaus stood.

Blaze stood with him, cupping his hands and bowing his head in thanks. This was an opportunity that few were able to acquire.

The merchants came back over to Blaze, as did Elise, and continued to watch the matches that continued throughout the day.

The day wound down, and more people were eliminated. As things heated up, there were more people wounded, but the healers were there making sure that no one died. There was always a chance of death or grievous injury, but the referees activated barriers around people who were about to be killed to stop the fight.

The fights had reached another level, gripping the hearts of those watching, as they cheered and yelled.

When the last match finished, the spectators filed out of the Battle Arena, talking in excited voices to one another.

Blaze looked over at the booth and saw Gu Chen. He had asked Elan to look into the Silver Dragons, and it was just as Yi Yin had said to Emilia; some kind of mistake had led to the order being passed down.

Blaze motioned to Elise with his eyes, telling her he would catch up with her later.

He walked among the people who were leaving and stopped in front of Gu Chen. "Could we have a conversation in private?"

Gu Chen felt good. Six of his people had made it through these first matches. Now, just a hundred people remained in the competition.

It was a good showing, and several people had spoken to him about the Silver Dragons' plans, looking to strike a deal.

With the emergence of the Adventurer's Guild and the possible tension between them, there were people standing on the sidelines, waiting to see how things would go.

When Blaze had asked to talk, Gu Chen agreed. He wanted to set things right. It had never been his goal to make enemies in Vuzgal.

"What do you think they will discuss?"

"Isn't there an issue between the Silver Dragons and the Adventurer's Guild?"

"Will they start fighting with one another? Both of them are fighting groups and are looking to do the same things in Vuzgal."

"Maybe one of them is giving up?"

Those in the booth talked to one another, interested in what the two men would talk about.

Gu Chen followed Blaze into one of the private rooms behind the booth.

"I am sorry. I remarked that your people were strong, and someone took it the wrong way and gave the order," Gu Chen said.

Blaze nodded. "I won't lie. I don't like people being told to kill mine. I know it was a mistake, albeit a heavy one. That being said, I do not want to create unneeded issues between us or for it to lead to anyone getting killed."

"I agree. And I understand how it would not sit with you lightly."

"Hopefully, we can move forward as friends."

"I think so, too, but I won't make my fighters go any easier on your people," Gu Chen said.

Blaze smiled. "Wouldn't have it any other way."

The two men shook hands. Gu Chen relaxed as they moved on to discussions about random items before they left the room.

"It looks like they're rather friendly with one another."

"I thought the two groups were about to fight it out."

"What could make them turn around like that?"

There were more questions than answers.

Blaze left the crowd behind.

Gu Chen made his way down to his fighters and the people who had been standing on the sidelines to make appointments to meet with him later.

Now that the two groups were amicable, it would put most of the observers looking to hire their services at ease. If a fight did break out, then it might be their goods or themselves caught in the middle of it.

Gu Chen met up with his people, and they headed out to their residence. A weight had been lifted off his shoulders, and he told the others what had happened and prepared for the auction that night.

"You're going to the Vuzgal auction?" Yi Yin asked.

"Of course. I wouldn't want to miss it," Gu Chen said.

"Wouldn't it make more sense to go to the Blue Lotus auction at the end of the competition?"

"The Blue Lotus is the Blue Lotus; they always have interesting items for people to bid on. The Vuzgal auction might not be the Blue Lotus, but this is their city and they have a reputation to uphold. Also, they have plenty of crafters. It is one of the few places to get peak Journeyman and Expert-level items. All of us have mostly Low Journeyman gear with a good collection of Mid Journeyman gear. Getting high or peak Journeyman gear would be a great advantage, and there are plenty of crafters here who are just a half-step away from becoming an Expert."

"Sometimes you don't need to buy the best of the best, just gear that is better than what you have," Yi Yin said, seeing to the heart of what Gu Chen was saying.

Gu Chen left with some of the Silver Dragons and headed off into the late afternoon. A large crowd had gathered at the newly upgraded Vuzgal auction house that had increased in size just for this competition.

As the matches came to an end, the group in the private lounge relaxed and talked among one another, sharing notes.

"How are we looking?" Elan asked Niemm and Roska, who had been watching the matches intensely.

After the special team recruits finished training, they would join the special teams. This was a way to learn about them ahead of time.

Nothing escaped their eyes.

"We have eleven special team recruits remaining. Eight of the Adventurer's Guild got through as well," Roska said.

"They're doing well," Niemm said. "After this, it's practical training in the field, right?"

"Yeah, scouting cities around us, locating hidden dungeons to clear and take the dungeon cores. Once we've completed that and verified their skills, we can send out groups to scout the Willful Institute's positions in the different realms. The recruits will put what they've learned about realm insertion, information gathering, and operating without any support from Alva to the test," Roska said.

Elan opened his mouth and then closed it.

"Something on your mind?" Roska asked.

"Well, they've had so much training, shouldn't they be placing higher? Isn't the Adventurer's Guild, without all the support they received, doing better?" Elan asked.

"In a way." Roska smiled. "Though the special teams have strong members, working together makes us stronger. We trained them with rifles and grenades, primarily. In the outside world, we'll have to use melee weapons, bows, and magic staffs. Like now, all of them are wearing weakening formations to weaken their Body Cultivation and Mana Cultivation. They also aren't allowed to use fighting techniques."

"Why?"

"It hamstrings them. They have powerful cultivation, powerful weapons. To be better, you need to struggle. You need to fight with a hundred and ten percent, every time. They have to draw out everything they have in these fights."

"If they used their techniques, could they win the competition?"

"I don't think so. People are holding back." Niemm glanced over to Roska for confirmation.

"I don't think so either. But if they were operating as part of a unit, with their normal weapons, I think they could take on most of the people here. Remember, up to this point, we have nearly always been the weaker group in terms of numbers and levels."

The two men nodded in agreement.

"We have used every damn trick we have to increase our Strength. We created powerful weapons and armor, and we created weapons that use combinations of formations, Alchemy, smithing, spells, and poison—layering those on one another so that even if we are level ten, we could defeat someone at level twenty. We have tempered our bodies and opened our mana gates. These are things that people pass by, looking to increase their power with levels or temper their bodies, only to finish the quest and not fully purge their body, gaining titles and breaking through their own bottlenecks. Every small way that we can gain power, we've held onto. And we've strangled out every damn stat point, title, or effect we can get. We came from nothing, so we take everything: Mana and Body Cultivation, levels, weapons, armor, techniques, and crafting. We never had it before, so we're hungry for it. Still, our levels are lower than most of the people we face. But it doesn't matter because we will do everything we can to grind through and become stronger."

"Well said," Elan said.

If a person had been hungry before or unable to eat food, would they throw away food later or make sure to never waste food they found in front of them? Even if that food was just scraps?

Rapid Expansion

Taran laughed at the breastplate in front of him. The sound echoed around his smithy as he cried at the same time. He held up the breastplate as if it were his newborn child.

I never thought in my life—no, in seven lifetimes...

He sat. His laughter turned tired and filled with fatigue. One only needed to look at his eyes, his worn-out body, and the layer of soot covering him to see how tirelessly he had worked to create this one breastplate.

He opened his notifications, and a glow appeared above his hand. Experience flooded through the smithy and poured into Taran's body, like life-giving water.

He closed his eyes. A feeling of deep satisfaction filled his bones. He opened his eyes and felt the weight as his Expert smithing reward was delivered.

"A compendium of Expert-level blueprints. Rugrat would be pissed if he knew I had beaten him to Expert smith. Well, actually, he might have reached it already."

Taran held the breastplate in one hand and his blueprint book in the other. He felt sad. He wanted to run out and bug his friends, but most of them were in other places.

With a wave of his hand, he put away the book and breastplate. "I'll go to Vuzgal and see Tan Xue. It'll be a research trip—totally not going to brag about reaching Expert level."

He chuckled to himself and stood. A light appeared in his eyes. What was achieving one's goals if you couldn't share it with your friends?

Jia Feng was in her office as her assistant came in.

"So, what are the numbers?" Jia Feng sat back.

"Taran escaped to Vuzgal to see Tan Xue; he reached Expert smith. There are four scribes who have reached Expert. Zhou Heng, the tailor department head. Shi Wanshu was able to raise two more woodworking Experts. There are three people other than you who are close to making a breakthrough to Expert in cooking."

"Seems like there are new Experts emerging from all over the place," Jia Feng said.

"Everyone was close to the brink. With the influx of information and competing with one another to see how fast they could get through the crafting trial, they were able to take the final step. The librarians are recording their different theories and compiling them with the older works. As time goes on, with the wealth of information we gather, we won't be searching in the dark; we can expand on what was previously learned and advance it," Jia Feng's assistant, Velia, said eagerly.

"That will be one hell of a thing." Jia Feng agreed the corners of her eyes wrinkled as she held her hands, falling into silence for a moment.

"With different soldiers getting their bodies tempered, the healers have seen a rise in levels as they've practiced their skills. More of them are going into the realms to heal people to gain a greater understanding of healing. The military complex takes up a large portion of our budget." Velia broke the silence with her rapid speech and groan.

"We need a strong military to support us," Jia Feng said.

"We still live in the Ten Realms, while Alva has supplied so much. Others would be more than willing to murder to steal it," Velia said.

"Life is cheap in the Ten Realms. Thankfully, we have the Alva military."

"What do you mean you no longer need our services?" Elder Hui from the Willful Institute asked.

"Someone else has been working with us for a few weeks now. We have no more jobs for you. I am sorry," the trader said.

"A few weeks?"

"We had jobs to be done, and you were not interested in them before. Now that you are losing other jobs, you decide to come to us." The trader snorted.

"Are you sure you want to cross us?" Hui asked in a low voice.

"Are you sure you can threaten anyone anymore? After all, you are looking for 'low level' contracts," the trader shot back.

"You will come to regret this," Elder Hui said in a huff.

He flicked his sleeves and stood, leaving the room. "Find out who is taking the contract and report to me immediately!" he hissed to one of his subordinates as soon as the trader was out of earshot.

The trader was right. Normally, he would never make a personal visit. Recently, their missions had been pulled by the people making them. Traders had found new protection and cheaper goods while charging the Willful Institute more for products. Something was going on.

Hui got onto his tamed beast, and they rode toward the Willful Institute's headquarters.

Jasper looked over the latest reports. A knock on his office door interrupted him. He put the report away in his storage ring. "Come in."

The door opened, and a woman with a hood pulled down against the wind walked in.

Jasper's eyes moved to her buckle that looked like a tower spewing mana into the air.

Alvan.

The door closed behind her, and a formation activated, closing off any sensing magic from entering the room.

The woman pulled back her hood and bowed deeply. "Vice Guildmaster Jasper," she said to the floor.

"Seems that I meet with more of Elan's agents than anyone else these days." Jasper laughed. "Take a seat, please. What do you have for me?"

She took out a book and passed it to Jasper.

Jasper opened it. It was an information book. Light shot between his brows as he closed his eyes. The book dissolved, and he opened his eyes.

"Very good. The Willful Institute is starting to feel the pinch on their purse strings now that we've taken a third of their contracts and a quarter of their trade routes."

"Using our links to the Alvan traders and their associates, we are cutting into their protection and supply jobs. It has created several new trading routes. Recruitment within the guild has increased too."

"How is the Willful Institute reacting?" Jasper asked.

"There are many factions within the Institute. None of them want to look weak, so they have been pushing the issues away. They'll attack if they have the opportunity but only in the dark, unless it reaches a stage where they need to make an open display of their power," the intelligence agent said.

"Good. The more they fight one another, the less they'll think about us." Jasper sent a sound transmission. There was a knock at his door.

"Come in!"

The door opened to reveal a guild messenger who quickly entered and closed the door, nodding to Elan's information operative and looking to Jasper.

"Send a message to Glosil. Tell him that we will be moving into the second phase of the plan soon." The messenger nodded and repeated Jasper's instructions back to him.

"Good," Jasper smiled at both people. "A great and powerful beast can be defeated with a thousand small cuts."

23

Top 100

Vuzgal was abuzz. With the prizes being announced, people who had been interested before came over in droves. Although they couldn't compete, they found out that the rumors of the items for sale in Vuzgal were not exaggerations. There were High level goods that would be hard to find anywhere else in the Sixth Realm, and they were available in large quantities.

The remaining one hundred competitors were broken down into groups of ten. From each group, there would be a victor, who would go on to fight the other finalists for the position of the strongest.

Among these one hundred, all of them had received offers from different powers looking to hire them.

"I heard that Vuzgal hasn't extended any invitations to the competitors in the matches," Klaus said absently as he sat next to Hiao Xen.

Hiao Xen looked over to the Fighter's Association branch head. "Are you asking something?"

"Would Vuzgal mind if we asked the competitors to join our ranks?"

Klaus had a relaxed air, but his eyes were locked on Hiao Xen.

Hiao Xen smiled. "If they are interested in joining Vuzgal, one needs to apply. We won't search them out. We want soldiers. We don't need people who are just strong in fighting one-on-one.

"Thank you, Hiao Xen." Klaus nodded. "Coming to Vuzgal has been a great boon to the Fighter's Association. I managed to get some sets of Journeyman armor from your crafters. Truly, your academy is producing great things!"

"Ah, I am just the manager. I am as impressed with the crafters as you are."

Klaus smiled and looked around. The people around them talking to one another seemed to have realized that they hadn't asked for permission to talk to the competitors. Hearing that the Fighter's Association was showing interest, some of them would try to lock down the people who had impressed them.

Klaus sent a sound transmission to his people. Not all the competitors had caught his eyes, but more members would increase their Strength.

The day's fight started. People clashed on the different stages. The contestants were forced to reveal their trump cards as they struggled to reach higher.

There were fifty matches on the first day, all based on a point system: two points for a win, one point for a tie.

Klaus watched the people from the Silver Dragons adventure group and the Adventurer's Guild. The Silver Dragons was a strong group. They weren't peak Experts but were putting on a good show, though most of them wouldn't make it into the top ten. The Adventurer's Guild, unless they had some deep secrets, he didn't see making it through to the top twenty. The competition would be fierce! A smile spread across Klaus's face.

"Something interesting, Guildmaster?"

"Ah, just fires me up seeing the younger generation proving themselves. I thought it would be only crafting and trading around here, but I'm starting to like this place!"

Roska walked up to the one-way windows that overlooked the arenas. The special teams and the team hopefuls were all in the operations room watching the matches. The second day had started. There were another fifty matches, but the bottom twenty fighters would be eliminated.

Derrick stepped forward as one of the participants in the first matches of the day. He was up against one of the hidden talents—Julia Oui from the Iron Spear sect.

He was using two blades, focusing on flexibility and speed, while Julia had a spear to keep him at range and use her strength against him.

The two of them shook hands and stepped back. They drew their weapons, and the referee started the match.

He used a foot technique from the start, looking to close with her before she had time to interpose that spear between them. Her spear shot out in a blur; he dodged it but was forced to retreat. His swords flashed, meeting the spear again and again. He kept trying to press forward, but her spear closed off his path of advance and kept him pinned in place.

The fight continued with no clear winner.

The stage was covered in scars from their imbued attacks striking the ground instead of each other.

Derrick straightened up, and his serious expression turned into a smile. As he stepped forward, her spear shot out again. He used a technique with his blades, increasing the Strength of his blows and, using his body to unleash his power, forced the spear to the side.

Julia increased her speed and continued to attack, but Derrick's defense turned from soft to hard and she was unable to land an attack. Derrick's blades forced her spear away. She moved with the spear so as to not leave herself open to counterattack, resetting and facing him once again.

As Derrick advanced, she stepped backward.

She activated a technique with a yell, increasing the speed of their spear and reinforcing it with greater Strength once again.

The swords and spear clashed with one another.

"That spear must be a High Journeyman-level weapon. If Derrick didn't have Mid Journeyman blades, they would have broken under those attacks," Niemm said.

"Using weapons as clubs is a waste," Domonos muttered.

Derrick cast an illusion spell. Julia recoiled, shaking her head to try to clear it. Derrick dashed forward, his swords blurring. His opponent pushed back, trying to make enough distance to use her spear effectively.

"She's good."

Derrick's attack struck her mask, leaving a bloody line.

She turned and thrust out with her spear.

Derrick was hit in the side, sending him to the ground. He used his momentum and his legs to spin around and get back on his feet.

Julia adjusted her stance and attacked as he rose.

Derrick turned. The spear ran along his back as he bent, and he stabbed his two swords outward.

Wind spread across the stage.

Her spear was by Derrick's leg, while his blades shone right next to her throat and stomach.

"Huh. Well, that's a coincidence." Domonos stared harder at the woman, as if seeing her for the first time.

"You know her?" Elan asked.

"She fought against Mercy—came from the Iron Spear sect. She was down in the First Realm, part of the group that went to the Beast Mountain Range trial. Didn't think that the next time I saw her I would be an officer."

"I forgot about her. She's wearing distinct armor and still using similar techniques. Hers was the last fight I saw before Mercy..." Domonos's expression darkened as he ground his teeth, his hands balling into fists.

The referee called the match in Derrick's favor.

"Well, she's gotten stronger. All but the Adventurer's Guild branch heads will probably be eliminated this round." Roska ignored his reaction. Everyone had their own demons.

On the third day, all the special team members had been eliminated and there were just five of the Adventurer's Guild left. Emilia had been knocked out of the fight with Yi Yin.

Roska gathered all the competition losers in the secret training rooms under Vuzgal's military compound.

The trainees were all hanging their heads low.

"So, now you know how it feels to lose. All of you have made it through to the next round of training. It doesn't matter how badly you fail; it matters how you react to that failure and what you do with it. You fought in there with your power restrained. You kept your identities and your strength hidden in a stressful situation."

They perked up and she continued, "You will be allocated into teams to take on missions across the Ten Realms. We need to understand the tactical situation around Vuzgal. We will be scouting the surrounding areas and infiltrating the different cities around us. We have operatives trained by Elan who will show us how to blend in and gather information. Other groups will strike out against the Willful Institute—attacking their convoys and taking out their links to one another. You will weaken the enemy through guerilla tactics. Upon completion of your missions, it will be up to the special team leaders to pick out those among you who they wish to be part of their team. During the missions, you will not be treated as recruits but as special team members. Do not fail our assessment of you. We do not need children in our ranks."

They all sat up, coming from the pits of despair to the focused soldiers they were.

Roska might not be able to watch the rest of the competition, but she could get back into the field and work. It had been too long since she had last went on a mission. Things were changing quickly with the Willful Institute. Glosil would have plenty for them to do. Roska's mouth lifted in a smile.

Ripples

Qin Silaz tucked an errant strand of hair behind her ear as she watched over the training grounds. As the Vuzgal Defense Force had increased in number, so had their need for training rooms.

There were five different camps now, and she had worked on the designs for the formations that were used.

"I heard you were lurking around here," Domonos said, startling her.

"Don't sneak up on me like that!" She thumped his arm as she fought to control her racing heart.

Domonos laughed and leaned against the banister, glancing at his soldiers before looking back to her. "So, what are you lurking around here for?"

"An idea." Qin organized her thoughts as her heart calmed down. "Your soldiers—they fight in formations. Well, Julilah and I have been working on sympathetic formations that work together to create a greater effect. It made me think of the armor our soldiers wear. It is good for fighters. And that is the thing...I've been thinking about it wrong."

"How so?"

"You told me that a group of soldiers working together can take down an enemy stronger than them because of their coordination. Fighters are capable by themselves and in small groups, but they aren't coordinated, so there is a limit to their strength. So, what if the soldiers' armor enhanced them as a group instead of as individuals?"

Domonos studied his sister.

"What kind of formations are we talking about?"

"They would apply buffs, small by themselves, but with more, they will have a stacking effect: The more soldiers linked together, working together, the more powerful they will be. Each platoon has buffs specific to them but also general stacks that work for everyone, increasing all of their stats," Qin said.

Domonos's brows pinched together, and he held his chin.

She wondered if she had said something wrong.

"I'll report this to Commander Glosil," he said in a serious tone.

"I don't think it's—"

Domonos cut her off with a wave of his hand. "If we can pull out a tenth of what you're suggesting, it will raise the power of our army to a whole new level. The more people working together, the greater the impact on the battlefield. The armor we have now is high quality, but using them to work together, amplifying the effects of one another, it will make up for our weaknesses. Even if we have lower-leveled people, their power will allow them to compete with stronger opponents.

"Our military leaders have been looking at how to fight stronger people and beasts for a long time now. There are those in the higher realms who can tear apart hills and destroy seas with a wave of their hand. We can't contend with that—yet. Now, if we have a party with buffed armor, even at the Journeyman standard, they'll be stronger than a group with Expert-level armor."

Qin didn't know what to say. She had only been thinking of new applications of formations. She had an idea of the scale, but hearing

Domonos running with it and thinking of uses, she realized the impact it would have.

"If I could add a sympathetic-attached formation to our cities? Or add mobile formations that link to the armor," she said quietly to herself.

"Can you make it?"

"You make it sound so easy. A new formation takes a ton of research. We need to look through other formations. Try to find something that works already, understand how it works, pull it apart, and then blend them together. If we don't have anything to go off, we need to make a whole new formation. The first version would be really rough, but it should work. It cuts down development time from years to months. You only see the results of that work. If I can pull in some people from the schools, I can speed things up a little."

"So... it's possible?"

"Everything is possible. The factor is time and luck."

She felt a fire burning within, driving her to do more, to create more. She wanted to throw herself into her work right away, to get the army outfitted so they could show the others. This was Alva.

Alva. Thinking of the word, of the dungeon and everything linked to it, her heart stirred in a way she had never thought it would when she had thought about the city of Chonglu that she had grown up in.

Chonglu had been the place she existed in. Alva was her home; it was where she had found *purpose,* where she had made friends. Some of those friends, even her own brothers, served in the military. Thinking of them, thinking of Alva as a whole, she felt the thrill of doing something more than herself. They weren't just a random group of people anymore; they were all Alvans.

Together, they were creating a community—no, they were creating a nation.

Domonos received a sound transmission. As he spoke, his expression turned from brother to colonel in a second, a man who commanded close to seven thousand men and women of the Alvan army.

"Something happen?" Qin asked as he sent out more messages.

"It's begun."

"What has?" Qin asked.

Domonos looked up. There was a solemn expression on his face. She took a half-step backward at seeing the bloodthirsty and vicious look in his eyes.

"The Alva military is free to act upon the Willful Institute, not just the special teams. Close protection details and even regular forces could be called on. All leave is canceled and training accelerated."

Qin's body shook. She had seen fights and heard of groups against one another, but she had never seen or been part of a war.

Just how far would it go? They both covered multiple realms.

She felt her resolve firm. Their path had been smooth to this point, but it was changing.

Qin might not be a fighter, but she could still help them from the rear.

Unexpected Breakthrough

I t was the third day that Erik had been inside Kuldir.

The healing stall was popular day and night. Rugrat had been helping out the special team members, allowing them to get two stalls.

Erik was reminded of Chonglu, where people had poured in once they found out there were healers in the area.

Then, as now, they triaged people and worked through them. There were several difficult cases, people who had been lamed or had lost limbs.

The special teams, like Erik, had a lot of knowledge on healing but had been unable to put it to good use as they were always stuck with other tasks. The Alva Healing House was filled with people from the school; the hospitals in Alva were never at capacity as people could be healed quickly. Vuzgal had so many students that there were few openings there.

So, now, they were experiencing an explosive growth in their healing skills. Skills were related not just to how many times a person carried it out but to how skilled they were in the craft. Most of them had jumped up to the Journeyman level rapidly.

Erik was working on a young girl who had gone out as a fighter, only to be hit by a shadow beast. She was suffering from a powerful poison and immobility.

"Okay, so we used poison to neutralize the poison in her veins; that will make sure her heart doesn't stop beating. Now, we just need to clean up the wound and heal her passively. Her body will temper with time and become immune to the poisons. Her wounds will heal normally," Erik said to Storbon, who was assisting him.

He used to think of health as one system and then as varied groups or parts of the same system. But, really, they were overlapping. Isolating or empowering one system would affect those and cause them to grow or wither. People were resilient, and magic allowed them to fly in the face of modern medicine. Using a combination of knowledge of the different systems, the healing spells could repair without being invasive or leaving behind any damage. Medicine, as he had learned it, and healing magic weren't two different systems; they were components of the same system. Physical healing, magical healing, and Alchemy healing—all were tools for the same job.

Erik's mind matched it all together.

Storbon nodded as Erik used his Simple Organic Scan to see everything happening in her body. He raised his hand and items fell from his storage ring, captured by the mana in his domain. The tools and spells darted around. It looked like a futuristic healing bay. Minimal healing spells were used in combination, with Erik using a Clean spell to clear the wounds and a Stamina potion. He used his Earth mana control to push wounds together and then used flames to cauterize the wounds so they wouldn't leave a scar behind.

These actions happened not one after another, but simultaneously and within seconds, after which all the items returned to Erik's storage ring.

The woman breathed easier. He had stabilized her completely; he had used his tools, working with her body instead of against it.

"She has spent a lot of Stamina with the poison, but the cauterized wounds will start to repair naturally. She has some breaks, but they will heal shortly. I focused on healing her, so her regeneration abilities will take over."

The young girl gasped as her body accelerated the healing process.

"She has Body Like Stone, so she will recover in a few hours with enough food. I am just facilitating the change in her body from sick to cured."

He checked her with his domain and sent surges of healing to her body.

"Even if she doesn't come to me, she'll be healed now. Using different tools, I was able to stabilize her body. A poison can be a vaccine, a spell, or a scalpel, and harm can be a bandage. My mind was too closed in." Erik clicked his tongue, mumbling to himself.

It was time to test his true healer abilities.

Erik used his Simple Organic Scan on the next patient, a man who had reached the Sixth Realm. His powerful body had been hit in the side, which had shattered his arm and broken his ribs. While he was in a weakened state, he was hit with an infection that ravaged his body. There was a raging war; his bones had fused together, making them painful and leaving him crippled. His body's natural immune system was dealing with the infection and the flu that had dug deep into his body, weakening and wearing him down.

He had a strong body, and although the situation was bad, it wasn't critical.

"Looks like you had a nasty hit," Erik said.

"I was a guard for one of the academy students. We were ambushed by Krohon. They conceal themselves by looking like plants and hiding within them. They have long limbs that hit like a damn war hammer. A broken guard isn't much use. They got me back to this outpost, and here I remained." The man's hollow eyes showed a flash of frustration before switching to apathy. He coughed. It shook his body, and he gritted his teeth against the pain when the coughing got worse.

Erik moved him onto his side and into the recovery position.

And that is the liquid in his lungs acting up.

Erik circulated a part of his power. He focused his healing spells on the man's overtaxed lymph nodes and bone marrow.

White blood cells were quickly produced, pushing into the man's body. Erik searched for signs of Stamina fatigue.

He used healing spells on the man's lungs. The coughing died down, and Erik dialed back his magic. The older man was tough, but with so much stress on his body, his Stamina recovery was compromised since it was being used to support all the different ailments.

Erik slowed his heals to a standstill as he got as close to Stamina deprivation as he wanted to.

The man was fighting to keep his eyes open, and the wheeze from his breathing, although not gone, had decreased. Erik ran another Simple Organic Scan.

He hadn't done anything about the broken bones yet. First, he had to deal with the infection, which would aid the Stamina recovery. Then, he could deal with the broken bones, torn ligaments, and tendons, and help him to recover the lost muscle mass.

Erik wrote up his treatment plan on a clipboard and attached it to the string above the man's bed.

Erik checked his skills.

Skill: Healer

Level: 73 (Journeyman)

You have become familiar with the body and the arts of repairing it. Healing spells now cost 5% less Mana and Stamina.

There was still no change. *We'll see what happens once he is healed.*

Each day Erik worked, he used tools and potions that he had designed or acquired, improving his knowledge and techniques.

For most, he was able to just use his healing spells. It took longer because he needed to wait for the patient's body to naturally recover their Stamina. He would heal some people, leave them to rest, move to other patients, and keep on rotating, clearing patients and bringing in new ones.

Four days passed, and the older guard was looking a lot better. His immune system was in fighting form, and the infections were in remission.

"All right, we should deal with your internal problems now, and then we can focus on your ribs and that arm," Erik said.

The older man, who had not had much hope before he arrived, stood as Erik walked in. "Thank you, Healer Erik." The man winced as he bowed.

"There is no need to do that, Gerek. You'll hurt yourself!" Erik complained.

But the man kept his bow, dragging out his bad arm with his good. "I have nothing to my name. There is little that I can offer you in compensation, but you have helped me without question. Your contract does not aid you or your people in any way. I can only do this for you."

"While we want to help people, we are doing this to increase our healing skills."

"I have seen healers in the academies above. They take one or two patients with certain ailments they know how to heal and use them to fool the Ten Realms system into increasing their overall skill. You heal people with not just one ailment. Your people have healed tens of people and are treating tens more. Yes, you are increasing your skills, but what do we care if you give us back our lives? I thought you were a scam at first. Who offers healing without getting paid? I would have felt safer if you had offered an agreement that turned me into your slave instead of the flimsy contract you proposed."

"We are helping each other. Don't worry about it too much." Erik felt touched, and he helped the old guard up. "Come on, time to get rid of that nasty infection and cold."

Gerek nodded and let Erik help him back to the cot.

Erik checked the man's body. The infection and flu were on the losing side. With repeated treatments, Gerek's body was recovering quickly.

Erik started using his healing spells and monitored. He got rid of the signs of infection first.

A flood of Experience entered Erik's body, and his notifications pinged. *Quiet down, will you?* He paid them no attention as he worked to defeat the signs of the flu. More Experience flooded him as Gerek recovered.

Erik examined Gerek's ribs again. Using Wraith's Touch, he numbed the area. "All right Gerek, how are you feeling?"

"A bit tired, but better than our last sessions," he said, lying on his side.

"Just going to work on some things on your side. Hold your arm, will you?" Erik moved Gerek's arm and had him hold it out of the way.

Erik summoned a mana blade. He melded the information of his organic scan with his own sight, seeing through Gerek.

He flicked Gerek's side, but the man didn't react.

The numbing salve was working. The mana blade cut through the skin and muscle and into the bone that had fused in the wrong way. He pulled out a clamp and pushed it through the incision, grabbing onto the rib and lining it up in the right place.

It was always easier to deal with patients who couldn't feel shit. Erik grimaced and bit the inside of his cheek as he felt the bones grate one another.

He used a Heal Bone spell next, just enough to fuse the bones together, then pulled the clamp out and used different healing spells to seal the incision. He shivered. *Like nails on a chalkboard.*

With a Clean spell, the blood was removed and the indent in the skin disappeared, showing a healthy side with no deformations.

Erik could barely keep his eyes open; the healing spells had taken a lot of Stamina from him. This Ten Realms style of healing was much slower—and dangerous.

"All right, Gerek, you get some sleep. We'll work on your side and arm next," Erik said.

Gerek grunted and closed his eyes.

Erik added some notes on his clipboard and left it above Gerek.

He remembered the rush of Experience, and after making sure there was no one around, he checked the blinking notification.

Skill: Healer

Level: 81 (Expert)

You are an Expert on the human body and the arts of repairing it. Healing spells now cost 10% less Mana and Stamina. Patient's Stamina is used an additional 15% less.

Upon advancing into the Expert level of Healer, you have been rewarded with one randomly selected item related to this skill.

You have received the tool: **Healer's Hands**

+10,000,000 EXP

79,786,922/86,100,000 EXP till you reach Level 60

A light flashed, and a pair of white gloves with golden runes on the back of the hand that traced over his fingers appeared in front of Erik. He reached out and grabbed them.

Erik checked their stats.

Healer's Hands

Weight:	0.3 kg
Health:	100/100
Charge:	100/100

Innate Effect:

Increase mana spell's effect by 5%

Enchantment:

Assisted Recovery—patient's Stamina recovery increases by 5%

Requirements:

Mana 40

Mana Regeneration 50

Damn!

He thought of IVs and other gear that assisted healers, but he had never thought of gear to directly aid in healing. This was a highly specific kind of mage's equipment, like how there were staffs to increase a mage's natural attacks. Fire mages got Fire staffs to increase their overall effects. It was a kind of a dumb oversight really.

Erik put the gloves on, and they adhered to his hand. He wiggled his fingers; they didn't limit his movement or sensitivity. They would help with the Stamina deprivation by a large margin, including the title and with Ten Realms's "natural" healing.

A smile broke out, which turned into a laugh and a chuckle. He had made it to Expert-level healer. *Mother fuckers!*

Damn, that feels good.

Erik kept staring at the notifications, using them to cover the aftereffects of becoming an Expert. There was a flood of information, and he sank deeper into thought. Connections he had not realized before seemed to snap into place, using the theory he had proved. His mind connected other items together. He was shaking, eager to test out his new ideas. He closed his eyes, taking the time to think about everything. He took out a pad of paper and wrote quick notes, scared that he might lose this inspiration.

Once he was done, he reviewed his notes and put them away.

"Well, that notification was a little sudden." Erik laughed. He had been hoping to get to Expert level in Alchemy but had made it with Healing first. *Makes sense.* Alchemy was something he had picked up in the Realms, but he had been learning and trying to put people back together for most of his adult life.

"Well, this is interesting." The increase would make it easier for him to temper his body.

"What you messing around in here with?" Rugrat came into the tent they had erected behind the stalls to keep their patients' modesty.

"Just made it to Expert. You owe me a six pack of Dougall's beers!" Erik said.

"Come on, I'm just building up my stock of them. I thought you were a long way off with Alchemy?"

"I was, but not with Healing," Erik said. "I figured something out. I was forcing myself to work in stages. I wasn't combining what I knew with how I can do things now. I think I know what to do with Alchemy." Erik held his chin, sinking into thought. "I didn't start Alchemy just for Alchemy's sake. I started it because I wanted to use it as an aid for healing. It is a component of healing, another tool. Everything is created from processes and stages. Medicine teaches that there are many systems: There are stages for creating magic and stages for creating concoctions. What if I were rushing those stages? There are not three stages, but innumerable stages. Like with healing, everything changes from one minute to the next. If your patient is stable now, they might not be in a minute."

Erik sat down and pulled out his cauldron.

Rugrat waved his hand.

"Fuck off." Erik waved him off without feeling in his words.

Rugrat snorted and headed out of the room with a smile.

Erik took out a preparation table, blade, and ingredients, quickly working to prepare them.

He tossed out other ingredients. Around him, flames appeared and his mana blade, too; within his domain, everything was under his control. He prepared several items at once. Flames appeared in his hands. They danced around, gaining form and detail, looking like beasts as they leapt free of his hands to gather ingredients and before diving into the cauldron.

Alchemy involved the melding of items to create an effect—that was the theory. But in the Ten Realms, things become stronger by consuming one another. If he were to force power into something or let it draw it into itself—which would be easier? Concoctions might not be alive, but through the tribulations of fire and the combination of the right items, they could go from simple elements into something that would change the Ten Realms.

They were parts of the Ten Realms affecting the Ten Realms.

As Erik focused, the cauldron reached the required temperature. Erik waved his hand. The cauldron opened, and flames rose around him. They snatched the different additives, their flames changing color as they rushed into the cauldron.

Erik supplied them with mana. He had a complete grasp over what was happening. The different flame beasts with components charged one another. The cauldron turned into a battlefield, the different flames tearing one another apart. When they defeated the other, the ingredient within was consumed by the winning beast.

The mixture at their core changed. The diverse materials lost a minimal amount of their efficacy as the fight continued.

The beasts fought, becoming stronger and more powerful.

Erik watched over them as their numbers reduced.

He opened the cauldron again, and more flame beasts appeared around the stronger substances. They were larger, meeting the size and power of those within the cauldron.

As they refined into their body, the flame beasts grew in size and detail. Snakes, birds, and wolves attacked one another and evolved, becoming dragons, phoenixes, and tigers.

More flame creatures charged into the cauldron. Each was a creation from Erik; each contained his knowledge of poisons. The essence entered their bodies, tempering them, increasing their Strength. The contents were being consumed—no, they were being transformed into the flame creatures. They used Erik's knowledge of ingredients to draw out every last bit of strength.

Erik felt the drain on his mana. He extended his domain and utilized the mana-gathering formation, focusing and drawing more through his body and directing it into his flames and cauldron. He tossed several mana stones into the cauldron, using their power to enhance the Fire beasts waging a war within.

The fight continued. Erik's face was pale and drawn out. There were two flames left, a dragon and a tiger, that looked as if they could leap free of the cauldron at any time as they roared and attacked each other.

The tiger latched onto the dragon's neck and used its claws to attack. Its body was made of shimmering colors; all of the previous flame beasts had been refined by it into its body. The dragon—with flames of green, blue, and purple—roared, and the cauldron shook as its body became more defined and stable.

It slapped the tiger away with a swat.

The tiger roared in pain; it was the lord of the land, but the dragon was the king of the sky.

They clashed again, but the dragon had the upper hand.

The tiger lost its form. The flames that made up its body swarmed up the dragon. The dragon roared as its flames became stronger. It curled up, and its body shrinking to remove impurities and increase the potency. Curled in the clutches of the dragon, a pill formed.

Erik infused Earth and Fire mana into the cauldron, compressing and heating the mana to bend to his will. The dragon continued to become smaller. Its essence and the colored flames were drawn into the spherical item in the middle of its body.

It became smaller and smaller, revealing a pill. The flames danced around, becoming part of it. Runes appeared on the pill, and a dragon appeared to run around the outside. Its eyes were closed, but when staring at it, one would think that they could open at any minute, unleashing the power of the dragon contained within.

The flames under the cauldron faded, and Erik breathed out. He was tired from the mental stress that came with creating so many different beasts from his flames.

A flood of golden power erupted from the Ten Realms. It rushed into Erik's body. He surged with power, and, once again, his mind agitated with what he had learned.

With healing, he had learned the body as a system and the body as a whole. With Alchemy, he had learned the Fire Beast Consummation technique.

These two techniques had the same basic theory: Small, exact changes happening at the right time will have a multiplicative effect upon one another.

"Why use a sword when I could use a kitchen knife? A Roman soldier is just a man with a shield. Alone, they are weak; together, they are strong. Instead of fighting against the Ten Realms, the ingredients, my tools—I have to accept them. I should look for synergies within them instead of differences." Erik's voice became faint as a secondary wave of fatigue fell over him. The Blood Infusion pill only focused on helping a person with blood loss recover and heal their circulatory system, acting as an artificial circulatory system until they could be properly healed.

The lights dimmed. Erik collapsed after he finished his last note. He smiled as he sat there, slumped over his work.

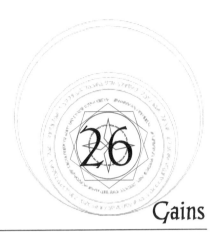

26

Gains

Erik opened his eyes to find that he was inside the room he and Rugrat shared at the inn.

"Collapsed after working on your pill? Thankfully, you were inside the mana-gathering formation or we might have more people bugging us about what happened. The guards asked, but we covered it up and agreed to heal some of their minor or hidden injuries to keep them on their way," Rugrat said.

"Sorry, I didn't mean for that to happen." Erik scratched his head awkwardly.

"Damn overachiever."

Erik laughed dryly, remembering the stream of notifications he had ignored.

Rugrat pulled out a smithing book and sat back on his bed, muttering about people achieving back-to-back breakthroughs and showing off.

Erik checked through his notifications.

Skill: Alchemy
Level: 75 (Expert)
Able to identify 1 effect of the ingredient.
Ingredients are 5% more potent.
When creating concoctions, mana regeneration increases by 20%

Upon advancing into the Expert level of Alchemy, you will be rewarded with one randomly selected item related to this skill.

You have received the book: Compendium of Tree Ingredients upon High Fire Attribute Mountains.
+10,000,000 EXP

"Well, that's one book heading right for the library. Experience is always good."

You have reached Level 60
When you sleep next, you will be able to increase your attributes by 10 points.

3,719,322/108,500,000 EXP till you reach Level 61

"Just made it to leve—!"

"Ah shit!" Rugrat yelled to the heavens.

"What is it?"

"You passed my level! And you're an Expert in two crafts! How can I keep going!"

Erik rolled his eyes at Rugrat's melodramatics. "Watch the area for me. I'm going to allocate my stat points."

"What was the pill you made?" Rugrat asked.

"Oh, this?" Erik pulled out the pill. Even sealed in a bottle, the area seemed to warm up. Erik grinned and threw it to Rugrat.

Rugrat caught it and looked from it to Erik.

"It is an Inscribed pill to help one recover lost blood. I was stressing over the small stuff. Trying to make a master pill that does it all, though blood loss is one of the major reasons that people die on a battlefield. This deals with just the bleeding. Not too fancy, but it can save so many people with that one effect."

"You really know how to treat a guy...always with pills and potions." Rugrat rolled his eyes.

"Were you able to get any more information on the orcs?"

"Still want to raid them?"

"You know it."

"Yeah, I got some. It looks like there are several camps and some roving bands. The basic orcs are between level fifty-three in the outer reaches to sixty in the inner reaches. All of them have the Strength of the same level human with Body Like Iron cultivation, and they have a berserker skill that stacks."

"Stacks?"

"The more orcs in an area, the more powerful the buff. If there are five of them, they get a five percent bonus to their attacks, and they don't feel pain. Ten of them, they get a ten percent bonus—all the way up to forty percent. Even if there are one hundred of them, they don't exceed a forty-percent Strength bonus. Well, unless they have some of their shamans buffing them."

"All right, go on," Erik said.

"Each of the bands have captains, which are stronger, powerful versions. Sometimes shamans. They're intelligent and a big pain in the ass. The camps can have up to five of these captains, at least three shamans, and a boss-level monster, a camp leader. They have different skills—some are shamans, some are fighters.

"They're going to be one hell of a fight, but if we can clear out a camp, they act as mini-dungeons. We get a bunch of bonuses—Experience and loot-wise—for clearing out the place. If we can clear out a string of them, we can even earn a title. And I heard that it is possible to learn the berserk skill."

"Just how old are you?"

"Who needs to count after thirty?" Rugrat rolled his shoulders and clicked his fingers into pistols making silent pew-pew noises.

Erik closed his eyes, letting out a breath as he gathered himself.

"We'll level up with the others and get used to fighting the orcs before we hit a camp. Reach Body Like Iron first. It'll take you a few days to digest that pill. I'll make sure nothing goes wrong."

"Camp raiding, this should be good!" Rugrat grinned.

"About time we did something other than hiding in cities and towns. I'm going to put in my stat points now. See you in the morning!"

It had been some time since Erik had leveled up. His level was higher than the creatures and people he dealt with day to day, and his skills were high enough that it took weeks or months to increase.

You have 10 attribute points to use.

Erik scanned his character sheet.

His Strength was really high at nine hundred and fifty, though his Agility was only six hundred and fifty-four. With the modifiers, he had put more stat points into Agility. He considered where he could use the extra Strength at one hundred percent, or if he needed greater control? Erik played with the idea for some time.

He was about to go into a fight, so he put it into Strength, certain that it wouldn't be too much for him to handle. Ten points to Gryf—Strength then!

Name: Erik West		
Level: 60	Race: Human	
Titles:		
From the Grave II		
Blessed by Mana		
Dungeon Master III		
Reverse Alchemist		
Poison Body		
Fire Body		
City Lord		
Earth Soul		
Mana Reborn		
Strength: (Base 54) +51	1050	
Agility: (Base 47) +72	654	
Stamina: (Base 57) +25	1230	
Mana: (Base 27) +79	1166	
Mana Regeneration: (Base 30) +61	73.80/s	
Stamina Regeneration: (Base 72) +59	27.20/s	

Thousand stat club! Who needs the thousand-pound club? Sleep took Erik as the changes spread through his body.

Rugrat's Tempering

Yuli, Erik, and Storbon were with Rugrat.

"Not the largest room for hosting," Rugrat muttered. His and Erik's cramped room was made smaller by their guests.

"Formations are set. I'll be outside," Storbon said.

It was the middle of the night, and there weren't many people around. The remainder of the special team was dotted around the inn, making sure no one approached.

"Let's start then," Erik said.

Rugrat opened the pill bottle with Delilah's Expert-level Heartflame Transformation pill. Heat spread through the glass and into his hand, making him feel a deep itch in his bones.

Rugrat glanced at Yuli and Erik. If anything did go wrong, they would deal with it.

He breathed out and tossed the pill back and swallowed. "Tastes like cinnamon hearts." He smirked.

Then his expression twisted. Burning heat spread through his body.

He yelled as he drew mana from the area. The candles around them tilted in his direction, the Fire mana reacting to him.

He let out a groan and fell back against the floor. Threads of heat traced through his body, reaching his veins and expanding. It coursed through his muscles while it burned, bringing an immense amount of power with it. He felt his muscles starting to transform, expelling impurities as his body and his mana were refined.

Waves of heat washed through his body. The room's heat increased several degrees, and Rugrat broke out in a sweat. His muscles strained, and his veins popped out.

He opened his eyes. Red embers seemed to float within his pupils before he closed them again. There was a burning smell as smoke rose from his body; his sweat evaporated through the heat he was expelling.

Conscious thought disappeared, and his head pounded. He felt like the magma was burning him from the inside.

A roar of flame filled his body. He saw small sparks burning through his mana channels. He circulated the channels; it provided some relief the sparks weren't all burning the same spot, but they were spreading throughout his body. His breaths came and went through his teeth. The sparks bloomed into flames, setting him alight from inside. Then they dimmed as the pill's healing effects repaired the damage. He didn't have time to examine any changes as his body was set aflame again.

So it continued. Steam rose from his body as he twitched and hissed in pain. His mana channels could be seen, with red and blue flames dancing inside.

Black impurities were pushed out of his pores as he endured it.

The surge of power invigorated him. His body felt alive.

A part of him knew that he had reached Body Like Iron, but the flames were still tearing through him.

He held on, forgetting time, and tried to focus on other things, making promises to himself—he would have beers, the food he would eat, the vacation he would go on—all to alter his mind and focus on anything but the pain.

The flames gradually died down.

He expelled a hot breath. He took some moments to focus his mind and remember what was going on.

"How are you feeling?" Erik used a Clean spell on Rugrat and removed the impurities his body had expelled.

"Warm," Rugrat said.

"Look at the floor," Yuli said.

Rugrat checked behind to see the wooden floor had been blackened with heat. "Well, I'm not sure if we're going to get the deposit back for that one." He laughed.

Erik helped him to his feet.

He was incredibly tired, but it didn't take much effort to stand up. He shook his body lightly, feeling the power coiled in his muscles. It felt as if he would be able to get through anything.

Erik helped him to his bed and gave him a High grade Stamina potion. As soon as it touched Rugrat's tongue, his forgotten hunger came back with a vengeance.

He gulped down the potion, and Erik had another ready for him when he had finished the first. It took three High Journeyman-level Stamina potions to sate his Stamina loss.

Fed and tired, Rugrat's body put the Stamina potions to work. He collapsed like a puppet with the strings cut and passed out.

28

Top Ten

The fighting had heated up in the Battle Arena. The city's population had only continued to expand since the competition started.

Gu Chen was watching it all.

Yi Yin had secured a spot in the top forty. An assassin appeared behind him, sending out strikes at his back, and he was thrown forward. The mana barrier around him flashed into existence. The assassin, who was moving to follow up the attack, jumped to the side, a victorious look on his face as people cheered.

"I didn't expect the fighting to be this intense. With the prizes, everyone is willing to put down their lives. It seems the Battle Arena is truly a holy ground for fighters to train in," he said to Blaze, who sat beside him.

"Well, there is always next year. And I hear the arena might open more training rooms to fit in more people. There's such a large demand."

"I wish I could secure some of them for my team."

"Get a guild hall, and you can train in there," Blaze said.

"If I had that kind of ability..." Gu Chen sighed. "I heard you are getting some new neighbors?"

"Yeah, looks like there are some other guilds interested in the area. They're holding an auction after the finals for people to buy a place in Vuzgal. I have a feeling the auction house is going to take away a large chunk of money again!"

Gu Chen looked around the stands as the other fights continued. Even though some of his people had made it into the top fifty, his gains had been great.

"This competition will bring Vuzgal to new heights."

"And it will raise the competitors to a new stage. I heard that no fewer than fifteen have agreed to join the Fighter's Association!"

"More guilds are coming every day to train. As a crafter, I thought of it as a holy land long before, but now I see that it is a holy land for fighters as well. I wonder what will happen in the future!"

"Looks like Lin Lei is up next," someone said to Blaze.

Blaze glanced over to the screen. Lin Lei was paired against a mage.

There were just four of the branch heads left in the competition: Joan, Stephan, Derrick, and Lin Lei. Only Lin Lei had a match left today.

Lin Lei was in her assassin garb while she was up against a mage.

"Begin!"

Lin Lei shot forward. The mage released a curse, striking and slowing down Lin Lei. Another Detect Life spell lit her up, making it impossible for her to sneak up on the mage.

"Dual casting, impressive," Blaze said.

"It is hard to cast one spell at that speed, but two of them…there are few able to do that, even with simple spells," Gu Chen agreed.

The mage cast a spell on the ground that made it hard to keep one's footing. Lin Lei was startled, but as she skated across the surface, the mage started to cast another spell and Lin Lei threw out a weapon. The mage dodged, stomped her foot, and a wall of ice shot up in front of her, protecting her from two daggers that hit its surface, leaving impacts.

Lin Lei jumped and used her blades as she scrambled over the five-meter-tall wall. She flashed, using a movement technique, and icicles shot out from the mage's hands; she had been ready for Lin Lei.

Lin Lei dropped to the ground. She dodged the icicles the woman threw out. Lin Lei got into range and spun around the woman. Her blade descended, and a magic circle appeared on the mage's back.

A spear of ice shot out, hitting Lin Lei in the stomach, and sent her flying.

"The mage used herself as bait, making her enemy think that she could only double cast, but she can triple cast," Blaze said.

"Triple casting is as rare as a phoenix's feather," Gu Chen commiserated with Blaze.

Blaze forced himself to nod. Casting more than one spell relied on one's control over mana. Among Alvans, there were many who could dual cast; a great number of people who dealt with crafting could double cast with High level skills. The ranged mages of the Alvan army were all taught to triple cast, and there were some able to cast quadruple spells; Roska was one of those people. She could cast High level spells that usually required a group effort.

Though none of them compared to Tanya, who could instantaneously cast ten spells at once. With her theories on pure magic, her spells were incredibly destructive.

Blaze's eyes moved to Stephan. The young man had his head buried in a book and was jotting down notes.

When he had gone to Alva to meet up with Tanya, he had rarely used his spells, but Blaze was interested to see just how strong this "tested and refined pure magic" was.

The fighting continued the next day. Joan was defeated in less than ten moves by a ranger with greater techniques and more combat experience.

Although she had lost the match, Joan had enough points to stay in the top twenty.

Derrick had revealed most of his trump cards, and the other fighters counteracted him, defeating him.

Stephan's match started with him facing a man wearing minimal armor and wielding a massive, two-handed broadsword.

He looked savage with cuts and markings across his armor and skin.

"Really, you want me to face this scholar? You think he's able to shave yet?" The man laughed.

Blaze watched the man's eyes. He didn't feel any malice in them; it looked as though he was playing mental games to throw Stephan off by being boisterous and loud. He was older, and in the previous fights, he knew when to attack and when to retreat. A man like that had plenty of combat experience.

"Meeting the Iron Berserker...you know, it is said that he has reached Body like Iron. So powerful and no one knew who he was before," one of the spectators said.

"Aren't they mismatched? A scholar who spends his time in his books and the other who fights for his life? I think this match will be over soon."

They didn't know Stephan. Out of all the branch heads, he had the most combat experience. When Blaze had found him, he was covered in scars and cuts. With proper healing, he recovered quickly. He trained more than anyone else, and because he was a mage, he relied less on positioning and needed time between casting to have the greatest effect while managing a battle. It was a lot harder than charging forward with a blade. He was the strongest among the heads and the most willing to learn new ways to increase his Strength.

"Hah, are you so scared that you can't speak? Don't worry! Uncle Iron will go easy on you!" The Berserker let out a loud laugh that could be heard across the arena.

The referee, sensing the atmosphere, didn't make them greet each other and instead started the match right away.

The Berserker charged forward.

Stephan looked around wildly, and the Berserker closed the distance in a moment. Stephan smirked, and his nervous appearance disappeared as he put his hands behind his back. The Berserker's blade stopped in midair just in front of Stephan. The Berserker was sweating, and his eyes opened wide.

Then Blaze saw it. A string of mana from behind Stephan had grabbed the sword, and curses covered his body, while three different spell circles rotated around the man. A pointed metal spear appeared in the middle, ready to launch at any moment.

"The winner is Stephan!" the referee said, recovering.

The Berserker lowered his blade with a sour smile. "Well played." He laughed and held out his hand.

Stephan took it, and they shook.

The man's robust appearance fell away.

"Smart play, but he rushed in, thinking he could confuse his opponent!" A woman in the crowd shook her head.

"Instead, he was the one who was confused. That Stephan—which team is he from?" her friend said as she checked through the information booklet on the fighters.

"Adventurer's Guild. It looks like they have some real strength behind them. I wonder how far they will go!"

"They will surely use this to launch their guild to new heights. The Fighter's Association has already talked to them, I believe."

"Creating strong fighters shows one's ability, but raising skilled fighters and mages? The Adventurer's Guild's background must not be small."

"I wish that it lasted longer. A match that ends so quickly at this stage—is he even taking this fight seriously?"

"What was that spell? It was like the mana he used to hold the blade was sentient! It was still attached to him, like a scorpion."

"Probably a secret spell. It happened so fast I didn't see him casting it."

The stands were filled with admiration, while others complained that the match had ended too quickly. In their eyes, they had to re-evaluate the Adventurer's Guild once again.

The day came to an end, but the city didn't sleep. Crafting workshops worked around the clock, and people were in the Battle Arena training rooms. Others attended auctions, buying and selling their goods, or frequented the restaurants and bars that dotted Vuzgal.

Fight for the Top

Joan reached her limit, unable to get past the top twenty.

Stephan defeated his opponents in just a few moves. With his control over mana, he cast multiple simple spells, stacking them on top of one another. People on the outside thought he was casting several spells, but he was layering them over one another. He used mana whips, which were the greatest things he had learned from Tanya. Using the mana to combine, creating secondary limbs, allowed him—as a mage—to fight in close quarters. He used curses to slow and distract, and then he used the secondary limbs to secure the attacking weapons.

Most people specialized in one kind of magic, never realizing how powerful the right spells were. The purer one's mana, the more options one had. Spells were a way to refine control over the mana and give them orders. Once one figured that out, High level spells combined the right kind of Affinity mana into something useful. Spells were like a cooking recipe: A bit of Earth, Fire, Wood, Metal, and Water could make anything. Mana manipulation reduced the need for the spells and decreased how complex they needed to be.

Even now, he was using his opponents to refine his mana manipulation and test out the theories that he and Tanya had worked on.

Although the power of the spells was higher, the cost to cast them and the mental strain was far less. Stephen was casting simple spells but giving them more power, using the tournament to hone the newfound pure magic that Tanya had taught him.

Stephan entered the top ten. His first match was against the ranger who had defeated Joan in the last round.

The match started. The ranger dodged Stephan's spells and replied with arrows.

Stephen dodged through the arrows, preparing a new spell.

The arrows exploded, and Stephen was thrown to the side. A blast of air to his side pushed him out of the path of several arrows.

The archer grinned, his hands speeding up. Stephen threw back spells, the two dodging and counterattacking.

He had made Stephen over-confident, leading him into his secondary arrows.

Stephan smacked his hands together, creating spells for Water, Earth, and a little Metal. The three elemental manas, mixed together, created clouds above the stage. With thunder rolling through the rapidly forming dark clouds, the winds pulled on the two fighters' clothes.

A storm appeared where the spells met, and the arrows were thrown off by the changes in the air.

Stephan created Wood and Water around a core of Metal and stomped the ground. The three manas combined in the ground in a straight line and tore up the floor.

It split like branches of a tree.

The ranger dodged and rolled to the side, using a movement technique to get more distance. The floor exploded upward, and shards of sharpened stone jutted out of the ground.

Metal, more Fire, Wood.

The manas combined to create fireballs that shot out of Stephan's hand in rapid succession. The ranger fired arrows faster than Stephan's spells; his arrows cut through the fireballs. Stephan reached his hand to the sky. Three spell formations appeared; blue and red shot out of his hand, adding more Water and Fire mana. The clouds ballooned, and the air threw the arrows back. The wind around Stephan shimmered, a column of wind blades that moved so fast they were barely visible.

The ranger dodged into the area of the stone barnacles.

Spell formations appeared in the midst of the barnacles as Stephan added Fire mana. It reacted with the Water mana he had used to create the area-of-effect spell. The Water evaporated with the Earth, and the Metal-enhanced barnacles exploded. The ranger was in a prison of explosions; his arrows hit the column of wind blades without getting close to Stephan.

The ranger was tossed from the stage, and medics ran over to check on him. The barrier had done the job, but the man had lost the match.

Stephan closed his eyes and drew in the mana. His spells collapsed, and dust blew across the stage.

"He's a mage? He should be called the Storm God. He didn't look panicked at all. I thought he had some tricks, but have you ever seen spells like that?"

"Storm God, that's accurate—a scholarly appearance but powerful control over mana. I truly underestimated him!"

"You underestimated him? I put a month's wages on his opponent!"

"Your branch manager's power could very well get him into the top five!" Chonglu praised Blaze.

"Stephan has been studying hard. Even I'm impressed with his performance." Blaze laughed.

Gu Chen smiled, pleased that he had decided to work things out instead of allowing a misunderstanding to grow.

Chonglu moved to the front of the box. The last match of the day had finished some time ago, and now it was time to hand out the awards.

"We now have your ten champions! Let us see who will make it to first!"

The last ten were rested, healed, and given Stamina potions to make sure they were in their best condition. The crowds cheered on their champions. Five matches started. Stephan cleared his first match in minutes, creating a wind tunnel to protect himself and then attacking his enemy at range, changing the environment to corner them before landing the final blow.

Vuzgal's bars filled with cheering and yelling as people watched the matches on the different viewing screens.

The arena filled with noise as the matches continued.

People were wrapped up in the fighting. Slowly, Stephan advanced. Other contestants were knocked out, and the rankings were established.

Stephan made it to the quarterfinals, easily defeating a mage who wasn't able to cast as fast as he.

In the semi-finals, he was up against an assassin, the bane of mages.

Stephan had a hard time pinning them down and had to react to their throwing daggers and magical attacks. Poison and curses covered the ground.

The assassin used the spells as markers, showing where Stephan was casting a spell, allowing them to know of his attacks in advance.

A smoke bomb went off, obstructing Stephan's view. A blade tore through his wind tunnel, breaking the spell. Stephan's secondary limbs shot out faster than he could move, but the blade cut through them. Stephan ignited Water and Fire mana behind his back, using Metal and Earth around him. An explosion went off, and the smoke cleared.

The assassin landed and rolled, keeping hold of their special blade that could cut through spells. The mana barrier flashed around them.

Everyone held their breaths, staring at where Stephan was.

The mage checked behind. A wall of stone crumbled; it had taken the brunt of the explosion and defended Stephan, blasting the assassin away.

Stephan frowned as the assassin charged forward.

Spell formations appeared on the ground, and limbs of different mana shot out, striking at the assassin, who showed off the power of his footwork, closing on Stephan slowly.

Mana curled around Stephan's hands into spell formations and shot out of his hand, looking like a snake as it roared and attacked the assassin. The different mana limbs showed heads as they struck the assassin, changing direction in the air.

The referee yelled out and a suppressing field was created, stopping the spells and restraining the fighters.

"Hah, he made it into the finals!" Emilia slapped Kim Cheol on the back and then waved her hand from the pain of doing so.

"Looks like he's still the strongest among us." Joan sighed.

"I'll beat him eventually. I just need to learn more techniques." Derrick tapped his swords, frowning.

"Stephan is awesome," Lin Lei said.

"Are you a branch head, too, or a secret fan girl?" Derrick narrowed his eyes.

She scowled and threw a blade at his head.

In a split second, he caught it, grinning, and flipped it around.

Her scowl only deepened.

"Don't stab Derrick, Lin Lei," Kim said. "Stephan wouldn't be pleased with you."

This seemed to do the trick, and she turned her focus back onto the stage.

Stephan came over to the group and pulled out a book, noting something.

"Well done!" Emilia said, her boisterous attitude on display as she put him in a headlock.

"You did well, Stephan." Kim nodded with a big grin.

"You best keep training, or I'll catch up to you," Derrick said.

"Fighting!" Lin Lei said in support, holding up two thumbs.

"You are supposed to be branch heads, but as soon as there is fighting, you turn into a bunch of kids!" Joan pouted.

"And you don't?" Stephan said, still writing notes in the book.

She stuck out her tongue. The others laughed.

Stephan looked up with a grin, losing his cold, scholarly outer appearance.

"Your next opponent is the sword mage Christoph. He's not weak!" Emilia said.

"He should be a good opponent to test the self-enhancement spells." Stephan nodded.

"Ever since you learned about this pure line of mana and spells, I can't understand what you're saying," Derrick complained.

Stephan shot him a look.

"Even less than I could understand you before!"

Time passed quickly, and the last match started—the dominating sword mage Christoph against the storm mage Stephan.

The two men stood on the main stage in the highest arena. People from across the city and the Battle Arena were all watching.

They stepped up and shook hands. Both of them seemed normal; at a glance, few people would detect their power.

"Let's have a good match," the referee said. The two of them nodded at the woman in appreciation. Her aura was even more retracted than theirs, and her eyes bore a warning as she stepped back.

Stephan laughed awkwardly. The strongest on the stage wasn't the fighters but the referee; the army has grown powerful quickly. Still, his place was with the Adventurer's Guild. Having to follow others' orders day in and day out—yes, he would become stronger, but he liked his freedom.

The two men went to their corners.

Stephan circulated his mana in preparation.

Christoph rolled his shoulders and did the same. He took out his sword. It had a slightly curved blade with a serrated edge on the back of it. Runes and formations lay along the blade, exerting the full Strength of a High Journeyman-level weapon.

Stephan tucked in his shirt, revealing a bandoleer of crystals along his waist. He reached down and grabbed two, his eyes locked on Christoph.

"Begin!" the referee called out.

Christoph waved his sword and charged. Using a technique, he accelerated rapidly while his sword shot out lightning.

Stephan channeled Earth, Water, and Fire mana into his own legs, imbuing the mana crystals he held with high amounts of Fire with a little Metal and Water, then cast Water and Fire mana into his hands.

Mana crystal was similar to gems. Gems were concentrations of mana that could be consumed over time. The difference was that mana crystal was devoid of mana, and they could absorb mana from different sources. For Tanya and Stephan, they were great research tools as they allowed them to mix different types of mana together at different ratios to see what the effect was.

The Water and Fire elements created a blast of air, shooting out of the crystal as if they were bullets. The crystals exploded into blinding light as Stephan's enhanced legs got him away from Christoph's attack and his path.

Christoph recovered from the blinding lights quickly and stomped the ground. Lightning tore through it. Stephan created an explosion under his feet, but the lightning caught him in the air, striking his hastily created mana barrier. He threw mana crystals at Christoph, each of them carrying a different attack, and Christoph was forced to deal with them before they reached him.

Fireballs, curses, and mana limbs appeared around Christoph, and his sword blurred. Stephan's attacks failed to make it through his defense, and they were split apart.

Stephan multi-cast spells instantaneously, and they exploded off Christoph's sword.

The ground was being torn apart by the deflected attacks as the two men went all out. Their dull expressions gradually turned into grins as they recognized their opponent's ability.

Lightning ran up Christoph's blade, exploding out as it impacted Stephan's attack.

Stephen smacked his foot on the ground. A boulder of stone shot out from the stage. The boulder exploded, dust covering the stage.

Everyone held their breath, waiting to see what had happened to Stephen under the dust.

Stephen's barrier spell, held in his other hand extended in front of him as he waved his hand, clearing the dust and sending an air blade at Christoph.

Christoph dodged to the side and lashed out again. Stephen raised earthen blocks, blunting the lines of lightning.

Stephen could only defend against the attacks.

A large bundle of lightning charged toward Stephen. He raised a stone block, while being torn apart. Not by lightning! Christoph was covered in lightning, like some lightning god.

Stephan channeled mana. His advantage of space was gone. Black mana wrapped together, creating blades. Blue mana covered them, forming ice. Stephan created one blade as Christoph got into range.

He waved his hand, sending the blade shooting forward.

Christoph's lightning burned through the ice, shattering it while his sword broke the rough blade underneath. He dodged back and to the side as a spear of stone pierced where he would have been if he had kept charging.

Stephan sent two more blades at Christoph, forming more.

Christoph, who had lost his momentum, fought to regain his footing, retreating to do so.

Stephan hurled swords at Christoph. His control over their attacks increased as time went on. The lightning sunk into Christoph's body, and his speed increased!

They were at a stalemate once again. Stephan widened his area of attacks. Christoph moved faster to meet the blades, sending out blasts of lightning to contain them.

"Are they both sword mages? The storm mage knows how to use a blade as well!"

"What is this? Mages are supposed to be weak in close combat!"

"He must be using his mana to fight Christoph."

"Do you know the kind of control that takes? I haven't seen him use one buffing spell. Might this be a technique?"

"It must be—they are using techniques every minute. If they were to lose focus for a second, the other would win."

The people in the stands were on their feet.

Christoph yelled; his eyes filled with lightning, and the clouds above stirred. His body increased in size as he lashed out with his sword.

"He's gone berserk! Is this a bloodline ability?"

Stephan gritted his teeth, using Water spells to slow down the lightning mana that Christoph could use. Instead, it simply boiled away as Christoph pushed Stephan back.

Stephan was just holding on when Christoph's Strength suddenly increased and he struck Stephan, cutting through his blades and shields of mana.

Stephan was pushed back. His mana barrier flashed into existence and trembled with the impact.

Christoph's lightning bloodline ability had increased his Strength, and he had reached Body Like Iron already. Stephan sighed as the ambient mana was dispersed from the stage by the referee, canceling the spells.

"The winner is Christoph, the sword mage!" the referee called out to cheers in the crowds, through the Battle Arena, and all of Vuzgal.

Stephen had lost, but he learned a lot and was eager to share his notes with Tanya.

30

More to Be Done

Things didn't start to settle down for some time. Vuzgal was busier than ever, with more traders making plans to visit this mysterious city. Adventurer teams found that the dungeons were no longer the main reason most people went to Vuzgal.

Most went to train in their different skills, from fighting to crafting. Vuzgal had established itself as a holy land for both groups.

The forests around the city were overrun with beasts that had been left to populate the area for centuries. Although there were some slots for people to enter the dungeons, there were plenty of beasts to kill, convoys to protect, and gear to be bought.

Hiao Xen and Elise worked with Domonos and Chonglu to make sure that Vuzgal ran smoothly. The massive city shifted according to their orders. In the last few months, they had come to control Vuzgal completely.

The competition left sects and powerhouses seeing Vuzgal in a new light. It was a new city, but it was already as powerful as some of the premier cities in the Fourth Realm.

If Vuzgal didn't rise, it would be a shock.

Underneath Vuzgal, in a complex underneath the Castle District, the managers of Vuzgal gathered. Tan Xue, Elan, Domonos, Elise, Chonglu, and Matt were all present. Blaze, as one of the council heads, sat in on the meeting. Hiao Xen was the only person not present.

"With the fighting and other activities, we brought in a large harvest. We made a profit of fifty Sky mana stones over the entire period. I talked to Matt about speeding up construction." She and Matt shared a look. "The last residences sold for ten Sky mana stones."

"There's always something new to build. Right now, it comes down to the number of builders I have. I've got different teams working in the untouched areas of Vuzgal—just takes time," Matt said.

The others nodded and glanced over to the next person around the table.

"There were some security issues, but they were resolved reasonably. I am investigating two incidents where there might have been a problem on our side. I should have the results of that in a week. We got a large increase in the number of people applying to join the Vuzgal military." Domonos looked at his father beside him.

"A number of deals were made with traders. People seem to like Vuzgal remaining as it is. I am interested by the fact that the Stone Fist sect sent people down. Not related to what has happened in Vuzgal—there has been a lot of activity between the Adventurer's Guild and the Willful Institute. We might need to show our hand in the future. If that comes around, we need to be ready in case they lead an attack against us," Elan said.

"How have things been on that front?" Elise looked between Blaze, Elan, and Domonos.

Blaze cleared his throat. "We have been undercutting them, taking contracts, and using guerilla tactics to hit their convoys and steal from them. They have probably figured out that it is us, based on the information Elan found, but few, if any of them, are willing to tell their higher-ups or others. These clans compete against one another to get resources and to climb higher in the sect. They don't trust each other. If a small group is messing with them, they will hide it so as not to look weak. They care more about their face.

"Because they're not talking to one another, it allowed us to strike at them more than we previously thought possible. Jasper is running the operations in the lower realms. The branch heads will be returning to assist him while I set up the guild here, working with the Fighter's Association."

"The Fighter's Association?" Tan Xue asked.

"They offered slots for our people to join them. They'll have to compete, but it is a rare opportunity for outer guild members who do not want to take the oath to join Alva and receive our training."

"Will the army assist the guild?" Elise asked.

Domonos sat forward. "Not at this time. Yui is preparing to clear out the Water floor of Alva. Once we have done that, we will have complete control over the dungeon. We are assisting the King's Hill Outpost in becoming the ruler over the Beast Mountain Range too. In six months, the Alva military will reach regiment Strength, which means we should have nearly seven thousand trained soldiers. In one month, we will be able to send two fully trained companies to aid the Adventurer's Guild. We still need time to train the soldiers into different roles, so until we reach regiment Strength, we have the two combat companies."

"That's a big risk with all of those people on the line," Tan Xue said.

"It might be if we were just fighting in the Fourth Realm and against a proper military. We are fighting a sect across several realms. They have allies, but they have more enemies. If we can hit them and weaken them then provide an opening to others, they will finish the job," Elan said.

The room fell quiet. Elise cleared her throat. "Chonglu, now that the competition is over, how have things been going?"

"We have plans to make more training rooms and open them. We weren't able to open them all before, but now the funds are freed up, we can hire skilled craftsmen to build the training rooms. Competitions will go on every week and month; plenty of people are still interested. Large groups are asking to rent out the training rooms for extended periods of time. The Fighter's Association has this benefit; all others, I told to follow what everyone else does. We sold several memberships, and based off the betting alone, we are making a hefty profit."

"Good. You and your people did well. This was a massive undertaking, and you did it with ease and showed the rest of the Fourth Realm our ability," Elise said.

Chonglu bowed his head in thanks.

Elise looked over to Tan Xue.

"Jia Feng wants to hold an internal competition between the crafters," Tan Xue said, "and I agree with her. The competition would allow the different crafters to show off their skill and push themselves. With current planning, it looks like it will happen in six months to offset against the fighting competition. In the future, we might have outer competitions to draw in crafters to Vuzgal. We have trained many Expert crafters and the academy is growing, so everything is heading in the right direction."

Elise looked around the room. "Well, everything didn't fall apart as we feared."

The others smiled and laughed.

"Also, I would like to ask—are we able to sell the weapons the army used?" Elise asked.

"Delilah passed on her decision. The old repeater weapons are outdated and don't have formations we can sell to others, but we can use them to establish alliances. It will be up to the Trader's Guild to create a contract that will satisfy these needs. You'll need to send it off to Alva for final verification. Firearms and their technology will remain restricted information," Tan Xue repeated the message given to her before continuing.

"Weapons will reach a point where it will be hard for anyone without the right equipment to mass-produce them. Everyone focuses on making just one piece of gear, while we have factories making all kinds of equipment in large quantities. It might be at a lower ability level, but we can produce a hundred where they can only make one."

"I'll get that contract worked on and ready for her as soon as possible. What about making it in the academy?" Elise asked.

"We can make some of them at premium grade, though I doubt many of the students will want to mass-produce them. Although I can supply the plans and the technical expertise, it looks like you will have to build more factories in Vuzgal. Then you can make them here and sell them to others. Though, have you thought about what will happen when you can pick and choose who you sell those weapons to?" Tan Xue asked.

"Oh, easy. My first customers might appear random, but they'll be people who have a grudge or issue with the Willful Institute. That way, we can make them stronger and make sure that the people we're fighting beside won't be able to attack us." Elise grinned.

"Remind me not to get on your bad side," Blaze said.

"We've got plenty of work ahead of us, so let's get to it." Elise hit her hands on the table, and everyone dispersed.

Esther Leblanc looked over Vuzgal from the Sky Reaching Restaurant room. Her eyes found the arena in the distance. It seemed that the people from the Fourth Realm were stronger than she first thought. The competition wasn't bad at all. Even in the Seventh Realm, the display would have been interesting. The top one hundred would have been able to find an academy if it had been hosted in the Fifth Realm.

She looked over to a kind but plain-looking old man who made happy noises as he slurped down some noodles. He coughed slightly and blinked, wiping his nose on the back of his sleeve.

"Spicy! But good! Oh, this is delicious. So much better than those potions. And the buffs last longer too." Old Jia laughed.

"Were you able to get the information I require?" Esther asked.

"Nope!" He laughed again, content to keep eating.

"You weren't able to get it, and you're sitting there so happy? What is the Marshal going to think?" Esther didn't fly into a rage. Old Jia was one of the men who had taught her how to be a master of disguise to get information out of people.

"The leaders of Vuzgal are incredibly smart. Well, at least their security and their military are capable!" Old Jia let out an amused snort and kept eating, even as tears fell from his eyes.

"So, you weren't able to get anything?"

"I got a sample!" Old Jia waved his hand. A repeater appeared in his hand, and he gave it to Esther.

She took it, looking it over as Old Jia dug into the food. "This is one of their outdated repeater models. The ones they no longer use for the army. They sealed most of the components, so it is hard to see what they have done, but it basically looks like a crossbow with a mechanism to pull the string back again and fire it."

"Where did crossbows come from?" Old Jia asked with a half-filled mouth.

A shiver ran through Esther's body. "People used to use regular bows. Because based on their abilities and their spells, they could get great power from the weapon. The Marshal created crossbows. They wouldn't augment a person's Strength as well as a bow, but a person who is a level one could kill someone who is a level ten. The power of the weapon was the determining factor in how lethal it is. A lot of people in the lower clans use crossbows still. Their popularity has increased, but they are more expensive to make and take more maintenance to keep working."

"Which means people of the lower realms think they're useful, but they're expensive and cannot be reused as they don't know how to put them back together. While higher realm people don't want to use equipment that will hamper their abilities and are weaker than the bows they could use. This design uses more expensive components, but it can fire repeatedly. Its power is enough to kill someone from the Third Realm in a single hit, and they are hard for people in the Sixth Realm to dodge. Also, I was able to get this sample, but most of the samples on display to be sold were the heavy repeaters. A limited amount of these personal repeaters can be sold. Umm, I also agreed to a contract!" Old Jia laughed at Esther's expression and continued to eat.

"What kind of contract?"

"Oh, one where I am not allowed to fight the people of Vuzgal. That is the stipulation that comes with the contract. Though that's not the best part!"

"There's more?" Esther asked.

"They've built a *factory.*"

"What is a factory?" Esther rolled the unfamiliar word over her tongue.

"It is a place where normal people operate different machines for the purpose of creating one finished item. A factory can create dozens of repeaters and their bolts in some hours. The people who work in the factories, while they do increase their crafting skills, are Novices creating Journeyman-level weapons." Old Jia put down his bowl, patting his beard and mustache. His eyes focused, and the air around him completely changed.

"That is an incredible capacity." Esther nodded. "Though, really—Journeyman weapons?"

"They have a group of crafters who focus on refining the raw materials. They are fed into the factory and turned into different parts and assembled together, checked at the end, and readied for combat. This is their true Strength."

"How so?" Esther asked.

"They can make hundreds of weapons in a day and thousands of bolts. Even if their crafters were all killed, people could man this factory and still produce powerful weapons. What if they found out how to create an Expert-level weapon through Novices? Think…if a Novice could create your silver long rifle and not just one of them, but tens of them a day?" Old Jia asked.

"They would have a lot of weapons, though they wouldn't be able to use their full Strength," Esther said.

"You've seen their military. The people at the competition made sure that nothing happened to the people there. You saw them breaking up fights between people from the Sixth Realm. What if you were to arm them with your rifle?"

"Their bodies and mana are strong, and they carry artifacts that make it hard to see their cultivation and level, but they are a powerful and growing force," Esther admitted.

"And they are well-armed. You saw some of the new weapons they use. They call them rifles, and"—Old Jia pulled out a cartridge case and smelled the opening—"they have gunpowder." He passed the cartridge to her.

She looked it over and smelled the opening. The faint aroma was nothing like the black or gray smoke that came from the weapons of the Sha clan's army.

It was different, but it came from the same family.

"I see you've got more questions than answers." Old Jia smiled as she examined the cartridge.

Esther looked at Old Jia directly. "What should I do?"

"I think that we are not as sly as we think. There is an information-gathering group in Vuzgal, and I feel that they know of us, at the very least."

"What?"

"Yes. I was surprised as well, but I noticed people paying a lot of attention to me. With my senses and stealth techniques, I feel like I'm being poked at by a dozen spears all at the same time, but they're hidden in needles!" Old Jia grabbed his chopsticks and snatched a delicacy from the table.

"So, we should give them the letter and head back to the Seventh Realm. My cultivation is starting to drop, and while it is tasty down here, there are many delicacies that the Marshal brought from France." Old Jia bit into the delicacy, and the outside crunched and the inside fell apart.

"We have found evidence that there is someone else behind Vuzgal. The city lords are always missing, and half their military marched out through the totem some months ago. Where they came from is a mystery, and they established themselves as a local power in record time. Do you think that one of them is a dungeon master? The dungeons here and the dungeons that appeared in the other locations seem coincidental," Esther pondered.

"They might be." Old Jia shrugged. "Is that such a big thing? There are dungeon master sects in all of the Sky realms."

"Though, can we really hand over the letter?" Esther asked.

"The letter in and of itself is a test to see if they will be able to reach the Seventh Realm and contact the Marshal. We know they have weapons similar to our own, using Alchemy and metal instead of magic and mana stones. The Violet Cloud Realm need allies and people who have a certain level of power. If their leaders reach the Seventh Realm, it will be a long time until the rest of their people can. Leaders get the best resources and conditions."

"But they are leaders. Even if they get to the Seventh Realm, how does that help us? We need hundreds of people who can fight in the Seventh Realm, thousands of resources," Esther said. "What use are some people in the Fourth Realm? Their leaders aren't even here."

"The Sha have become stagnant, and you know as do I that the Marshal's power has been waning these last few decades. The Black Phoenix Clan has been targeting us ever since we got the token. I don't think that these people can help, but what does it hurt to test them a little?" Old Jia asked.

"Finish up your meal. I will head to the Blue Lotus." Esther rapped her knuckles on the table.

"Oh?"

"Vuzgal don't know people of the Seventh Realm. The acting city lord is a man of the Blue Lotus. They will know who I am and be able to get me a meeting with Hiao Xen. Many people are seeking him out and looking to cooperate, but not many are able to see him. I need someone to vouch for me." Esther gritted her teeth.

"Hah! Looks like it is one place that even you can't barge into!"

"Who said that?" Esther said.

"You've felt it too. Vuzgal is an iceberg—there is much more hidden and unknown about the people here. If you charged the castle, I don't think you would get past the first few gates. They employ Expert crafters with ease." Old Jia left his words in the air and dug into his food again.

Esther cooled her mind and thought it through. With a snort, she checked her weapons and pulled her cloak tight. She headed out of the room, opening the door.

"Could you get the waitress to come back? I have some more items I want to order!" Old Jia called.

Esther rolled her eyes and sighed. "You're paying for it!" Esther yelled back. She left with two of the guards waiting outside the doors.

She pressed a panel next to the door to call the waitress.

They headed out to the lifting platforms that took people up and down the Sky Reaching Restaurant.

She marched over to the Blue Lotus and up to the main desk. With a medallion and a quick word to the attendant, she found her way to the branch head's office. A woman waited for her there.

"Hello. I am the head of this Vuzgal Blue Lotus location, Nadia Shriver. How can I help you today, Miss Leblanc?" The woman guided her to a seat.

A female guard poured tea for the two of them.

Esther's eyes raked her armor. *Dangerous. Lower level, but definitely powerful enough to be the personal guard of a Fourth Realm branch head.*

Memories appeared from her time in the Fourth Realm as she smelled the tea. "Seventh Divine Recovery tea?" Esther's mana channels moaned in desire.

"Please," Nadia said.

Esther picked up a cup and took a sip. Power seemed to drop into her stomach as it ran through her mana channels. Her core, constantly under pressure, relaxed as the mana imbalance between the inside of her body and externally nearly balanced.

She let out a satisfied sigh and took another deep drink. The tea was a rarely found delicacy in the lower realms and was a peak-level item in the Seventh Realm.

Nadia took a cup herself and sipped it lightly, bringing a flush to her cheeks.

"Thank you," Esther said. "I would like you to introduce me to Hiao Xen. I have a message to give him."

Nadia and her guard focused on Esther, but if Nadia had any questions, she kept them to herself.

"For what reason?" Nadia smiled as she put down the cup. She had only consumed a little of the tea; it was too powerful for her body.

They wanted to know whether Esther meant to attack them and seemed to disapprove.

Interesting.

"I wish to pass him a letter. I don't wish to fight to the front of the castle," Esther said.

"Very well. I can organize that." Nadia smiled, but it slipped slightly as she leaned forward.

Esther did as well.

"Though I must remind you that he is a branch head of my Blue Lotus and the city lord's *personal* friend. My superior pays close attention to the happenings in Vuzgal." Nadia leaned back with the same simple smile.

Esther had heard that Vuzgal assisted the Crafter's Association and the Blue Lotus. She thought that had been over-exaggerated, but it must not have been.

"I only wish to talk." Esther smiled.

Ten minutes later, she stood in front of a large office door. It opened to reveal a man who was reviewing notes.

He looked up from his work, his eyes sharpening when saw Esther. A formation activated and covered his desk, hiding what he was working on.

"Hello. My name is Hiao Xen. I am the acting city leader of Vuzgal. I understand you are Esther Leblanc, the envoy of the Marshal Dujardin of the Sha clan." He bowed his head slightly and indicated to the couch. "Shall we talk?" His voice was light, but his eyes were focused and there was steel in his words.

Interesting, a person from the Blue Lotus working in a city. Just what kind of people are these city lords? And he is defensive of his position and the people commanding him instead of angry.

"I have something that I want to pass on to your city lords from the Marshal. Nothing to be worried about—an invitation. A test, if you will." Esther pulled out the letter her uncle had given her nearly three months ago.

She didn't miss the interest in Hiao Xen's eyes as he received her letter.

"I will make sure to pass it on."

"Very well." Esther stood up. "It was interesting seeing Vuzgal. I hope you are able to reach the Seventh Realm soon." Esther realized that she meant most of her words. Dealing with the Black Phoenix sect, they were up against a wall; they needed people on their side. The Sha clans, as all clans and sects did, kept their information closely guarded. If the people from Vuzgal could reach them, they might have more people they could bring into their secrets in return for their loyalty, increasing the Strength they could deploy against their enemies.

She turned and left.

Hiao Xen stood as she marched off.

Dungeon Overflow

A larms went off as Storbon worked. He stood and looked over to the rest of the team, as well as Erik. Rugrat was off training in a smithy.

"A dungeon overflow," one of the waiting patients said in a shaky voice. Others dispersed and hurried in different directions.

Storbon caught one of the fleeing patients. "What is a dungeon overflow?"

"Beasts, beasts everywhere!" They struggled free and kept running.

Scenes from the beast waves that had slammed into Alva passed through his mind.

A group of guards rushed down the road heading in the direction people were running from.

"Make a path!" a woman in the lead yelled. People quickly moved to the sides.

Her armor, like the other guards', was simple and well worn. The guards had different expressions, from fear to determination.

The woman stopped in front of Storbon as the rest of his people came out of the tent.

"You and your healer friends, we must ask you to assist us in defending the wall," the woman said.

"To fight on the wall?" Storbon asked.

"No, to assist at the aid station if there are any wounded."

Storbon glanced over to Erik, who nodded.

"All right, lead the way," Storbon said.

The woman and her guards ran through the small town. They reached a market square that had been bustling just minutes ago. The vendors were clearing their items away as the guards put down beds and food supplies, creating an ad-hoc secondary base.

"Set up where you want. The wounded will be brought to you for treatment. You will be paid according to the city's rates in a time of defense. If you are found to not perform your best or you flee your post, an open bounty will be placed on your heads within the city and passed to the academies." She rested her hand on her blade.

The air chilled around Storbon as smithies opened their doors and prepared to receive equipment to repair as needed. "You don't need to worry about us."

The woman looked them over and then turned with her group and hurried off, sending them off to different places.

"Set up a field hospital," Erik said.

They cleared an area, moving the stalls back. They used some of them as counters and got cots and stretchers out. Another alarm rang out; guards who had been around the city rushed to the walls. The people hid in their homes.

Rugrat appeared, waving to them and heading into the smithy. Tian Cui went with him, and everyone else gathered in the field hospital.

"I need two people to come to the wall with me," the female guard yelled.

Storbon stepped forward and Erik was right behind him.

He frowned and pressed his lips together, holding back his words.

"You'll do. Try to keep up!" The woman turned and ran as Storbon shot Erik a look, but the other man simply smiled.

Storbon snorted, and a glimmer of a smile appeared on his own face. Being next to Erik, he felt confident. Erik had changed his entire life. He would lay down his life for him in a moment. A part of him, since that time so long ago, had always wanted to prove himself.

They followed the guard to the wall. Both of them wore their armor plates under their clothes; it made them look bulky and weird, but no one cared.

They ran up the stone steps. There were guards spread across the top of the wall. Available mana rested atop; archers readied their bows, mages their magic.

The ground was dusty beyond the walls. The road was well worn leading up to the gates. Trees, withered and twisted in the dungeon's environment, stuck up; being lower than the walls, they could see over the rolling forest. Flying creatures were fleeing from their positions as a faint but growing thunder was heard.

It grew quickly, and the commanders readied themselves.

"Everyone is on the walls, but the commanders are determined by their Strength, not their ability," Erik whispered to Storbon.

Storbon looked around. The guards were ready, but they weren't organized in any real sense.

"Here they come!" someone yelled.

The trees near the edge of the open ground shook.

Archers and mages prepared themselves.

Fleeting shadows moved in the dim light underneath the trees.

Then, in a rush, a black cloud of animals shot out from underneath the trees.

Upon seeing the wall, some started to veer away; others—a group of leopard-like creatures with large flaps upon the sides of their bodies—gathered light on their three horns.

"Fire!"

Mages and archers fired, but it was disjointed. Some of the mages and archers waited to get a clean shot at the enemy, making sure that no one else would get a portion of their Experience.

Storbon watched as the groups gathered but worked for themselves. Every kill or assist they got was more Experience for them to level up with.

"Leave the mid-level beasts to me!" one of the more advanced mages yelled as she pushed out her spell. Twin whips of dirt shot out, tossing low level beasts aside and piercing two mid-fifties beasts.

"They are trying to kill the higher-level beasts first to increase their Experience gain. Fucking idiots, only caring about leveling up," Erik spat.

"Their coordination is way off. They're trying to take kills from one another!" Storbon said.

"The more kills one gets of the higher-level animals, the greater the rewards the academy will give them and the faster they will grow," Erik said. "This is the path of warriors, not soldiers."

A few of the glowing horn beasts let out a blast. The yellow and blue shattered into light, tearing through those on the wall and tossing people backwards. People cried out, begging for aid or calling for the beast's deaths.

Mana cannons rumbled, firing blue balls of mana into the beasts.

It had turned into hell. Explosions of magic ignited across the open ground. Archers fired as fast as they could find an appropriate target. Mages swore as they missed creatures or got ones they didn't care about.

"Stop shooting in my area, you bastards," one mage hissed at a nearby mana cannon team. They altered their aim and he let loose, raising a tornado that compressed and spat out dirt and stone bullets.

A section of wall was hit by the three-horned creatures, sending a person tumbling to the floor below and crying out.

The beasts reached the walls. Most tried to get around it, instead finding more defenders. Others started to clamber up the wall.

"Old Wei is hungry for some Experience!" A man laughed as he brandished a saber and clashed with a powerful beast.

Erik and Storbon ran down to the person who had been blasted off the wall. They were covered in dust and groaning from the impact.

He opened the man's eyes and created a flame in his hands, using it to see better.

"I didn't realize how fundamentally different our military is from others," Storbon said.

"We hire people into the military full time; they hire people in times of war and emergency. They get them gear and take a share of what they win. The armies of the Ten Realms are supported by looting, mostly. Mercenaries train to fight in wars or are in them all the time. They're the closest to our military. It's the difference between having a professional military and a conscripted militia," Erik said.

"The wounds are getting worse every time," Yuli said to Erik as they worked on different patients.

"They're tired. They used all their Strength to secure the best kills. Now they're running out of steam." Erik fused his patient's arm back together; the man yelled as if he were being eaten by a beast.

"You'll be fine." Erik grabbed the man's shoulder and noticed he had left a bloody mark on his clothes.

The man's pain subsided, and Erik moved to the next patient.

Yuli checked the face of the man she had been working on. The wall he had been beside had exploded, turning into stone chips that tore up his face.

She finished applying healing potion to the cuts, and they started to heal themselves and return to normal.

"Why aren't we fighting?" she asked Erik.

"We're more valuable here. We would only get in the way, maybe piss someone off for 'taking their kill.' We would also reveal more of our skills and abilities than we have already," Erik said.

"All right, it's time to go back! Let's fill ourselves with Experience!" A group that had just been resting in the market was led out by their leader toward the wall.

Yuli frowned.

"The people of the Ten Realms prove their ability through their feats; in Alva, people prove their ability in their actions. Soldiers work together, not to increase their rank but to bring their weakest to a higher combat ability. Levels and cultivation are great focuses, but they are not our primary focus. If they were, we would recruit the strongest people, instead of the best." Erik sighed.

"Everyone here bases someone's potential off what the Ten Realms says about them, while we give people an opportunity to prove their potential," Yuli said, as if she was having difficulty connecting the two realities.

"Look at our military leaders. Glosil is from the First Realm. He is no stronger than Domonos or Yui, but he has a better grasp of tactics and strategy, which is how he has kept his position. The one thing we take from the Ten Realms that we didn't have on Earth is competition of ranks. On Earth, the longer you did a job, the higher you would get. Instead, we changed the system, so people are elected by their peers and their leaders to get a promotion. If you are not commander material, you will not be put forward to be a leader. I saw it too many times when someone thought they were a leader, got into an officer position, and it was a mess. Kind of like how Rugrat and I were commanding the military, which didn't make sense as we don't have the expertise or ability. Plus, we are always off to different places," Erik said.

"One thing I only recently realized is that people in Alva look to shore up their weaknesses. They are not seen as a fault, but something that can be worked on. In the Ten Realms, people focus on their strengths and turn a blind eye to their weaknesses, looking to overcome them with greater power," Yuli said.

A barrage of mana cannons went off. Their lights dazzled the eyes while the rumble of cannon-fire rolled over the city like thunder.

The weight of fire seemed to reduce, and people were called off the wall.

Wounded were carried and hauled into the medical tents. Erik and Yuli got to work, separating out the different patients and treating them.

People dropped off their weapons and armor at the smithy, getting them repaired and honed for the next battle. The next group to rest dropped down into the other half of the square where there was a barrel of hearty stew with a tantalizing smell and ample mana rolling off it.

The guards quickly devoured the food, not caring whether it got into their beards or ran down their chests.

"How is he?" One guard grimaced as Yuli pulled off her friend's armor and checked the wound.

He'd been gored in the stomach. She used a Clean spell, but the blood started to come out again quickly. The armor must've been stemming the flow of blood. She grabbed bandages and gauze they'd been supplied with and pulled out forceps. She doused the gauze in healing potion.

"Hold this."

"What? I'm not a healer."

"You want him to live or die? I only have so many hands."

The guard took the gauze.

"There's a piece of bone in his side." Yuli stuck the forceps in, making the man cry out in pain as she grabbed it and pulled it out.

The man writhed and complained, but Yuli's hand stopped him from agitating the wound.

"Gauze," Yuli said, the other guard was looking pale and had turned away with her eyes closed.

"Help these days." Yuli pulled the gauze from her hands and put it on the wound. She pulled out a bandage, expertly looping it around the man and securing the gauze.

"Try and kill animals all day but can't handle a little blood," she muttered as the female guard coughed and shivered.

"H-how is he?"

"Your boyfriend will be fine."

"H-he's not my boyfriend!" the woman stammered.

Yuli blinked. "Well, now I'm sure he is. Anyway, he'll be fine. Just need the healing potion to take effect." Yuli turned to her next patient.

"What about his hand?" the female guard asked.

"He doesn't need it to survive. Once I've dealt with the worst cases, I'll check on it." Yuli checked the person beside her; they had broken a thigh bone and were turning pale.

"Shit." Yuli checked him. The broken femur had caught on the artery.

Yuli used her Clean spell on her scalpel and forceps, then on the man. She grabbed a rag and put it in the man's mouth. It was doused with a painkiller, allowing him to relax as he breathed it in.

She cut into the man's thigh. Blood drained out as she used her Simple Organic Scan and the forceps inside the man's thigh. He groaned as she tried to reach his artery.

"Shit!" Her forceps slipped and she missed it. "Erik!" she yelled.

Erik quickly finished up what he was working on and rushed over.

"Femur through the artery—it's up in his hip." She tried to grab it again.

Erik checked the man and grimaced. He pressed his hand to the thigh, casting a spell.

"Won't that deplete his Stamina?"

"Stamina over life. Focus!" Erik barked.

Yuli saw the artery had retracted into the groin, expanding in size and firming up instead of being a ragged mess. She finally grabbed it with her forceps, clamping down and cutting off the blood flow.

"Fucking scare me like that." She pulled out a new set of forceps, grabbing the artery that had descended. She pulled them together and Erik used his healing spells to fuse the two arteries together.

"I fucking hate the femoral." Erik shivered.

She checked the man's thigh again. The man cried out as she righted the bones.

"Seems livelier now." She pulled out a needle, checking the healing solution inside.

Her hands glowed, and her Simple Organic Scan allowed her to see through his thigh.

She injected the healing potion in the man's thigh. It went to work, pulling the bone fragments together and fusing them.

"Good. Now there's little chance of him moving and cutting it open again. Release," Erik said.

Yuli unclamped the forceps.

"Immobilize the leg and align the femur, bandage up his leg, and get a Stamina drip via IO into his shoulder. His bone marrow will convert the Stamina potion into blood," Erik said.

"Got it," Yuli said. A Clean spell removed the blood from her and her gear as she followed what he had ordered.

The next few hours went by in a rush. A group left and another came back. The sounds of fighting had calmed down.

She returned to her first patient with his broken hand.

"Looks like the overflow is over." Yuli put salve on the man's wrist. They were using the city's supplied gear unless it was dire circumstances. They wouldn't get compensated for using their own equipment.

"It isn't over yet. These overflows change everything in the dungeon. It could last for some days or even months," the patient's friend said as she watched what Yuli was doing.

"What's the salve for?" the man asked.

"So, you don't feel this."

Yuli located the shattered bones, re-aligned them, then injected a healing potion. The shattered bone melded together and repaired the broken hand.

"Your side is looking better. Grab a health potion on your way out and get some food into you. The more food, the better—your Stamina is going to be low," Yuli said.

"That's it?" the female guard asked.

"Yup."

"But you didn't use one spell. Are you really a healer?"

"I am, but sometimes using spells is wasteful." With that, Yuli wiped off her hands and checked on her other patients.

"This is going to be a long slog," she told Yao Meng when she saw him.

"What do you mean?"

"Just heard that this can be days and up to months long."

"I'll tell Storbon and see if we can't figure out a rota for people to get some rest. Thanks for letting me know," Yao Meng said.

"No worries, second boss man." Yuli smiled and wandered off to find Lucinda.

32

Life Isn't Always Peaceful

ui was guided by the Alvan soldier into one of the large open seating areas that was surrounded by food stalls and shops.

"This way, sir," the soldier said nervously as he guided Yui around the back of a noodle shop.

I think I need to take myself off the duty watch rota.

They found a cowed group of soldiers and an irate shop owner tapping his foot at the rear of the shop.

"What is it?" Yui walked ahead and into the shop to the sound of snoring. He'd been woken up and pulled from his bed for this "emergency."

Davin, the little Fire imp, lay on the floor, several dozen cleaned-out containers around him. His little belly protruded, and he had one hand in a bucket of noodles. His snores sent out a stream of fire with every exhale.

I don't get paid enough for this.

"He ate all of yesterday's leftovers, and he even ate the raw noodles I made last night!" Old Wang yelled, waving his spatula before someone covered his mouth.

"What do we do, sir?" another asked, not paying attention to the struggling Wang, who was windmilling as two soldiers held him up, forced smiles on their faces.

Yui's eyebrows twitched. "Davin!" Yui yelled into the kitchen. "Davin!"

Davin shifted and turned, pulling out noodles and putting them into his mouth, absently chewing on them.

"Davin!"

Davin snort-snored and shook his head. Opening his bleary eyes, he peeked at the group with a sleepy smile and sucked back a noodle that was half in his mouth.

"Davin, these are not your noodles to eat," Yui said.

"They were laying out in the open."

"Behind a closed door that you melted!"

"Well, I just leaned on it and it came apart." Davin laughed.

"Egbert! Get your ass over here now!" Yui said to the ceiling.

Davin's face turned a little pale, and he put on a big smile. "There's no need to bother Egbert. He's probably bus—"

"Excuse me, coming through. Watch out there, Mark! Come on, James, blocking the door. Hi, Mister Wang, how's it hanging? Ah, Major Yui Silaz, how might I help you?" Egbert landed among them.

"Davin has gone through all of Mister Wang's leftovers and his freshly made noodles," Yui said.

"Okay, and?"

"And he spent a lot of time and hard work on them, and Davin doesn't seem too repentant."

"All right." Egbert drew out the word. "You do know I don't eat food, so is that like a bad thing?"

Yui looked between the two of them, feeling as if he were going to explode. He looked up and then back down. "It's as if he took your favorite books, got sauce all over them, and then went and read the books you were anticipating and bent the bindings and you can't even read the words anymore."

Yui ignored the confused looks from Wang and his fellow soldiers.

Egbert's jaw literally hit the ground.

Davin, doing his best to impersonate a chipmunk getting ready for winter, eyed windows and doors, looking for a way to escape. His chest and belly expanded to inhale the noodles as if they would be plucked from his mouth.

"I believe you should be able to handle his punishment and a method for him to pay back Mr. Wang?" Yui said.

Egbert's jaw flew back up into his head as he straightened. "Davin Leopold Firepot Slunzair!" Egbert turned to the little Fire imp.

"Ahh!" He turned to run. Flames appeared around his body as he was promptly plucked from the floor. "Catch me if you can, you old sack of bones! Hah!"

He was up in the air but didn't seem to notice he wasn't moving.

"You'll never catch the great Davin! Taste my ash!"

"That just sounds wrong," Mark, one of the guards, said.

Yui had to nod in agreement.

"You little rapscallion!" Egbert said, making a motion as if he was pulling in a rope.

"What is happening? You're using magic—no fair!" Davin huffed.

"If you'll excuse us." Egbert waved a hand, and Davin bobbed behind Egbert.

"Egbert, I don't feel so good," Davin said.

"I have heard that it is an issue of overeating, my devious charge!"

The two left.

Yui glanced over to the others. Old Wang was put back on his feet.

"I'm sorry about this, Mister Wang. I'll make sure he pays you back for the food. It seems that he found it so delicious that he wasn't able to stop himself from eating even the uncooked noodles," Yui said.

Old Wang appeared to have aged ten years. "As long as he is gone! And

I need a new door! This mess!" Old Wang walked in, and Yui headed out.

"Where do you think you're going? I am an old man. You don't expect me to do this all on my own, do you?"

Yui turned back, a weak smile on his face. "Of course not, Mister Wang. Come on, let's help Mister Wang," Yui said to the other guards.

They put on forced smiles, turning into Mister Wang's laborers for the day.

Light dissipated around Yui Silaz as the sounds of people talking suddenly surrounded him.

Combat Dungeon training.

Yui adjusted his armor as he walked through the merchant area around the teleportation pads. Potions, weapons, armor, pills, meals to recover Stamina, people purchasing materials from the dungeon divers, or offering services, weapon sharpening, armor maintenance.

Instead of having to pay the teleportation fees, dungeon divers could pay a little more and get all their needs seen to. Past the market, there was an open seating area. At the sides, there were food sellers. Beyond them, there were armories.

Soldiers passed through these before reaching the next area.

Tens of people were hanging out, watching the boards and the gates next to them carved into the semi-circle area.

Yui went up to a desk, checking the board.

Level 55 Dungeon: *Defense*

Underneath were times listed for the military. Other times were listed for Alvans to use the dungeon. Over it was a sign.

UNDEAD TRAINING.

"Do you have any slots open?" Yui asked.

"Colonel!" The man at the desk jumped up.

"Don't worry, only military members need to salute. Any free times? What's the undead sign?"

"I can slot you in. The undead are training in there right now. There aren't many people willing to take on such a tough dungeon."

"They the Blood Demon sect undead?"

"Yes, sir." The man nodded.

"Okay, pull them after the next fight. I'll take in a group on the next one."

"Yes, sir," The man grabbed a sheet. "I have four groups of undead. Level forty-five to fifty, two of those, and a group of level fifty. The rest are in there right now. They were level fifty to fifty-five."

"I'll take the forty-five to fifty." Yui looped his thumbs into his vest's armpits.

"Coming right up."

There was a stir among the Alvans as the undead group that had been waiting in the armories walked over.

"Sir, do they freak you out?" the man asked.

"Nope, they were our enemy. Now they're our strength. We could have let their bodies disappear, but turning them into fighters makes them a powerful backup. Hell, if I die, I hope my body gets turned into an undead."

"Really, sir?"

"Hell yeah. No sense in wasting my bones if they can be used to defend Alva."

The door beside the desk opened, and undead walked out. Their armor showed signs of hard fighting, their weapons were in need of repair or replacement, and one of the skeleton's sword had been cracked in two.

"You've been sending them in every time there's a free spot to level them up?" Yui asked.

"Yeah. Once they reach level sixty-five, they're stored in Alva or Vuzgal as a reserve. That's the highest any of our dungeons go."

"Good. Well, I should get to work." Yui checked his gear, slapping his pouches, telling how they were by touch. "What's their designation?"

"Squad Four."

"Two mages, four ranged, and six melee fighters, shield and sword. Simple but effective in groups. Like the Romans,"

"The who?"

"Don't worry about it. All right, Squad Four." Yui felt the tattoo on his chest warm before dulling again. Like many, he had tattooed the Alva emblem into his chest, so even if he were not wearing his amulet, the formations would recognize him.

The undead's eyes, orbs of faint flame, moved to him, awaiting orders. He wondered if the first undead maker gave them flame balls because plain skulls were just freaky.

Yui cleared his throat, shaking away his thoughts.

"Follow me."

Yui walked into the room past the open doorway. He pulled out his rifle from his storage ring, shaking it to loosen the sling. He looped it around his neck and under his arm and pulled on the charging handle, checking the chamber and empty magazine as well. He played with the action, feeling how smooth or gritty the action was from maintenance and use.

He took out a magazine and loaded it as he reached a big, blue button embedded into a pillar.

Yui moved the rifle, using a band of rubber to secure it to his side. He wanted to simulate being in a real fight and wouldn't have time to unsling his rifle and put it away.

Yui secured his helmet, taking out his spear. Holding it in his hand felt *right*. "Best gift Qin ever gave me."

He laughed, thinking it wiser *not* to repeat that to his sister.

"Ready your weapons."

They freed their swords from their scabbards and raised their shields. The ranged archers laid arrows along their bows and the mages' staffs glowed as the runes carved into their bones gathered power.

Black and red lines laid deeper.

They needed mana to repair, and this dungeon had plenty of it. No pain receptors. It just took time to walk undead into a pool of poison then into a pool of lava. Yui sank into his thoughts. With them acting as testers, the medics and doctors had made rapid advances in tempering. *And I'm getting distracted.*

Yui touched the blue button.

The door to the room closed, and he disappeared in a flash of light with Squad Four.

Defense Dungeon

Kill waves of incoming beasts.

Every 5 waves you gain a random chest.

Kills will get you dungeon points, redeemable through dungeon kiosk

Escape the dungeon by crushing your dungeon medallion (found next to the obelisk). You will lose 20% of gained Experience.

Wave will begin in 00:00:59

Yui waved the timer away.

"Squad, grab your medallions, follow dungeon procedure."

His squad moved as he checked the defenses.

"Well, this place got fucked up."

There was one entrance into the walled fort, a stone bridge with a moat ten meters below on either side.

The battlements were in various states of destruction. The two rounded towers on either corner of the fort had seen better days. From the outside, one could see into the second floor of the left projecting tower.

The right tower was in a better state, a floor shorter but the broken parts of the second floor would give cover to those inside.

Yui looked across the bridge.

Fog and smoke hid everything ten feet away from the other side.

"Won't be much warning of what the hell is coming before they arrive. The two towers at the rear are a lot better than the two in front." The undead had grabbed their medallions and put them between their teeth so they could crack their medallion no matter the situation.

"I want a mage in each of the rear towers. Archers, I want two of you in the right forward towers. The rest of you gather rubble from inside the fort and put it at the gate entrance."

He went to the obelisk. An obsidian rock floated above a formation, turning slowly as the light played on its sharp surface. A dungeon core lay beneath it, controlling everything.

Alva had placed their dungeons across the Beast Mountain Range. They seem closer with the teleportation halls but were stuck in regions with the highest mana and attribute density, creating a network.

Yui grabbed the medallion and affixed it to his carrier, checking to make sure he could smash it easily.

Wave will begin in 00:00:10

"Awesome." Yui's ranged forces were positioned. His melee and two archers on the ground were hauling over what had been part of the wall, dropping it on the bridge and between the gate. The wooden doors had been shredded. One lay in the middle of the fort; the other had broken hinges and parts of wood that was barely attached still.

Yui stored his spear and reached down to the door in the middle of the courtyard. It was made of five trees that had been roughly cut into squares, bound by iron bands and nails.

Each timber was bigger than Yui's thighs.

Yui squatted down and lifted the door enough to get his hands underneath.

Noise came from outside the camp.

"Those moving rocks, drop them at the gate and take up defensive positions. Shield bearers up front, assume Testudo. Mages, archers, when you see a target, attack it. Shield bearers, hold your position." Yui adjusted his grip.

He let out a powerful exhale. His muscles and veins bulged as he raised the half-broken door. He grabbed the hinges and walked backwards. His legs shook as he dragged the door that must've weighed hundreds of kilograms over the broken ground.

Yui grunted, picking up his pace.

Wave 1 will begin in 00:00:00

Yui increased his speed, digging deep, until he was behind the archers at the gate.

The wall was two meters thick. Yui was just a meter or so back from the funnel created by the walls.

"Stone Projection." Yui raised a stone trench, one side under the door's side, and the other spaced out in front of the door.

Yui released the door onto the one raised stone side, and it released a wave of dust as Yui drew his spear.

He looked through the gateway. Archers on the right tower popped up and fired arrows. The mages were linked to the rest of the squad, using them as spotters. It allowed them to remain in the protected rear and attack accurately.

The archers behind the melee fighters were shooting occasionally but not as much as their friends up high.

"Fucking dogs." Yui saw the enemy; they looked like hyenas running in the fog. A few would rush out, testing their defenses, only to be followed by spells or arrows.

Yui raised his spear and jammed it into the stone. He released the band holding his rifle and aimed over the melee fighters.

More of the creatures jumped out of the fog.

Yui squeezed his trigger, dropping a beast. He felt Experience enter his body as he searched for the next.

It continued for some time before a full pack of the hyenas ran out from the fog.

Yui and the archers picked them off. They didn't make it halfway across the clear ground before they were cut down, turning into fading particles.

More groups formed and charged; three packs in all, making it some meters farther than the first group.

> *Wave 2 will begin in 00:00:15*

"Mages, regenerate your mana. Archers, check your ammunition. Shields, grab more rubble around the obelisk and put it along the bridge up to the gateway."

Yui tapped his magazine.

"Half full." Yui shrugged and reloaded, taking magazines out of his storage ring and leaving the ones in his vest untouched.

Yui helped the undead to move rubble onto the bridge. He created stone projections that were a few feet high and had the mages fuse most of the rocks to the bridge.

He watched the time, making sure they used every second they had.

> Wave 2 will begin in 00:00:00

"Get into position," Yui said.

He stood beside his spear again.

The next two waves were similar to the first. The number of hyenas increased. They created packs faster; by the fourth wave, they appeared in packs.

"Now!" Yui said.

An archer fired a flaming arrow, hitting the rocks on the other side of the bridge. The hyenas covering the area yelped as they were set aflame.

A mage called down a tornado, and the influx of air turned the flames into a blaze. The flame-nado multiplied as the mage sent them out across the clear area, driving through the three other packs that were rushing the bridge.

The packs were broken; the remaining hyenas ran toward the bridge, meeting the undead's arrows and Yui's bullets.

The flame-nados died down, the ground still shimmering on the other side of the bridge.

Wave 5 will begin in 00:00:15

"Mages, cool oil patch on, fuse the stones afterwards. Archers reload, then those in the right tower, pile up stone against the walls you're using as cover. Melee fighters, gather stones and throw them out from the gateway to the other side of the bridge."

They carried out their tasks quickly. The oil patch recovered and cooled down. Yui took out a small cask and threw it out. It smashed on the fixed stones.

"Mages, fuse the stones the archers in the right tower have laid down."

"Water Movement." Yui spread the oil across the stones at the edge of the bridge.

Each pause, he was updating their defenses.

"Wave five is always something different. The hyenas have been increasing in number and getting stronger. Wonder what's next."

Wave 5 will begin in 00:00:05

Yui had his squad ready.

A howl called out in the fog. Another howl greeted it some moments later, then a third.

Yui heard yipping and the sound of claws upon stone in the smoke.

He checked his rifle, tapping his index finger against the magwell before adjusting the positioning of his hand.

The pack burst out of the smoke, but they weren't all enlarged hyenas. Some had taken an evolutionary step to become Werehyenas. They stood on their back feet, twice the size of a man, and used weapons and armor they looted from the dead. They were constantly hunting for food. The hungrier they were, the more desperate they became, rushing to their deaths.

They were smart enough to use weapons but not enough to talk, and their beastly desires controlled them.

Yui fired into the leading Werehyena carrying a halberd like a great-axe.

The creature took some rounds before his body realized he was dead and collapsed.

Driven by hunger, they fear nothing and care for less.

The archers fired arrow after arrow into the pack.

There were seven members in total, four hyenas and three Werehyenas.

They made it halfway across the open area before other Werehyenas and hyenas ran out of the smoke, doubling the number of beasts.

Yui and the ranged force ground down hyena beasts.

They had the Strength, but they didn't have the numbers of the previous waves.

The last Werehyena collapsed, turning into motes of light.

A section of stone around the obelisk opened, and a pedestal rose with a chest on it.

"Ranged, recover and reload. Melee, use fuse stone on the walls around the gateway."

Yui touched the ground.

"Stone Spikes."

Spikes rose out of the rubble and between the stones.

> **Wave 5 completed.**
> 1 random chest awarded.
> *Wave 6 will begin in 00:01:30*

"Mages, cast magical traps on the open area on the other side of the bridge." Yui checked over his handiwork with the spikes. "Hopefully that works."

Yui walked around the gate and toward the obelisk. The little bit of house cleaning they'd done looked better than when they first got there. Without anyone to come in here and check the condition of the place, the undead were fighting in deteriorating conditions. Having it all busted up was kind of sweet, though. More remodelling.

Yui opened the loot chest. A nebulous light rose, and within it, one could see different things. Gear, weapons, armor, books, scrolls, random tools, ingredients, pills, powders, staffs.

He bit the inside of his lip. He couldn't see anything clearly, but the anticipation built as the light reached its peak. A bottle of pink-and-red-flecked pills disappeared, and the box settled on a set of Mid Journeyman chest armor.

"Crap." Yui let out his breath through his nose and tossed the gear into his storage ring. "Though Wren could sell it for me."

> *Do you want to leave the Dungeon?*
> **YES/NO**

"Not yet."
Yui checked his gear then the timer.

> *Wave 6 will begin in 00:00:46*

Yui used the undead to create a wall in the gateway, fusing stone and spikes. He had the melee fighters change to spears and placed them at openings in the wall.

Wave 6 will begin in 00:00:00

Werehyenas and hyenas crept out of the smoke.

The mages called down stone spears from the dungeon roof above as the archers picked off the hyenas with their bows.

Yui used a section of the wall to rest his rifle, pivoting to find targets. He reloaded as casings landed on the melee undead next to him.

"Sorry, dude!"

Yui kept shooting. The beasts made it a third of the way across the open area. They were smaller in number, making it easier to thin them down.

The undead had grown stronger with the last couple of rounds, fighting beasts so many levels higher. It was still taking one or two hits to kill even a hyena, but the Experience was massive. No such problem with a rifle, though.

Left, two taps. Right, movement, fire, motes of light. Movement, track, fire. *Click.*

"Reload!" Yui ducked. He saw an archer stumble behind him; an arrow had dented their armor.

Yui pulled on his charging handle, and he looked through the spear slit nearest him.

"Gotcha." Yui turned under the cover of the wall. He stood up, rifle raised.

Casings rained down on his neighbor as rounds tore through the Werehyena archer.

Yui switched targets. An archer collapsed as he fired into the hyenas that had entered the stone field. They yelped as their padded feet found the hidden spikes, and they had to slow to cross the rock covered area.

They were the last of the wave as their numbers dwindled rapidly.

Yui's rifle clicked empty. He ducked and reloaded.

Wave 7 will begin in 00:00:15

"Dammit, Uremovich, stealing my kill!" Yui said, using the slang for undeads.

Yui looked over his wall.

"Those archers are going to be a problem." He unloaded his magazine, pulling on the charging handle to see how dirty his rifle was.

"Mages, more magical traps!"

He frowned before reloading.

"Not too bad."

The next waves went in a blur, with only so much time for Yui and his squad to recover and upgrade their defenses. The hyenas increased in level, taking more hits before they died. The Werehyenas increased in number, with archers entering the fray.

"Taste my traps, bitch!" Yui yelled from behind the wall as he was reloading, hearing a magical trap going off. He didn't have to aim as he looked over the wall; they were a third of the way across the bridge.

"Second oil band!" Yui yelled, firing as fast as he could and then ducking behind the wall as he reloaded.

The two archers with him alternated their shots—one firing up, one down.

Yui heard the *whoump* of oil being ignited, and the wave of heat through the holes in his ad-hoc gate-wall.

Flame-nados sprouted and ran through the hyena beasts.

Bloodied and battered, two Werehyenas pushed through, tearing their feet apart on the spikes and tripping over the small stone projections that were hard to see with the naked eye.

Yui put a round into each of them, dropping them to the ground.

The rest of the hyenas were farther back. Squad Four and Yui cleared them up.

Yui reloaded his rifle, letting it hang. He grabbed the tube inside his helmet and drank deeply, not caring about the lukewarm temperature of the water.

He coughed, clearing his throat.

"Mages, cast the magical traps that were used up. Archers, reload. Take out a basket of arrows and put them around your position. Use them before you use the arrows in your quiver.

"I swear time is moving faster. Is that a Werehyena riding a hyena? That thing's as big as a horse! Die, shitbag!"

Yui's rounds struck the leading Werehyena and mount.

Lightning descended from a spell formation and struck one beast, carving a path through the beasts as it left a smoky path of destruction littered with tombstones.

They collapsed, and Yui changed his target to the Werehyenas who seemed unaltered, while the hyenas had almost tripled in size compared to the first wave of beasts.

The ground glowed under one hyena whose paws triggered a magical trap. A spike of wood shot out of the ground, impaling the beast.

Yui switched to a different target, not taking the time to aim, instead just lining up his body and watching the trace of his rounds.

The numbers thinned. There were only a few hyenas left now.

"Cease attacking. One archer in the tower keep attacking."

Yui watched a hyena take an arrow to the side. It kept coming as it was hit with a second arrow; the third slowed it, and only with the fourth did it collapse.

"Shoot that one in the stones."

Yui counted out the arrows before the beast collapsed into a tombstone.

"Four arrows. Not the worst. At least I'm getting a boost in Experience. They're a higher level than I am."

Wave 10 completed.
1 random chest awarded.
Wave 11 will begin in 00:01:30

"Magic traps!"

The mages cast traps as if deranged marionettes.

"That's what I like to see—determination. Shield dudes, fix my bridge—spiker, rockier, shittier!"

The chest rose from the ground again. Yui opened it to the ever-changing objects. Yui watched rare weapons, powerful potions, and tools pass.

If I could get a nice blade for self defense, maybe new boots, or a powerful trinket and necklace.

Even with his pay, he couldn't get everything he wanted. His gear was issued by the army, except for his spear. The cost for him to cultivate sorely bit into his military credits that worked like money within Alva. He poured out his savings to increase his cultivation.

The light dissipated to reveal an old scroll.

"What's this?" Yui took the scroll and opened it carefully. It was designs for a floating formation. That would be nice to have on their support wagons and weapon systems. In the past, they could use it on the mortars, but now the troops were so strong they could pick up and carry the gear and ammunition easily.

Yui rolled up the scroll.

"I'll give it to Qin. Maybe she can figure out a use for it. Waste not, want not."

> *Do you want to leave the dungeon?*
>
> **YES/NO**

"Nah. I think I've got more rounds in me yet. They haven't got to the gate yet, and I have some surprises."

> *Wave 11 will begin in 00:00:34*

"All right, lets see what else they have. Crap, I need to relay down the first three oil bands!" Yui went to the entrance and threw out small oil casks.

> *Wave 11 will begin in 00:00:00*

"Fuck you!"

Yui checked his rifle and put it on the wall.

"Mages, use mana potions. Archers, shoot any hyenas that come into range!"

Three Werehyenas riding their brethren ran out of the smoke and fog, leaving eddies behind them.

"Explosive shot." Yui's finger glowed with magma veins. He fired, following the red trace of the round.

It blew off the hyena's front leg, causing it to tip forward.

The Werehyena jumped free.

"Explosive shot." Yui struck the Werehyena head-on, turning him into a spray of light.

Yui fired into the hyena packs.

> *Wave 15 will begin in 00:00:15*

"Mages, traps!"

Yui reloaded and replaced the magazine he'd used from his vest.

"Shit, almost made it."

Yui stared at the motes of light three-quarters of the way down the bridge, just out of reach of the melee undead's spears.

"Sorry, lads, next one."

Yui let his rifle hang and lifted his helmet. He took out a cloth to wipe his face.

"At least you all levelled up quickly. Hell, I think I might level up soon." Yui grinned. "Kind of fun, actually."

He pulled his helmet back down, securing it and drinking from the water tube.

He grunted as he moved through the empty cartridges on the ground.

Could turn them into metal spikes and coat them in poison?

"Damn, you are a bastard. Uremovichs, throw the casings on the bridge."

Yui unloaded his rifle and used a Clean spell on it, shaking out the carbon dust. He poured gun lube on the bolt, using Water manipulation to cover the interior of the weapon where metal touched metal.

Something's wrong. Yui looked up and saw the archers, the melee types, and the mage.

"Shit!"

He had called them all, not just the ones at the gate.

Wave 15 will begin in 00:00:02

"Mages, return to your positions. Archers from the right tower, return there!"

Yui stood up and reloaded.

Dammit!

Wave 15 will begin in 00:00:00

The mages and archers ran back to their positions.

Hyenas and Werehyenas tore out of the smoke.

Yui fired through the open gateway over the wall. Explosive shot tore chunks out of the hyena pack and the ground around them.

"Those around me, hold position and attack as soon as the enemy gets into range."

His two archers added in their attacks. Their levels had increased, but the hyenas had advanced faster.

"Fire Strike!"

Red mana traced through the skies, forming an interlinked spell formation. Power gathered, turning into a pillar of flame that descended onto the world below, and the Werehyenas rushed to dodge it.

Some at the edges jumped clear. The ground shook as the temperature increased rapidly.

The pillar disappeared, leaving a scorched ring of molten stone.

Hyenas avoided the falling pillar.

The archers in the right tower joined back in with the fighting.

Yui fired on the hyenas leaking around the circle.

"Screw your armor."

The Werehyenas shrugged off some hits and near misses, wearing simple armor that protected them from shrapnel.

Arrows hit the gateway. Yui ducked and put his weapon through the spear slit in the wall, kneeling and firing.

A lightning trap went off.

Yui targeted the stunned hyena. Two normal rounds took out the beast.

Vines shot out of the ground under another beast, trying to pierce it. Instead, they were wrapped around the beast's leg, causing it to trip and fall into a fire trap. The trap went off, leaving motes of light.

"Shitty day. Reloading!" Yui reloaded his rifle and kept firing through the wall.

"Hit oil band one!"

The beasts charged forward; the fire arrow hit the first fire band as they reached the second band.

Yui drew on the Fire mana in his body within his veins.

Let's see how strong this iron body makes Fire spells.

"Fire Manipulation." Yui used the spell to twist and control the fire. It spread across the nearest hyenas, causing some to jump and fall off the bridge. The fire spread to the second oil band.

"Fire Wall!" The flames grew larger, covering the area between the first and second oil band. Flames licked at the hyenas, burning them and setting them on fire as they forced their way through.

Yui fired as fast as he could pull the trigger, his gun nearly as fast as an automatic version as he tore out his empty magazine and slammed in another one.

He didn't need to aim as hyena beasts were clambering forward regardless of the damage.

Their smarter Werehyena brethren tried leaping over the flames; some made it, others misjudged.

They let out yelps as they landed among the stones and spikes.

"Shit! Melee line, attack anyone that gets into range!"

The mages created flame-nados. Hyenas and Werehyenas were just meters from the gate-wall.

Yui threw his rifle to his left side, securing it with his band. He grabbed his spear, tearing it out of the stone.

He lowered his stance, coming into a half-squat as he leveled his spear with the slit in the wall.

We made the wall high enough that they'll need to climb through the gap at the top.

Yui jabbed his spear out, burying it in a hyena's chest. Undead spears stabbed through their own slits.

A Werehyena jumped on the back of a hyena, forcing him into the spikes of the low wall.

Yui heard a noise on the wall and rock came down.

"Shit!" Other Werehyenas were right behind, using what they could to gain leverage and jump onto the wall.

"Mages, create spikes on the wall above the gateway!"

Yui ran into the courtyard.

"Archers in the tower, kill the beasts that jump on the walls!"

The first Werehyena reached the top of the wall and jumped toward the obelisk. Yui turned, his foot kicking up dust and leaving a line through it. He stood between them and their goal.

The Werehyena snarled, raising his thorn-covered stick. He wore a mishmash of looted armor picked for function over form.

"Well, you're not going to win any beauty contests." Yui turned his spear, gathering the wind around it.

He jabbed out, a spark of fire appearing on his spear.

The air he'd compressed around the spear blasted out at the Werehyena, igniting the beast with the spark.

He was tossed backwards, crashing into the ground, leaving a smoking carcass.

Two more appeared on the wall and jumped.

Yui twirled the spear between his arms, making big steps before they became tighter.

"Flame Spear!" Flames ran down the length of his spear, projecting out of his weapon and stabbing through the one on the left.

"Wind Slash!" Yui's spear flowed from the stab into a slash, and the air shimmered in its path. It reached out, bisecting the Werehyena on the right.

Three Werehyena bodies turned into motes of light.

Four more had jumped. Yui killed two before they reached the ground.

He slid beside the first that was holding a spiked bat. His spear slid along the back of their leg and jabbed out, cutting through their neck.

Yui cartwheeled to the side, drawing out a bloody arc with his spear as an arrow passed his side.

More Werehyenas landed in the courtyard, and hyenas had joined them. Two archers were on the walls.

"Mages, buff the melee fighters!" Yui felt his blood pumping as he ran toward the nearest Werehyena. He smacked away the short sword aimed at his head, with his spear, jabbing forward and piercing their neck.

Enemy Arrows thudded into the dead Werehyena.

Looks like they don't care if they hit their own.

Yui used his turns and dodges to maintain his momentum. *I slow, I die. I slow, I die.* The mantra repeated in his head, forcing him to push harder and leave destruction in his wake. He could give up. It was just training, after all.

You'd do that? Give up when it's just getting interesting? This is nothing!

Yui gritted his teeth and surged forward, his armor staining with blood as he charged the enemy.

He halted the Werehyena beasts' advance. There was nothing to do but fight, and Yui did as he had trained for so long. He kicked out, throwing a Werehyena backwards, hitting a Werehyena. Yui spun and lashed out with his spear, driving it through another Werehyena's neck.

He tore out the weapon and turned as flames raced from his hand down to his spear.

"Flame Blade!"

Yui hit the Werehyena that he thought was out of range. He jumped to the side, expecting arrows to hit him. When he checked where the archers had been, there were only tombstones.

The sounds of fighting at the wall had died down as well.

Yui controlled his breathing.

Wave 15 completed.
1 random chest awarded.
Wave 16 will begin in 00:01:30

"Let's see if we can't make it to level twenty-five. Everyone, use magic to repair the bridge and add in magical traps. Now where did I put that poison? I didn't make any poison-covered spikes. I could make caltrops."

A Thousand Needles

Blaze knocked on the door.

"Come in." Jasper's voice carried through the wood.

He opened it and saw Jasper standing before several maps.

"Looks like you have been busy." Blaze glanced at the information pinned to locations on the map.

"Most of this is Elan's work, gathering information on the Willful Institute. We know where their people are, and we have a pretty good idea of the different factions within the sect. We are hitting different faction-controlled areas, outlying cities, and trade routes—small things that impact them slightly—and grow our own influence in the area. Now, individually, it's not much. The Willful Institute branches don't share much information with one another, wanting to look as good as possible for upward progression.

"We're like a thousand small needles, annoying but not threatening until you look at the effect in total. Elise has mobilized the Trader's Guild. As we take jobs, she buys the supplies that would have been intended for the Institute. Meanwhile, Elan's people are spreading rumors and increasing the friction and tension between the Institute's factions. They're so focused on their old grudges they aren't dealing with the issues popping up in their own cities. Elise says that we have taken twenty percent of their business away already." Jasper's face twisted into an ugly smile.

"Twenty percent—is that enough to make a difference?" Blaze's eyebrows pinched together.

"Sects have tight budgets. They have some funds on hand, but most of their money is spent on training the younger generations. If a city can produce a powerful student, they get greater backing from the higher-ups. The stronger the younger generation is, the further they will take the sect."

"So, while they look grand on the outside, they are just putting all of their money back into their younger generation to hold their position and possibly advance," Blaze said.

"Yes, but as with all things in the Ten Realms, things are made by custom order. We targeted their training supplies: monster cores, mana-gathering formation plates, alchemists, and the suppliers of these things. Everyone is training and burning through resources. The sects only give them out based upon other's performances. They get stronger students, but they have a greater inner strife. The factions and fights between clans. With the reduction in overall resources..."

"The more the factions and clans will fight one another," Blaze finished.

"Those resources aren't going into some hole either. They're getting funneled into our guild."

"Damn, Jasper, that's some sneaky shit. Weaken their rate of progress, increase the infighting, and quietly increase our own people's power."

"We have to be ready for when they retaliate as well."

"No one in the Ten Realms goes down without a fight." Blaze rubbed his face.

"They don't, and they make a lot of enemies along the way. Elan has been talking with some of their enemies—sects and groups that would take advantage of the Willful Institute if they fell on hard times."

Blaze saw the pitying look in Jasper's eyes.

The two men fell into their own thoughts.

"They thought they were going up against just a group of mercenaries, but they ran into the Alvans, attacking them from every possible angle," Blaze said.

"Erik and Rugrat call it asymmetric warfare," Jasper said. "How is the recruiting in the Fourth Realm progressing?"

"We have around two thousand applicants. They need to be trained and vetted. We already have some jobs; most of them are simple protection details from Vuzgal to other places. The Fourth Realm isn't a nice place to live—going to send some of our core members who trained in Alva to bolster our numbers in the Fourth to establish ourselves. How is training going with the guild members in other realms? Been out of the loop."

"We have people joining the Fourth Realm from the First now. We are building a new Adventurer's Guild hall in King's Hill Outpost. The leaders in the First Realm don't like us being in their capitals, but with our heavy recruiting and training, our numbers are swelling with First Realmers. With training, we can easily pull them up to level twenty. With monster cores, we can boost them to thirty and get them into the Fourth Realm. We have fighting in the First and Second Realms to temper our people, but the Fourth Realm will give them more of an opportunity to fight and train. I have a new proposal." Jasper pulled out a stack of paper and gave it to Blaze.

"This is a guild management system—recruiting standards that reward people. They will get guild credits for completing different tasks, and they can use them to buy equipment at lower market prices. People's contributions, the restrictive contracts they are bound to, will weigh more than their overall skill level," Jasper said.

"It is something that has weighed a lot on my mind," Blaze said. "All right, see that it's implemented. Move slowly on the Willful Institute. Keep the physical confrontations to a minimum. Focus on training our people. When the time comes, we'll have the support of Alva, but we need to show our own ability," Blaze said.

"Understood. We have plenty of people from the lower realms who are willing to do anything to get to the higher realms."

"They're just like us: If you have nothing, you appreciate every little thing you're able to get," Blaze said.

"Elder Ahgren, please let me fill your glass," Elder Gulo said to the dignified woman sitting next to him in the spectator box.

They sat in Karem City's Arena, a Willful Institute city. Two of the strongest clans in the Fifth Realm were to be united in marriage, and the stands were packed with members.

The other clans had rallied their strongest fighters to break up this union, which had led to fierce battles all afternoon.

"Please, I would be most honored. Soon, I will be calling you brother, Gulo!"

They laughed together lightly, in contrast to the young, skinny man who was struck by a spear and was sent flying off the stage in the middle of the arena. He hit the ground, his body covered in cuts and his eyes swelling shut.

"Seems your granddaughter has many suitors! With her talent and looks, anyone would be blind to not try their chances. Marrying into the Ahgren family is an honor!"

"Ah, well, it is a good thing that your grandson has trained for so long. Truly, Trito is a great warrior. With our families united, it will bring about a change that could be felt throughout the Institute!" Elder Ahgren laughed and smiled, her eyes filled with hidden meaning.

"Indeed!"

The two elders drank from their glasses. Some of the other elders held their tongues and had grim expressions. Others looked pleased—feeder families and allies. With such an alliance, they would be able to drive out those who had plagued them for years.

The competition continued as the different fighters of the Ahgren, Gulo, and their allied families removed the competition. The elders had poured their full resources, and the Institute's, into their younger generation.

When they met on the stages, the weaker members would bow out, allowing them to push ahead safely. It created a wall within the competition.

"Are you sure of this?" Elder Dayal asked the trader beside her.

"I am a man of my word, Elder Dayal. The best weapons and armor. I even brought you training aids that would be hard to find in the Sixth Realm. While the Fifth Realm has plenty, your boy has the best chance of winning," the trader said.

"Very well. If it is as you say, then we can break up the alliance between the Gulo and Ahgren family and tie the Dayal family to the Ahgren boat. With our boy sure to make it into the Sixth Realm academies—although it will not give them their alliance—it will save us from any backlash, and we can grow strong enough to carve out a position."

"Yes, you said the Gulo family has some problems with you."

"They claim that we tried to force out their elder some four hundred years ago. Whether we did or didn't, it is so long past, why does it matter?" Elder Dayal snorted.

"You haven't forgotten about the terms of our deal?"

"I won't, Trader Ajeti. For your participation, we will happily admit your sons to the Willful Institute and help them into the Sixth Realm if we can. As long as my son wins this fight. With us working together, we can surely change the Dayal family's fate."

A man wearing all black armor with gold etchings walked out onto the stage. He wore a sword of blue and white at his hip.

"Rahul, I didn't think you would show up. I heard you were in hiding, that you didn't want to get caught up in all of this. There might be a clearing of the people who are using the Institute's resources without our express permission." The boy opposite wore a spellcaster's robes.

"Begin the match," Rahul said in a deep voice.

The trader and Elder Dayal watched the match intently.

"Begin!"

Rahul shot across the stage. Before the other boy could do anything, he was struck by a fist and sent off the stage.

The caster rolled to a stop, staring up into the sky as he wheezed and coughed blood.

His clan members walked out with resigned steps, forcing him to drink a healing potion before they carried him and their disgrace away.

"Trash like you should know when to step down." One could hear the sneer in Trito Gulo's voice.

Elder Dayal nodded in appreciation. "His speed is higher than before. His Strength has increased too. He didn't even draw his weapon. Kitaros's grandnephew never stood a chance. Though nothing is sure. We shall have to wait and see if he will make it all the way to the end or not," Dayal said.

"Well, I hope for our sakes that he does," the trader said.

Slowly but surely, Rahul made his way through matches. He didn't draw his sword in the first fifteen.

On his sixteenth, just two matches away from the end, he pulled out his weapon against a spear user.

He turned just enough, and the spear scraped past him. He chopped out at the spear wielder's arms. They flinched to the side.

Rahul used a movement technique and shot forward. His blade cut across the boy's chest and up his shoulder. The boy's quick reaction stopped Rahul from cutting his neck open.

"Hmm, worthy," Elder Dayal said, as if he saw the world from another standing.

Were all the children raised in the Fifth Realm as arrogant? Ajeti thought to himself as he sat next to Dayal. He was looking forward to getting the hell out of here and back to Alva. He couldn't believe they had wasted so many resources on this arrogant little shit. Born and raised in the Fifth

Realm, he was a coward. Now that he had some power, he was lashing out at everyone and expected his family to give him everything. If he ever reached the Seventh Realm, he would be even worse. At least the people who had climbed up here, although they were cutthroat, knew you couldn't trust them, unlike these mice that were little fuckers underneath it all.

Rahul Dayal made it through to the last match.

"Looks like it is Trito at the very end," Ajeti said.

"It will be best if we can cripple him, better if we can kill him. The Gulo family will rush to bring up another champion while our Rahul increases his fighting ability."

"I thought killing wasn't allowed in these matches?"

"Ah, but weapons are blind in the heat of battle, no? How can they be at fault?" Elder Dayal raised an eyebrow, a sly smile showing. "Don't worry. Your boys won't be a part of this. As long as they grow strong and work on their crafts, they will catch the eye of the teachers in the Sixth Realm. It matters more what one brings to the table than talent, don't you think? What is a talent worth if he has a talentless family?"

Ajeti forced out a laugh. "I couldn't agree more, Elder!"

Rahul pulled out his sword from the beginning.

Trito pointed his spear at the ground.

The two of them stared at each other from across the stage.

"Begin!"

Rahul dashed forward. He needed to get inside Trito's reach. His movements blurred as he used a movement technique.

Trito used a spear technique, creating sparks as his spear head ran along Rahul's blade.

Rahul and Trito separated. Rahul waved his sword, flames appearing around his sword and covering his body.

Trito's spear thrusts created air blades, narrowly missing Rahul and splitting the flames around his body. Trito's movements infused with the air, allowing him to almost glide across the stage with ease.

Rahul's weaknesses were clear as he lashed out with his blade, using

Strength to compete with technique.

The flames grew around him, fanned by Trito's wind.

Rahul dodged backward, and it gave him space away from Trito. Power surged around him. The flames that covered his body congealed and flowed up his arms. Instead of flames, they looked like red mercury.

Rahul stabbed out with his spear, and a twisting wind curled around his shoulder. It spun across and down his arm, around his sword. It drew the flames behind it. The flames burned hotter, shooting forward along the path of his sword and twisting air lance.

Trito's eyes widened as the spear of air and burning flames pierced through his armor and into his stomach. He screamed as he fell to the ground.

The crowd was quiet for a moment, then people started to clap. The pale faces from before gained some color as their gloating eyes looked over at the Gulo elders.

Ajeti watched Elder Ahgren out of the corner of his eye. She had paused with a drink right before her lips. Now she looked over to the Dayal family and raised her cup in salute.

Elder Dayal graciously held her glass up in salute as well. The two elders drank their cups, watching each other.

The Ahgren and Dayal family would get along well and grow into a great power. The Dayal family controlled a lot of Institute locations, while the Gulo family had a lot of trade connections. With the Ahgren trade connections, the Dayal family could breathe again and grow in power. All Ajeti needed to do was to make it look like the Ahgrens had killed him. Sow distrust between them. The Gulos would think the Ahgrens had plotted out the fall and death of their champion. The Ahgrens wouldn't trust the Dayals. The Dayals wouldn't trust the Ahgrens, thinking they attacked their backer. Then the other four powerful families would be sucked into power squabbles and issues.

Should make for quite a mess in the Fifth Realm training centers.

Ajeti didn't fake his smile as he drank with Elder Dayal.

34

Operations

Roska led her team through the forest. They reached a rise and lay down. They pulled formation-covered sheets over themselves that would render most sensing spells useless.

They used their different scopes to look at Aberdeen. The city had been heavily damaged. The city-wide barrier had failed long ago.

"When we passed through here last, it was the start of the fighting between the Sanem family and an alliance of the Marceola and Halberd sects. What happened since then?" Roska asked, wanting to know how much they had retained from her briefing.

"The Sanem family controlled Aberdeen and several other cities to the north. With the mountains and valleys, it was easy for them to defend and hard for others to attack. It was also hard for the Sanem family to attack them, so they focused in one area, hunting and clearing the forests, when they found a useful dungeon," one said.

She stopped them with a tap. "Who are the players, their motivations?" She pointed to another trainee.

"The Marceola sect was to the south and wanted to expand north. They were surrounded on all sides. The Halberd sect to the west is a powerful force; they have several cities over the Fourth Realm. This is just one outpost, a beachhead for them to expand."

"Good." Her eyes moved to her next victim. "What was their fight up to this point and the significance of Aberdeen?"

"The alliance took two cities and reached Aberdeen. It covers a key pass. The alliance paid a heavy price, and it took five months to take Aberdeen and push forward. Behind the city, there are growing areas for different Stamina ingredients."

"And why is that important?" Roska stared at the last member of their four-person team, not including herself.

"There aren't many areas to grow items in the north. Without the ability to grow ingredients, the sects rely on purchasing the ingredients or concoctions. If they have the option, they can get these items from groups they are allied with in the lower realms."

"Very good. Supplies are a weakness in any war. In the Ten Realms, people can move supplies through realms, and they can use auction interfaces to buy and sell items if they control a city. If that city is under attack, trading interfaces and auction houses won't work and the totems are unable to be used as well." She pointed to one of the team.

"With teleportation arrays and formations, people can still move, right?"

"That is correct, which is why the Halberd sect is winning this war." Roska looked out at the city. "Never underestimate your enemies or your allies. I want to know the force in Aberdeen: their weapons, armor, morale, civilian population, and defensive and offensive capabilities." She moved back from the group.

This was their mission now.

She got comfortable underneath a tree.

"Vuzgal, this is West Eagle One," one said into the comms channel she was tapped into.

"West Eagle One, this is Eagle's Nest, go ahead." The communications channel was permanently manned in Vuzgal, part of the communication network built by the Alvans to connect them across the realms.

To send messages across the realms, one needed to pass through the totems. Alvan traders across the different realms carried special communication devices that would collect messages and spit them out once the traders passed through the totems.

Elan's intelligence department had people who ran from realm to realm, passing sensitive information. The military, civilians, and intelligence department's communication lines operated separately, but there was overlap, making sure there were multiple communication routes.

The command center had several communication devices that allowed them to instantly know the situation outside their walls. Everyone was vetted as they had access to information on all military movements in the area, like the four special team trainee groups that were scouting out to the west, the two teams that were dungeon hunting in the Chaotic Lands, and the remaining three groups across the Fourth Realm, observing the Willful Institute's city.

There was also running commentary and information that came through Elan's people, detailing military movements through the eyes of intelligence agents who were also members of the Adventurer's Guild and the Trader's Guild that were seeded across the Fourth Realm.

"Eagle's Nest, we are in position at location one. Will update if the situation changes. Confirm."

"West Eagle One, understood. You are at location one, will update as needed."

"Eagle's Nest, that is correct. West Eagle One out." The special team trainees went silent, using their scopes and communication devices to gather and share information with one another. A group of two broke off and moved to another position.

Roska shifted her weight, finding a better spot against the roots of the tree and got ready for a long and boring scouting mission.

Domonos checked the reports coming in from the surrounding area. "Feels good to have more eyes out there," he said to the newly minted Captain Choi.

"I heard that you got the artillery platoon working on a ranging exercise," Choi said.

"I thought it was about time we updated the ranges for our mortars. Having clear arcs can never hurt."

"And it just happened to clear out an extra three hundred meters of the forest with the rifle platoons, while having the support platoon laying down trap formations?" Captain Choi's smile betrayed his amusement.

"Wanted to expand the view a bit. And the woodworkers love those materials." Domonos smiled in a way that wasn't quite a smile.

"You think they're going to attack us?" Choi's smile faded.

Domonos paused, letting out a heavy sigh and shrugged. "Frankly, I have no idea, but better to plan for it than be caught with our pants around our ankles."

"A healthy dose of paranoia keeps people alive in the Ten Realms," Choi agreed. She chuckled. "Only need to look to the west. You read the report about the fighting between Sanem and the family?"

"Some of it. The Halberd backed the Marceola sect, and they took three cities. When they reached Aberdeen, they were stretched too thin. Their supplies had to travel miles, and their people were wounded and tired. Aberdeen was built with interlocking castles, and it bled the Marceola sect.

"The other sects smelled blood in the water and were preparing to attack. The Halberd sect gave them an offer: Become part of the Halberd sect, or they would make an agreement with the other sects and leave them to be torn apart," Domonos said.

"So, the Marceola sect became part of the Halberd sect. They got seven cities while only needing to take three personally. Using the war as an excuse, they're sending the Marceola troops into Sanem's defenses. It weakens the defenses and reduces the number of loyal Marceola fighters." Choi shook his head. "Sneaky tactics."

"And just the kind that we want to use and emulate." Domonos said. "It's similar to the actions against the Willful Institute. They think they're dealing with a local guild, but they don't know how far it reaches. If we attacked them, they'd band together. Right now, it looks bad on each of the city guilds that they are losing defense contracts. At the same time, another unrelated group of traders is starting to snap up their business transactions. A hundred small attacks."

"Weaken them before the final strike." Choi grinned.

Domonos met his eyes, their shared grins cold and savage.

"Soon." Domonos checked the other reports on his clipboard. "Time to go check on the recruits and tour the city."

"The Marceola sect was looking at us when they took Aberdeen; there is a reason they attacked people outside our gates. What do you think about the Halberd sect?"

"I think it is interesting they have not traded with us and have never sent a trader over to Vuzgal. Keep an eye on them. They're not tame sheep. If they see an opening, they'll take it," Domonos warned.

"Have fun. I'll watch over the communication channels," Choi said, as he pulled out a book on gardening.

It was an Alvan book produced by alchemists and farmers. The book market was exploding in Alva, and printing presses had been stepped up so people away from Alva could learn even while traveling. If one poured water on the book, the pages would clear the words to make sure that others couldn't get the information contained within.

They were all breathing heavily. It was warm inside the ship.

There were three levels for the ship: one in the hull and two in the pyramids. Yui walked the deck of the destroyer, as the armed ships were being called. He used the hand rope strung across the boat as they were pushed from side to side. It was a jarring experience having the ground moving underneath him. A few people's stomachs had already disagreed with the swaying motion. As soon as the woodworkers were finished with the first ship, they had started training in them. Nothing replaced training, Yui found.

The weather was clear, and the waves were created by big, wooden arms on either side of the ship, pushing it from side to side.

The weapons were roughly similar to what they used already. The mana cannons used mana stones to fire. There was a readout that would tell one how hot the cannon was and when it needed to be cooled down with spells or slow down the rate of fire. The repeaters were standard weaponry. FAL look-alike emplacements acted as secondary weapon systems. They could be used in the semi-auto function, but these ones had enlarged charging handles and were belt-fed. It looked like a wooden snake that went from a metal box to the weapon system. Gears with rotating formations lined the wooden snake arm. It was much easier to make them with wood than metal. When treated, the wood was more flexible and as strong as steel back on Earth.

When activated, the gears turned, moving the ammunition from the large box on the ground to the weapons, allowing them to fire without needing to reload. Once the ammunition box ran out, they just had to move the lower section of the wooden snake to a new ammunition box.

Erik and Rugrat had passed on as much knowledge as they could to the Alvans. At this point, they were making multiple advancements all on their own.

Yui was proud of what his people were able to do.

For them to come back to having the entire dungeon under our control...
Yui stood straighter as the boat shook again, tilting wildly.

People panicked.

"Right side!" Yui yelled.

They shifted their weight, and the ship hit the water again. Water came in through the open gun ports to swearing from the now-soaked gunners.

Some had fallen over with the wet floor and the chaotic movement, but they were getting back up or others were helping them.

His sharp eyes looked over the groups. They were recovering a lot faster than they had before; they were quickly loading their weapons and going through the motions without actually firing them. Senior sergeants would call out orders for different gun teams, so they needed to react differently.

Staff sergeants controlled half the deck's flank guns, and a lieutenant controlled all the guns on one side of the deck.

These different layers allowed them to watch for different threats and break up fire control and regain it as needed.

As a leader, Yui could see how beneficial a chain of command like this could be.

He passed a group clearing a stoppage. The two-person gun team worked as a singular unit. As they pulled the feed from the gun, empty rounds started to pour out.

"Turn off the damn formation!" a sergeant yelled, spotting the issue before Yui could say anything.

The two chastised themselves and worked harder to show they weren't idiots. They slammed the weapon system back together and started "firing."

"Cease fire! Cease fire!" The call came from abovedeck and filtered down. Everyone stopped what they were doing and calmed down.

"Endex!" another call went out.

"Unload weapons, clear hatches!" a sergeant called out.

"Clean up your area of any obstacles. Make note of what you dropped!" another called out.

Hatches opened, revealing the outside.

They were in the largest pond on the Alva floor. The floor was growing bigger to fit in more housing and industry. They were already three-quarters of the way to the barracks and beast stables.

Pillars of fused rock dotted the area, supporting the ceiling above.

The "pond" was part of a small river that ran around the city. Its banks turned into a park for people to rest in.

Around the main pond, there were some people watching. A dock that moved pleasure craft for people to sail around in had been taken over by the army. There were tents along the shore to support training.

"Well, needs must, I guess," Yui muttered, staring at the mooring lines connecting the ship to the shore. Two platoons had been hauling on the ropes randomly from each side of the pond, creating chaos inside the ship's hull.

"Well, it's a good workout," Second Lieutenant Sun Li said.

"Frigging tug-of-war, and we're in the middle." Yui smiled.

Li snorted and shrugged.

Smaller boats made their way to the ship, and soldiers disembarked. Once they were ashore, the next group boarded the ship.

Glosil was on the shore. He snuck out of a tent and saw Yui.

"Sir." Yui snapped off a salute. The group with him came to attention.

"Captain." Glosil returned the salute and indicated for Yui to follow him.

Yui waved the group off and walked with Glosil.

"Pretty magical how two officers makes everyone want to hide," Glosil said dryly.

"Ah, yes, and you weren't hiding in that tent so your arm wouldn't go numb from saluting everyone coming ashore?" Yui asked.

Glosil smirked, letting out a chuckle. "How are we looking?"

"We'll need some more time. We have the weapon systems sorted. Getting used to the movement is the main issue. We still have people losing their lunches."

"You have three weeks. Gives them a goal to strive toward. We'll have another talk then," Glosil said.

"What about the Willful Institute?"

"We haven't seen them doing much of note recently. They're annoyed, but they probably don't know who is attacking them or that they're even being attacked."

"That will change, one way or another," Yui said.

"Yes, it will. The situation is fluid. Plan is to operate within the Adventurer's Guild. Domonos with a mix of close protection details from his Dragon Company and your Tigers Company will act as command and control. The spine of the Adventurer Guild's offensive. Over time, more will be turned over to the guild. While Domonos leads that front, you will be in charge of defense."

"So, training, drills, and managing Alva and Vuzgal."

"You got it. Also, rotate forces to the front as needed, if Domonos needs help or one of our groups. You'll be the one coordinating and sending people out."

Yui paused, and Glosil stopped walking to look back at him.

"Commander, I feel I need to say that we're spread thin."

Glosil turned from Yui and looked out over the open barracks. New walls and training areas were being erected. The first barracks was nine times its original size, and two more barracks were being erected near the totem and the teleportation pad.

"The other kingdoms are eyeing King's Hill Outpost. More roads connect it to the surrounding outposts every week. Vuzgal is a prize that any sect would want to have. Alva is hidden for now, but if others were to find out about it, then who knows what they might do? Then we're poking the Willful Institute with the Adventurer's Guild and Trader's Guild. And then the Stone Fist sect wouldn't have forgotten that we might have been the reason for their ice empress leaving, slapping their faces and pissing off one of the larger factions inside the Stone Fist sect." Glosil sounded tired. "The Ten Realms has never been a quiet or peaceful place. One has to fight to earn their place here. There will come a time that we need to fight. For now, we just need to make sure that we're as ready as we can be."

"More training." Yui glanced at Alva taking the living floor in. "We're going to double the number of basic courses. We have the applicants; our bottleneck is turning them from recruits into soldiers."

"You know, sometimes I still can't believe all of this is real." Yui sighed.

"You should probably sleep more," Glosil said with a sideways glance and a grin.

Yui snorted and shook his head.

Glosil stared at Alva beyond the growing walls. "Don't worry, there's plenty to do after you take the Water floor."

"The Willful Institute crossed the bottom line of the Adventurer's Guild. They attacked Erik and Rugrat in the past. If we exist, they cannot. One way or another, we will tear them apart." Glosil sighed. "We need to show our strength. There are people eyeing Vuzgal. If we defeat the Willful Institute, we not only remove a thorn in our side, we gain capital and position. We affirm our position, sending a warning to those who are thinking of attacking us."

"You don't think the guild can handle this by themselves? Won't we expose the fact that they're part of us?"

"I don't think the Willful Institute will be able to deal with it all. They are a powerful group—don't get me wrong—but they're split right now. But once united, they'll be strong. We need to hit them before they have time to pull themselves together. We will show our hand in the guild, but there are plenty of forces that control guilds and groups of different kinds. Showing that we have hidden cards and that one of them has become powerful will look good for us and warn others. We have the ability to raise an army, a guild, and Expert crafters—not too bad," Glosil said.

"Taking the Water floor isn't about taking the floor. We need to secure our rear lines, our home, before we attack externally." Yui glanced over to Glosil for confirmation.

He nodded and cleared his throat. "Once we have taken the Water floor, we'll deploy army units to assist the Adventurer's Guild against the Willful Institute. It is time to put our new units and training to use."

"Aditya? Hey, Aditya."

Lord Aditya snorted, startled, and began to stir. *Huh, why am I—huh?*

He sat up, waking violently. An overload of information and his lack of sleep had caused him to fall asleep on an information book. He peeled a scroll off his face, staring at Evernight.

She tilted her head, and he wiped his face. He'd gotten used to her presence and took some moments to wake up properly.

"You do have a bed, you know," Evernight said.

Aditya shrugged. "I do? Huh." He'd been using his couch to sleep when he could.

Constructing King's Hill Outpost was a full-time job. Over three-quarters of the outposts allied with them had a connecting road now. Traders coming from across the First Realm and even some from the Second had showed interest. As Yao Li from the Trader's Guild had said, there were a lot more traders than Aditya thought there would be. Their wares would cause interest in the Second Realm. Powerful items, such as the mana barrier formation that covered Vermire and King's Hill Outpost, weren't dealt with publicly.

"I heard that the first army is out and patrolling the outposts and roads. The second army should be finished training soon as well," Evernight said.

"Yes. The biggest problem has been the relocation. To make sure there are no old influences in the occupied outposts, we kicked out several supporting families, banning them from coming back to the Beast Mountain Range for ten years. We have been shuffling people between outposts so that the different factions and groups are broken up. Instead of helping with our money issue, it's been costing us more." Aditya sighed.

"Don't worry about that," Evernight said.

Aditya felt the mana density in the room increase. He felt alert; his body relaxed as his five mana gates opened, and he drew in the surrounding mana hungrily.

Evernight tossed a mana stone in her hand.

He had seen Mortal mana stones before, but this was clearer and the mana denser.

"Is that an Earth mana stone?" His voice caught in his throat.

"Yes, though it will be hard for you to use here." Evernight passed him a storage ring.

He checked inside and saw it was filled with gems and jewels, from cut to uncut.

"We have a whole bunch of these from acquiring another piece of land. With your contacts, it should be easy enough to turn this into liquid funds, no?" Evernight smiled and put the mana stone on the desk. "For you to cultivate with."

He couldn't estimate how much was in the ring, but staring at the Earth mana stone, his eyes went wide. It was worth one million gold. Such an item was simply too extravagant.

"Don't worry, there are plenty more where that came from. Literally could rain from the sky, though that would suck. So, how are things going here?"

She dropped down into the chair opposite his. She wore the emblem of King's Hill Outpost but wore rough traveling clothes.

"We have expanded rapidly. There are thirty thousand people within King's Hill. Every day, we have several dozen trading caravans moving to and from King's Hill, trading at the outer outposts and beyond. Several people have sent messages looking to create alliances or to threaten us. Well, all of them are threatening us. They offer us an agreement, but they see we are facing difficulties or will in the future, so they are looking to snap up our outpost for cheap. Crafters and healers have appeared from *somewhere* and are setting themselves up in King's Hill. I've given them all the assistance I can provide. Some of them came with plans for crafting workshops, and we are building those now," Aditya said.

Evernight smiled at the mention of the crafters and healers.

"Good. It seems that you are developing well. Focus your efforts on King's Hill. If others attack, the outer outposts can flee and pull back. Small parties will find it easy to move through the Beast Mountain Range. An army? Well, they'll piss off every animal around," Evernight said.

"Are we going to be attacked?"

"Maybe?" Evernight shrugged.

"I wish you weren't so cavalier about it all." Aditya sighed, and he felt his heartburn acting up.

"My employers are interested in controlling the Beast Mountain Range, nothing more. Alva wants to trade and recruit capable, loyal people. That is it. Now, if something threatens the Beast Mountain Range, truly threatens it, there are plenty of things they can do. I'm not sure, but just one team could probably destroy a country without the subterfuge they used to make the Zatan Confederation collapse."

It was too clean and well-timed to be anything but. It has been some time, but to destroy a country out in the open without exterior help… Were they more confident in their power or did they just not want to lose their investment here?

"Keep up the good work. Reinforce the outer outposts but keep building King's Hill. The greater benefits you have to the other powers and the harder you are able to fight, the less willing they will be to attack you."

"What about this Adventurer's Guild?" Aditya asked.

"They're a good group; they'll help if you need it."

"I heard they that adventurers can go to higher realms through them?" Aditya asked.

"I've heard the same." Evernight raised an eyebrow.

Aditya closed his mouth and cleared his throat. "So, the guild?"

"Is an *internal organization.*"

He had gained some trust, but there were still things he didn't know about his mysterious masters or the people who worked for them. He nodded and didn't press for more information.

"They should be able to exert greater control over the mercenaries and other fighting groups in the outposts. If people want to join their ranks and go to the higher realms, they need to prove themselves."

"If they survive. With all the recent activities in the Beast Mountain Range, the beasts have increased in Strength and numbers. They're stronger than before."

"Is that an issue for your traders?"

"Only for the road-building crews. We increased the number of fighters protecting them, and we haven't had too many issues. Pan Kun is using it as a training opportunity. We're quickly getting some of the highest level guards out there. Though, many of the fighters are looking at the guards and the Adventurer's Guild, between the choice of staying here for the rest of their lives and being under our command or heading to the higher realms and having greater freedom. I don't know if having the Adventurer's Guild will be a good or a bad thing," Aditya said, voicing his true concerns.

Evernight pulled out a piece of paper. "This is from the leader of my people." She put it on the table.

Aditya stared at it and then back at Evernight, unconsciously asking her permission to open it.

She chuckled and waved for him to get on with it.

He opened the letter and read the contents. His expression turned serious. "So, the leader of your people is interested in recruiting from the guard ranks, picking out those who have proven their loyalty, and giving them complete training, not just the training they received before we took the outposts?"

"That's pretty much the way of things. They will be offered an opportunity to go to the higher realms and learn more about crafting and other skills they wouldn't have had access to before. Which means that you can keep pulling in recruits, and you'll have a group of guards who, if you come under attack, will return to assist you and be much more powerful, possibly as strong as people in the Fourth Realm."

They would lose some of their best guards if they did this. Their roots would still be here, though, and if they were ever under threat, they could get their help. It would also bind them more closely to this mysterious power. Some of their guards would remain, and they could train the new recruits coming in.

"If we come under attack, what will our masters do?" Aditya asked.

"Depends, really. Every situation can have a different solution."

"What if it is something that we can't deal with, that we'll be destroyed for?" Aditya pushed.

Evernight's playful smile faded, and she looked up at the ceiling.

"No one in the first three realms should be able to threaten you. The Alchemist Association has no interest. Those in the higher realms have better resources than what can be found in the first two realms, and it wouldn't make sense for them to come down here. A group that is too powerful or too large would make us act. King's Hill and Vermire allow us a direct connection to the outside world. Through you, we have had fifteen thousand people join our ranks, and you are sending more every day. You have effectively created a shadow city. A city that we can exert power through into the First Realm. We have placed a lot into this endeavor. If something comes along and threatens the Beast Mountain Range, we can still disappear. We would take all of those we could who were innocent or loyal and place them under our direct protection. If the power learns of us, though, well, we can't very well just hide. At that time, you'd see the true power of my people."

Aditya felt the weight in her gaze.

"Thank you," Aditya said, feeling relieved. He didn't want to seem like just another outpost lord trying to save his own skin, but everything he had was on the line: all of his people, his guards, all that he had made. When he started, it was to accrue power and spit in the eyes of those who had pushed him down or to the side because of his injuries. He'd become attached to the people around him and couldn't insulate himself from them all. Although King's Hill was a large undertaking, the reason his people in Vermire hadn't become a problem was because he had supported them for so long, and now they supported him. A large portion of the people in King's Hill were from Vermire.

"So, how are the numbers looking for the market? I heard you've been making a large profit, and that the first auctions went well. People were talking about them on my travels. Some were calling it an unofficial meeting of the outpost lords as they managed to create a bidding war among themselves." Evernight smiled again.

"I wish they wouldn't make such a show in public. We have private auctions for the items that we don't want to put on the public market, but they're traders and fighters to the bone!"

Their conversation had a relaxed tone as Aditya reported on Vermire, King's Hill, and the rest of the Beast Mountain Range.

Qin and Julilah were in the Vuzgal Library. It was packed with people and supervised by librarians who drifted around the building. People joked that if the Vuzgal Defense Force were defeated, all it would need was someone stepping into the library and raising their voice for the attacking force to be defeated.

The librarians spent their time caring for the library, but in their spare time, they traded insights into what they had learned.

By themselves, they were powerful combat Experts. When they had learned of combat techniques, they had created a whole section of how people could create new combat techniques and all the techniques they had created.

Many of them were part of Tanya's new school of pure magic. Like crafters, they spent an inordinate amount of time figuring out the combination of different elements with the infusion of mana that combined to create a spell.

Julilah jotted down a note on her pad of paper and sat back in her chair. "That should work," she muttered.

Qin had her eyes screwed up, trying to mentally picture the formation that she was thinking of creating. She drew out partial sketches, focusing on different parts.

Julilah made some more notes, staring at the gathered information, and waited.

Qin finished sketching and studied the interlinking runes and circles that would create the formation. "Ugh, too many damn linking circles. Going to be a big power loss," Qin grumbled.

"Qin, what if we made a power formation and then added formations to it?"

"We already have that," Qin said.

"Yes, but with component formations, you can, say, have one formation that is a mana barrier and another that adds in, buffing the people in the area of the mana barrier. With an attack formation, you can have a formation that summons a flame; you add in another and the flame becomes a fireball, then another, and you can direct where the fireball attacks. Where does the power come from?"

"The first formation, and right now, the base can have three other formations to support the original or add another effect like buffing people in its range. Beyond that, and the power is too much. Why?"

"My formations are much smaller, and I'm reaching a power ceiling with my current materials. I can change materials and the power would increase, but it would hit that ceiling again in the future. I wondered if there was a way to boost the base formations that aren't that flexible," Julilah said.

"Basically, a reusable spell scroll. Power it up again and use it all over, as long as it's not damaged." Qin nodded.

"Yeah, so I took another route: amplification formations." Julilah leaned forward, getting heated about the topic.

"Formations to amplify the spells cast inside them?" Qin nodded. She'd made several of them herself, for the defense of Vuzgal and key supplies for the Alvan army. All peak crafters who received the benefits of Alva were requested to make High tier supplies to support the military. She and Qin had made several amplification formations, tied into the mana-storing formations at Vuzgal and Alva.

"I reviewed our notes on the formation sockets. The power component is usually the first to burn out or deform until the formation can't be used. They have to be inlaid perfectly and not cross any of the controlling circles or runes, or they might diverge and turn into scrap. Like the rifles and weaponry of the army, what if we were to plug in controlling formations into a power formation?" Julilah looked at Qin with expectant eyes.

"It should work." Qin glanced at the desk, not seeing it as she organized her thoughts. "So, yes, having a formation as the power source and using formation sockets to direct that power would work. Still, the effect would be limited by the formation socket."

"What if it was a power formation as the base and we linked in amplifications?" Julilah's breath was heated, staring at her friend.

Qin frowned, her eyes tracking left and right. "I...I don't see a problem with it." Qin smiled. "With that kind of formation, our mages could use it. Crafters could use it, as well, to have greater control over their spells. Then, if they plug in a formation socket, it turns from amplifying their spells to another type of formation. Go from hurling meteors to plugging in a healing formation socket. What if we could combine that with the armor the army wears? Wait, where are you going?"

"Formations to make and theories to test out!"

"You! Wait up!" Qin yelled and ran after her.

Someone cleared their throat, and the two of them saw a librarian frowning at them and glaring at the books they had left on the table.

The two girls glanced at each other and meekly bowed their heads to the librarian. They went back to the private room to tidy away the books and put them on the cart to be re-shelved.

The librarian smiled and walked on peacefully. Even the librarians had a high mana cultivation. She should focus on that after this next formation.

Qin and Julilah quickly shuffled out of the library, making sure to not make too much noise. Once they were outside, they broke into a run, racing toward the formation workshops.

35

Raiding Orcs

The stalls were quiet compared to the month and a half the group had spent healing countless people.

Rugrat cracked his back as he looked at the smithy he had practically lived in the entire time, repairing and creating weapons.

He hit his mug of beer against Erik's before they both tapped the mugs on the table and took deep drinks.

"Looks like things are turning out for the better now. Even for the crippled people you and the rest of the team healed. Some created groups and stood on the walls, killing beasts and leveling up," Rugrat said.

"Once everyone got into a rhythm, it got easier. Six damn weeks, though." Erik drank his own beer. He opened and closed his free hand, sending healing spells into it and his arm.

"They are hauling in the bodies of the beasts and cutting them up. Traders will swarm here soon enough; people might start asking questions about us," Rugrat said.

"Time to leave?"

"I think so," Rugrat said.

The two of them drank their beers, taking their time.

Erik turned the mug in his hand, staring at its contents. "Three days? Get everyone rested and ready."

"Makes sense to me," Rugrat said. "What about our reward?"

"Five percent of the total haul? Get it in cash."

"You know they'll shortchange us."

"I know, but do we need mana stones that badly?" Erik drank from his mug again.

"Try to get ingredients and materials from them as well. Sure, we can grow a lot of stuff down below, but it's just lying around up here."

"You have a point, Rugrat. All right. We'll get it in resources, and everything else in mana cornerstones if we can."

Three days later, Erik, Rugrat, and their special team snuck out of their inn under the cover of night with their gear hidden under cloaks.

"Night" was a relative term. The glowing plants and crystals that lit up the city didn't stop; although, the light formations were dimmed so people could have something close to a normal sleeping schedule.

Compared to the system in Alva, it was unremarkable.

"We're clear." Storbon jogged back from the alley entrances.

Lucinda watched the entrance with her beasts, making sure that no one was following them or could enter the alley.

"Helmets on," Erik said.

"Badass." Rugrat grinned as he pulled his helmet on.

"As long as it's not part of that kickass set you made me." Erik shifted his cloak so it wasn't hiding his body armor anymore and he could move his arms freely.

They pulled on the helmets. They were a new build that covered their entire heads. The helmet had no eye slots, making them look like faceless killers. Formations like the screens used in Vuzgal allowed them to see outside the helmet with a small limit to their vision. Another formation controlled the environment inside the helmet, keeping it from getting too hot or cold and pumping in more air. It would also purify the air if they were attacked with poison.

Commander Helmet MK2	
Defense:	387
Weight:	4.5 kg
Charge:	10,000/10,000
Durability:	100/100
Slot:	Takes up helmet slot
Innate Effect:	Increase defense by 5%
Socket One:	*Vision Projection*—See through helmet's armor.
Socket Two:	*Clean Air*—Air is cleaned and temperature regulated.
Requirements:	
Agility 42	
Strength 42	

"Feels like I'm a modern knight." Rugrat's voice reached their ears through the built-in comms.

Erik smirked.

"This is badass," Yao Meng said to the laughter of others, saying what Erik was thinking.

Erik adjusted his gloves.

Tropic Thunder	
Defense:	157
Weight:	1.8 kg
Charge:	1,000/1,000
Durability:	100/100

Slot:	Takes up glove slot
Innate Effect:	Stores blood energy
Socket One:	*Blood Drinker*—Consume blood from opponents to increase attacking power.
Socket Two:	*Mana Strength*—Increase the power of mana spells/attacks.
Requirements:	
Agility 41	
Strength 51	

He kept the Tropic Thunder gloves. He had not put them to proper use yet, and with the ability to change sockets, he had just changed the second socket. With access to hundreds of Earth mana stones, restoring the power in his armor was easy, so he had increased his offensive capabilities.

Erik checked the rifle in his hands.

MK7 Semi-automatic Rifle (FAL)	
Damage:	Unknown
Weight:	4.25 kg
Charge:	10,000/10,000
Durability:	100/100
Innate Effect:	Increase formation power by 12%
Socket One:	*Punch Through*—Penetration increased by 10%
Socket Two:	*Supercharged*—Increase bullet's velocity by 12%
Range:	Long range
Attachment:	Underbarrel Grenade Launcher
Requires:	7.62 rounds
Requirements:	
Agility 53	
Strength 41	

The requirements didn't change from the MK1 Marksmen rifle. The rifle used the same round as the marksman rifle, so the forces that one had to deal with were the same. If there were a different round type, the requirements would increase or decrease. This allowed the High level fifties and people from the lower realms to use the weapon accurately; although, the recoil might be too much for them to handle and they'd lose accuracy, meaning they couldn't use the full power of the weapon.

The formation masters had improved and updated the formations; one only needed to pop them out and put in updated versions.

Erik checked the underbarrel grenade launcher.

Underbarrel Grenade Launcher	
Damage:	Unknown
Weight:	1.4 kg
Charge:	1,000/1,000
Durability:	100/100
Innate Effect:	Increase formation power by 5%
Socket One:	*Supercharged*—Increase projectile's velocity by 7%
Range:	Medium to long range
Requires:	40mm Grenade shell
Requirements:	
Agility 65	
Strength 42	

"Rugrat, do you know why the Agility required for the grenade launchers is so high?" Erik asked.

"Well, grenades are larger, heavier rounds. An MK-19 is a destructive force of awesome, but it coats the impact area in explosives. A machine gun creates a cone of fire. The rifle's barrels are dialed in, so they have a tighter grouping to be accurate; it's easier than being on target with a grenade launcher. The higher Agility means you need a higher control over your body to reduce the sway, so when you're shooting long distances, your grenade hits where you want it to hit. Agility isn't just about reacting to attackers and getting on target; it's about accurately getting on target. Agility takes care of aiming; Strength takes care of the recoil. The two work hand in hand to make you lethal as shit," Rugrat said. "I think."

Erik opened the grenade launcher, checked that the shell was in there, and then pulled it back, verifying that it was locked in place.

Erik checked their stats as well.

Grenade Launcher	
Damage:	Unknown
Weight:	5.8 kg
Charge:	1,000/1,000
Durability:	100/100
Innate Effect:	Increase formation power by 10%
Socket One:	*Enhanced Shot*—Power of the round's formation increased by 10%
Socket Two:	*Supercharged*—Increase bullet's velocity by 12%
Range:	Medium to long range
Requires:	40mm Grenade shell
Requirements:	
Agility 65	
Strength 42	

"You know, one of the cool things with being this strong, instead of using standard grenade rounds, we went with the larger rounds that are used in Mark 19s." Rugrat laughed to himself and shook his head.

"Mark 19s can reach out to like two kilometers away. While we can't really get all that range, we can get close to it. The formation rounds are much more powerful than the Earth counterparts. We don't need the complicated firing system; it just has a certain number of spins, arming the formation, and then 'boom.'"

"I was wondering why this thing kicked like a mule, even with our higher Strength," Erik said.

The others in the special team finished their checks.

"Good to go?" Storbon asked everyone. They all held up their hands, giving the "okay" signal.

He glanced over to Erik and Rugrat.

"Let's go orc hunting," Erik said. "We're in your hands, Sergeant."

Storbon nodded. He quickly organized everyone. They put their weapons back in their storage rings exiting the alley.

After a short walk, they reached the gates. The area was busy, with more people heading out into the unknown, looking to find riches.

The guards glanced at the group but didn't say anything.

Once the city disappeared behind, them and the forest closed in, they moved into the forests and broken landscape.

Out of sight from the roads, they removed their cloaks, revealing their armor and fatigues. They retrieved and checked their rifles, looping the slings around their necks.

George and Gilly expanded to their full size. The special team took their mounts out of storage. They helped their beasts into their armor and mounted their dual repeaters on their back.

George and Rugrat took off in a cloud of smoke, flying well above their heads. Lucinda's flying beasts spread out to cover the area.

"Mount up!" Storbon ordered.

The group moved up one hand on their heavy ballistas as they headed into the dungeon's forest.

"Watch out, you've got a group of roaming beasts to your right. Circle around to the left and you'll miss them," Rugrat said through their comms, watching the situation.

They followed his guidance.

"Group up ahead. Big creatures—won't be able to evade them. Grenade coming in."

They kept riding. A few hundred meters ahead of them, an explosion went off. Pained roars could be heard, and the group on the ground, riding in an arrowhead formation, scanned the forest around them.

Rugrat used his formation-engraved silencer, dropping wandering beasts without a sound as they advanced.

They reached the series of caves where creatures half the size of their panthers rushed out. The area was covered in rot; mushrooms and fungus grew over the surrounding area, and some rare species grew within the caves.

The beasts' skin had mottled greens, yellows, and purples, looking like moving fungus. They had several tongues, four limbs, and a tail with spikes.

"Yuli, Fire spell!"

The others opened fire with their repeaters. The bolts hit the creatures, and they cried out in pain. Their bodies released spores into the air and covered the ground in black blood.

The air was thick with spores.

A spell formation appeared in front of Gilly's mouth as she fired ice and Earth spears. Erik's rifle cracked killing a fungal creature, more pushed past their fallen. They took several hits from the repeaters to fall. Erik was using standard rounds, and although it took a few shots to the body to kill the annoying creatures, one hit to the head was enough.

Rugrat continued to provide covering fire from above and scanned the area, checking to see whether other creatures or people had been attracted by the sounds of fighting.

Yuli finished casting her spell. An orange spell formation appeared in the middle of the hazy area. The ground trembled as the runes rotated and the circles moved within one another.

The caves lit up, and the ground shifted upward.

The ground exploded, sending rocks flying. Magma poured out of the ground like a fresh spring and fell on the fungal creatures.

Yuli's spell was the spark; the fungus ignited in a blinding flash. The formations on the helmet could see through the darkest nights and the brightest days; even staring right at it, they could still see.

They held onto their mounts as the explosion uprooted trees and tossed boulders.

Magma rained down from above and rose through the caves. Beasts fled in a panic, the magma chasing them out of their homes.

The group stopped firing and kept riding, staring at the destruction left in their wake as the molten lava bubbled and spurted, burning away the last of the creatures.

"Looks like we won't be getting that loot," Tian Cui said.

"Be a bit warm," Yao Meng said.

"How are we looking, Rugrat?" Storbon asked.

"Should be good. I don't see anyone rushing over. Best to get a move on. We're halfway to the camp. Do we want to go back and get the loot?"

"I'm not stripping down in the nude in a dungeon to go lava spelunking," Erik muttered. "It's probably destroyed by the lava anyway."

"I'll do it! I've got that Fire Body now!" Rugrat nearly jumped off George in excitement.

"No!" several voices said at once.

"You're just jealous!" Rugrat huffed with heavy sass.

Under Rugrat's guidance, they only ran into a few more bands of creatures.

When they were some kilometers away from the orc camp, they grouped together at the base of a hill. Rugrat, Storbon, and Yao Meng went up the hill to check the terrain and the camp while the others checked their gear and drank some water.

Rugrat crouched as he moved slowly before lowering himself to the ground between a tree and a boulder. Storbon moved to his right while Yao Meng was on the other side of the boulder.

The three of them used different spells as they scanned the area between them and the camp. They used their comms systems, making it impossible for others to hear them.

"Roving patrols, just like the people in Kuldir said there would be," Storbon said.

"Spaced out and random. If we rush in, they can alert one another," Yao Meng said.

"We'll need to lure them away. There's no way of knowing if they have a way to communicate with other groups. We'll have to test as we go—pull a group, hit them, and be ready to run. If we get pinned down by multiple groups, we're screwed," Rugrat said. "We thin out their patrols, see how they react. If we can clear out the patrols, we can look at hitting the camp. I count seven patrols."

"I have nine. There are others in the distance," Storbon said.

"We can use a Detect Life spell on them," Yao Meng said.

"There was a high-powered shaman in the camp. Orcs might be dumb, but they are an intelligent species. They know how to coordinate. Shamans are a bit smarter; don't want to risk them detecting it," Storbon said.

They checked their maps and noted where the different patrols were and watched their paths.

"Look, another patrol is coming out," Rugrat said.

The gates of the camp opened. Several large furred beasts with their own tusks and scars moved on all fours. The orcs used whips to move them as they pulled cages made from bones.

"Shit, there are people in those cages," Rugrat said.

The bone carriages rolled forward, pulled by the boars. Orcs marched with them, following a road that curled around the camp and headed into the orcs' territory.

"People did say that orcs kidnapped people to use as offerings to their gods and as food. They think consuming the flesh of strong opponents will make them stronger," Storbon said.

"Shit," Yao Meng said.

Rugrat agreed with him.

Orcs were little more than beasts, but seeing this systematic collection and processing of humans, Rugrat's blood chilled. "We'll wipe them off the damn map."

They took their time watching the groups.

"If we use that ravine there with a couple of formations to stop any sound from coming out and ambush them from the sides, we should be able to take out one patrol without much trouble." Storbon outlined his plan.

"How do we lure them?" Rugrat asked.

"Food? Raw meat should do it, if we kill some beasts and put them in there," Yao Meng said.

"Why food?"

"They smell the air all the time. I've seen some of them hunt down small beasts. Each time they get a beast, there is a fight over the meat. So, they're meat-eaters, they have a strong sense of smell, and they're hungry, seeing that they're fighting over scraps," Yao Meng explained.

"Good observation," Rugrat said. "Storbon?"

"You think you could kill a creature and bring it back here with George to bait the trap?"

"Only too easy," Rugrat assured him.

"Then I think we have a plan. Let's go tell the others. Yao, stay up here and keep watch. Yell if something happens," Storbon said.

"Got it, boss."

The two others slid back from the tree line, got in a crouch, and headed back down to the group at the bottom of the hill, who were fanned out watching the forest.

They shared what they had seen and their plan moving forward.

They got to work while Rugrat went off to find a bait beast.

Using George's sense of smell, they found a large beast with mean-looking tusks.

Rugrat checked the silencer on his rifle, an attached piece of metal with a Silence spell, powered up the formations, and fired.

The round went through the beast's eye and into its brain. It was dead before it hit the ground.

Rugrat checked the area with his different Sight spells.

Seeing nothing coming their way, he ran over to the beast. It was larger than George, and George grabbed it by the neck. With a flap of his wings, he got it off the ground and headed toward the ravine. Rugrat followed on foot, covering George.

When they reached the ravine, the ambush was set. They had picked a ravine that was sealed on one end. It was thin enough that only three humans could walk beside one another before it opened into a bowl. Water dropped down from some unknown source and into an underground river.

The special team had scaled the sides of the ravine, finding ledges and firing positions, or making them by using their Strength to shift rocks or using spells to alter the surroundings.

Yao Meng and Tian Cui were on heavy repeaters that they had positioned to watch the entrance. Lucinda was scouting. The others were laying down formations that would stop any signal or noise coming from the ambush.

They were just finishing off as Erik placed explosives along the walls as a last resort.

All of them had secondary firing positions prepared and escape routes.

"We're all set. How are we looking, Lucinda?" Storbon asked.

"Got a patrol three hundred meters away. If we splash some blood over the place, they should pick it up," Lucinda said.

"Get to your positions," Storbon said.

George dropped the beast on the ground and began to shrink as he headed towards Rugrat.

Rugrat climbed up the ravine to the shooting position Erik had prepared for him.

Storbon checked everyone and then signaled to Erik.

Gilly screeched and stomped. Earthen spears pierced through the beast, spraying blood over the area.

They waited, hoping the smell of blood would draw the orc patrol.

"Looks like they're coming this way!" Lucinda said via their comms. "Should be here in a few minutes. Group of fifteen."

The orc group grunted and hit one another as they made no attempts to hide their presence.

They bunched up in the skinny passage, scanning the area and smelling the air.

They were a man-and-a-half tall with bulging muscles covered in grime and scars, two tusks jutting out from their lips. They wore animal hides that had turned greasy and dirty. Their weapons were clubs they had crafted themselves, rough metal cleavers, and a few used rusted swords that would have been a two-handed weapon in a human's hands.

They advanced, cautious but unworried, confident in their own power.

"There are some hanging back. Wait for them to enter too," Lucinda warned.

The leading orcs checked the area and then let out roars, rushing the beast. The others behind them yelled.

Their group devolved as they crowded the beast, tearing off chunks and eating it raw. They were more like beasts themselves as they fought one another, bloodying each other to assert dominance but not kill.

"The ones at the entrance are coming in."

Rugrat tapped the side of his rifle, moving from one orc to the next, practicing and readying himself to move from target to target, scanning the group at the same time.

Four more orcs ran in, adding to the fight.

"Activating formation," Storbon said.

There was a faint buzzing noise, and they were now isolated from the outside world.

"Fire."

Rugrat stroked the trigger. An orc fell and a tombstone appeared. He switched to his second target, firing and seeing the tombstone. His third was killed by someone else.

He killed another and then scanned, but there were no other targets and nothing was moving.

The patrol of orcs, fifteen strong, ended in a ravine just like that. Some died, still fighting one another, not realizing they had become the prey.

"I don't see any movement outside the ravine. Keeping an eye out,"

Lucinda said.

"Loot the bodies and disperse them. We'll see if we can pull in another patrol. Well done," Storbon said.

"Found what looks like a horn, some metal pieces and copper, and bone weapons," Lucinda reported.

"Clear them away. We don't need any of that," Erik said.

Lucinda guided flames over the bodies and dismissed the tombstones. The orc bodies fell apart in seconds.

"Reset it all. Let's see if we can't draw in others," Storbon said.

Like this, the team lured and killed five patrols. They changed positions occasionally, moving to different ravines or points where the orcs were forced to bunch up.

They were readying another ambush point between some low hills when a horn came from the camp.

"What is that?" Yao Meng asked.

"Nothing good." Erik scrambled up a hill, Rugrat right behind him. The two of them looked over the area around the camp and heard other horns responding to the first. They came from the direction of the other patrols.

"Shit," Erik said.

A silence fell over the area, as if they were waiting for something.

"Get ready to move," Erik said.

The group abandoned their preparations, clearing up their gear and pulling out their mounts.

The horn at the main camp called out in a different sequence. There were no responses for several minutes.

The horn sounded again in a different pattern. Rugrat watched a patrol turn and head toward the camp. "We can let them go back or hit them on the way, weaken their numbers. I'll go from the sky. If we move on our mounts, pepper them with repeaters, just weaken them, and not get into a drawn-out engagement, we should be able to take them," Rugrat said.

"Let's take down as many of them as we can now. If we wait, they'll be behind their walls. There must be at least six other patrols out there. That's ninety orcs," Erik said. "Mount up! Yao Meng, you're up front. Lucinda, call out targets. Yuli, hit them with spells to disorient. Use spell scrolls if you need to."

Rugrat and Erik moved down the rise, getting onto George and Gilly, respectively.

"Head to the southeast," Lucinda said.

They rode out on their mounts, navigating through the tortured landscape of broken trees and rocks.

"They should appear on our left-hand side after we pass this rise!"

Yao Meng was the first to see the enemy. The orcs growled and roared as Yao Meng fired his repeater. One orc tried to use his horn, but the noise was cut off suddenly.

Yuli fired out a spell, and the others peppered them with repeater bolts. Rugrat and Erik fired their rifles as Gilly shot out Water spears and George sent fireballs.

It was a one-sided slaughter. None of the orcs were left alive. Several tombstones appeared in their wake, but the team was riding away already.

"They're retreating!" Yao Meng yelled.

"Lucinda guided us to the closest group. Once they're inside the camp, they'll add to the defense."

Lucinda guided them across the ground, closing with the nearest orc patrols.

Storbon used a grenade launcher, illuminating the dungeon. Orc tombstones appeared in the blast radius.

Horns called out as the orcs spotted them. Horns in the city changed their tone; the orcs stopped trying to return to the camp and started striking out toward one another, following the sound of horns to kill the group.

"If we use their horns, we can get them to come to us," Yao Meng said.

"There is a valley to our right; we can use that," Lucinda said.

"Do it," Erik said.

They moved to the valley. Erik threw down explosives in some of the rock outcroppings, and they rode their beasts up to different vantage points, jumping off and getting into a good firing position.

They got ready as fast as possible, moving rocks around and checking their lines of sight.

"Good to go!" Yuli called out over the comms. The others did so as well.

Rugrat checked his grenade launcher and magazine, slapping it back into his rifle. "Good!"

"Yao Meng!" Storbon called out after everyone was confirmed.

Yao Meng pulled out the horn they had picked up from the destroyed patrols and blew it, matching the other calls. The baying noise covered the area.

"The other groups are coming. It looks like it is working," Lucinda said.

They waited, scanning the area, their skin itchy and their eyes wide. They could feel their hearts in their chests, and every movement was so loud in their ears that they thought the enemy would hear them.

Rugrat breathed through his nose, scanning to make sure that he didn't get tunnel vision.

"Here they come," Lucinda said.

"Let them get in closer," Erik said.

Two or three patrols snarled and growled at one another before the largest orc hit another one and roared at the others, cowing them into submission.

The orc raised his club and roared in the direction of the team. They turned their frustration into forward momentum, picking up speed as they raced one another forward, jostling each other as they came on like a herd of buffalo.

Rugrat cast spells on his rounds and rifle.

The orcs were now in range and still charging forward.

Rugrat started to get apprehensive waiting for the first shot.

Yuli sent out vines across the ground, snagging the orcs' feet; they tripped and fell.

"Fire in the hole!" Erik activated a formation. The charges he had tossed into the underbrush and the rocks nearby exploded, tearing apart the surprised orcs.

Yao Meng got onto his knee and fired his grenade launcher into any groups of orcs he could see. Rugrat fired into his targets until they dropped, shifted to the next movement, and fired again. Gilly roared, and arrows made of stone shot out from the sides of the valley, striking the orcs.

The others fired their rifles. Dust and chaos filled the area. The orcs' blue-black blood covered their bodies as they were cut down. Some raged and activated their Berserker skills, ignoring their wounds until an explosive or a round damaged their body so much that they couldn't move anymore.

"Cease fire! Cease fire!" Storbon said.

The shooting stopped, and they peeked at the group. Tombstones littered where the orc patrol had been.

"Shoot and scoot! Let's move," Storbon said.

They pulled another group using the same tactic. As the dust settled on their ambush position, the gates that were open for the orcs slammed shut. Orcs stood on the camp walls, looking out at the surrounding area.

The team gathered their gear, looting the corpses. They had some mana stones, their simple weapons, and rare ores with them, as well as orc talismans that would increase the wearer's attributes. All of their effects were weaker than the stat bonuses that the team received from their Alvan-made armors.

Rugrat went ahead of the group, scouting for them and found a rock outcropping they could camp behind and use to watch what happened in the camp.

"Check your gear. Get cleaned up and get some food into you. We'll have one person awake in the camp and two up on top of the rock observing the camp," Storbon said through his comms so his voice wouldn't carry.

Rugrat heaved himself up on top of the rock outcropping, getting on his belly. He crawled forward and moved some rocks around, clearing out a better vantage of the camp.

Using his sight-based spells, he watched the camp. The orcs were aggravated. Instead of the light-roving watchers on the wall, tens of orcs watched the surrounding area, ready and waiting for a fight.

Yao Meng tapped his leg.

Rugrat checked behind and nodded, pointing to another position on the outcropping that one could observe the camp from.

Rugrat took out his rifle, unloaded it, and used a Clean spell. *Weapon cleaning made easy.* He oiled up the weapon and loaded it again before storing it away. He studied the camp. *All right, so, how would I take it?*

Erik, Rugrat, and Storbon gathered, watching the camp together. Lucinda and Yuli were up in the observation post, while Yao Meng and Tian Cui were getting some induced sleep.

Rugrat's map lay between their feet. They had some details that had been added from passing by the camp and other details from the different maps they had purchased, rounding out the map nicely.

"They're amped up over there. Got a full guard on the walls watching everything and anything. We make a move now, and they're going to respond with all they have. We should wait till they relax, get careless, and scout out shooting positions. Everyone here has completed their sharpshooter course. We shoot and kill them; then we sneak out of our positions, mount up, and move to new locations. Wait for them to calm down again, rinse, and repeat. Reduce their numbers some more. It'll take time, but we have time on our side," Rugrat said.

"What if they get reinforcements or that carriage train comes back?" Erik asked.

"We have plenty of spell scrolls. We can use those to break them up. We could use one of the stronger spells and hit the camp with it?" Storbon said.

"Worth a shot. Didn't think of that," Rugrat admitted.

After everyone was rested and fed, they moved out in smaller groups. Rugrat was with Lucinda, Erik with Yao Meng, and Tian Cui with Storbon and Yuli.

They moved slowly, making sure they wouldn't get the attention of the orcs. It had been several hours since the orcs had returned to the camp, and already, they weren't as alert as they had been.

"This looks good." Yao Meng gestured to some boulders they could sit on.

"Let's get dug in and wait for those to get ready," Erik said.

"In position," Yuli said some minutes later.

"In position," Rugrat said shortly afterward.

"Deploying spell scroll," Yuli said.

The mana shifted. A spell formation appeared above the camp.

Cold spread through their bones, and the orcs looked up in alarm. As the spell formation gathered more power, its lines brightened and the formation became more complex.

White smoke appeared, freezing the air.

A beam shot out from the center of the formation. It broke against a mana barrier that covered the small camp.

The chilling ray washed over the sides, causing the ground to freeze and creating jagged ice crystals that shone like a field of frozen blades around the camp.

The orcs, seeing that they were protected, hooted and hollered, daring their attackers to show themselves.

The massive outpouring of mana made Erik's hair stand on edge. *Where are you?* The barrier held as he studied the camp, looking for the formation supporting it.

"Lucinda, do you have eyes on the formation?" Erik asked.

"I have a bird in the air..." She trailed off. "There is a circle of sticks in the middle of the camp. There are shamans inside it. They're glowing and chanting. I think they're creating the barrier."

"We're moving," Storbon said.

"Understood," Erik said.

"Beasts that can use mana barriers…" Yao Meng shook his head.

Erik grunted in agreement. "This day keeps getting better."

The spell scroll depleted its mana while Storbon's team repositioned themselves.

Orcs growled and struck the ice, starting to clear it.

Everyone shifted, readying themselves to test the orc defenses.

Erik shifted slightly, getting comfortable behind his weapon. His sights followed a roving orc on the camp wall.

"On my mark. Three...two...one...mark." With Storbon's order, all of them fired.

Erik's target dropped, and several other orcs fell without a sound from the silenced rifles. He switched to his secondary targets and fired again, rewarded with another spray of orc blood.

"Must be a caster if it isn't working all the time." Erik scuttled away from his firing position

A strong one to stop that spell scroll.

"Moving to fallback," Erik said. He called out Gilly while Yao Meng called out his panther mount, and they rushed off.

Erik watched the mana barrier rising around the camp again, shimmering in the low light.

The orcs yelled out and turned away from the camp. They looked ready to charge out, snarling and raising their crude weapons toward the group.

Erik and Yao Meng got to their next position.

"Looks like they want to come out and kill us. The shamans are holding them back and maintaining the mana barrier." Lucinda used her eyes from above to report what was happening.

"We could hit them with spell scrolls, drain the shamans? Keep them on alert?" Rugrat said.

"We could, but we don't know how strong they are. It could take a lot of spell scrolls. Get reset, shoot them up again, and whittle down their numbers. Get them scared to walk on the walls, then we'll see what our options are," Storbon said.

Rugrat had been on the move for a day, moving from one position to the next, waiting for the mana barrier to come down around the orc camp, hitting some more guards, and then moving again. It was tiring and grinding work, but it was wearing the enemy down.

"Looks like they're getting smart," Rugrat said on the comms channel.

"Or scared," Tian Cui added.

"Guess it's time we looked at the next option," Erik said.

There were just a couple of guards on the walls; the other orcs were all inside the camp. The head shaman had come out of his tent, assisting those in making the mana barrier, and would periodically send out attacks to where the teams had been shooting from.

"We don't know how powerful that barrier is. We know it can stop a level-three spell scroll. We don't know how long these shamans can last. If they were just using a formation, we could see its power from the runes. Creatures are harder," Yuli said.

"How many are left in there?" Storbon asked.

"Looks to be about thirty of the melee types, five shamans, and the head shaman," Lucinda said.

"Could your beasts get up close and drop off charges?" Storbon asked.

"Should be able to, now that there aren't as many guards on the wall. If we hit the guards on the wall, my beasts can get to it without being seen," Lucinda said.

"What if we use the charges, blow a hole in the wall, and at the same time pepper the place with grenades, aiming for the shamans? Maybe we hit them, and even if we don't, we have a line of sight into the camp, and we use that to shoot at the shamans."

"Sounds good to me," Rugrat said.

"Worth a shot," Erik agreed.

They waited for everything to calm down. Lucinda pulled out several of her beasts and had them take the charges toward the camp. They were quick and small, making it hard to see them as they snuck in close.

She guided them personally as they got closer.

"Bomb carriers in position," she said.

"Three, two, one, mark," Storbon said.

Erik fired his rifle, the dust around him moving. His higher Strength handled the small recoil of the rifle easily.

Orcs dropped off the wall, and Erik and Yao Meng ran from their position.

"Bomb carriers away," Lucinda said. "Head shaman's casting a spell!"

A whirlwind appeared close to the camp. The winds screamed as it cut a path through the rock, adding it to its razor-sharp winds. It smashed through the position Erik and Yao Meng had been in moments before, eating through the rocks and churning them up.

Erik and Yao Meng hunched over their mounts, fleeing at their fastest speed. Rocks sailed overhead and hit their armor. They turned down a cut in the rocks. Their mounts' legs fought to find purchase. Yao Meng's panther ran along the stone wall of the orc camp before jumping onto the ground.

They came up out of the cut in the rocks, far away from the dying whirlwind. Their old position was now a divot in the ground as rocks fell all around.

"Bombs are in position and the carriers are coming home," Lucinda said.

The mana barrier was back up. But mana barriers, although they stopped spells and fast-moving attacks, didn't stop living creatures.

"We'll need a minute to get to our next position," Erik said.

Storbon checked his grenade launcher while staring at the camp. Lucinda had confirmed there were no prisoners in the camp, so they could go all out.

"All right, shall we kick this off?" he asked over the comms channel.

"Ready here," Lucinda said.

"Ready," Erik said.

Storbon glanced at Yuli and Tian Cui. Both of them had a six-shot grenade launcher in their hands.

"All right, blow the charges on my mark. Three, two, one, mark!"

Explosions shook the camp and the ground as the bombs the beasts planted at the base of the camp's walls went up. The wall disappeared in a wave of shrapnel, killing and wounding the orcs standing on or near the wall.

Storbon stepped out of his cover and aimed his grenade launcher, looking through the sight window, his launcher pointed nearly straight up.

He pulled the trigger, moving slightly to cover a larger area, firing as fast as he could before chucking the grenade launcher into his storage ring and pulling out his panther mount.

"Hopefully, we don't hit the ceiling," Yuli said, the last to get on her mount. Their panthers raced away from the camp as explosions fell on and inside the camp.

"Watch out!" Tian Cui said.

A crack spread from the shamans across the ground toward their position. Whirlwinds appeared outside the camp and rushed toward the other positions as well.

"Yuli, use a spell scroll. If the shamans are casting, they're not putting up a barrier!"

Yuli pulled out a spell scroll as Storbon pulled out his grenade launcher, dropping out the old shells and putting new ones in.

Tian Cui followed what he was doing. They glanced at each other and peeled away from Yuli.

Their panthers took them away from each other as they aimed and fired at the camp again.

"We've got orcs coming out of the camp. It looks like they're not playing around anymore!" Erik said. "Yao Meng and I will cover the opening."

Orcs moved out of the walls around the camp. Around twenty or so orcs were left now. Each of them was covered in a glow, and their eyes were red with madness.

"They're buffed!" Rugrat reported.

The second wave of grenades landed, striking the camp. Most of them missed anything but served to distract the shamans.

Yuli's spell scroll activated. It spread out, creating multiple formations in the sky. The wind churned up as the spell formation dragged in the surrounding mana.

The cracking ground terminated. It went off like a bomb, throwing molten rock everywhere.

Everyone ducked as lava spewed forth, covering a twenty-meter area.

"Fuck, someone forgot to turn off the damn heating!" Rugrat yelled.

Whirlwinds that had cut through several of their old firing positions, leaving divots in the ground, were canceled as the shamans rallied together, casting a mana barrier over their camp. The orcs gave in to their bloodlust and rage, and they charged out of the camp.

Erik's and Yao Meng's rifles fired. Their rounds struck the orcs, and the orcs' buffs enhanced their Agility and Strength, making them harder to track and lead and causing Erik and Yao to miss.

Yuli's spell scroll activated. A pillar of golden, cleansing light struck down, hammering the mana barrier. The impact of the attack shook the sky, throwing a wall of wind out. The wind picked-up rocks and dust and washed over a hundred-meter area around the camp.

The pillar of light kept descending. The head shaman turned back and supported the other shamans under the onslaught.

"Storbon, pull your team back! Make a second line!" Erik yelled.

He and Yao Meng were firing on automatic now, but the berserker orcs could take three or four hits before their buffs wore off.

Storbon turned and raced to catch up to Yuli. His panther weaved from side to side as the orcs grabbed rocks and hurled them.

He saw Tian Cui also racing back.

A roar shook the ground as George took to the skies. Rugrat fired his rifle from atop George as mana condensed around them into blue balls of flame that shot out at the charging orcs.

Gilly let out her High pitched clicking call, and the ground around the orcs turned into spikes. A few speared themselves on the wall; the others, using their superhuman strength, dodged the attack or jumped over it, only to be caught in George's blue flames or were shot by Rugrat.

The spell scroll finished, and there was a roar from the camp. The shamans charged out of the camp on bloodthirsty boar mounts. Larger and stronger than the ones that had pulled the carriages filled with people.

They cast spells on the orcs. A green light appeared around them, healing their wounds and bringing those that were on the brink back.

"Pull back to the choke point position," Storbon yelled. If they were caught out in the open, they would die. "Tian Cui, mount your heavy repeater!"

He pulled out his repeater and secured it onto his panther's armor. He saw Yuli come to a stop, holding her position; she waved her staff, sending out lightning and throwing up the ground in the orcs' faces to slow them.

Tian Cui and Storbon raced down the divot in the ground she was in and turned to face the enemy, their mounts below the ground but their repeaters above it.

"Covering! Get your asses moving, Erik!" Storbon yelled as they fired their repeaters at the orcs.

Erik and Yao Meng jumped on their mounts and raced back, off to the right flank of Storbon.

Rugrat and George dropped from above. Rugrat fired his grenade launcher at the shamans while George breathed fire on the charging orcs, slowing them down as they banked away, avoiding the shamans' attacks.

Storbon's team laid down covering fire. The shamans had met up with them now and were healing them from the latest attacks.

"Luc?" Storbon asked.

"I'm halfway back to the choke point!" Lucinda yelled.

Rounds and explosions hit the orcs, killing one and wounding another that was quickly restored.

"Covering!" Erik barked.

Storbon and his team turned and ran, zigzagging across the ground. The orcs were still coming with their shamans, and they were getting closer.

Rugrat circled around the rear of the group, shooting at the shamans. Chains appeared around the orcs, binding them and biting into their flesh. He dove, getting away from them again but slowing the orcs' advance.

Storbon passed Erik's and Yao Meng's position, tossing away his empty repeater magazine and securing a new one. His panther turned, facing toward the enemy again. He pulled the trigger, but the repeater failed to fire.

Yuli and Tian Cui were up and shooting. "Covering!" they both yelled.

"Moving!" Erik and Yao Meng yelled. The two of them charged back on their mounts.

Cursing in panic, Storbon's hands followed his training, clearing the repeater, reloading it, and firing.

"I'm at the choke point, putting down the traps and explosives. When coming in, Erik, your team will go right. Storbon, go left. Got it?" Rugrat said.

"My team right, Storbon left. Got it."

"Erik's team right, my team left," Storbon repeated, burning it into his mind.

"Covering!" Erik, Gilly, and Yao Meng's attacks hit the orcs, aiming at the shamans who were using them as shields, causing them to slow down.

Storbon's team started running as a whirlwind hit their position. It struck Tian Cui and her mount, sending them flying. They were cut up badly and slammed into a rock outcropping.

"Move it! I have her!" Storbon yelled. His mount rushed toward them, and he pulled out his beast storage device. Tian Cui and her mount disappeared into it as Rugrat fired into the orcs. Chains appeared around the shamans, stopping them from moving. He flew over and dropped grenades down, killing three of the shamans and wounding another. The head shaman yelled and sent a blast of lightning after Rugrat and George. They were too close to dodge properly. George turned into the hit so Rugrat wouldn't take it.

It was reduced in strength by Rugrat's domain, but it threw them back.

George dropped toward the ground.

Rugrat used Gliding Steps. He grabbed George, who was shrinking, and continued on his way down to the ground.

Storbon didn't have time to worry about George or even Tian Cui as he got to the next position.

Yuli threw out a formation plate. Her panther stood on it and channeled power into her, amplifying her spells. "Covering!" Lightning shot out of her hand, striking an orc and arcing between them. They yelled out as it got past some of their buffs, killing one and stunning four others.

"Moving!" Erik and Yao Meng yelled.

Storbon pulled Tian Cui out of the storage device and onto the ground. He pulled off the medical kit on her side. Grabbing a needle, he jabbed it into her neck and pushed the plunger. The healing and Stamina potion injected into her internal carotid pumped through her body.

Her complexion looked better already.

"Rugrat, status?" Erik asked over the comms.

"I'm heading to the choke point now," Rugrat said.

Storbon put Tian Cui back into the storage device and fired his repeater.

Blades of air cut at the orcs. The force stalled their forward charge throwing back bloody orcs, leaving mirror smooth lines in the ground.

"Covering. One more bound to the choke point! Lucinda!" Erik yelled.

"We're set up as good as we can get!"

"Moving!" Storbon and Yuli yelled as they turned and ran.

The orcs were still coming, their twenty melee fighters down to ten. They still had the head shaman and two regular shamans supporting and laying buffs on their fighters.

Now that there were fewer orcs, the shamans could increase the Strength of buffs instead of spreading it out.

Storbon and Yuli got into their fallback position. They were positioned on either side of a pass that ran through the rock.

Erik and Yao Meng raced back, moving behind them and down through the pass.

"We're through—pull back," Erik ordered.

Yuli tossed trap formations on the ground and against the wall, using a spell to hide them. She charged down the pass, and Storbon followed.

The pass went for some time before opening.

Gilly and Erik were to the right; Yao Meng climbed up the rock face beside them to a position in the rocks.

Rugrat and Lucinda were hidden in the sheer walls of the opening.

Storbon and Yuli dismounted and put their panthers away, climbing up the cliff face to the left of the opening.

Storbon pulled out his rifle and aimed at the pass. It looked like a "Y," with the pass as the bottom line. Erik and Yao Meng were on the right side, and Storbon and Yuli on the left. Rugrat and Lucinda were somewhere in between the opening at the top of the "Y" and angled up gently.

The trap formations went off, and Storbon could hear them.

"Trap formations are active. Explosive charges are ready," Lucinda said.

The orcs weren't quiet as they ran through the pass that had been carved into the ground.

"Steady," Rugrat said. "Fire on my order."

The noise increased, but Storbon was focused on the entrance to the pass moving his sight and forcing his breathing to stay clear headed.

Erik studied the opening in the pass. Gilly had used an Earth spell to make a trench for them to hide in. He had his rifle in his hands, waiting for the enemy.

An orc yelled and ran out of the pass. It made it twenty meters, and the rest of the group ran after it.

"Fire!" Rugrat fired on his selected target. Trap formations went off. Restrictive formations cut off the orcs' advance, attacks cut at their bodies, and rounds slammed into their armor and skin, draining away their buffs. The shamans at the rear cast healing spells.

Erik's head hurt as he altered his Hallowed Ground spell. The modified spell landed on the orcs. A black spell formation appeared underneath them, and a yellow haze appeared around it, attacking the orcs and draining their health.

He focused on the head shaman, who was self-buffing.

"Fire in the hole!"

Everyone ducked as the explosives in the pass and around the orcs went off.

Orcs were tossed around like sticks. The shamans were killed, crushed by rocks from the pass, the head shaman was thrown to the side, bloodied.

Three orcs were left standing.

The head shaman rose to his feet unsteadily, beginning a chant.

Blades of shadow stabbed into the shocked, shaman, raising him up.

The head shaman's eyes dulled. The chains lit up tracing runes down their length and the spell formation they rose from in the ground.

The spell exploded in a shower of light killing the three nearby orcs and removing any sign of the shaman having existed.

Suddenly, it was silent, and they stared at the pile of orcs caught in the choke point.

"Everyone okay?" Erik yelled.

They called back to him, letting him know that they were still alive and had come out of it relatively unharmed.

"All right, let's move back to rally point Echo. We'll check the wounded there. Rugrat, how is George looking?"

"He's in bad shape but alive." Rugrat's voice had none of the light joking that one might find on a normal day. He was switched on, pissed and hungry for revenge.

"Let's move. It's a few minutes' ride."

They mounted up. Rugrat jumped on the back of one of Lucinda's beasts, and they ran toward the fallback point between a ring of boulders.

"Yao Meng, get up and keep an eye out. Lucinda, have your beasts watching," Storbon said as they got into the opening.

Erik jumped off Gilly and pulled out a cot, indicating to it.

Storbon pulled out Tian Cui. She was in pain, but her eyes were open.

Erik used his domain and Simple Organic Scan, seeing all her injuries in just a moment. "Get some Stamina into her. Lots of cuts, nasty hit to the head, nothing serious. Dose with healing concoction when she's ready."

He turned to the other side. Rugrat had pulled out George. He'd injected him with a mixed potion that had more Stamina recovery than healing abilities.

Erik saw where the lightning had hit. There was a point of impact and then a ripple, like tree roots that ran through George's chest.

Erik set to work, focusing on George. He had heavy internal damage. His heart was struggling and not pumping correctly. He had deep cuts that were partly cauterized.

Rugrat tore himself away, finding it hard to look at his mount. He pulled out his rifle. "I'll help keep watch with Yao Meng."

Storbon nodded. Rugrat needed to be away from George; being there wouldn't help him. Keeping him distracted and focused on something else would make it better for them all.

Rugrat climbed up onto the rocks while Erik worked on George and checked on Tian Cui periodically. He didn't need to leave George, just extend his domain.

It took several minutes for him to heal the life-threatening damage to George.

"Tian Cui took a nasty hit to the head, but she will be fine. George will need time to recuperate, but he's good for now," Erik said on the comms channel. "Storbon, Rugrat, on me."

Unhallowed Ground

Expert

Someone who steps into the area of effect will have their very life force sucked from their body. Wounds and hidden traumas will be negatively affected.

Cast: 500 Mana 200 Mana/minute – 20m radius

1500 Mana 500 Mana/minute – 40m radius

For teaching yourself an Expert-ranked spell, you gain: 5,000,000 EXP

11,592,334/108,500,000 EXP till you reach Level 61

Rugrat got back down from his perch, and Storbon walked over from the others who were checking their gear, cleaning their weapons, and getting some food into them.

Erik clasped hands with Rugrat, pulling each other in for a quick embrace.

"Thank you, brother," Rugrat said.

"Any day, brother," Erik said and turned to face Storbon.

Rugrat moved to George and scratched his mount's head.

"So, what's the plan?" Erik asked Storbon.

"We head back to Kuldir, rest up, and come out again later," Storbon said.

Erik pulled out a field chair. Storbon did the same, and Rugrat came over to join them.

"If we do that, other orcs could come out of the caves, reinforce the camp, take it over, and it'll be even harder to take," Erik said.

"We have wounded. We shouldn't push ahead. We came damn close to having more injured. If you two were to get hurt…" Storbon trailed off.

"We get it. We're city lords, dungeon masters, and whatever—that doesn't matter. We trained you; we trained the damn military. First and foremost, we're soldiers, and soldiers take the enemy's position and push forward. Hiding back in the town, that's no way to grow," Rugrat said with some fire in his voice.

Erik glanced at him. Rugrat caught the look and reeled in his emotion. *They're coddling us like we're damn children.*

"What I'm saying is that we need to take that camp's position, see if there is any intelligence in there, and find out what the hell the orcs are doing. If we don't do anything about the people who were taken away in the cart, I doubt anyone else will," Rugrat said.

"George will take a few hours to recover, but he's made of stronger stuff. He'll be fighting ready by then. Tian Cui will take some more time," Erik said.

Storbon seemed to be having an internal battle.

"We have a foothold. We need to capitalize on it. Those people in the carts…they won't be coming back out of those caves by themselves," Erik said.

"Shit, all right, you're right. It's hard. I know you're both stronger than my people, but my mission is to protect you both."

"Sometimes, that becomes secondary," Erik said.

Storbon sighed and lowered his head. He raised it moments later. "We head to the camp and clear out anything else that is in there. Yuli looted the bodies of the group we killed at the choke point. There was a horn that the head shaman had that might be useful. The rest of it was trinkets and mana stones."

He pulled out the horn.

Horn of Obedience

Use this horn to gain the obedience of surrounding orcs. Affects an area 15m x 15m.

Uses: 4/12

Duration: 1 Hour

"Well, that could be useful." Rugrat pulled out the horn they'd looted from a patrol.

"This is just a regular horn for communication. That must be how the orc leader got them to come back to the camp.

Storbon put the horn away again.

"Save it for a rainy day."

"We are in a dungeon, you know?" Rugrat muttered.

Erik elbowed him.

"What? Not like we're going to get a shower without some magical intervention."

"Once Tian Cui is good to go, we'll head to the camp."

36

A New Quest

Tian Cui recovered quickly. Rugrat stored George away in a beast storage device and rode on Lucinda's beast again.

"Dismount. We'll take the rest on foot," Storbon said.

They got off their mounts and studied the camp. Up close, they could see the damage they had done over the last half-day.

They walked through the shattered walls, weapons up and ready. Dead orcs that had been pulled off the walls made a pile in the corner, the flies getting to them already.

The camp smelled like unwashed bodies and a non-working sewage system.

Erik and Rugrat used their domains to the fullest, making sure no one was hiding in the camp waiting to jump out and attack them.

"Yuli and Lucinda, on watch. Make sure nothing sneaks up on us," Storbon said once they had confirmed that the camp was empty.

Everyone took a moment to put a cloth over their faces to block out some of the smell.

Storbon looked through the barracks. It was nothing more than a hide tent that had been strung up across wood, with bone used to seal the entrance and pin the tent to the rock. The person or creature these had come from had to be at the Body Like Iron or higher level for them to be driven into the ground and not destroyed.

He searched around, finding rusted and broken weapons, discarded clothing, bones, and putrefied meat from their unfinished meals.

"Got something!" Yao Meng said from a side tent.

"What is it?" Erik approached from where he had been searching. The others went over as well, leaving Yuli and Lucinda to watch the area.

"Looks like a map and some written words. I got a quest when I picked it up." Yao Meng passed it to Erik, who got there first.

Erik looked up from the papers. Seeing a notification, he waved his hand, reading through it all. "Well, I'll be damned."

Erik passed it to Tian Cui, who arrived after him. So it went, with them passing around the page to everyone.

Quest: From Orc Jaws

Adventurers, lost souls, and villagers have been captured from the lands surrounding the orc territory and sent deeper into orc territory. Find these prisoners, free them, and escape the orc territory.

Requirements:

Free the prisoners

Lead them out of orc territory

Rewards:

Wandering Hero Title

EXP (Depends on final result)

"Well, it looks like we have a goal," Rugrat said.

"I've got something!" Lucinda called out.

"What?" Storbon asked.

"Orcs."

"Fuck!" Rugrat said.

Erik was up on the wall with the others. Orcs boiled out of the caves cut into the side of the dungeon, massing their numbers as they stared at the camp.

A horn called out.

The orcs waited until after the horn faded away, staring at the camp attentively.

"And we don't have a reply to give them," Erik said.

"We have our horn," Storbon said.

"Don't think we really want them charging our way. If we run, we'll be attacked from behind. We might lead them to Kuldir," Rugrat said.

"The walls are smashed to hell here. If they flank us, we're screwed," Storbon rebutted.

"They have numbers, and they'll have shamans. I guess it is about time we stopped limiting ourselves," Erik said.

"You are the leaders of Alva." Storbon stepped forward.

Erik and Rugrat saw the coldness in his eyes. He had been one of their powers in the Alva military since the beginning, going from a young man who had never left his village to a spear-wielding veteran of some of the bloodiest battles they had participated in. He had proved his ability and it had changed him, making him much older than his outward appearance would suggest.

He deserved their respect and to be treated as an equal.

"We might be the figureheads of Alva and Vuzgal, but they are both places for those who call themselves Alvans," Erik said.

"First and foremost, we're fighters. We don't run from a fight; we run toward them. There are people who the orcs have, and we're all they have.

We're not leaving them behind. That is our code," Rugrat said.

Storbon grit his teeth. It looked as if he were debating whether he could drag these two idiots away from the fight by himself.

Erik smiled and put a hand on Storbon's shoulder. He felt responsible for Storbon, fatherly almost. He had healed him, trained him, and watched him grow into the man he was now, and he could see the difficult expression on his face.

"We're idiots for lost causes." Erik's smile widened as he saw Storbon going through decisions he clearly didn't like.

Storbon sighed. "You are the commanders of the Alvan army. Guess I should just shut up and listen to my bosses," he said finally.

"He's the boss. I hang out for the free lunches," Rugrat said.

Storbon cracked a smile.

"So, what is the plan?" Rugrat asked.

"Defend, as well as we can. Get firing positions up, and hammer the enemy with ranged weaponry and spells," Erik said.

"Trap formations around the walls?" Storbon said.

"Good idea. That will slow them down from entering our broken walls," Rugrat said.

"Thin out the trap formations there, create a natural funnel. The rubble makes it harder to cross. If we make it easier for them to enter, we have melee fighters there, supported with ranged attacks, to kill them," Storbon said.

"Smart." Erik nodded. "If you can see who you're supposed to kill, you're more likely to charge at them instead of a massive wall in your way."

"Put explosives behind the breached wall. The shamans like to hide out in the rear. If we can time it right, we can get some of them in the blast. If we get it wrong, we get more orcs," Rugrat said.

"Let's get to work. Have Lucinda send out her birds to keep us up to date on what is happening. Everyone else gets working on defenses," Erik said.

"We should clear up the chain of command," said Storbon. "I've been doing this a while, but I am used to offensive operations. You both have more experience doing this."

"Rugrat." Erik stared at the confused marine.

"Huh?"

"You'll be back from the fighting. You're fast and you have ranged attacks that can help to control the battlefield. It gives you a better view of everything that is going on," Erik said.

Rugrat raised his lip to start arguing and sighed instead. "All right, fine. Let's get to work." Rugrat used his comms and relayed the plan to the rest of the special team.

Erik and Storbon ran off outside the camp and started to wave their storage rings, tossing out formation plates.

George, who was now back on his feet, went around the camp and used his flames to open holes in the side of the wall that Rugrat had marked, creating firing positions for the special team members.

Yuli lay down several amplification formations while Yao Meng put together a mana barrier formation in the middle of the camp.

Erik finished his first loop of the camp and continued prepping the defenses. Pausing for a moment, he looked over at the orcs, seeing that they were still amassing.

"How many do you put that at?" Rugrat asked.

"Too damn many," Erik said.

"'Bout fifty?"

Another group joined.

"Seventy?" Erik said.

They got back to work; they didn't have time to stare at orcs.

Gilly created pits in the ground, and Erik planted explosives and an activating formation. Then she fused the upper layer of stone, so it didn't look any different from the surrounding area. But as soon as someone stepped on it, the formation would activate and set off the explosives.

Erik could have used his mana, but he was saving it. He was their main healer; he didn't want to be fatigued starting. Also, Gilly's mana pool was bigger than his, and although he had great control over Earth mana, Gilly used it on almost an instinctual level, much closer to the pure magic that Tanya was studying in Alva.

A horn called out from the caves.

Erik looked over. It had taken some time, but the orcs seemed pleased with their numbers. There had to be over a hundred orcs waiting at the entrances of the caves.

"Pull back into the camp. Move to your firing positions. Gilly, work on the ground around the broken walls," Rugrat yelled.

Erik ran and jumped, grabbing onto the wall and using his Strength and Agility to climb up.

Gilly used a pillar of stone and a jump to get over the wall. The pillar collapsed into itself so the orcs couldn't use it. She ran over to the broken wall and smacked her feet. Spiked protrusions grew from the ground, and the stone on the ground fused to it, looking like loose rubble. But if someone tried to kick it away, they'd find it was part of the ground.

The spikes and berms that rose from the ground created covered firing positions and single-path firing corridors.

Erik pulled out his rifle and dropped to the ground. The special team members checked their weaponry.

Storbon, Lucinda, and Erik were on the wall. Yao Meng, Tian Cui, and Rugrat had grenade launchers in their hands, while Yuli gathered the surrounding mana. Her robes billowed out, and the runes on the formation below her glowed with power.

George looked much better, and he prowled the ground beside Rugrat. Erik could feel the rage rolling off his body. Someone had dared to attack the proud flame wolf; worse, they'd attacked his beloved master.

He wasn't about to let that go easily.

Erik checked the drum magazine on his rifle, one of the newer products for the rifles, ensuring it was fully loaded, and flicked it from safe to auto. He put the bipod of the rifle down on one of the firing positions. The orcs' roars reverberated off the roof of the dungeon's cavern.

Night, or the dungeon equivalent of it, had begun. Luminescent plants that illuminated the area and light shafts from above had darkened. The orcs had adapted to the darkness, and the special team's helmets cut through the darkness easily.

Erik checked the socket formations and the runes that directed power from his magazine into them. He was just looking for things to do before it all kicked off. Erik made sure to breathe so he wouldn't tunnel, checking those around him.

Lucinda and Storbon had the same setup as him, waiting and ready along the wall.

"In range!" Rugrat yelled.

Whoumpf! Whoumpf! Whoumpf!

The grenade launcher team fired their grenades as fast as they could, altering their aim just slightly from left to right to displace their attacks.

They ejected smoking cartridges from their launchers, loaded a full six-shot cartridge, and readied themselves again.

Explosives landed around the orcs. A few hit close enough to affect the beasts.

Lucinda called out changes to their aim.

They fired again, hitting the forward lines of the orcs passing through their formation. The orcs ran into the grenades.

"Tough fuckers," Storbon hissed.

The orcs took the hits and kept on coming, their shamans buffing themselves and their fighters.

"George! Yuli!" Rugrat yelled as he fired off his third round of grenades.

Blue flames ignited around George's body. Wisps of flames floated away from his body, gathering into fireballs the size of bowling balls. They shot out over the wall, curving toward the orcs.

He did all this in seconds and sent tens of blue fireballs at the same time.

The grenades impacted the orcs, thinning their numbers once again.

George's fireballs hit the ground and exploded into flames that melted the stone they landed on. It was like a rocket barrage, coating the area with blue flames. The orcs' madness turned to panic as they tried to slow their forward momentum. Two fell and were trampled by those behind them.

Letting out fresh roars, the orcs increased their speed. Horns blared as shamans cast different spells.

The fireballs coated the area, and orcs were set aflame. Shamans sent out spells to contain the fire, and hasty barriers were set up.

Some pulled off what looked like big headdresses from their backs.

Those look like totems.

They slammed the totems on the ground, making them look like carved tree trunks. They were covered in different symbols and seemingly random ornaments of bones, gems, and other parts.

The totems created barriers or shot out blasts of green light, thinning out the incoming fireballs, but the shamans needed to stay next to them to control them.

A mouth formed of stone opened in the ground underneath one of the stationary shamans and his totems.

The shaman cried out, falling into the mouth before it snapped shut and disappeared into the ground.

Other mouths formed before lines of fire were traced across the land in front of the orcs, forcing them to squeeze together to get past the flames.

Erik stared at the marker they had placed outside the camps. *Still out of range.*

Grenades targeted the openings in Yuli's firewall as her stone mouths snacked on running orcs and shamans, disrupting their barrier cover.

George continued to coat the orc horde in flames.

They were tough fuckers. Some of them were missing limbs, but they were still charging forward as they were being healed and recovering from their wounds. If they had been fighting all buffed orcs from the beginning, it would have been hard to take more than ten of them in one of their ambushes.

The orcs had fully left the caves, with just over sixty melee fighters and about ten shamans.

Erik felt the air pick up behind him. He glanced out the corner of his eye to see Yuli with a crate in front of her. It was covered in poison symbols. A cloud of golden dust with a green haze around it rose in front of her, held in a Tornado spell.

Yuli waved forward as she chanted. The formation reinforced and multiplied her power. The Tornado shot out air blades that crossed the area in front of the camp, hitting the orcs that had made it past her flaming obstacles.

The wind blades filled with poison dust cut at the orcs. They defended themselves against the attacks but were left with cuts that quickly healed under their buffs' effects.

Blades turned the air into a shimmering mess, making it hard to see the dungeon's roof.

The flame lines started to dim, running out of power.

As the wind blades were still attacking, Yuli held out her hand, chanting and casting a second spell. At the same time, she controlled the last of the wind blades that had separated from the Tornado.

Spell formations appeared on the cavern above, unseen by the orcs. The spell formations sank into the roof. The area around them turned red as parts of the ceiling started to collapse. Rocks dropped and exploded as they hit the ground, sending shards everywhere before magma fell from the ceiling.

Some orcs were hit with the magma, being burnt into nothing, not even leaving a tombstone behind.

The other orcs' fear of fire made them bunch up again, away from the lava falls from above.

"Get ready!" Erik yelled as the orcs neared the machine gunners' range.

Yuli's raised hand glowed silver and black, and she closed it.

Several other spell formations appeared on the other side of the camp wall. A streak of lightning as thick as a tree burst out, hitting one of the leading orcs.

The lightning arced, jumping from one orc to the next, creating a chain of light. Some died outright; others were able to hold on through the attack.

Two totems were struck. One exploded, hurting its controlling shaman, while the other melted. The shaman turned irate, sending out all the buffs he could muster.

"On my command!" Erik used his comms under the chaos of explosions, orc yells, and those in the camp communicating with one another.

It seemed as though it had gone on forever, but the orcs had left their cave less than five minutes ago. A fifth of their number were dead, and they had plenty of fight left in them.

The wounded recovered quickly, and they didn't even recognize their pain unless their wounds were so severe that they couldn't survive.

"Fire!"

Erik, Lucinda, and Storbon were lit up as they fired from their burnt-out positions in the camp wall.

Three lines of green tracers hit the orcs head on.

"Focus your targets!" Storbon yelled.

Traversing his fire from one side of his arc to the other hurt the orcs, but it didn't put them out of the fight.

Erik picked a target and fired into them. His Strength and Agility made him as accurate shooting his automatic weapon as he was shooting on semi-auto. His rifle shot straight instead of making a cone of destruction like a true machine gun, allowing him to pour rounds into the orcs until their brain realized they were no longer able to survive the kind of damage they had sustained.

He changed targets and fired. The orcs were so close now that the grenades were making him starry-eyed, and the dull wave he felt in his chest from the grenades felt like someone was smacking him.

Erik saw a stream of tracers come from his rifle, signifying he didn't have many rounds left. "Reloading!" He pulled out another drum magazine. He used a Cooling spell on his weapon, smacking the old magazine out and slapping a new one in place. Thank fuck they had a mag release like the M4 and not like the real FAL.

"Barrier!" Lucinda yelled.

The shamans had organized themselves and finally created a barrier to protect their horde.

Erik fired. It created flashes of light on the barrier, but none of his rounds passed through. Grenades hit the top of the barrier, while a line of fire appeared ahead of the orcs. A tornado sprang up from the orcs' right flank and smashed into the barrier, lighting up its entire domed side, grinding against it with little effect.

"Reload! Re-arm!"

The orcs rushed forward, largely uncontested. There wasn't anything the special team could do to take out the barrier that wouldn't take a tremendous amount of effort, which would leave them weak when they needed to fight the orcs directly.

The orcs hurled spears at the camp. The mana barrier over the camp was revealed as the attacks flashed against it.

The barrier formation was made from hexagonal pieces that linked together. It was Julilah and Qin's creation. The pieces could be changed out or added to, adding functions to the formation, like buffing those who were linked to the formation via their Alvan medallions.

The grenadiers changed to their rifles. Rugrat and George jumped up to a wall on the opposite side from where the orcs were attacking. The wall was a shoddy construct, so they were higher than the wall facing the orcs, allowing them a greater view of the battlefield.

Yuli had changed to a new amplification formation that glowed brighter than the first one. A secondary mana barrier formation was active, protecting the area one meter around her.

Gilly watched the orcs. The air around her was humid as she readied herself.

Erik patted her absently. Everyone was tense behind their guns.

"Shit. The leading orcs are right at the front of the barrier. They're going to be covered right up until they reach the wall," Lucinda said.

"Shit," Yao Meng muttered.

"Lucinda, Yao Meng, fall back to the inner position. Storbon, Erik, be ready to fight hand-to-hand. Tian Cui, you're on ranged, but be ready to fight and run back to the second position if we get overrun. Hit those shamans with so many Silence spells they forget how to speak. Yuli, start dropping fire on their right flank. Shift them to the left and force them to go in the direction of the broken walls. I will provide cover from back here," Rugrat said.

People organized themselves and got to their positions. The secondary positions were stone walls that Gilly and Yuli had pulled up from the ground, creating half-trenches behind them and covering them in spikes to make them hard to climb.

Erik opened and closed his hands in his Tropic Thunder gloves, pulling them on tighter. The blood-red formations seemed to glow in excitement. Erik circulated his mana, feeling the power in his grasp.

He checked the buffs that the Alvan main defensive formation applied to them.

All base stats increased by 15%

It didn't seem like much, but with their base stats so high and stacking their titles on top, the special team's ability had reached a new level. Not to mention all the Experience points they had earned so far. As they leveled up, it would make their base stats even more impressive.

Explosives went off under the orcs as they stepped on trigger points, and the orcs were torn apart. In their charge, they were largely spread out. Some were missed; later groups of orcs found the traps as the leading orcs met the formation traps.

It looked like the poison has taken some effect. Erik stared at the color of the orcs. Their speed seemed a little slower, and their regeneration was slower.

The formation traps activated, killing those in their radius. Dead orcs fell to the ground. Ignoring their losses, they kept on charging.

"Be ready at the front," Rugrat said.

Erik checked his weapon again. He'd loaded special formation-enhanced rounds that would punch through even Body Like Iron skin.

He saw the leading edge of the orcs' mana barrier as it met the side of the camp, interfering with the mana barrier they had placed over the camp.

As it passed, Erik fired his machine gun into the closest orc. The rounds punctured and then ruptured. The orc died after three hits.

Erik kept mental notes, sending accurate bursts into the orcs.

The leading attackers were being thinned out.

Formations shot out tendrils looking to slow and clump the enemy; others released area-killing attacks.

Thankfully, the orcs didn't have real armor. If they did, Erik and his team would have been truly fucked.

Spears of ice shot out beside him as Gilly attacked. Her spears stabbed into the orcs, exploding as they struck. The orcs' tempered and innately stronger bodies defended against the attacks. Direct attacks would gravely wound them, but they could recover with enough time. The shards of ice wounded the other orcs, but they ignored these wounds.

Erik cut down orcs and moved to the next one. Storbon was doing the same as the leading orcs, just a few meters away from the camp walls, jumped.

"Orcs on the walls!" Rugrat yelled.

Attack formations went off, killing more orcs.

Erik and Storbon put their rifles away. Storbon pulled out his spear and moved it in his hand, limbering up. More orcs were on the walls now. One jumped over, a spear of stone from Gilly cutting through them.

It was the start of the flood. Several orcs hurled themselves over the camp walls, waving their rusted weapons.

The second line of Yao Meng, Tian Cui, and Lucinda opened fire, shooting above Erik and Storbon, who pulled back to the entrances to the second line.

Rugrat was shooting from George, as they were on the move.

"Yuli, keep up the flames!"

Orcs were making it through the fire and dropping into the camp. Storbon yelled as he used his spear to smack an orc's weapon to the side. His spearhead flashed as he took the orc's head off.

Erik pulled out a Defender's Might pill and threw it back. It filled him with power, and he followed it up with a Stamina pill.

He crushed them in his teeth as three orcs rushed him and Gilly. Gilly launched stone spears at one and sent out her tail, smacking them back into the wall of the camp some thirty meters away.

Erik applied his Strength, for the first time, unleashing all his power.

The ground cracked underneath his feet. There was a savage and wild grin on his face, but within, he was ice cold. He unconsciously used Combat Scan. Based on his previous fights, he knew the orcs were strong, but their Agility was low. They were heavy, but their knee joints were weak. Their chests were covered in a large skeleton plate, and their heads were built like battering rams, with their brains being cushioned to take impact better.

Erik used Semi-Illusionary Fist, creating two more fists around his own, making it hard to know which one was attacking.

The first orc raised his war axe.

Erik dodged to the side. His separate fists overlaid his own as he slammed it into the side of the orc, cracking something.

A gray smoke appeared over the wound.

Erik had applied Unhallowed Strike to all his fists. He dodged under a machete from the second orc and used his One Finger Beats Fist technique.

Stone appeared around his hand, tattooed with poison and with veins of molten magma.

Erik yelled as he struck with his finger. The Fire mana encased in stone slammed into the orc, piercing its stomach and driving upward. The uncontrolled Fire mana expanded explosively. The shards of stone tore through the orc. The poison that laced it seemed like overkill, and the orc dropped to the ground.

"Go left," Rugrat said.

Erik planted his foot and moved to his left. A split second later, the first orc's head shattered as Rugrat's round went through its eye and out the back of its skull.

Four more orcs had made it over the wall.

Gilly used a Yell on them, slowing them. Earth and Water mana revolved together, creating a dirty spear that lanced through an orc and exploded, tearing them apart.

She charged, and Erik joined her.

They hit the orcs like wrecking balls.

Every hit could break bone. The hits caused shockwaves in the surrounding area.

Erik used his Combat Scan to see his enemies' weaknesses. He killed the orcs faster as he added poison and Fire and Earth mana into his attacks.

Erik stomped the ground. A shield of stone shot up, and he kicked it at an orc charging him. The stone shattered and turned into weapons, tearing up the orc. The poison he had applied to the stone quickly entered its veins.

Erik got hit in the side, but he barely registered the hit; his armor took the brunt of it. Still, he grabbed the offending hand and pulled with a yell and threw the orc at another attacker.

A rock hit Erik's helmet.

With the power the orc had given it, Erik saw stars. He used Focused Heal. There were three orcs to his front and one in the rear with a sling.

A round cracked overhead. The slingshot orc was dead.

George breathed fire across the camp wall, turning it into an inferno. The wall started to burn.

The orcs charged, and instead of dropping back, Erik pushed forward. His Agility was pushed to the peak, moving through the tiniest of openings, striking out at the orcs, and dodging the enemy. He knew his body better than ever before. He knew his limits perfectly, having tempered himself completely.

His movements were almost fluid. A rusted sword went for his side, a spear for his chest, and a war hammer from overhead.

Everything seemed to slow. His Combat Scan showed openings in the orcs. Based on their motions, he could tell how they were manipulating their muscles, the placement of their bones.

Erik sent a fireball into the war hammer wielder's face. He used an imbued One Finger Beats Fist. The slug of stone and magma exploded under the arm of the sword user, making them stumble into the spear user, whose spear went wide. Erik tore it from their hands and reversed it, his mana and his muscles flowing as one.

The orcs fell to the ground in a pile.

He drove the spear through the spear user's head and kicked them. They flew back ten feet, and Erik raised his hand. Spears of stone shot out of the ground to catch the orc.

Erik felt goosebumps across his head; he was combining his attacks on an almost instinctual level.

Some orcs were able to get through the defenses; most were taken out by weapons fire, magical attacks, and traps. Those that were left were in small groups.

He contemplated the rest of the fighting.

"The orcs will be pushing to the opening. Erik, get over there. Yao Meng, support him. Yuli, be ready to switch your attacks," Rugrat yelled. He fired as he talked, killing an orc aiming at Storbon.

Erik felt the adrenaline draining as he ran to the opened camp walls. There were stone barriers all over the place, creating a spiky funnel.

Erik started to feel the pain of fighting. Pushing his body to the limit had its drawbacks.

"The orcs' bodies have reached the Body Like Iron stage, which comes with naturally increased Strength and Regeneration," Erik told the others as he used a healing blade and stabbed it into his leg. He didn't feel any pain as healing radiated through his body. He pulled out his rifle, using some rubble as support.

He fired as soon as he could.

Rugrat surveyed the camp. The walls the orcs had been climbing were now on fire. Inky smoke curled toward the ceiling. Yuli's wall of fire had pushed the orcs toward the broken wall. With their fear of fire, they were reaching the broken camp walls and meeting the ranged attacks.

"Yuli, switch targets," Rugrat said, seeing the group of orcs turning to the new opening.

"Understood!" she said through the comms channel. She sounded tired.

"Everyone, focus on the funnel," Rugrat said.

Rugrat's eyes found Erik, waiting with his rifle ready.

Seeing Erik fight hand to hand with the orcs, a shiver of excitement ran through Rugrat. They'd become stronger, much stronger than he thought, but until now, they just hadn't been able to use their power.

He was shocked by Erik's ability to take on multiple orcs at once. As he had been fighting, he had refined his fighting style and even combined his attacks in different, unorthodox ways, using a minimal amount of effort for maximum impact.

Storbon killed the last orc that had made it over the wall.

Erik fired first, followed by Gilly. The orcs ran forward into the defenses, catching on the spikes, opening wounds and running forward.

Rugrat used his link with George to guide him and fired his rifle.

A spell formation covered the funnel. Vines grew on the walls and the ground, pulling the orcs toward them, holding the orcs on the ground or pulling them into the spikes.

The ranged attackers fired. Tracers lit up the funnel.

Shamans planted their totems.

"No, you fucking don't." Rugrat rose on George, exposing himself more but allowing him to switch targets and greater freedom of movement.

Three black formations appeared under the orcs. Chains clanked against one another as they shot out and wrapped around the orcs.

Rugrat cast spells on his rounds as he fired them, hitting the shamans he could see. He got two of them and felt his mana fighting to recover.

Multi-colored chains wrapped around them, covered in mana blades of varying effects. The shamans cried out in pain. They were used to sitting in the rear and buffing the orcs; their ability to withstand pain was much weaker.

If the orcs weren't weak already, his chains wouldn't have worked on them. *Got you now!*

He drank from his Camelbak of mana recovery potion and fired, altering his aim and firing again. With every trigger pull, an orc dropped to the ground.

Erik gave up his firing position and called down Unhallowed Ground on the final funnel.

The ground looked like a swamp. Tendrils of poison reached up, sticking to the orcs that entered it.

The poison Yuli had added to her wind attack slowed them down more; their hits weren't as powerful.

Erik stood in their path, an iron wall. He took hit after hit and kept fighting, even as his armor started to deform from the strikes.

Rugrat watched him out of the corner of his eye and switched targets. He had lived with and fought alonside Erik for most of his adult life. He fired, the round passed through Erik's legs hitting an Orc in the leg, causing his blow to go wide.

Erik used their momentum and threw them to the side, impaling their skull on a spike. As he turned, Rugrat fired over his shoulder, hitting an orc in the eye. Erik kicked its body into its fellows and stepped forward. He took a hammer blow to the side but held firm, the stone around his legs that he had used to brace himself cracking.

Erik's hand jabbed out; stone flame hardened and pierced through his attacker's neck, and he grabbed their hammer.

Rugrat fired to Erik's right side, striking an orc in the arm. The blunt force pushed them to the side.

Erik swung the hammer he had stolen from the last orc and hit the off-balanced orc in the head, cracking their skull.

The two of them flowed together—one acting, the other anticipating—the two of them more powerful than the sum of their parts.

"Focus on the shamans. Use your Ranged Silence spell. That should stop them chanting!" Rugrat ordered. The ranged fighters changed their aim and shot at the shamans.

Rugrat ignited the second part of the chain spells. Explosions tore through the orc formation, killing seven of the shamans.

One of the shamans got off an attack, slamming his staff into the ground. The ground cracked and split apart, just as it had with the orc camp leader.

George, in tune with Fire mana, quickly understood what the shaman's aim was.

"Erik, dodge!" Rugrat yelled.

Erik jumped, using an explosion in front of him to toss himself backward.

It wasn't a moment too soon as a pillar of magma shot out of the ground.

Yuli sent out a spell of Wind, cutting the pillar apart and spraying it back over the orcs, causing them to scream out.

Rugrat looked at the breached defenses; the cracks in the ground tore apart the funnel they'd created.

"Tian Cui, get around the camp and hit those shaman fuckers from behind. Yuli, try to throw up some barriers. Gilly, take the right. Storbon, the left. George, help them. Yao Meng, Lucinda, get grenades into them!" Rugrat pulled out two grenade launchers and jumped off George.

People kept telling him that he and Erik could do things that no normal person could do; it was about time they did some superhuman shit! Rugrat flicked the safety off the grenade launchers.

He was like a mobile turret, firing on the orcs that were still smoking from the magma as they ran forward. Destruction rained down on the orcs. Their defenses were already screwed. Rugrat only cared about thinning the creatures.

The melee fighters ran in. Tian Cui rushed across the camp to an unseen part of the wall.

Erik had the room to move around as orcs made it through the fire. Rugrat and the others had to make sure that none of their attacks were close enough to harm their allies. They aimed at the middle to the rear of the orc horde pushing forward. There were around half of them left, including the orc shamans who were deploying their totems.

Attacks shot forward, hitting the defenses on the second line. Yao Meng and Lucinda, to their credit, didn't even flinch and kept on shooting. The dust and explosions made it hard for the shamans to see clearly.

With the orcs packed together, each grenade could take out up to five orcs.

They were starting to take control of the fight again.

Erik was up there, fighting away. He took more hits from the orcs to make sure that they couldn't get past him, using his own body as a shield.

His hands were covered in a red haze as his attacks increased in power. He created stone shields against the nasty hits, blunting some of the force. The area around him was covered in a dark miasma that leaked poison across the area. The longer the orcs fought him, the weaker they became. Some that had been inside his range for too long collapsed from poisoning.

Erik's movements flickered. His strikes made the three-meter-tall orcs stumble backward and lose their balance.

Rugrat left his inhibitions behind, fully pushing himself into the fight, feeling the rhythm of it. His body reacted on trained impulses. The team worked together, and as they had all trained together, they could react and act in accordance with how the others worked. There was no need for verbal communication.

This was what they were looking for. People working together as one. Rugrat felt the flow of power through the area.

Yuli created a ball of Water and shot out Water arrows from it repeatedly. With the other hand, she raised mana barriers, her fingers dancing across the air.

It was a show of complete skill and understanding over her environment and her own abilities, melding them together. She cast a mana barrier over the front-liners, protecting them against the totems' attacks while not obscuring their fight.

That was how a support class was supposed to do it!

Yao Meng had jumped onto an amplification formation. It increased the power of the spells that he put on his grenades. He raised barriers around where the grenades hit, directing the explosion, so instead of wasting themselves on blowing upward, their force went parallel to the ground, cutting orcs apart.

Lucinda's flying beasts were daredevils, circling the battlefield and dropping explosive packages.

The orcs were at a standstill.

Gilly used her body and her spells to hold down half of the front line. Erik held down a five-meter-wide area, shooting and using fireballs to control his front or exploding them around him to increase his instantaneous speed, hitting and retreating from the enemy just as fast.

His domain stretched over the battlefield. He threw out healing daggers, hitting Gilly and Storbon, who had just taken a hit to the arm, making him yell in pain. His hand was split, his fingers hanging at unnatural angles.

The blade hit Storbon in the side. He kept fighting; if he stopped, he would die for sure. He lashed out with his working hand, aiming at the orc's head.

The orc shifted, so the spearhead raked his chest instead.

Storbon and the orc backed off.

The orc's head snapped backward, and two others fell.

Storbon used his armpit to push his hand together with a yell. Rugrat nodded to him, reloading and shooting at other orc stragglers. Storbon was pale and covered in blood as he shifted the grip on his spear. He gritted his teeth. His tempered body was already fusing his hand back together. He looked over the barricades, ready to meet more orcs that tried to jump over.

Storbon's spear flashed, his face cold. *Not just a boy anymore; kid's seen some shit.* Erik looked over between the fight, seeing if Storbon needed help.

His spear left streaks of blood around him, as any orc that came in close was cut down, the poison on his spear doing quick work.

George roared. His body ballooned as he sent a stream of flames through the orcs, melting the very stone he stood on.

Using that opening, he rushed into battle. There were more blue flames among his red fur. His jaws bit through the orcs' half-iron skin as if it were nothing. His claws sent out streaks of flame and tore them apart. He was a lone wolf wrecking crew!

Who's a good boy?! Rugrat thought, with all the pride of a dog dad.

Rugrat felt that he was on the cusp of something. He couldn't help but think about his forge and sitting at the top of Vuzgal, looking over the city with Matt.

Rugrat tossed his grenade launchers into his storage ring and pulled out his rifle. Ejecting the magazine, he caught it in his storage ring with a practiced ease. He slapped in a new magazine with an "S" on the side of it.

He had personally forged these bullets and given instructions to the formation masters engraving them. One magazine was worth ten Earth mana stones.

There were three hundred meters between him and his targets, and there were orcs, his allies, chaos, and totems in the way.

He exhaled. Feeling the shot line up, he fired. The round cut through the battlefield and went through a mana barrier. The outer formation and round peeled away, revealing a smaller round underneath that punched through the shaman's head. The orc opened and closed its mouth as poison melted it from the inside.

Rugrat switched targets and fired again. The first round hit the next shaman in the chest. A necklace fired up with power and stopped the round from doing too much damage. Rugrat sent two more rounds at the shaman before he could do anything else.

The third poison round decorated their chest, causing them to cough and sputter. Black blood flowed out of the wound.

He saw Tian Cui appear out of the shadows. Her blades dug into a shaman's neck, and she tore them back out. The orc's veins changed to a new color.

There was poison everywhere, and it was looking like Erik's Alchemy had affected them as well. Thankfully they all had poison resistance!

Tian Cui worked, and Rugrat covered her. Orc shamans realized something was going on and called to their orcs. A few of the larger orc guards returned to them. Others had either lost their guards or they were caught up in the fight and had given themselves over to their bloodlust.

Rugrat fired. His rounds hit the larger orcs. It took three of his poison rounds to take out the guards, but he was finishing them off quickly.

He surveyed the battlefield.

"Meng, Luc, get out into the fight," Rugrat yelled.

The two of them had limited targets that wouldn't put the others in danger.

"Rog!"

"Moving!"

The two moved from their cover and grabbed their weapons: Yao Meng with his sword and shield, Lucinda with her short spear and shield.

They entered the fight, quickly taking the pressure off the others. Yuli controlled her elements, using the openings she found to hit the orcs, allowing her to support the special team without putting their people at risk.

Seeing the battle had turned against them and their fellow shamans were getting killed, three shamans broke off from the fight, taking orcs with them.

Rugrat opened his beast storage devices. Five full-grown panthers in armor appeared on the camp walls with Rugrat. He pointed at the fleeing shamans. "Kill."

The panthers growled and ran along the walls. Their eyes turned red at the smell of blood and fighting.

Rugrat called on his mana, casting his Chains. They appeared among the groups of orcs, focused on the shamans. The chains snapped out to try to capture others, and those in the area were silenced and slowed.

Casting it three times nearly drained Rugrat, but the shamans were no longer able to cast their spells or use their totems to create barriers.

The panthers struck the outer orcs that were separated from the group and tore them apart, their claws and teeth only marginally less effective than George's. It was easier to raise a beast to a higher level than it was to raise a human.

Rugrat kept focusing on the shamans. Tian Cui killed the last shaman, and the buffs over the orcs fell away. Yuli's poison-filled air blade attack ravaged their bodies, killing those that were weaker. Others that had been hit with poisons or with grave injuries no longer recovered at increased speeds.

Their Strength dropped as well. It turned into a one-sided slaughter.

Erik's Strength had reduced as his Defender's Might pill ran out. Still, even in his weakened state, he was deadlier than when he had started. He knew his enemy. He could predict their actions.

He stepped forward and started pushing back the orcs. He flowed through them. His armor showed sparks as his fists, fingers, and feet left dead in his wake.

The hits were exact; he was striking the critical points in the orcs' bodies.

They broke the orcs that were still trying to push through their defenses. Erik jumped onto Gilly, and George flapped his wings, shooting toward the panthers to help with the fleeing orcs.

The rest of the special team ran forward. Storbon slowed his pace and scanned the area before rushing to catch up with them.

The orcs got in some good hits, but Erik was there with the healing and support, so no one was gravely injured.

Rugrat looked up from his rifle, the smell of gunpowder around him. As he shifted, he pushed spent casings. With a wave of his hand, he pulled them into a storage ring.

"Consolidate on the camp," Rugrat ordered. He scanned the area again and used spells to enhance his vision. He thought he saw movement. "Yuli, how are you doing?"

Yuli sat in a chair on one of the amplification formations. "Tired," she muttered. She grabbed a tube from her Camelbak, drinking Stamina and Mana Regeneration potions.

Everyone had made it back to camp, tired, bloody, and covered in the signs of fighting. Erik looked like fresh death with the aftereffects of his Defender's Might and the hits he had needed to heal himself from.

His armor was dented in places, and there were cuts that his natural healing was quickly repairing.

He had to focus to make sure that his footsteps didn't make him bounce. Once he had used all his Strength, it was hard for him to limit it.

"Stamina and Mana Regeneration potions, everyone! Storbon, organize a watch. Yao Meng, Erik, and I will clear out a part of the camp for us to stay in. Lucinda, Tian Cui, loot the tombstones. George and I will patrol for the first bit. Yuli and Gilly, I want to repair our barriers and erect a stone wall over the burnt one," Rugrat said.

They were all fatigued from the fighting, but they pushed onward.

"You did good." He felt as tired as they looked.

"Which always means there's another job for us." Erik grinned.

"One good act deserves another shitty job." Rugrat winked.

They all laughed, more to bleed off the stress of the fight and catch their breath than at the actual joke.

They organized themselves and got to work.

Rugrat checked George and got onto his back. Together, they took off into the sky.

He looked over the battlefield. They had changed the landscape of the dungeon with their fight, leaving craters, cracks in the ground, and melted rock, and covered the place in orc tombstones. The camp walls were still smoking. Gilly blasted them with Water and hit them with her tail, breaking them apart before she pulled the bottom of the logs out.

A wall started to rise from the ground. Rugrat looked over to the caves. He pulled out the horn in his grasp. He had a feeling he might need it in the future.

Quest: From Orc Jaws

Adventurers, lost souls, and villagers have been captured from the lands surrounding the orc territory and sent deeper into orc territory. Find these prisoners, free them, and escape the orc territory.

You have found caves that appear to have been carved out to allow carriages to pass.

Requirements:

Free the prisoners

Lead them out of orc territory

Rewards:

Wandering Hero Title

EXP (Depends on final result)

"Sorry. I found what appear to be tunnels that are carved out and cared for better than the others. They've been smoothed down to take carts, I think."

"Well, it's as good a place to start as any," Erik said.

"We'll rest up, check out the gear, and then head out," Storbon interjected.

"Works with me," Rugrat said. Erik and the others agreed as well.

With nothing else to say, Erik cut the channel. He pulled up his Experience bar as he stood.

11,847,729/108,500,000 EXP till you reach Level 61

Most of the beasts were a lower level than him, even with the modifiers for their combat ability. He was fighting alongside people who were a lower level than him too. Experience gain was a pain in the ass in the low-level areas. If they were in the higher realms, he'd be raking it in.

Erik reached the center of the camp where there was an orc effigy of bones, stones, and blood.

A notification appeared in front of him.

Do you wish to:
   Take command of the Camp
   Destroy the Camp

Erik put his finger on "Destroy the Camp," and a new screen appeared.

Destroy Stronghold: Volzig
You will receive:
   1x Wand of Bear's Endurance
   1x Armchair
   2 x Bag of Common Spice
   1x Bag of Wheat
   8 x Barrel of Oil
   15 x Bottle of Common Wine
   2x Cheap Wig

1x Courtier's Outfit

3x Flint and Steel

1x Handsaw

8 x Lamp

5 x Large Carpet

1x Salted Ham

1x Shrine

8 x Small Carpet

1x Snowshoes

8x Hide Tents

5 x Vial of Exotic Ink

24x Necklace

Do you wish to destroy this Camp?
YES/NO

"Well, no one said that anything orcs collected had to make sense"

Into the Caves

Everyone managed to get some broken sleep in the orc camp. Dawn came quickly, and they used Clean spells to get rid of the sweat and grime from the previous day.

It wasn't the same as washing with water, but it was the best they could do.

Rugrat and Storbon repaired their armor and gear. Lucinda monitored the area with her beasts while Yao Meng patrolled the wall, looking for signs of movement. Yuli prepared their food as Erik checked the loot from the orcs.

There were orc tusks that could be used as an Alchemy ingredient. Their rusted weapons, Rugrat had already appraised. All of them were worthless; they could only be melted down to be turned into something useful. Then there were the orc totems. None of them could use them, but Erik kept the ones in the best condition to bring back to Alva. At the very least, they were made of rare materials and could be broken down by crafters. Then there was hide armor with such low durability that Erik had tossed them to the side.

A collection of rare gems, ores, Earth-grade mana stones, and ingredients were the main parts of the haul. The most valuable items were also the most basic: monster cores.

The orcs didn't have monster cores inside their bodies, but the shamans and the camp leader had kept a few.

Loot:
1x Common Earth-Grade Monster Core
2x Grand Earth-Grade Monster Core
1x Greater Earth-Grade Monster Core

Translated into Experience, they were worth 33,000,000 Experience.

At one time, that might have been enough to power level them from one realm to the next. Now, it was barely a third of what he needed to increase one level. Erik stored them away.

With how slow it was to level up, he was starting to wonder if he should start to use monster cores. Considering the massive amount of Experience required, it was no wonder the people of the Ten Realms needed extended lifetimes to become stronger.

Erik stopped checking the loot in his storage ring and stretched. His armor was one of the sets that needed to get buffed out. The solid plates were strong, but the orcs had been close to level sixty with Bodies Like Stone, and a higher constitution compared to humans.

He felt the dent in his plate pressing against his chest.

He was tight from fighting. The bruises and internal damage, he'd dealt with already.

He grabbed his rifle and walked over to Rugrat and Storbon.

"How does the loot look?" Rugrat had pulled out his mobile forge and was working on people's gear.

"Most of it is going to need to be pulled apart. Should be enough to get a few rounds at the bar when we get back." Erik dropped into a squat, his rifle over his legs. "How's my armor?"

"Dented. They can hit like a damn transport truck." Rugrat used his domain, creating flames around the armor plate and hammering it back into form.

"Most of their weapons are blunt. They can stagger you easily with a hit or send you flying," Storbon said. "Have to watch out for internal injuries and broken bones."

Erik grunted in agreement as Storbon sharpened Tian Cui's blades. With their tough bodies, just hitting the orcs degraded the condition of their weapons.

Storbon continued talking. "Good thing that all of us have tempered our bodies to Iron. Well, Yuli is half-step Body Like Iron, but she should be in the rear of any large fight we get into."

"It's going to get harder before it gets easier. The orcs know we're here. When they group together and have their shamans, they're a pain in the ass to kill. Going into the caves, we'll lose our defensive position. We'll be fighting them head on. Means we'll probably face the orc fighters while the shamans hide in the rear. They can circle around us and hit us from behind," Rugrat said darkly, staring at them both and then inspecting the armor plate he was working on.

"As we go, we could collapse the secondary tunnels that lead into our path. Give us a way to control the battlefield, preventing flanking and allowing for retreat if required," Erik said.

"Could work," Rugrat said.

"I'm scared that it could all come down on us if we do that," Storbon said.

"Gilly and I should be able to do it. If we think it might all collapse, we can set up a bunch of walls that the orcs would need to break through?" Erik threw out the option.

"I'd feel safer with that," Storbon conceded, looking directly at Rugrat. "With Erik and I up at the front, I'd feel good if you were in command again. Have Yuli as your second. Lucinda won't be able to use her beasts much in close-quarters fights, but she can scout out the caves before we start moving."

"All right, let's get her started then."

Lucinda's beasts headed down the tunnels. The team took breaks to eat and relax. Rugrat and Storbon finished working on the armor.

It was midday when Lucinda's scouts had gone as far as they could, and they picked out a route.

They gathered the formations, unused mines, and explosives before they mounted up.

The caves were foreboding and darker than the cavern.

Erik used his Night Vision spell. The cave brightened, and he stepped forward. Lucinda was on his right, Storbon on his left. Rugrat and Yuli were behind them, with Tian Cui and Yao Meng taking up the rear guard.

"Let's start the grind," Yao Meng said.

They had their rifles ready as they walked forward, scanning the area. They destroyed the entrances to the tunnel they were in, following one of the routes Lucinda's scouts had checked out.

Erik opened and closed his hands around his rifle, feeling the pressure of it, trying to remain as alert as possible.

Finally, the tunnel curved and then opened up, getting brighter.

Erik slowed down as they got to the mouth of the tunnel, taking a knee with Lucinda and Storbon as they surveyed the cavern in front of them.

It looked to be a farm to raise the big bulky boars the orcs rode.

There were several plots of mud where the boars lived. They had their snouts to the ground, trying to search out something to eat.

Some had orcs whipping them or riding them, breaking them in. Scarred, older-looking boars shoved one another out of the way. Fights broke out among squeals and snorts.

A group of large hide-crafted tents sat in the middle of the muddy pens. Orcs milled around them and headed off into the caves in groups or returned from the caves.

There had to be close to a hundred orcs and nearly twice that number in boars, maybe more. Based on the way they tossed the boars around or roughhoused one another they were probably between level fifty-seven and sixty.

"Shit, empty carriages," Erik said.

"There are clean tunnels up ahead. They must've been transported deeper," Rugrat said.

One boar attacked another with its tusks. The boar squealed in pain, whipping its head to the side.

The orcs, hearing the commotion, moved over to see the boars fighting and raised their weapons in excitement.

"Pull back," Erik said over the comms. Once they were back in the cover of the tunnels, he relayed everything to the rest of the team.

"All right, everyone, get set up," Rugrat said once they were forty or so yards back from the entrance to the open area.

Gilly raised spiked walls to guide the attackers through. Yuli and Rugrat tossed down amplification formations. Erik created trenches through his magic behind the walls, creating firing positions and a secondary line that was more suited for hand-to-hand combat.

Gilly created raised platforms for Yao Meng, Tian Cui, Yuli, and Rugrat to see the battlefield from and be above the three front-liners so they could shoot and use ranged attacks without hitting them.

They were almost done when Lucinda's voice sent a chill through their bodies.

"There's a patrol coming."

"Yuli, do you think you could target the village and the pens?" Rugrat asked as everyone moved to their positions.

Yuli grimaced and looked at the tunnel and at the wall between them and the tent village. "I can try."

"Good enough for me. Fire it up," Rugrat said.

Erik was in one of the trenches, his rifle fitted with a drum magazine. The noise from the orc patrol grew louder.

He felt the surrounding mana gathering around Yuli as she prepared her spell. Without a line of sight, she would have to rely on her long-distance artillery training to guesstimate the ranges she was working at and hit the enemy village.

From the mana she was pulling in, it looked like she was aiming to hit them with something big.

Erik pushed those errant thoughts from his head as the patrol group turned the corner of the tunnel.

The orcs made some confused noises, those in front not knowing why the tunnel had changed.

"Open fire!" Rugrat said.

Erik fired into the foremost orc. Tracers cut through the tunnel, hammering the orcs and dropping them. Smelling blood, the orcs in the rear charged forward.

The shaman was casting his spell when a round found his head, and he collapsed backward. The spell died with him.

The orcs' racial buff affected them, but they had lost half of their ten-orc group before they had charged. Not one of them made it to the first line of defense.

Erik changed magazines, checking the magazines he had laid out along the trench's wall and making sure that they were all still in reach.

"Damn." Erik felt the Fire mana Yuli had channeled into the cavern next to them. The mana built up quickly. He felt small impacts hitting the ground and then larger ones that made the tunnel they were in shake and drop dust from above.

"Shift the fire away from us and to the north." Lucinda was using one of her beasts she'd snuck into the cavern to alter Yuli's attack.

"Got some orcs coming this way!"

Orcs rounded the corner. They were in a panic, trying to escape the cavern. Rifles fired and added more tombstones to the ground.

Lucinda watched Armageddon. Yuli had called down Meteor Rain on the village. Meteors from the size of a fist to a cart appeared from the massive magical circle above. Streaming smoke and fire, they crashed into the ground, exploding into superheated rock and magma.

The first part of the attack tore through a pen of boars. With her callout, the attack carpeted the village, tearing it apart, and turned it into a crater-filled fire.

The orcs had turned toward the tunnel when they had first opened fire, but now, they were running in panic. Their fear of fire was embedded deep in their bones, and they forgot about the first sounds of an attack.

"The orcs are running in all directions. Some of the tunnels have collapsed," she relayed to the rest of her team. "There are more orc fighters rushing into the cavern from other places. Get ready, some are coming our way!"

Another orc team ran into their tunnel.

Lucinda didn't need to aim down her sights and used the line of tracers to cut through the charging orcs.

Tian Cui used a spell scroll that shot iron spears down the tunnel, piercing the orcs and pinning several to the wall. Some of them were strong enough that it took them a few seconds to succumb to their wounds.

Yuli's attack faded, and one of the orcs raised a horn to their mouth.

Beour—mphf

The deep, bassy horn was cut off with Rugrat's shot.

"Shit. It looks like that got their attention!" Lucinda said.

Horns called out to one another, pulling in more groups. The orcs, enraged at the destruction of their village, rushed toward the tunnel.

Lucinda checked her connection to her controlled beast. "Looks like they figured out where we are. They're piling toward us—must be three more groups the same size!"

"Looks like they're pissed at your redecorating, Yuli!" Tian Cui said.

Lucinda grinned despite the situation as orcs piled into the tunnel.

The shamans of this group were thinking ahead, buffing their orcs early. Magical designs covered their bodies.

Lucinda squeezed her trigger, sending controlled and measured bursts into the orcs. They were enough to get through their enhanced bodies and kill them.

A roar shook the tunnel as George stepped forward, sending out a pillar of flames that crashed with the orcs like a force of nature. It burnt through orcs, turning them to ash.

Gilly let out a shrill shriek as stones shot out of the ground. She smacked them with her tail, and they shattered, turning into shrapnel that cleared a path through the orcs.

"Ranged, focus on the shamans and the leaders with the horns. Front-liners, just control them as best you can. Yuli, drop area-of-effect spells near the entrance to the tunnel on Lucinda's command. Thin out their numbers," Rugrat ordered.

Unhallowed Ground appeared under the orcs' feet. Erik drank mana potion from his Camelbak, still shooting.

"Reloading!" Lucinda yelled as she ducked and moved from her first firing position. She ejected the magazine, slapping in a new one, and hit the bolt catch. She got back into position. "Back in!" she yelled as the first rounds sailed down at the orcs.

She saw several multi-colored areas no more than two feet wide. If anything stepped into these areas, blades of mana formed and attacked with abandon.

It looked as if Rugrat had figured out a way to create a domain-like area-of-effect spell.

The Unhallowed Ground increased in size until it covered most of the tunnel.

Orcs pressed forward. There were just too many of them, and their bodies were too strong to be stopped with less than an extended burst of rounds or powerful spells.

"Will you just fucking die already!" Tian Cui yelled.

Yuli gathered her mana again and cast Lightning Bolt. It jumped between the orcs, creating a sea of lightning that hurt to look at. Those farther back roared as they broke free of the Control spell and pushed forward. They threw their fellow orcs to the side, slowing their progress.

The special team recovered their sight and cut down the orcs that were still standing.

"Shaman!" Yao Meng yelled.

A shiver ran through Lucinda, feeling the perverse magic of the shaman drawing in the power of the land. The totem on their back glowed, and everything else dimmed as it shot out a blinding beam across the tunnel.

Gilly's pillar of Water cut through the totem's beam and the totem itself. The totem stopped, the power contained within it burning through the materials, lighting up the area and exploded outward, leaving a crater on the ceiling and the floor that rippled through the tunnel as it tore through orcs. The beam smashed into the shaman's barrier.

His totem flared with power, growing brighter. Smoke started to rise from the totem, and the shaman poured out everything he had.

Gilly's beam didn't dim, and the barrier gave way. The totem exploded, and Gilly's beam cut through where the shaman had been.

Rock fell from the ceiling. The reinforced area the team occupied wasn't affected as badly, though Lucinda wondered whether the tunnel hadn't partly collapsed behind them.

The orcs made another push forward. They were bleeding for every inch.

The Unhallowed Ground had increased in strength, reaping lives.

"Prepare to fall back," Rugrat said. The tide of orcs got ever closer, filling up the gaps in their lines with new bodies.

"Fall back!"

"Moving!" Lucinda waved her hand, gathering her magazines. She ran through the trench and up to the second line. She kneeled behind a stone firing position and fired on the orcs.

"Covering!" she and Storbon yelled.

Erik turned and ran. Everyone fired and attacked over him, dropping orcs.

"Damn, these buffs make them a pain in the ass," Lucinda muttered and quickly checked her scouts in the village area.

More groups were coming over, but there weren't as many of them now.

"Yuli, be ready to call down that spell on my mark," Lucinda said.

"It'll take four seconds to channel," Yuli yelled.

"I can work with that!"

"Watch the left!" Yao Meng yelled.

George exhaled a blast of fire that hit a group of orcs that had made it to the trap formations. The orcs were blasted backward.

Gilly yelled, and the rocks around the entering orcs turned into spears and shot out, striking them. The ground started to transform, turning into a slurry that cut down the orcs' running speed.

Another shaman got a clear line of sight and fired at the defensive position. It hit their mana barrier, but the shockwaves made the tunnel shake again, causing it to collapse in more places.

"If they keep going on like that, they're going to block us in," Erik yelled.

"Tell me something I don't know!" Rugrat yelled back.

Formations went off as the orcs reached the traps.

Magic flared to life, tearing up the orcs.

Lucinda smacked the bolt catch, braced, and held down the trigger. With her Strength, even the High caliber automatic rifle was rock steady.

She followed the lines of spells that covered the rounds, using them like tracers. She fired into the groups of orcs until her targets stopped moving. There was no time for controlled bursts.

"Reloading!"

She ducked down and moved from her position. She ejected the magazine, tossing it into her dump pouch, and the storage pouch made the empty magazine disappear. Her hand flashed, and a fresh drum mag appeared. She slapped it into place, hitting the bolt catch, and popped up again.

Tracers cut into orcs, spraying blood on the ground. Formations activated magic that annihilated those within its area of effect. Unhallowed Ground and Rugrat's twin blades had bodies piled around them. Gilly and George fired out elemental attacks, and Yuli joined in.

Tian Cui and Yao Meng used spell scrolls at the same time.

"We need to push forward or we're going to get buried," Rugrat yelled.

Lucinda's rounds cut down one orc; she switched targets and fired. Her scout pulled on her attention as the rounds thudded into the orc. The force stopped their forward momentum before a tombstone appeared and they were tossed to the side. An orc behind them charged forward, wielding rusted axes.

Lucinda looked at her scout. "Yuli, call it now," Lucinda said. The reinforcements were making it to the tunnel.

"Cui, Meng, buff the front-liners. We're going to push out as soon as Yuli's attack clears us a way," Rugrat yelled.

Lucinda gritted her teeth. She didn't want to leave the protection of the defenses, but if they stayed, they'd get buried. Their fight had already partly destroyed the tunnel around them.

She took a quick glance back. *Nowhere to go but forward.*

The rear was blocked with rocks and debris.

Yuli used a spell scroll instead of her own power. A fivefold magical circle appeared over the ground and made it tremble. The stone pushed out ten stone golems that brandished weapons of polished stone.

They let out roars, charging the orcs rushing to reinforce those in the tunnels.

"Move!" Rugrat ordered.

Lucinda ducked down in her trench, switching magazines. She jumped out of the trench and fired her rifle. The orcs were closing the distance quickly, so she barely needed to aim.

Erik and Storbon were beside her, but they weren't able to cut down all the orcs. They stored their rifles and pulled out their melee weapons.

Buffs fell on Lucinda. Her Strength and Agility were rising. Power swelled within her veins as she yelled with the increasing pressure, aching for release.

Erik and Storbon joined her, and they ran forward.

Erik grabbed an orc's wrist that was swinging a club at his head. Erik's fist hit like a train, crushing the orc's stomach and ribs before he threw them to the side. His kicks and punches laid out the orcs, leaving them with broken bones and crushed organs.

He was a human wrecking ball. Mana shifted around him, coursing through his body. He jabbed out with a finger, sending a chunk of metal through several orcs before he kicked out with his foot that seemed to stiffen while it was covered in flames.

He broke an orc with his leg, sending them into those on either side. With a wave of his hand, spikes rose to greet them.

He was powerful, but he couldn't be everywhere, and the orcs kept coming in from across the lines.

Lucinda used her shield, turning an orc's axe. Her sword flashed, tearing through the orc. She pushed past them. She took an overhead chop on her shield, absorbing the impact with her legs. Her sword never hesitated as it crossed right to left.

The orc collapsed, and a tombstone appeared.

Another orc died at her side from a hole in its head. Lucinda didn't have time to thank whoever had shot him as she skirted a small hill of rubble and advanced.

An orc, who had been climbing the rubble from the other side, jumped up. A blast of mana from behind cut through them. Two orcs rushed around the pile, wielding a club and axe. Lucinda got behind her shield as the orcs attacked her.

Their attacks were timed differently. Lucinda reinforced her body with mana and slammed her shield against her first opponent's club before she turned. She used the edge of her shield to strike the side of the axe aimed at her shoulder.

The wood of the axe shattered, and the two orcs were thrown wide by her counterattack. Lucinda blurred forward, using a movement technique. Her blade flashed, cutting through their necks.

More orcs gathered. She used her movement technique to create a blurry trail. She came in under the lead orc's guard, her blade cutting through an orc's knee.

They dropped, and Lucinda reversed the direction of her blade, separating their head from their body.

She turned to the side. A spear glanced off her shield and she rolled along it, catching the orc with a backward blow.

There was a yell from the side as Erik barreled through the orcs.

It was as if he had removed some kind of limit. His punches cracked bones and sent orcs flying. Even as he yelled, her bones chilled, seeing the look in his eyes.

It was the same look he had when he was performing surgery, calm and collected.

At an attack to the head, he reached out, grabbing the offending limb and turning at the same time. He used the orc's body and his own, turning the orc and tossing it back, clearing a path.

Rounds weaved around Erik as he and Rugrat were on the same wavelength, their attacks synced together.

Erik got in close, using his smaller body compared to the orcs to block their forearms so their weapons couldn't be used. A kick to the leg brought one down; his hand, covered in stone, darted forward and tore out the throat of an orc. He turned his same hand, blocking a weapon, as he hit the orc in the chest so hard that they were lifted off the ground with the sound of broken bones. He used a movement technique, shooting to the side. He threw out his hand, and his finger stabbed underneath an orc that had attacked where he had been. Stone and magma exploded in the orc's chest.

Erik waved his hand. Exploding stone darts shot from his fingers, hitting several orcs and killing them. As he moved past them, he tore a blade from one of the orcs. Black and red lines traced the blade, poison, and Fire spells. He threw the blade and struck a shaman, who looked blankly at the blade as he dropped.

Two bullets went around Erik, one under his arm and the other behind his back, hitting two orcs that were winding up to strike him.

Rugrat's rounds were unerring in finding their targets.

Storbon appeared out of a crush of orcs. His body glowed with power, and his eyes lit up with blue light.

His speed accelerated to a new level as he used his air-based movement technique. His spear left afterimages; the air crashed around his blade as his attacks shifted the very air around him. As Storbon darted forward and side to side, leaving destruction in his wake, he rarely needed a second attack to kill his enemies.

Storbon's spear stabbed and slashed with lethal efficiency.

Cold mana filled his eyes, seeing everything as he walked forward at a seemingly sedated pace. His spear flashed and howled as orcs died around him in droves.

Lucinda used her shield and sword as if they were an extension of herself, blocking and attacking, forging a way forward.

They were in the thick of the orcs now.

A horn sounded from behind her. Threads of power filled the air, reaching the orcs. Some stopped, while others slowed as they seemed to fight something internally.

One by one, the orcs stopped fighting and came to a standstill.

"Kill those that aren't controlled by me!" Rugrat yelled.

The orcs yelled, turning away from the tunnel and rushing out.

Lucinda had her weapons up and ready to fight, holding position with Erik and Storbon.

The three of them sported new dents as they turned their armored, faceless helmets to check on one another.

She felt Erik scanning her with his domain before he focused forward.

"I don't know how long it will hold. The stronger orcs and shamans will break the horn's effects the soonest," Rugrat said.

"So, we move forward," Erik said.

"We move forward," Rugrat agreed.

Erik took the lead, and they moved forward to the entrance of the tunnel.

The stone golems were tearing into the new reinforcements, but three of them had fallen already.

The orcs that had been in the tunnel were fighting those that had been outside the horn's area of effect, tearing down their allies.

They made a quick fight of it and ran to attack the orcs that had come to reinforce them.

"I'm going to go around the group and use my horn to get them all under our control." Rugrat mounted up onto George.

The others mounted up as well.

"Just like corralling cows," Erik said. "Follow my lead!"

He set off, Gilly quickly picking up speed. Erik reached down and grabbed two stone war hammers from the ground, holding one in each hand.

He spun the hammers in his hands as they circled around the orcs. A few saw them and charged out of the group. A shaman was putting down their totem, and Yuli shot out fireballs at him, the fireballs washing him away in a sea of fiery explosions.

Tian Cui and Yao Meng aimed at two other shamans that were on the outside. Gilly shot out a Water ball that exploded on an orc, killing it and the three orcs around it.

Erik swung his hammers, striking the orcs as they shot past. Storbon's spear jabbed out and sliced as Lucinda cut down with her sword. The group smashed through the spread-out orcs like a sledgehammer.

George launched a fireball that exploded into a group of assembling orcs, leaving a smoldering crater behind.

It started to get worse as more orcs left the main fight to attack them.

Rugrat blew on his horn. The orcs seemed to fall into a daze, pausing their attack on the group. Then they rushed toward the orcs they had been fighting beside and attacked them.

They pushed on through the orcs, with Rugrat blowing on the horn.

On his last blow, the horn turned to dust and faded away.

The orcs' fighting lasted for a few seconds, and they killed the few orcs that hadn't been tamed by the horn.

"Okay, this thing has a time limit, so we should make the most use of it," Rugrat said. "We'll have them as our vanguard to follow the kidnapped people. Everyone good to go?"

"Good to go!" Storbon said.

"Tian Cui, Yao Meng, plug those other tunnels." Rugrat turned to the orcs as the two pulled out grenade launchers and fired them into the different tunnels.

"Orcs, head through those tunnels. Kill any orcs in your way," Rugrat ordered.

The orcs let out yells and charged forward.

Lucinda reloaded her rifle and then grabbed her sword, following in the orcs' wake.

The orcs rushed through the tunnels. Sounds of fighting could be heard as they reached other groups along the way. The team rode over the bodies that were left behind. The tunnels weaved together, and they fired into tunnels they didn't go through, blocking them.

"Looks like it's opening up ahead!" Yuli said.

The tunnel did open. The sounds of battle rang out as the shamans started to deploy their totems.

They made it out of the tunnel to find a large camp ahead of them, nearly five times the size of the camp they had just fought.

The tunnel was on a rise, so they could see over the large walls.

There were boxy buildings that had been hacked out of stone and pieced together. Smoky fires were littered around the place, with orc tents between the buildings and the stone block wall that seemed to have been smashed together.

Several large tunnels led to the orc stronghold. Lumbering, big beasts could be seen in cages near some of the large stone buildings.

Forty controlled orcs roared and charged the stronghold. Outside, twenty controlled shamans placed their totems, using them to activate green fire that arced down to fall on the tents inside the camp.

The defenders didn't have time to close their gates. The controlled orc warriors attacked anyone that wasn't controlled by the special team.

The defending orcs started to rally and counterattack. The controlled warriors didn't care about their lives, and the shamans' fire was slowly covering the interior of the camp.

The stone golems followed the controlled orcs, their swords cutting through the orcs as chaos ensued.

Orcs covered in pustules ran out from one of the stone buildings at the rear of the stronghold. They were covered in disease and corruption.

"Shoot them!" Erik yelled.

The group turned and fired on them.

Storbon and Erik missed, and Lucinda's rifle jammed. Yao Meng and Tian Cui fired their grenade launchers, but they also missed, instead hitting a stone building and causing it to collapse on a group of orcs.

Yuli raised her staff, and three bolts of mana shot out. They hit the orcs.

As the orcs were struck, their bodies expanded and exploded, covering the area in a green mist with red, flickering light.

Orcs that stepped into this area coughed and shuddered. They looked almost drunk as the corruption infected them.

They ran toward the fight. As they were killed, they exploded, creating smaller areas of the infectious gas that spread to more orcs.

"Rugrat, pull back the healthy orcs. Have some run into the poison. Let them gather it up and then run them with teams to the other orc groups. If the carrier dies before they reach the target, have another get infected and keep going, like plague relay," Erik yelled.

"Get them to spread the disease as fast as possible," Rugrat said.

"Yeah!"

Rugrat organized four groups of five and sent them off with new orders. They entered the infectious clouds, covering themselves in disease, and ran off down other tunnels.

They were ordered not to fight anyone, but to spread the infection as far as possible. The more camps and orc villages they could reach, the better.

The corruption started in the middle of the stronghold, so it hit them the worst.

"Yuli, help it along with some Wind to blow it deeper into the camp," Erik said.

There was a roar from the camp. Lucinda looked over to see that the cages holding the massive creatures had been opened.

They were large beasts with oversized guts and chains hooked into their bodies. They stepped out of their cages, grabbing clubs the size of an orc.

Shamans sent magic down the chains. The massive beasts cried out in pain as they moved according to the shamans' commands.

"That looks like an ogre to me if I've ever seen one." Rugrat fired his rifle. The round crossed over the shamans and the orcs flooding the stronghold to strike the large shaman guiding the ogre. A necklace lit up to fend off the attack. More artifacts lit up to stop the attack. Chains wrapped around the shaman in all kinds of colors. They glowed with power, destroying different charms and artifacts with popping light displays.

The chains weakened from the attack's power. Rugrat's face screwed up in concentration, channeling power into the chains.

The shaman fought back.

"I'll crack his barrier. Hit him with what you've got," Rugrat said.

The chains erupted into a storm of mana blades and exploded. The shaman was flattened to the ground, covered in wounds.

It raised its head just as the rest of the team fired. Grenades and rounds bloomed around the powerful shaman, killing him.

The ogre's arms had chains wrapped around them, each link as big as a child.

With a roar, the ogre waved its hands and smashed the chains against the walls of the stronghold, breaking them and killing orcs indiscriminately.

It roared again, clubbing the ground at its feet, making orcs lose their footing. It swiped its massive club, smashing through several orcs with its crude hammer.

The other ogre turned toward it.

Rugrat fired at the second shaman, but it seemed to be ready as other shamans threw up wards that defended the shaman from attacks.

A spear of stone shot out of the ground and stabbed the shaman controlling the ogre.

They released their chains in pain. The ogre hit the shaman, turning them into paste.

Orcs were coming through the tunnels. Most of them were affected by the plague, having passed the plague groups that were busy spreading their infections.

Yuli's Wind picked up the plague and spread it over the camp, covering it with a thin, green haze.

"Heed my commands! Shamans, buff the remaining orcs with the highest speed. Work in groups of five to spread the plague to as many orcs as possible. Do not fight unless you have to. Spread the plague as far as possible!" Rugrat ordered.

The shamans worked feverishly, buffing the thirty or so remaining orcs. Twenty had already run off, infecting people. Another twenty had died in the fighting.

The orcs ran into the infectious clouds and then ran through the tunnels as fast as they could.

"Shamans, charge into the fight and attack anyone that attacks you." Rugrat's last orders sent the shamans down and into the fight.

Gilly and Erik erected a simple defensive position of spiked ground and trenches.

Everyone got into cover.

Yuli used simple Wind spells, carrying the plague across the camp, concentrating it on the ogres that were running wild, destroying anything they could find.

"Stay down and stay quiet. Looks like they aren't paying attention to us," Rugrat said. "Tian Cui, do you have any Stealth spells?"

"Yeah, one second."

Tian Cui cast spells over the group. Their vision seemed to become darker, and Lucinda felt fewer eyes staring at her.

The special team-controlled shamans harassed the remaining orcs stuck in the stronghold. They were growing weaker as the plague spread and two controlled ogres attacked them.

The new orcs coming in didn't know what was going on; some were infected and others not.

"Looks like they're confused," Storbon said.

"Yuli, target the other shamans with your infection. Let's destroy their command and control," Erik said.

"I think our shamans will fall soon," Lucinda said.

The shamans excelled when they had orcs to command. Without them, they were powerful, but only able to take on a few orcs at the time. But numbers and strength won out in the end.

The fighting between the groups died down. The plague winds had claimed more than a hundred lives, spreading farther as orcs died and released the infection that had built up in their bodies.

"Damn, Yuli," Yao Meng said.

The Wind spells were covering the shamans. Their barriers weren't stopping the infection; they only stopped incoming attacks. The infection passed to them, and they forgot about buffing orcs and tried to save themselves.

"Orcs don't even realize that their buffs are running out," Tian Cui said.

Lucinda nodded grimly. The ogres were covered in wounds, but they were working together, in a limited fashion. Their clubs smashed orcs apart, even with their strong bodies.

The orcs tried to grab the ogres' chains but were struck by them instead.

The team waited, watching the fight happening below.

"Damn, those things are tough," Lucinda said.

The ogres were now showing signs of infection as well.

A group of orcs riding on their war boars entered through one of the tunnels. The boars looked like ponies underneath them.

Seeing the ogres, the leading orc—one with a mohawk and a halberd it wielded like a simple axe—raised his weapon at the ogre.

Shamans called out their spells. Buffs landed on the orcs as they rushed across the open ground toward the stronghold. They passed the orcs running across the ground to reach the stronghold.

"Yuli," Rugrat said.

The clouds of infection gathered, spinning up, becoming thicker, turning from a haze into a mist and then a storm.

It dropped to the ground and raced toward the orcs on boars.

The leader yelled as he brought his halberd back and leaned forward on his boar.

The group ran headfirst into the cloud, lost in the swirling greens and reds.

They burst out the other side, leaving streaks of the cloud behind them.

"Cover the tunnels in it," Rugrat said, his voice grim.

"Bring me some," Erik added.

The cloud split into streamers and rested over the tunnel entrances.

A small amount of the cloud separated and moved around the outside of the open area to Erik. He put his face into the poison and breathed it in before anyone could stop him.

"Cover me." Erik sat down, and Lucinda saw him drinking from his second Camelbak filled with healing and Stamina potion.

He took a few moments then pulled out a potion bottle. He breathed into it, and a red gas with green light spots, the opposite color of the cloud in the room, filled the container.

"Drink this. It will protect you against the infection." Erik passed the gas-filled potion bottle to Lucinda.

"What did you just do?" Rugrat asked.

"I used my Reverse Alchemist ability and infected myself. My body fought off the plague easily, and I could understand it more. I made a poison that would counteract the plague and breathed it out. It was an ability that came with my Poison Body. Quickly inhale it, then your body will have the same resistance I do. Those infected orcs are great against orc groups because the infection is highly contagious and bred inside orcs, but it's not as effective against humans because our bodies are slightly different."

Lucinda watched the orc riders reach the ogres. They slashed and cut at the beasts. If they were a moment too slow, the ogres' hammers would shatter their bodies and the boars they were on, whether they were wearing armor or not.

The team watched the fight, antsy to be so close but not fighting. All of them expected to be attacked at any moment.

They quickly breathed in the gas inside the potion bottle, remaining vigilant throughout.

"I'm getting Experience, but it's limited," Yao Meng said, using the communication device so that no one else could hear them.

"We're all close to level sixty. That's the peak of people in the Sixth Realm. Most of the orcs are below level sixty, and we are using tools to attack them," Yuli said.

"If we want to level up, we need to head to the Seventh Realm. Everything would be a higher level than us, and we would earn Experience from everything we kill," Rugrat said.

"So, what do we do now?" Lucinda asked.

"We wait," Erik said. "They seem to have forgotten about us. We let the plague spread as much as possible, then we can keep going."

"Feels strange sitting here," Yao Meng said. "Will the plague affect people?"

"It'll have some effects but shouldn't kill them."

All of them got comfortable at the mouth of the large, open area, watching as the orcs and ogres fought it out. The ogres took out a lot of them, but the orcs won in the end. Most of them were barely standing. The plague had taken hold; their skin was crawling, and open sores appeared.

Other orcs arrived by way of the tunnels, passing through the green clouds.

The special team waited and watched.

Orcs that had survived in the stronghold started to fall over from the infections. The reinforcements were coughing and looking sickly as they left.

Life was cheap here. Seeing orcs dying, fights broke out over their gear. Others just left, not wanting to get involved.

There were some times when it looked like the orcs were going to head to the tunnel they had created their walls and defenses at the entrance of.

The defenses were hidden from the stronghold.

"Why aren't they coming over here?" Yao Meng asked.

"Illusion formation," Tian Cui said. "I have one covering the area. When they look over here, they see a regular tunnel and it gives them the compulsion to not come this way. With their limited intelligence, they're not able to see through the illusion and just keep on going."

"Hiding in plain sight. Would never work back on Earth, but just about possible in the Ten Realms," Erik said.

"Speak for yourself. I know some snipers you wouldn't be able to find unless they wanted you to," Rugrat said.

Over the next hour, orcs moved back and forth among the tunnels, most of them appearing pallid and sweaty as they trudged about their duties. Yuli pushed the clouds forward.

"Infections and disease claim more lives than any other tragedy on Earth. One untreated infection can spread like wildfire and take out everyone. Even the people that have no visible wounds," Erik said, a grim look on his face.

He turned to Lucinda. "It could very well wipe out the orcs hiding in these tunnels."

A chill ran down her spine.

Fighting them all would be nearly impossible, but killing them with a silent and deadly infection? They wouldn't even know it was happening until it was too late.

38

Empire of Alva

Delilah and the rest of the council were assembled. They sat in the beating heart of Alva. Its dungeon core floated in the middle of the room, drawing in a gigantic amount of power from the separate floors, refining and shooting them toward the mana-storing formation in the ceiling.

All the council leaders cleared away their papers as they started to disperse.

"Dinner tonight at the Steel Boar?" Delilah asked.

Sounds of agreement came from the various council leaders.

"Got to keep up tradition after all." Blaze laughed.

"We could only do our planning at meals when Alva was a village," Elise rebutted.

Delilah smiled as she cleared the last of her papers

"Alva is becoming more complex. There is always something happening." Delilah sighed.

"Enough to make your head spin!" Egbert smacked his head. It twisted around as he tried to walk and instead started to stagger.

"Urgh, no, nope! Stahp!" He grabbed his head and put it facing the right way. "That was a terrible idea."

"Guess that's an aftereffect of being undead—less brains." Blaze tapped his skull.

"That is Undeadist! You take that back!"

Even with all the new roles and changes they had been through, thankfully, the core people hadn't been changed.

Delilah smiled as she stood. The meeting came to an end, and people broke off into groups, chatting to one another, making plans to meet up or talking about different projects and trying to get the other's help.

It was a madhouse, but somehow Alva had prevailed and pushed forward.

Delilah left the meeting and returned to her office. She toured the room, running her hand over her desk. She organized the papers on it and fell back into her chair.

She studied Alva beyond her office windows. The simple, square homes had been altered; many growing up like runner beans. Multiple tall buildings rose around the dungeon core. There were several markets, busy as ever.

Parks and streams had been created and cultivated, and the first Alchemy garden was moved to be part of the academy. And people, there had never been so many people in the streets!

There were chairs and tables across the first marketplace. Restaurants were doing a quick business; chefs and cooks from the academy turned it into their battlefield of flavors and food—to the joy of their fellow Alvans.

Delilah watched a group of people walking by. They must've been new Alvans because they looked around the city with wide eyes. A police officer and a recruiting officer were with them, guiding them to the intake building, where they would be able to stay for two weeks to get themselves settled, learn about Alva, and start their journey to become a supporting Alvan citizen.

Her eyes moved to the academy. It had grown, sprawling across the floor. The library had grown outward, too, becoming thicker and larger, but it had remained in the same style it had been originally built.

The barracks, which had been barely manned in the past, was now filled to bursting. Glosil had put forward a request to create secondary barracks on the other floors and a second barracks on Alva's main floor.

Her eyes drifted to the Alchemy gardens, the parks, and the people. Alva had flourished and thrived here, away from everything else.

There was a knock at the door, interrupting her daydreams.

She turned to the door, clearing her head. "Come in!"

The door opened and Egbert walked in. He closed the door behind him.

"Is there something I can help you with, Egbert?"

"I just wanted to bring you some reading material," Egbert said.

Even without lips, she could tell he was grinning as he snuck to her desk and pulled out a stack of romance novels.

Delilah burst into a smile and bit her lip.

"These are the best ones I picked out for you. We've got summer romance, a king who falls in love with a female warrior. A male warrior who is sent to kill a female shapeshifter, but he is wounded on the journey and she tends to him, then he has to either defend her against more hunters or stand with them against her. This is about a woman cook. She is put down all the time, then she has a fortuitous encounter and surges forward. The powerful men in her class are all attracted to her, and they must all compete for her affections," Egbert said excitedly.

Delilah couldn't wait to dive into the books. "I should've never read that first book," Delilah said. "My mother found it and started reading it. Now she's begging me to share the ones you pass to me!"

Egbert laughed. "Well, when one finds a good read, they must share!"

"Little romance book trickster! You just want more people to talk to about your books! I think you want to create a book club just to talk about them." She laughed.

"Well, what did you think of the *Merchant Warrior*?"

"Oh, come on." Delilah circled in her chair. "You can't use books against me! But it was pretty good." Delilah, a faint blush on her face, fanned herself.

"Right?" Egbert agreed as he dropped into a seat opposite.

"Though, the *Loyal Judicator*—damn, Terrance and Victoria, red hot," Delilah said.

"Oh! That *was* a good one. Yeah, I can't deny that. And the twist at the end, with Ivana falling for Terrance's brother instead of meddling in Terrance and Victoria's life!"

"I thought she was a lot nicer once she found someone to settle with instead of chasing and disrupting others. Felt kind of sad for her." Delilah sighed.

"So, what's up? You're all business-y." Egbert's voice turned authoritative and bossy.

Egbert's words were a hidden sword and a cold bucket on Delilah's head.

Her excitement faded. She didn't answer immediately and instead gathered her thoughts. She stood and turned to the window. A group of soldiers joked and played around with one another as they ordered food; the older lady dealing with them playfully chastised them, using her towel to attack some of them, and they fell around laughing.

Delilah watched other people: teachers, students, traders, workers, farmers, soldiers; people from all walks of life were gathered.

Alvans greeted one another and then went about their business or joined friends with smiles and hugs.

A shadow slowly appeared next to her. Egbert looked over her shoulder. With him there, she felt that he was the strongest shadow.

She had come to rely on his mind, on his suggestions. He was a big goof, but she relaxed around him. He wanted what was best for Alva at his core. Even if he wasn't sworn to carry out Erik's, Rugrat's, and her orders, she could see his own excitement and the joy he took from helping Alva grow.

He was like a father to them all—or a goofy uncle who hung out in the corner and made everyone laugh, using humor to drain their anxiety.

Delilah caught sight of a serving lady sneaking an egg into each of the soldier's dinners. She took the piping hot meals with a younger lady. They served the soldiers, joking and laughing. The soldiers saw the eggs; she admonished them, and they all had thankful expressions as she pinched one man's arm. He flexed his muscles, and she appeared shocked with how strong he was. They all fell about laughing, and she patted the man on the back; they started eating and thanked her.

She waved their compliments away and headed over to greet some new customers, putting her towel on her shoulder.

"That's Miss Sabina. Her daughter was Corporal Helena Sabina. She died when taking Vuzgal," Delilah said. "She fell apart when I gave her the news. She was inconsolable. But when the army returned from Vuzgal, she reopened her store."

Delilah felt her eyes growing wet, a sad smile on her face.

"I asked her if she was okay, that she could rest. That woman's a tiger!" Delilah chuckled. "You know what she said? She said, 'Well, Miss Delilah, my Helena loved my pork noodle soup. She brought her friends every week. I might not be able to make it for my Helena, but don't her fellow army members deserve a welcome? Are they not her brothers and sisters? Are they not missing her as much as I do? So, I'll open my restaurant, and I'll make my pork noodle soup and I will make it until I can't anymore. It is the part of a home that I can give them. When they go out and fight, they'll know that I'll be here with my pork noodle soup and an ear.'"

Silence fell over the room, thick and stifling.

Delilah took a shaky breath and recovered her composure. "The path we're walking will lead to war. It hasn't gone too far yet, but it will. Once the fighting starts, everything could come apart." Delilah turned to Egbert.

"If we let the Willful Institute get away with killing people from the

Adventurer's Guild, we might as well give up on the guild. All we ever wanted was to create a place where fighters could come together and support one another; they might fail, but they have the support of the army to drag down the Institute."

"Do we need to, though?" Delilah asked.

Egbert stared into her eyes. "This is the Ten Realms. If we show even a slight weakness, our enemies will exploit it. We will prove the strength of the adventurers. We temper their abilities; in secret, we bloody and train our people in combat. We will gain cities, selling them. Through Vuzgal, we prove the power of Vuzgal and reinforce our position."

"The cost?" Delilah asked.

"A part of our soul and the lives of those who signed up to defend Alva, to be her sword and shield," Egbert said.

"Shit," Delilah said.

"We are doing all we can to weaken the Institute and increase our own Strength, but with fighting…" Egbert shook his head. "There is nothing sure. But we have our orders. Erik and Rugrat have given us a mission, and we will complete it."

The soldiers talked to one another excitedly as they ate their meal. There were veterans of the Vuzgal conflict, others who were brand new to the military, and other seniors. She had seen the power of the newly trained units. She was stunned with what they could do.

Her eyes moved to Miss Sabina, who was talking to the chefs, ordering meals, and organizing her shop.

39

Orc Plague

The stronghold was a silent grave. All the orcs were dead now. It had been two days since the special team had reached the stronghold.

The area around the stronghold was large, so it was easy for them to find a pile of rocks to hide under, removing the defensive works they had created.

The first day had been nerve-racking as they hid in the defensive works, relying on the illusion formations to keep their position secure.

"Nothing much happening." Rugrat shifted away from one of the slits that allowed them to survey the cavern the stronghold was located in.

"The plague is probably running through all of the tunnels now. The Experience gain has decreased to almost nothing now. It wasn't much anyway," Erik said.

He checked his notifications quickly.

Skill: Alchemy
> *Level: 79 (Expert)*

Able to identify 1 effect of the ingredient.

Ingredients are 5% more potent.

When creating concoctions, mana regeneration increases by 20%

Skill: Stealth

Level: 69 (Journeyman)

When in stealth, your senses are sharpened by 5%

Movements are 15% quieter

15,916,578/108,500,000 EXP till you reach Level 61

He would have to wait until the Seventh Realm to start increasing levels again. "All right, let's see what loot we can get out of this."

Do you wish to:

Take command of the Stronghold

Destroy the Stronghold

Erik put his finger on "Destroy the Stronghold," and a new screen appeared.

Destroy Stronghold: Naraz

You will receive:

1x Bolt of Canvas

16 x Bolt of Linen

1x Box of 20 Candles

12 x Cold Weather Outfit

1x Flask of Oil

12 x Flint and Steel

1x Hammer

9 x Pavilion Tent

4 x Portable Ram
1x Rope Ladder
3 x Sack of Apples
1x Sack of Wheat
1x Salted Ham
15x Vial of Exotic Ink
89x Necklace

Do you wish to destroy this Stronghold?
YES/NO

"Do you think it is safe to move on?" Storbon asked.

Erik looked out at the stronghold and the tombstones there. The bodies were starting to fall apart as the Ten Realms drew their power back.

"If we move carefully, we should be okay," Erik said.

"Kind of hard to do in tunnels. If they see us, we'll have to fight it out," Rugrat said.

"We lucked out that the orcs weren't paying attention to us when we got here," Storbon added.

"Nothing much we can do about that. Have Lucinda push her scouts out ahead, and have Tian Cui checking that we're not running into the enemy," Erik said.

"We'll move out in four hours. Make sure that everyone is ready. The longer we're here, the greater chance there is of someone finding us," Rugrat said.

They checked their gear and prepared themselves.

Tian Cui moved to the front and Lucinda moved to the rear, but there were no changes to their formation otherwise.

Lucinda sent out her beasts that Erik had immunized against the effects of the orc plague. They were rats and smaller creatures that would be hardly noticed.

"Should we loot the stronghold?" Yao Meng asked.

"Can't hurt. Might find another horn," Storbon said, looking to Rugrat.

"All right, but make it quick," Rugrat said.

It didn't take them long to collect everything, accessing the tombstones.

They found ingredients and hides. There were monster cores in the boars, as well, and two of the controlling horns.

Horn of Obedience
Use this horn to gain the obedience of surrounding orcs. Affects an area 15m x 15m.
Uses: 8/12
Duration: 1 Hour

Horn of Servitude
Use this horn to gain the obedience of powerful surrounding orcs. Affects an area 15m x 15m
Uses: 3/5
Duration: 1 Hour

Horn of Boar's Call x3
Use this horn to gain the obedience of surrounding boars. Affects an area 30m x 30m. Increases chances to tame.
Uses: 15/15
Duration: 2 Hours

"Well, we might be able to add some of those boars to our ranks," Erik said as he got a hog horn. Yao Meng got the Horn of Obedience, Lucinda a Boar's Horn, and Rugrat took the Horn of Servitude and a Boar's Call.

"Been missing me some bacon," Rugrat said hungrily. "Okay, let's head out," Rugrat said once Lucinda had found the path where the carts had gone, deeper into orc territory.

Erik smelled it before he saw it.

There were bodies all over the tunnel, some here and there before they increased in number at an intersection in the tunnel. The green-and-red cloud was thinning, covering the dead orcs.

This scene repeated itself again and again.

Erik knew what the effects of purposefully spreading the plague might be, but he had underestimated just how powerful and fast it would spread.

They looted the tombstones—it was ingrained into their minds now—and pushed onward. There were some cases of orcs fighting the plague. They were stronger members, some above level sixty, commanders of the orcs.

The team used their blades to finish them off. The Experience they earned left them with a hollow feeling.

They passed several encampments and other larger bases. The special team used their helmets to block out the smell.

Do you wish to:
Take command of the Stronghold
Destroy the Stronghold

Erik put his finger on "Destroy the Stronghold," and a new screen appeared.

Destroy Stronghold: Lograkh
You will receive:
7xIron Bar
6 x Light Catapult
1x Noble's Outfit
5 x Pitchfork
8 x Rope Net
1x Rug
32 x Sack of Animal Feed

1x Siege Ram
6 x Small Cask of Dried Figs
14 x Small Cask of Tobacco
29 x Small Glass Rod
5 x Small Magnet
1x Weapon Rack
2x Vial of Exotic Ink
37x Necklace

Do you wish to destroy this Stronghold?
YES/NO

"The boars aren't affected by the plague. We could use our horns, turn them into a vanguard ahead of us, and soak up damage for us," Storbon said.

"Lucinda." Rugrat turned to face her.

"I can do it, though the horn's effect will weaken if I use it multiple times."

"Do it," Rugrat ordered.

The boars moved ahead of them. A few tried eating their old masters, but it was too much for the group. As Lucinda enforced that they weren't allowed to eat the dead, they fell onto the wounded and dying with glee, killing them and taking large bites.

Erik's face was hard as he walked stiffly, scanning. He couldn't focus on the fact he had started this.

So it went, looting the dead and controlling more boars, driving them ahead of the group, growing the boars to several hundred.

"There's a castle up ahead," Lucinda said over the communication channel.

"Halt," Rugrat called out. The group took a knee.

"A castle, like the strongholds we've seen?"

"No, this is like a human castle. I don't see anything on the ramparts, though," she said.

"Humans this far in?" Rugrat muttered. "Send in your scouts."

"It looks human in design and the buildings are made from stone, but they're built to fit orcs. The castle is filled with dead orcs. All of them are as strong as commanders. Shit." Lucinda went silent.

"What is it?"

"Some of them are still alive," she whispered, as if the orcs would be able to hear her. She was silent for some more time. Her eyes closed as the rest of the team scanned the surrounding area.

"The castle... it looks like it is blocking a tunnel entrance, and there's something in the main square."

They waited as Lucinda moved her scouts around.

"Damn. Okay, it looks like there are people in those carriages in the middle of the castle."

Erik felt relief run through his body. He bowed his head and breathed out.

"They must be gathering them there," Rugrat said.

"What the hell for?" Yao Meng asked.

"Fuck if I know." Rugrat shrugged.

"What's the plan?" Storbon asked.

"We try and rescue their asses. Didn't come this far for them to be caught in the crossfire," Erik looked up, gripping his rifle tighter.

The members of the special team nodded in their armored helmets.

Rugrat was quiet for some minutes.

"Lucinda, try to make a rough map of the castle."

"On it, boss," Lucinda said.

Rugrat studied the map Lucinda had drawn. They'd fallen back to one of the strongholds as she worked.

"Okay, so the castle has three main walls that are fused with the tunnel sides. It's basically one massive guard house for the tunnel behind it. There is one central castle in the middle of the walls, with views over the surrounding area. It is five to six hundred meters from the five tunnel entrances to the walls of the castle. There is one gate, on the main wall in the middle. There is a main road leading from the gate around the castle and to the tunnel. The other roads angle off the main road, leading to stone homes that the orcs live in. There is an open area behind the castle. There are cages covered in tarps. I'm not sure if there are people in there or not. There are a lot of orcs in the area, and they might notice and kill my beasts if I push in. There are around thirty to forty commander-level orcs that have been seen moving around. It looks like the plague reached here, but the commander orcs are stronger and recovered." Lucinda paused. "There are orc bodies around the castle walls. It looks like they tried to approach the castle, and the defenders cut them down. The gate is closed."

"Looks like these orcs are a little more advanced," Erik said.

"Smarter means harder," Storbon muttered, studying the map Lucinda had drawn.

"It's not like the places we have seen the orcs in before. The other groups were linked in tribes, strongholds where the main forces were. There were signs of infighting with the orcs; while they live together, they are competing among one another. The construction, the positioning—it screams human to me," Rugrat said.

"Maybe it is the leading tribe of the orcs, and they adapted knowledge they learned from humans?" Erik asked.

"With commanders as foot soldiers, they must be the most powerful orc tribe in here," Storbon said.

Erik and Rugrat had ugly looks on their faces, agreeing with Storbon.

"Hitting them head on isn't going to work. Tian Cui and I will sneak into the defenses; you guys make a distraction if we need it. We get into the city and plant charges on the walls. We scout the interior of the castle, spread that plague, pop the walls, and drive the boars into the castle to soften the orc commanders. We'll use the chaos to isolate the commanders and kill them," Rugrat said.

"That's risky," Storbon said.

"Rugrat and Tian Cui are our best at Stealth." Erik backed him up.

"You are never going to make protecting you two easy." Storbon sighed.

"Not when we can be of use." Rugrat patted him on the shoulder, knowing it must be tough for the young man. "When I'm attacking, you'll be in command. Make sure that the boars don't get out from under your command. Thankfully, we found some more controlling horns."

"I'll pass those over to Lucinda. She knows more about beasts and will understand what is going on with them better than me," Storbon said.

They cleaned up the final details, and the group broke apart. There would be three groups: Rugrat and Tian Cui would be the scouting force, with Erik leading Lucinda and Yao Meng as assault team one, and Storbon would be with Yuli as assault team two.

Rugrat and Tian Cui snuck forward toward the walls of the castle, using gear they had purchased just for these kinds of operations.

Cloak of Sneaking	
Defense:	120
Weight:	2.1 kg
Charge:	1,000/1,000
Durability:	100/100
Slot:	Can cover current gear
Innate Effect:	Blend into the surrounding environment.
Formation One:	*Nightstalker*—Reduce the chance of others noticing you, increase your stealth abilities and skills' effectiveness by 12%. Effect will be broken if discovered.

Requirements:
  Agility 37
  Stamina 28

Boots of Silence
Defense:	159
Weight:	1.5 kg
Charge:	1,000/1,000
Durability:	100/100
Slot:	Takes up boot slot
Innate Effect:	Increase Agility by 3%

Formation: *Silencing*—When wearing these boots, your movements and your footfalls are silent.

Requirements:
  Agility 45

Neither had the formation sockets and relied on formations that had been sewn into their fabric. The effects couldn't be changed out; still, they would help them out greatly in their attack.

Rugrat had switched out the formation on his rifle as well.

MK7 Semi-automatic Rifle (FAL)
Damage:	Unknown
Weight:	4.25 kg
Charge:	10,000/10,000
Durability:	100/100
Innate Effect:	Increase formation power by 12%
Socket One:	*Punch Through*—Penetration increased by 10%
Socket Two:	*Silenced*—Weapon doesn't make any noise.

  Range: Long range
  Attachment: Underbarrel Grenade Launcher
  Requires: 7.62 rounds, 40mm grenades

Requirements:
Agility 53
Strength 41

Tian Cui bounded forward, moving between the rocks that dotted the landscape.

Rugrat's rifle traced over the wall, looking for targets. He hissed as he saw an orc moving around on the wall.

Tian Cui, hearing it through the communication device, dropped to the ground. Her cloak settled around her. It flickered and changed colors, blending into the area she was lying on.

Rugrat's breathing was deep and calm. His rifle tracked the orc, ready for any signs of alarm on the creature's face.

The orc didn't notice anything out of the ordinary. It met up with another orc, continuing their patrol together and heading out of sight.

Rugrat continued breathing, though he didn't feel relief, and continued to stay alert. He couldn't relax this close to the wall. He scanned again, looking for other threats.

Tian Cui was facedown on the ground, trusting in him completely.

"Go."

Rock and dirt shifted as she stood up and moved forward again. With her cloak blending into the surroundings, it was hard to see her.

Rugrat was reminded of the times when he had done his training for sniper school. It had been hell moving so slowly, but those skills had become ingrained to his everyday actions and movements.

With the power of the Ten Realms and that same training, the Alvans were like ghosts. Rugrat was impressed with Tian Cui's ability.

He even lost her for a bit before she reappeared.

"Set."

"Moving." Rugrat shifted forward, gliding across the ground. When another orc appeared, he lowered himself to the ground, melting into it. Dropping to the ground would pull one's attention to the movement.

The orc passed and the game of tag started up again, the two moving forward slowly toward the wall. Moving fast was liable to get them caught.

Rugrat swept the wall for formations, traps, and tripwires. He nodded to Tian Cui. The area was clear.

They advanced the last few meters to the wall.

For the first time in hours, they allowed themselves to relax slightly. There were no machicolations in the walls, so the orcs had a good view of the surrounding area, but they couldn't look down.

Rugrat and Tian Cui nodded and moved to part two. They pulled out equipment and got to work, cutting into the wall with mana blades that didn't make any noise as they cut through the stone and planting charges.

They moved to the gate, checking it and placing charges in the places Rugrat had identified as weaknesses in the structure and materials.

Once done, they moved to a section of the wall where the orc guards patrolled the least.

"Charges down," Rugrat reported.

"Nothing in the area where you're ascending," Lucinda said. Her scouts were watching the wall from up high.

Rugrat and Tian Cui pulled out climbing gear that had been modified with silencing formations. They turned to the wall and started to climb, digging in picks and barbed climbing shoes as they started to scale the wall.

Lucinda provided them an update on what was happening above them.

The other assault teams moved into their final positions. If things kicked off, they were ready to fight.

"Orc!" Lucinda called out. They were just a few meters from the top of the wall.

Rugrat dug his feet in, and the two of them pulled themselves tight to the wall, the cloaks covering them.

Rugrat's foot shook. A part of the wall shifted, a rock coming free under him.

Shit. He tried to adjust his foot to make sure the rubble would stay in place.

The orc above them walked around. It snorted in boredom.

Rugrat's foot shifted. He hadn't adjusted to the broken piece enough.

The piece of rubble fell away and dropped down.

It hit the wall and then the ground, sounding like thunder in Rugrat's ears.

"They're alerted to something," Lucinda said in hushed tones.

Fucking orc and your damn hearing. Just turn back around; nothing to see here. Nothing at all. As Rugrat continued his mantra, he mentally readied himself to hurl himself up the wall and take on the orc.

"Orc is looking over the wall."

Although there were no machicolations to look down through, if someone leaned over the wall, they could see directly down. Luckily, none of the orcs had done that while Tian Cui and Rugrat had been planting charges. They probably believed they would see their attackers crossing the ground ahead of the castle walls before they reached the base.

Time stretched before there was another snort and shuffling.

"Looks like he's moving away," Lucinda said.

A few moments later, Lucinda said, "Yeah, you're in the clear."

The two continued their advance. More of the wall fell away as Rugrat shifted his foot. His leg had gone numb holding it in position, but he ignored it as he pushed forward.

They were just a meter or so from the top of the wall when Lucinda stopped them. "Two orc commanders!"

They flushed themselves against the wall again, hearing the footsteps, *feeling* them through the stone wall.

Rugrat heard them leaning over the wall and felt the breeze that shifted his and Tian Cui's cloak.

The orc made an alert noise.

Rugrat moved before Lucinda could say anything, activating his domain as he scurried up. He threw himself over the wall, summoning mana blades that he sent out at the startled orcs.

They were two big bastards.

Rugrat's blades shot out at them. One cut through the orc that had spotted them, tearing him apart. The second dodged to the side and pulled out his blade.

Tian Cui threw a dagger as she reached the top of the wall, but due to her position and where she was, her dagger hit the orc in the shoulder and didn't do anything to stop him.

Rugrat dropped his climbing gear into his inventory and had his rifle up. The orc started when the special round hit it in the neck, looking at them in surprise.

Rugrat stepped forward and fired three more silent shots, following the orc down to the ground.

The silencing spell on the rounds made sure that the orc didn't make any noise as he died.

The second tombstone materialized. Rugrat scanned the area.

"Orcs heard something. Moving toward you but not running," Lucinda said.

Rugrat used his storage ring to collect the bodies and cast his Clean spell, removing blood from the scene.

He jumped off the wall into the stronghold, with Tian Cui behind him.

She had her rifle out now as well.

They dropped to the ground, taking the fifteen-meter drop with ease, then used movement techniques to cross the dead and empty ground.

They entered one of the buildings around the castle. There were orc commanders sleeping all over the place. Rugrat's rifle snapped from one side of the room to the other, taking it all in. He relaxed slightly, as none of the orcs were awake.

Blades of mana appeared in the air around him. He positioned them over the sleeping commanders. As one, they stabbed down into the orcs' vitals.

The sounds of struggle were gone, replaced with silence and blood.

Tian Cui and Rugrat cleared the building and set a trap formation at the doorways.

They climbed up a ladder, opened a roof trapdoor, and snuck onto the roof. It was square with crenellations along the sides.

From it, they could see the wall and down two walls.

They split and moved into position. Rugrat got into position, checking his mobility and taking off his cloak while under it. He used it as a tarp, covering himself and his rifle, blending into the rooftop.

He pulled out a cushion, using it to support his rifle as he laid out magazines. "We're inside the wall. We have firing positions, readying ourselves," Rugrat reported to the two other teams.

"Let us know when you're set," Erik said.

"The orcs on the wall have wandered away. They didn't seem to notice anything," Lucinda said.

Rugrat felt a weight shift as he checked his preparations and switched channels. "Ready?"

"Ready," Tian Cui responded.

He looked over, seeing a slight rise on the roof that was her cloaked position.

He switched back channels. "We're good to go here. Blow it when you're ready," Rugrat said.

"Moving up," Erik said.

Erik moved from rock to rock, watching the wall. The boars snuffled around, moving forward. The two assault teams commanded them, Lucinda in charge of them all as she knew beasts the best out of them all.

Erik saw movement on the wall and heard orcs yell.

"Seems they know we're here!" Yuli said.

"Fire in the hole! Fire in the hole!" Erik hit the formation trigger in his hand three times. It went off with the first.

The walls blew inward, charges going off along its base. The shaped charges did their work as it collapsed back around the castle.

The gatehouse was torn apart, but falling rubble blocked it, making it inaccessible.

Orcs that had been on the wall near the charges had been thrown clear. The first tombstones appeared where they fell.

Lucinda and Storbon used a boar horn, claiming control over the startled boars. In times of panic, they could start to fight against the control over them. The assault groups reasserted control and sent them charging forward.

The boars let out war squeals and rushed toward the walls, dust covering the castle.

Orcs yelled among the walls and horns called out to one another.

Erik saw orcs moving among the rubble. He ran forward with the others, shooting at the moving shapes.

Boars hit the enraged orcs, running through them. More orcs charged out of the buildings to try to assist, but they got stuck in the doorways in their rush.

Damn, that is a lot of orc commanders—not a lower-level orc among them.

Erik was with Yao Meng and Lucinda. Lucinda was holding back, coordinating the boar horde.

Erik and Yao Meng crossed the rubble that had been the wall.

Erik saw an orc cutting boars down with his blade and sending a boar flying with a kick. There were holes and cuts across his body where the boar's tusks and teeth had found purchase.

Erik fired at the orc with a burst of automatic fire.

The orc dropped under the fire as Erik followed behind the boars.

"Contact right!" Yao Meng yelled.

Erik turned to see orcs break through the wall of the building they had been living in. They brandished weapons and wore armor.

"Grenade out!" Yao Meng fired his grenade launcher. The round went through a small window and into the building. The explosion blew smoke out of the building and caused it to collapse. Orcs were killed or thrown down, and the boars trampled and gored them.

They pushed on. He saw Storbon and Yuli hit the main castle.

Storbon's grenades blasted holes in the walls, while Yuli buffed their boars as they charged inside.

The two followed the boars in before the orcs could get a foothold.

Yuli started to transform the castle's doorways, blocking some and trapping others, so the orcs could only leave through the routes that she and Storbon were covering.

Rugrat and Tian Cui were on their rooftop, using it as a firebase. They targeted orcs moving inside the walls.

"Looks like there is a resistance building up close to the rear cave," Rugrat said.

Erik peeked at his map. The boars' initial momentum slowed as the orcs started to get organized and more of them in their full gear got into the fight.

"We'll try to punch a hole through them," Erik said.

Yao Meng and Lucinda followed him as they pushed through the buildings.

Orcs appeared, and they cut them down in a hail of rounds.

They found orc and boar bodies as they pushed up; there was no time to loot them.

They found a series of buildings that had been broken and damaged in the fighting.

Erik turned a corner and saw orcs in a line. Boars attacked their former masters with gusto, but the orcs were holding their own, coordinating and buffing one another with their close proximity.

Erik fired on them, and Lucinda pushed up beside him. The two of them held and fired on the orcs. The orcs yelled and tried to charge forward, but they were impeded by the boars. One threw his weapon in anger. Lucinda dodged in time, and it stuck into a wall.

Erik cut the thrower down with his rifle.

The orcs' line collapsed; the boars rushed through and turned to attack the other pockets of orc resistance.

"Castle is cleared and secure," Storbon reported.

"Sweeping across the rooftops," Rugrat said.

"We're rolling up the remaining orcs near the cave to the rear of the castle," Erik said.

A shadow passed overhead. He saw a flash of armor and weapons as Tian Cui and Rugrat moved from rooftop to rooftop.

Erik used his domain, allowing him to sense what was behind walls. He stopped as he sensed something strange, and he held up a hand to the others. He turned to the wall, lowered his rifle, and motioned to the two others, waving them around the wall.

"In position," Yao Meng said.

Erik pulled out a grenade and let his rifle hang on his sling. He punched the wall, creating a hole in it. He threw a grenade into the hole.

Erik grabbed his rifle and moved around the wall. The grenade went off, and dust shot out of the hole.

He turned to see Yao Meng and Lucinda flow into the door that had been blasted open.

There was the sound of shooting. Erik made it into the room, smoke and dust in his vision, as well as tombstones. Orcs lay around the room. They had been getting their armor on when Erik saw them.

Now, they were just more tombstones.

One quick sweep showed there were none left.

"Move it!" Erik pushed forward instead of acknowledging the destruction that filled the room.

The fights were sporadic, but no one had injuries that needed Erik to act.

The boars' population had been decimated by the attacks, but the ones remaining were much stronger than when they had started. They had grown in size, turning from small horses into small elephants.

They feasted on the dead. Their power grew, and Lucinda had to use her horns to keep them under control. She had used taming scrolls on the strongest among them to make sure that all the boars couldn't rush off if they wanted to, creating a command structure among the alphas in the herd.

The boars started to take on different appearances, growing armor of stone and metal. Their tusks changed as their level increased.

Erik lowered his rifle slightly. Boars could be heard squealing and eating. He looked away from it as he stared at the cave that had been protected by the castle.

It was a large tunnel that could fit two carriages through it.

"Yuli, Yao Meng, Lucinda, dig in facing the tunnel. Rugrat, what about those cages?"

"No prisoners, but I think I've found something."

Rugrat stepped into the cages, observing.

Quest Update: From Orc Jaws

It seems that the orcs want to use the humans for something more than food and sport.

Requirements:

Free the captured humans. Find out the motivations of the orcs

Rewards:

Wandering Hero Title

EXP (Depends on final result)

The Ten Realms created quests to keep things balanced, and it looked like saving people was secondary to finding out what the orcs were doing. It seemed the Ten Realms system didn't like what was happening.

Rugrat waved the updated quest away.

"What do you think the orcs were doing?" Erik asked.

"I'm not sure, but they weren't using these people for sport or eating them. There has to be something more to this all."

"How long do you think it was since the people were moved from here?"

"A day or two, I would think," Rugrat said.

"All right, let's check everything that we have, get loaded up, and we'll head deeper. We're close."

"Got it." Rugrat nodded.

Erik moved to some rubble and sat down. He pulled out his notifications.

15,919,383/108,500,000 EXP till you reach Level 61

Skill: Stealth

Level: 72 (Journeyman)

When in stealth, your senses are sharpened by 5%

Movements are 15% quieter

Skill: Hand-to-Hand

Level: 68 (Journeyman)

Attacks cost 20% less Stamina. Agility is increased by 10%.

Skill: Throwables

Level: 48 (Apprentice)

Your throws gain 5% power

Do you wish to:

Take command of the Stronghold

Destroy the Stronghold

Erik put his finger on "Destroy the Stronghold," and a new screen appeared.

Destroy Stronghold: Kodril

You will receive:

    1x Barrel of Oil

    6 x Bow Saw

    5 x Cart

    1x Light Catapult

    9 x Throne

    54x Sack of Animal Feed

    9x Vial of Exotic Ink

    54x Necklace

Do you wish to destroy this Stronghold?

    YES/NO

40

Water Floor

Glosil found Yui sitting by himself in the cafeteria. He was reading a book as he absently ate.

"You look well prepared for the fight tomorrow." Glosil sat down opposite with his tray of food.

"I haven't read a damn page. I was getting scared that someone might notice. Pretty hard to eat with one hand." Yui chuckled nervously, setting the book down.

"Just can't let them see you sweat."

"Are you sure about staying up here?" Yui asked.

"Instead of going down with you? Yes. You're the one who trained everyone in fighting on water. You have the experience, and you have the people. I have been working on different projects. I know some things, but I don't know them all. Also, this is your operation—I made the mission, and you are completing it." Glosil put a forkful of food into his mouth.

Yui leaned forward and pitched his voice low. "But I know how much you want to go on it."

Glosil drank from his glass, seeing images of the fights they had been in before. For the last few years, there might not have been constant fights, but every single one they had been in was on the edge of a blade.

"I want to. I won't deny it. Not because I like fighting or winning or any of that. You know it, that feeling that if I am not there, then the worst thing will happen. When I started out to build the military, Erik and Rugrat came to me. They told me that I would be the commander of Alva's military operations. Said that I would be in charge of them. You know how terrifying that is? The two lords of Alva under my command." Glosil shook his head, but there was a smile on his face. "They told me they had been stifling me, said that I needed to be a commander without their support. I had everything resting on my shoulders. It wasn't easy, but I got used to it. If I am there, then I undermine your ability to lead. You know what to do—why would I be there? I need to show my trust in your ability to lead, and you need to lead without me there to support you."

Yui nodded slowly. "It's one hell of a weight to carry."

"Good. If it wasn't so heavy it was crushing, then you are in the wrong position. The lives of your people rest on your shoulders. Don't fuck it up." Glosil pointed his fork at Yui.

The two of them fell quiet before they continued eating.

"Once we clear the floor, then what?" Yui asked.

"Then you're on training duty." Glosil smiled.

"Great," Yui grumbled.

"Well, the training has taken longer than anticipated. It's only fair. Also, Domonos's unit is quickly reaching regiment size, while you are still at the battalion size. You'll get some new transfers into the unit to balance it out better. Get you some new blood."

"Got to love training," Yui said.

"So, what is your plan, one more time?"

"We will enter via the teleportation array. From there, we will head across the Water floor at our greatest speed, passing the different islands to reach the central command island. We will have Egbert and Davin, his Fire imp companion, to assist. On the water, Davin will be helped by Egbert, since high Water Affinity suppresses his power. Once on the main island, Davin will melt the ice on the command formation. Once it is cleared, Egbert and the engineers will repair the formation and power it up."

"Sounds simple," Glosil said.

"You always said that the simplest plans are the best plans. Less to go wrong."

"So, you *are* learning." Glosil smiled. "Stick to the plan, watch out for your people, and you'll do fine."

Yui picked at his food.

"Eat up. The troops are watching," Glosil said.

"I don't want to—"

There was no more noise. Yui looked over to Egbert and at the burn marks on the deck of the ship; the Fire imp was missing.

"He just needs some time. He's not very good with cramped spaces, despite his size," Egbert said.

"Just how did you get a Fire imp in here?" Yui asked.

"Well, when making the Fire floor, the gnomes needed to get some materials to kick-start the project. We went on an expedition into the heart of a volcanic mountain range. We were gathering materials and capturing beasts when we came across a little Fire imp. His parents were dead, killed by a purple-flame gryphon. We scared off the gryphon and found the youngster, just a few weeks old, crying his little magma tears out. The gnomes feel for other small races, and they had me look after him. The Fire floor became his domain. He looked after it and became the floor guardian. With time, he gained the ability to learn and speak, and his power grew rapidly. The gnomes treated him well, and he was friends with them, thinking of the older generation like a group of grandparents and the younger ones as his little brothers and sisters. He protected the gnomes who were on the floor with him when he was cut off from the others, though there was no way for them to return and the environment poisoned them with Fire mana." Egbert shook his head. "He remodeled the Fire floor so that they could live a little longer. They did, but none of them had children. When they died off, there was only Davin left behind on the floor. With the Fire mana, he was able to grow to his current Strength and maintain the floor."

Yui thought about the trickster Fire imp, about finding him in Old Wang's noodle shop. "He's a strange one."

"Oh, undoubtedly, but he means well," Egbert said. "Looks like we're almost ready!"

Yui studied the assembled groups, a battalion's worth of soldiers, nearly two thousand in total. It was over twenty times the force that had held onto Vuzgal.

Seeing them prepare, he couldn't help but feel proud. They had come so far in such a short period of time. Alva and Vuzgal had undergone an explosive growth period.

Yui turned back to his four captains.

Captain Sun Li had been there since the beginning. Long Da was a strong woman with a fierce temperament; her ability with her spear was only second to her ability to command. Du Su was a quiet man, but in the heat of battle, he came alive. Gazi was a larger, darker man with a personality to match his size. One of the more recent recruits, he had sought out a future for himself and his family, going to Vuzgal and joining Alva. His family lived in Alva as well—his three sons, five daughters, and one harried but strict wife.

Yui glanced over to his side where his second-in-command, Major Selena Carvallo, stood. She was a shorter woman, but she had a fierce personality. She was organized, direct, and blunt. She didn't take shit from anyone, could poke holes in most ideas and plans, and had become the other half of Yui's brain in the past couple of months. She had passed through training like a fish in water. She made it into the close protection detail and applied to be an officer.

She wanted to become a member of the special teams, but there were limited spots and there was plenty she could do as a leader.

She took the time to work with her varied groups, her natural talent giving rise to her position. Yui had wanted Sun Li as his second-in-command, but Sun Li didn't accept, telling Yui he would be an idiot to not make use of Selena.

She needed time to mature, but she listened and learned at an incredible rate.

"How are we looking?" Yui asked, moving in his armor, rolling his shoulders with it.

"All ready and waiting," Selena said.

Yui faced the captains. "Alrighty, this is it, what we've been training for these last couple of months. Today, we take the Water floor, the last floor of the dungeon. Our key element will be speed. We are fighting on Water. It is not our natural environment, so once we are on the Water floor, we will proceed directly to the target. Anything that stands in our way, we attack without holding anything back. If you have anything to say or need to let me know, this is it." Yui looked at the men and women around him, the core of his battalion. They were both younger and older than him; he commanded people who were twice his age, and they believed in his orders and abilities.

There were no questions in those eyes. There were no smiles, just grim faces filled with determination.

"Okay, Sun Li, you're up first. Selena will go with Long Da and Bravo Company. I will be with Du Su in Charlie Company. Gazi, you will bring up the rear. Let's get this done, Tiger Battalion."

The group fell apart and went back to their companies.

The soldiers wore the same camouflage uniforms, helmets, and carriers. Each of them was loaded with backpacks filled with gear: medical pouches on their sides, grenades, magazines, their rifles slung over their necks.

Everyone was ready and broken into their groups. The medics had their bright-red crosses on their shoulders, artillery had a black mortar tube, riflemen had one rifle, sharpshooters had two crossed rifles, and engineers had a magical staff crossed with a hammer. The mages had a thunderbolt slash, and the close protection detail had a simple CPD stenciled on their shoulders.

Yui looked over to Sergeant Niemm. He and his special team were there. He had fourteen people with him. They had modified their gear further. On their shoulders, they had a laughing skull. Some of them had modified their masks to look like skulls by painting them.

Yui pulled his helmet out of his storage ring and pulled it down over his face. The issued mask covered his entire neck, head, and face. With their helmets on, they resembled ominous iron golems, unfeeling and uncaring.

Yui secured his mask to his face and checked his rifle.

The first two platoons moved onto the teleportation array. The next group moved up to the ready position, and the other groups marched behind them.

"Launch!" Sun Li yelled.

A flash of light, and the array was clear. The next group rushed forward and into position. Egbert monitored the array below and on the main floor.

Another flash, and the second half of the combat company was away.

The first two platoons of the Bravo Company stepped onto the array. The people of Alva watched as they disappeared into the unknown.

Finally, it was Yui's and the two platoons he was with turn.

The light flashed, and the living floor disappeared. A world bathed in blues and freezing cold appeared.

The platoons rushed off the array toward people who had been set up to guide them into their positions.

"Report!" Yui ordered Selena, who had gone ahead.

"No hostiles. We found a supporting formation. The engineers are working on it now. We have a point to launch from."

Yui changed it to a leadership channel. "All right start getting on the boats!"

"Understood!" the captains said at the same time.

Alpha Company remained in their defensive positions, watching the island and the water for threats. Bravo Company split into two groups as they'd trained, each half-company.

Gazi arrived, and Selena passed on Yui's orders to him. Egbert arrived with the last group.

"Egbert, help the engineers working on the secondary formation," Yui ordered.

"On it." Egbert flew across the ice-covered ground. The engineers had used mages to melt off the ice and snow and were trying to bring it back online.

Bravo Company used specially acquired, large-capacity storage rings to hold siege equipment to deploy sections of their ships along the side of the port. The engineering platoon used Fusing spells to pull the ship together.

In just a few minutes, the first ship was ready, nearly two hundred meters long and covered in firing ports and casting towers. Formations carved into its sides glowed with power.

Bravo Company engineers moved to assemble their second ship as the other squads braced the first ship next to the water.

"Push!" a staff sergeant called out to the Bravo Company's rifle platoons.

With a grunt, they pushed the ship off the ice, and it tilted and dropped into the water. It righted itself as the rifle companies pulled the ship back toward their side of the broken ice.

They moved the ship forward, clear of the second Bravo Company ship that was coming together. Planks were laid down, and platoons started to load up.

Bravo Company repeated it with their second ship.

"Bravo Company, move your ships out of the port to protect us," Yui ordered.

"Yes, sir," The boat's runes powered up, and the ships moved out of the port, presenting their sides to open as much of their firepower up to the Water floor.

Charlie Company pushed their first boat into the water and started loading, followed by their second.

Yui boarded the second ship. He moved to the command deck. It had more formations to control the flow of information and give him a clear view of the battlefield to command and control.

People rushed to their stations, and weapons were pulled from storage rings, mounted, and pinned in position.

Formations came alive as mages checked their functionality.

Ammunition belts were fed into weapons that were readied. The gunners checked their line of sight and arcs.

Charlie Company moved to reinforce Bravo Company's ships.

Delta followed afterwards, though instead of pushing out on their ships, they assembled Alpha Company's ships before they loaded up their own.

"All right, Alpha, collapse inwards and board your ships." Yui stopped talking on the comms, speaking into the air. "Egbert, any luck?"

"One second."

"Formation is active," Sun Li reported, a limpet to Yui.

The map displayed on the wall changed as information filled it.

"Shit," one of the platoon lieutenants said, seeing the moving blips on the map. "They're underneath us."

"Delta is boarded. Alpha will be boarded momentarily," Selena said in Yui's ear.

"Tell me once we have everyone boarded," Yui switched to the company commanders' channel.

"Just as we practiced. Keep a watch for hidden ice and obstacles."

"Yes, sir," the different captains replied.

"Last of Alpha and the engineers are loaded," Lieutenant Colonel Selena reported.

"Bravo Company, start pushing toward the objective," Yui said.

"Yes, sir!" Captain Long Da said.

Her two ships watching the area turned, and their formations glowed with a deep-blue light, illuminating the dark water around them and creating a halo effect from the spray.

The ships surged forward, charging into the waves.

"Charlie, follow behind. Keep your spacing." Yui checked the securing line at his waist that held onto the map desk.

"Prepare for acceleration!" The order was passed through Charlie Company ships three times. People found hand holds and checked their lines.

He looked down from his command center through the stairs, seeing the gunners, their assistants, and mages watching through their portholes.

The ships turned, the wood creaking as the formations increased power.

They rode on the small waves, water splashed against their clothes and their masks as they picked up speed.

Water rushed over the decks. Some people, whether from the nerves or the motion, lifted their helmets in a panic, leaving their last meals on the deck. Thankfully, the water washed it away, and the wind cleared the smell.

The ships moved into formation, pushing out of the crack in the ice that had acted as their port.

Yui checked the map. They were stretched out in a long line, following one after another. His map was updated with information from the sensing formations.

The different gunnery commanders saw the same information displayed on the walls and had their people watch where magical concentration was being detected.

"Use Detect Life formations," Yui said.

A ripple of power spread out from the ships that bobbed across the water. People tensed as they saw just how many animals were around them, seeing them through the walls and the water.

"We've got company," Gazi said.

Yui looked over and saw a group of animals charging for the ship. They were moving at great speeds. "You're free to open fire."

The ships opened fire on the approaching creatures. The side of the ship lit up as mages used lightning attacks to stun, and the gunners left streams of tracers cutting through the water. Formation sockets to improve bullet penetration in the water were added every few rounds, and there was an explosive round that would penetrate a dozen or so meters and then explode.

This killed many the creatures, but they sped up and spread out, chasing the boats.

"We've got more of them showing up. Watch your arcs!" Yui saw the map display more groups of fast-moving creatures.

They couldn't take many hits, but there were a lot of them and they were *fast*. The gunners had quick reaction speeds, many times the human norm, and even they were having to fight to keep up with them.

Yui heard the weapons going off in his ship. He glanced to see everyone working together and turned his attention back to the battle at hand. He needed to focus on the overall fight.

"New creatures detected at our front," Long Da said.

"Understood. Bring them under fire as they come into range," Yui said.

Long Da and the captains commanded their ships while Yui and Selena coordinated positions and watched it all.

"Second beast type has a ranged attack, a close-range Water attack—looks nasty. They're much slower than the first beasts and in lower numbers, about five to ten in a group compared to twenty to forty of the first beast," Selena said.

Yui felt an unnatural movement, and the ship shuddered.

"We just got hit. Minor, but there is something ranged out there. Locating!" a lieutenant said, fighting to be heard over the sounds of battle.

"I have it! Six hundred meters away, four o'clock position," a gunner commander yelled.

Yui checked the direction where the hit came from. Using the Eagle Eyes spell, he saw it. "How the hell did it hit us?" Yui muttered.

It looked like a large sail with a pipe in the middle of it. There were holes across its body as it contracted.

"Brace!" he yelled, sensing the mana being drawn into the beast's body.

Its mouth broke through the waves; its white, almost translucent, body contracted as it opened its mouth. It ejected a projectile of Water that had been compressed and frozen into an ice shell.

It struck the mana shields, causing them to bloom.

The sea had come alive with beasts that were hunting them down.

"We're halfway to the mainland. We just need to keep fighting," Yui said as more beasts were attracted and coming over from where they had been hiding.

The machine guns spat out rounds, and the grenade launcher teams left water geysers across the water, traveling some meters down and then exploding. The helmets were fighting to keep the noise down.

"Fire Teams Five to Seven and Twelve to Fourteen, take out those long-range beamers! One, Three, Eight, and Seventeen, target the lancers. The rest of you, go for the crabs!" the lieutenant yelled out.

Yui watched as a crab jumped out of the water. They were a mix between octopus and crab. They were shaped like an octopus, but they had the armor of a crab. The octopus-like mouth shot out water to propel them, and the armored tentacles were covered in blue mana to increase their speed or change their direction. They had four claws that stuck out of their heads.

The crab flipped in midair and landed with its tentacles on the deck, stabbing them into the wood as they ran up the hull, wielding their claws.

It was an ominous sound, to be sure.

A man attacked one of the beasts with his sword as it reached one of the gunners. In a few strikes, he tore the crab apart and kicked it out of the opening.

In another place, a man used a large war hammer; the crab turned into flying debris and covered the water.

"Use blunt weapons against the crabs when they attack."

A lancer got in close and attacked, hitting the ship with its horn, making the hull squeak and shake.

"Toss out depth charges!" a lieutenant called.

"Stagger the ships' line!" Yui ordered.

The ships created a "Z" in the water, no longer following right behind one another and allowing the depth charges to go off without causing friendly fire.

"Fuck!" Yui grabbed onto a railing as a beamer fired. It hit the shields, and the force caused the ship to shake.

The sea was fighting them, but they forged a path onward.

"A new beast just appeared. It's a hydris," Selena yelled into Yui's ear.

"Hydris?"

"As big as two ships, all tentacles and anger. It's deep and just shrugging off our depth charges," Selena said.

"Egbert!" Yui yelled.

Egbert rolled with the waves and the ship. He was at the top of the very last ship. He had tied himself there so he wouldn't fall over.

From his vantage, he could see all the ships. The waters raged, sloshing over the ship decks, and storm clouds brewed over the fleet at a rapid rate with the fighting.

Mana barriers flared with hits from the beamers and lancers. Mages poured out spells while gunners created whips of tracers and lines of explosions in the water.

The water rippled as groups of biters rushed forward, another charge through the ship's weapons fire.

Grenades dropped among them, churning up the sea and making them fall into disarray.

A beamer surfaced, and Egbert saw a multi-layered spell formation snap into existence, as several lances of fire, enhanced by a supporting formation, shot out from the side of the ship. The water vaporized underneath them as they struck the beamer. Only two struck, one meeting the water projectile and turning it into an exploding ball of boiling water, while the second pierced through the beamer, killing and cooking them as they exploded from the rapidly boiling liquids in their body.

A wave of force rippled off one ship, shaking it but throwing the biters that were on it off into the ocean. Lightning dropped around the ship, turning it into a land of sparks and electricity.

Egbert felt a large fluctuation. His head turned to look toward the mainland. The lead ship carved around an iceberg and rocks, making it out to the other side as others followed behind, their propulsion formations glowing silver, blue, and white across their ships. They took their hits and pushed on.

Egbert looked through the dim light and past the ships. He saw something moving unnaturally in the water far ahead.

It raised its bulk, appearing in its full form.

"Oh, that's ugly." Egbert peered at what seemed to be an oversized catfish. But instead of just a mustache, it had several tentacles around its face.

And it was the size of a small island.

It rose out of the water with its mouth first. Its sideways eyes surveyed the area, its tentacles slapping the water.

Waves like arrows shot out from where the tentacles hit the surface, spreading outward.

The lead ship moved out of the way of a direct hit. The glancing hit made the ship tilt wildly as it curved back around in the water, bringing its one broadside to bear on the creature.

"Egbert!" Yui's voice entered Egbert's mind.

"What?"

"Kill that damn hydris!" Yui said.

Egbert's eyes changed color as he channeled mana from the Alvan dungeon.

Floors above, the mana flow into the mana-storing formation ceased. It seemed to have evaporated; thin threads curved back around and surged down through the floors.

Mana gathered around Egbert as runes appeared across his body and skull. Mana revolved around him, and he lifted his hand.

Golden, rotating spell formations appeared in front of his hand. A torrent of energy was released through him, shooting out of his hand and slamming into the first spell formation as more mana was gathered.

The first blast shook the ship he was on and sent out a wave of force. The beasts attacking his ship fled in fear.

The second spell formation was completed as power was drawn in from the environment. Threads of blue added to the golden pillar as it squeezed through, striking the third and passing between it and the fourth. An unknown and unseen change happened as the meter-wide beam shrank to the size of a beer can and fired out of the final magical circle.

It left the ship almost peacefully. Under it, the water was carved apart, shaking the ships as the compressed spell passed the rear of the lead ship that was firing on the hydris as it was about to strike out at them again.

As soon as it saw the projectile leave Egbert's pop spell formation, it had been trying to escape, but it wasn't fast enough.

The projectile bloomed into a flower pattern, with one projectile in the middle and eight dots of light surrounding it.

A drill of Water was created at the front of the spell, supported by its golden light. The drill struck, and golden light exploded out of the hydris.

The light was so bright that few could see what was happening. Egbert watched as the half-formed spatial realm, powered by a failed domain within the spell, activated and then failed, containing the raging power of the spell and taking the destroyed hydris to a newly created spatial realm that collapsed at almost the exact moment it existed.

The light shut off abruptly.

"Push for the central island as fast as possible," Yui yelled.

The convoy of ships moved at their fastest pace, not wanting to let the local residents have any more time than necessary to attack them.

"Group coming in again!" someone called out.

Yui was getting tired of the constant attacks; he'd hoped it was over after the Hydris.

Charlie Company's second ship's barrier flared as several beams struck it from the depths of the Water floor.

"Mages, hit those beamers!" an officer ordered.

Spell formations appeared under the water, raising water plumes as they attacked the beamers.

"Lancers targeting Delta Company's second ship."

"Have them rotate forward and drop Bravo Company's second ship to cover them," Yui yelled over the depth charges that were being dropped all around the ship.

The ship shuddered under the impact of beamers.

Sea water rolled in through the portholes, spraying Yui as he held onto the command table.

"Biters! Hold your stations!" a sergeant yelled from below.

A group of biters swarmed through a gunnery hatch. The soldiers' yells were drowned out by creaking wood, depth charges, and spells.

They used spears and hammers, killing the biters and sending their corpses out to sea.

"Oh fuck!" Sun Li's voice made Yui look over through the windows at the line of ships.

"Bravo Company's second ship's been holed. Lancers came out of the deep, tore the hull out!" a communications man yelled.

Yui jumped onto the communication channel.

"How bad is it, Jeff?" he asked Lieutenant Hollingsworth, who was in command of the second ship.

"We're taking on water. We're going down. I have the lower floors pushing up, we have wounded and dead." Jeff's voice was calm

"Beamers are targeting!" someone yelled in the command center.

"Give them fucking cover. Have the rest of the fleet circle around the ship!" Yui yelled and changed to the communication channel. "Get your people to the upper floors. Deploy your lifeboats if you need to. We're coming for you."

"Yes, sir!"

Yui closed the channel. "Tell me if he contacts you again," he said to the communications officer who had warned him.

The ship shifted its bulk, and the entire formation shifted. The forward ships cut to the left, while the rear ships cut out to the right.

"Pour on the power. I want to see what these ships can do. Egbert, hit any threats you spot around that ship! Tell the ship leaders to get their rescue boats ready, and we'll secure a cordon. On my command, they will deploy to take everyone off that ship and cross load them to the remaining boats."

"Sir!" Sun Li said.

"Prepare rescue boats for launch!"

Shutters opened on the upper levels as Close Protection Details prepared to go out into the raging seas.

Beams cut across the water, hitting the ships.

"Egbert, send Davin out. I want those beamers shut up!"

"Yes, sir," Egbert's voice appeared in the ship.

The rear ships that had turned right cut hard and fast to the left, turning in front of the sinking ship. Men and women were fighting to stay afloat; others were jumping free of the ship and launching rescue vessels.

The ship listed to the side, and its lower decks were submerged already.

Mages were fighting from their formation towers as the ship went down. Biters, while unimpressive on land, were deadly in the water.

The formation closed in. All seven ships created a cordon around them, driving through the waves, their own force of nature.

"Go!" Yui yelled. Boats were released from storage rings, and close protection teams jumped into them and pushed off from the ships. They rained down on the sea, taking the impact with their bodies.

Runes on the rescue vessels flared to life as they took on waves twice their size, charging toward their comrades.

Formations were secured to the deck with mages preparing spells.

Yui felt his stomach twist as he saw the life signs coming from the depths.

"Lancers!"

The horned beasts surfaced, driving into the ship. The lake stirred, and mana was directed along their massive horns.

The lancers' water drills tore through the ship in several places.

Mages and melee went into a frenzy, attacking the lancers, killing them and dying the water red with their blood.

The ship's fate was sealed; the last sections dropped away, claimed by the Water floor.

Rescue ships rushed to save their people from the water.

"Did we get everyone?" Yui asked Sun Li said.

"No remaining life signs in the area."

"I want Charlie Company's ships out front; they'll break out of the cordon formation once we've recovered all our people. Tighten up the formation."

"Colonel, Davin has dealt with the beamers," Egbert said.

"Good. I want the best speed toward the central command formation." Yui felt a chill that wasn't from his wet gear. "Give the standing order to constantly release depth charges. I don't want any more lancers getting close."

The convoy was rushed by biters, and they started to serpentine through the water to avoid the lancers and throw off the beamers. Depth charges and spells threw the water into chaos, spraying the ships and those on them with water.

Beamers attacked them from a distance, and lancers tried to charge forward, but it wasn't the crush of attacks that it had been before.

Yui watched over it all. The ships were doing their jobs; their shields were holding, but they had needed to repair parts that were broken or leaking from the attacks that had struck their hull.

A spell formation appeared around the ships. Ice spread out across the water, freezing even the beasts attacking the ships. Ice spears dropped from above, stabbing into the captured beasts.

The Water floor turned silent as the creatures rose to the surface, leaking blood through the water.

"Get ready for landing!" Yui looked past the ships to the shimmering ice mountain with incandescent turquoise water flowing down its sides. Black clouds remained pinned above, releasing rain and snow on the ice mountain. It filled the crater, passing through the mountain and running down its sides. Ice covered the ground where the mountain reached the water, creating an island around it.

He glanced over to the sides. He was unable to see the sides of the floor easily, but there were dark shapes where other rocks and icebergs poked out of the water.

They reached the island and got off their ships.

"Okay, we'll head to the top. Delta Company, take the lead." Yui rotated out the companies, so they were fresh. They had each trained for different parts: defending, navigating the water, and ascending the mountain.

They headed up in sections, close enough to support each other should something happen but far enough away that they wouldn't be taken out together.

Captain Gazi and his company started off first, marking out the path as they went. They picked out a route amongst dozens of twisting paths that made it look like a drill up close. They crossed icy plains, passing streams and rivers that ran over the ice and crashed into the sea below.

Their mages worked to alter the mountain, so it was easier for those behind to ascend.

"Water!" someone yelled ahead.

Yui looked around in confusion.

"Hold onto the lines! Pin into the rock!" someone else yelled.

Yui did so, and then he *saw* it. Water poured down the path they were on, slamming into people and sloshing down the side of the mountain. Paths had been cut into the mountain by the water, and then the water had frozen along the side of the mountain, creating perfect paths up and for descending water to rage through.

Yui and the others braced themselves, sticking their securing lines into the wall. Some people fell, and others were washed down.

"Grab that man!" a sergeant ordered.

"Secure your lines! Secure your lines!" Yui barked. The water hit Yui, freezing him down to the bone as it soaked through his clothing. Soldiers shrieked and yelled or grunted as their body was shocked by the sudden cold.

The rush of water passed, turning to an icy trickle that reached the troops' mid-calf.

"Get on your feet! Push on! Move it!" Yui's voice cut through the command channels and over the mountain. Soldiers pulled one another to their feet, and they pushed on.

"Knock holes in the sidewall to take out some of the water," Gazi said.

Mages used spells, cutting through the sidewall, the icy water flowing over the side of the mountain, creating a series of new waterfalls.

They forged on.

"Let's push on. We need to get to the top," Yui ordered the company captains. He had lost enough today He didn't want to lose any more people.

They were nearly there. Once they completed the mission, then he could think of the dead.

They continued to ascend. Gazi's Delta Company reached the top, using spells to alter the surrounding area and stopping water from washing the rest of the battalion down the mountain

Yui reached the top and looked around. The mountaintop was cut out like a bowl. Water rained into it, creating a freezing pool of water that shone with brilliant blue light.

A wave of potent Water mana covered the top of the mountain. Yui stuffed a pill into his mouth to counteract the Water mana, so it wouldn't harm his body.

People staggered under the power of the mana. Medics were there, waiting for them and feeding them pills.

In the center of the brilliant blue water, the central formation rested.

It had taken several hours to reach this point. The climb had left them all exhausted.

Yui walked over to Gazi. "You haven't started creating a path?"

"We started, but that rain drilled through the boards we were putting down. Watch." Gazi took out a stone staff and pushed it into the rain boundary; pieces were cut off as he submerged it into the pool of water. He pulled it back out. The sharp cuts from the falling water had been smoothed over, and the stone staff looked as if it had been worn away by centuries of wear and tear.

"Looks like we'll have to wait for Egbert," Yui said. "In the meantime, get people warmed up and fed."

Gazi nodded and passed the orders through his communication device while Yui gazed into the pool in front of him.

Egbert turned his eyes but couldn't turn his head "What is going on?" He looked up at Yui.

"You might need to reassemble yourself." Yui smiled.

Egbert's magician's robe covered him, and his bones glowed as they came back together. "I'm a little out of practice with using that much mana. It must've caused me to go into standby mode as my body repaired itself." Egbert stretched, pushing some of his bones out of place. They fell to the ground, lit up with runes, and floated back to his body.

"We need your help." Yui turned, and Egbert looked at the main formation for the Water floor.

"That is some highly concentrated Water mana indeed. Wouldn't try going in that unless you're a Water elemental or pure Water. Yeesh, be a tonic for them and cause anything else to explode or dissolve. Water is weird." Egbert looked up at the rain.

"It looks like regular rain, other than the ominous clouds, but it goes through stone and wood pretty easily," Yui said.

"Lovely. You take me to the best vacation spots." Egbert tapped his chin, looking over it all. He waved his hand, and Davin appeared.

Davin opened his eyes groggily. "Urgh, cold. Napping." Davin tried to turn and go back to sleep.

Egbert held his shirt and shook Davin, not allowing him to go back to sleep.

"Hey!" Davin looked around, and the air around him started to heat up.

Egbert held him to the side. "You know how I tell you to not test your limits?"

"Yes," Davin said, as if trying to figure out what he had done wrong.

"Well, this is not one of those times. Let's see how warm you can get!"

Egbert jumped in the air and flew over to the central formation, using Davin to cover his head.

"Hey! That's condensed Water mana!" Davin yelled. His whole body glowed red, and steam rose around him as he ramped up higher and higher, causing the condensed Water mana to evaporate.

"Stop using me to stop you getting your head wet!" Davin yelled as Egbert crossed to the island. There was no rain from above; a hole had formed in the clouds over the central formation.

"Flames, please!"

Davin released flames from his mouth, melting through the iron-strong ice, and it flowed into the surrounding pond.

"I wondered why there wasn't any condensed Fire mana on the Fire floor. You ate it, didn't you!" Egbert turned Davin around.

Davin put his fingers together, his head dropping to his chest. "Well, I didn't *mean* to do it. I was going past it one day, and I went in there for a nap. It was nice and warm. I kept getting closer to the source in my sleep. And I might've accidentally been snoring, and a drop *could've* fallen in. I didn't know. I thought it was just spicy water, so I had some sips of it now and then. It took so long for any of it to form." Davin smiled as widely as possible.

"Only someone who's consumed and dealt with condensed Fire mana could deal with condensed Water mana." Egbert sighed. "No more eating condensed Fire mana! Do you know how hard humans have to work to even withstand those places? Took Erik weeks just to get close to the source. That guy is a masochist, though."

"What's that?" Davin asked.

"Uh... it's...too much for your young mind. Come now, flames!"

"I'm centuries old!" Davin complained. He produced flames once again, covering the central formation.

Once it was clear, Egbert went over the formation.

"Pretty much intact, just worn down over time." Egbert took out Earth mana stones and put them into different places. The rings of the formation lit up. He placed the last one, and lines of light traced out from the mana stones, splitting into runes and shapes, connecting to one another and lighting up the formation.

The surrounding mana swirled toward the mana formation before it redirected that power. Lines appeared down the side of the mountain; the centuries-old formation reignited once more. Out in the darkness, Egbert saw another formation light up. A secondary array activated, then another and another, like beacons in the darkness.

To Egbert, the entire floor came alive as reconnected to the rest of the dungeon. He held up his hand. The locking doors separating the Water floor from the Wood floor unlocked and pulled apart.

Power, pure mana descended from above as ambient non-Water mana shot out from the formation underneath Egbert's feet.

The two lines passed one another. The pure mana descended through the center, and the non-Water mana created a pipe around it.

The Water floor calmed, and Egbert looked out into the darkness. It was massive, and although some of the formations had survived, many were broken or not operating.

Egbert pulled out a dungeon core and placed it above the central formation.

You have come into contact with a dungeon core. With your title: *Dungeon Master Servant*, new options are revealed.

Do you wish to:
Create Dungeon

Egbert selected "Create Dungeon," and he took out an ancient blueprint. "I didn't think I would have to use this. Good thing that I made copies of the original blueprints!"

> *Blueprint accepted*

Power from the formation diverted through the dungeon core, remodeling the floor as if a separate dungeon.

Egbert jumped over to Yui, with Davin above his head again.

"Is that it?" Yui asked.

"That should be it." Egbert felt as if he had put down a weight that had been resting on his shoulders for a very long time.

He couldn't bring the gnomes back, but he could honor them.

Seeking Aid

Domonos sat at his desk, staring at the information on the three battalions under his command when there was a knock at the door.

"Come in!" Domonos said.

Lieutenant Colonel Dominik Zukal, his second-in-command, marched in first, followed by Lieutenant Colonels Choi, Acosta, and Hall, commanders of First, Second, and Third Battalions, respectively.

They stood at attention, and Zukal snapped off a salute.

Domonos returned the salute. He waved to the chairs and activated a formation to make sure that no one could listen in on their conversation.

"We have new orders. It will take a few months for the repairs to be completed on the Water floor. We are now shifting to a war footing. Tiger Battalion will prepare to defend Alva and Vuzgal and support the Adventurer's Guild in the field if needed. Officially, Dragon Battalion's base of operations will be Vuzgal, while Tiger Battalion's will be based in Alva."

Silence remained in the room.

They're eager to get into the action.

"At this time, only select Close Protection Details will head out on external operations. There is a rotation schedule. Anyone who is not selected for external operations, or doing assigned tasks, will undergo training, attend the academies, or work on their fighting techniques and cultivating."

Zukal raised his hand. Domonos waved for him to talk.

"Will the Tiger Regiment not fall behind in their numbers?"

"The training battalions will be intermixed, half from the Tigers, half from the Dragons. We are the same army, and we will be operating together and apart in multiple roles. Although Vuzgal has an overall larger population, Alva will be taking on recruits from the general population, from the people from the First Realm and the military units operating out of King's Hill. It wouldn't surprise me if they quickly reach our own numbers," Domonos said.

Choi raised his hand. "Sir, what about ongoing operations against the Willful Institute?"

Domonos felt their focus sharpen. They had been training and preparing for it, reading the reports and information daily.

"Currently, we are undermining them in every sector. The Adventurer's Guild went for their missions and have sowed dissent among the merchants and the Institute. The Trader's Guild followed up with a second volley, attacking the roots of the Institute's trade and bolstering the reputation of the Adventurer's Guild. With the support of the academies, they have carved out a portion of the Willful Institute's income that is no small amount. Our information network has infiltrated their network, making it appear that some of these actions have not been done by external forces but by other factions, igniting fits of anger and frictions within the Institute. With their anger focused on one another, we have been chipping away at their power base."

Domonos stood. "The Trader's Guild and Adventurer's Guild have been using information from the different spies to find potential recruits and taking them away before the Institute can recruit them.

"We have uncovered the groups with a grudge with the Institute and built their animosity, using them as our puppets to take from the Willful Institute. It has created a smoke screen for us to operate behind.

"I want our people to know those places inside and out. I want to have positions prepared to assault each location. I want to know where their food stocks are, how many days' supply do they have? Their Stamina potions? Are there hidden routes in and out of the city? Are there powers in the surrounding area that we can get to fight the Institute for us?"

"That won't be easy," Acosta said.

"We might not complete it this month or the next. It might take a half-year. But when the fighting begins, we can hit them with a series of lightning attacks before they realize what is happening."

The two men peeked at one another

"One way or another, we will destroy the Willful Institute."

"Salute!" Colonel Yui saluted the seventeen new names carved into the memorial in Alva Park. Behind him stood the rest of the military men and women within Alva.

Yui gripped his jaw tight as rifles fired, making the civilians to the side jump in shock.

"At ease!" Yui commanded, and everyone behind him stood easy.

Yui marched to a podium. He glanced at the names, took a breath, and looked at everyone there. Alva had practically shut down for the day.

"I will not waste words. These men and women lived and died doing their duty to one another, to us, to Alva. We went into an unknown place to deal with a threat that lingered over all Alvan heads. They excelled through training and became masters of boats and fighting on them. They were brothers and sisters to us in the military, but they were mothers, fathers, sons, daughters, *and* brothers and sisters before they ever joined our ranks.

"Because of them, we claimed the Water dungeon, once again making Alva whole. I wish they could be with us having a beer tonight instead of us missing them. Rest easy."

Yui saluted the memorial once again. He walked in front of the Tiger Regiment that had grown from forty members to close on six thousand.

"A-tten-chun!" Everyone snapped their legs together.

"Turn to the right, right turn!"

Everyone snapped to their right, Yui's left.

"In columns of three, by the center, quick march!"

The first three lines marched off, the fourth, fifth and sixth followed after them, and so on, like a belt of ammunition fed through a machine gun.

They headed toward the barracks, where a second memorial had been carved into the first barrack's walls. There, the soldiers could have the privacy to grieve.

Yui walked into his office, and he took off his headdress and put it on the table, slumping into his seat. He rubbed his face, seeing the scenes on the Water floor again. He reached for his desk drawer and pulled out a bottle and a glass, pouring the alcohol before putting it away.

Yui sat forward, drinking from his glass, letting out a hiss from the burn.

"Takes the strongest shit to make me feel a buzz anymore."

There was a knock at his door.

"Who is it?"

"Caravallo."

"Come in."

She walked inside.

"Want one?" Yui held up his glass.

"I'll need one later. There's a Miss Hollingsworth to see you. Jeff's mom."

"You know what she wants?" Yui sat up.

"Says she wants to carry out Jeff's last wish."

"Last wish?"

"Wants to tell you herself."

Yui put the glass into his drawer and closed it. He took out a canteen, swishing it around his mouth and taking a few gulps.

"Bring her up."

Carvallo left Yui, who looked out of his window at the barracks, staring at the military memorial that displayed the names of those who died protecting Alva.

He sunk into his thoughts, deeper than he expected. The door opening shocked him some.

"Mister Silaz." Miss Hollingsworth tried to curtsy.

"Please, there is no need for that, ma'am."

She nodded with a weak smile.

"Would you like a seat?"

"No, no, I don't want to take up much of your time. I, well, I just wanted to convey my Jeff's wishes." He could see her gathering herself.

"He did what he did out of a sense of duty to the people in his unit and the people of Alva. He asked that if he died I wouldn't let his body go to waste. Letting the Ten Realms take it back. He worked hard tempering his body, increasing his mana cultivation. Said to me that if he were to die that he'd want to become an undead. He gave his body to the military anyway. If he were to let it fade away, it would waste all the taxes put into him."

A soft smile appeared on Miss Hollingsworth before it faded with remembered pain. "Could you allow it?"

"Jeff was always ahead of the curve. I didn't think of that, but yes. I'll check with the council. Egbert should be able to do it without a problem."

"Thank you. Knowing that even in death he'll be out there, ready for the call, ready to defend Alva. I know it's what he would have wanted. Would've made some comment about it being badass."

She sniffed, happy, but the loss was too recent, too raw. Tears ran down her face.

"Thank you for your time, Mister Silaz. My boy talked highly of you. Thank you."

"Jeff was a fine man and a loss to all of Alva."

She was unable to answer, giving a jerky shake of her head as she turned and left his office.

Call of Horns, Sound of Marching

Rugrat absently chewed on some jerky. He was lying facedown on a roof, staring at the cave opening behind the defendable castle and curtain wall.

George was behind him, wrestling and chewing on a large bone, cracking it between his teeth.

Rugrat sighed and glanced out of the corner of his eye, unable to stop himself from grinning at the big doggo's efforts.

A noise came from deep within the cave.

Is that a horn?

More horns sounded from the large cave opening.

"I have a bad feeling about this." Rugrat activated his communication device. "Just heard what sounds like horns from the cave ahead."

"Well, that's ominous," Erik said.

"We found a horn on the orc leader," Storbon said.

"Anyone good with horns?" Rugrat asked as he checked the position of his magazines and shifted around in his position.

No one said anything.

"Guess that answers that question," Erik said. "Lucinda, give it a shot. You've been using the horns up to this point."

"All right, but don't blame me if it doesn't work. They probably have a code or something."

A few minutes later, Lucinda blew the horn. It was loud and powerful, echoing through the castle. The others moved around, laying down fields of mines and trap formations, and having Yuli change the terrain to create natural funnels and hard-to-traverse terrain.

The panthers were out there as well, shifting rubble and scratching out ditches. Gilly helped to change the terrain and created traps—sharpened stone spikes underneath a thin plate of stone that was incomparable to the rest of the ground. Stone spikes were placed over balls of water that, once superheated, would expand explosively and shoot out the spikes.

The final plan, if everything went to hell, was charges embedded into the top of the long cave. The explosion would drop the roof on the orcs and close off the cave.

Rugrat looked through his rifle sight. He grabbed his water hose, his fingers resting on the buttstock, and took a sip of Stamina and mana potion, the adrenaline making his mouth dry.

He pushed breaths in and out as he scanned the cave. It had been cut from the rock and smoothed out, creating a tunnel deep into the rock.

The horns fell quiet. Then they started up again, this time at a faster pace.

Lucinda once again blew on the horn; the different horns let out long and short blasts, communicating.

They got quieter after a few minutes, and Rugrat scanned the tunnel. There was no movement still.

"What do you think? Do you think the orcs are coming?" Rugrat asked, talking to George out of the corner of his mouth.

George forgot about his bone and padded over to Rugrat for scratches.

"Yeah, I think so too." Rugrat reached up and scratched behind

George's ear and along his neck, right in his favorite spot.

More horn blasts called out to one another before they settled down. Lucinda added in her horn from time to time.

Finally, it settled down. Rugrat finished his watch, stretching and getting food before helping with the defenses. They could always be improved.

Tian Cui replaced him on watch. Time passed slowly, and he almost looked forward to when he had to go on watch again.

"Go get something to eat or get some rest." Rugrat got down to the perch. The building had been broken apart and a new position in the rubble created. This way, if it were hit with heavy magic, it wouldn't collapse, and it was harder to spot Rugrat and others who might be hiding in the broken houses.

"Might do that. Don't have a good feeling about these damn horns," Tian Cui said.

"Me either," Rugrat muttered, shifting some rocks and getting comfortable.

She left him alone. George was off helping with the defenses. Erik was out there, too, using his Earth magic and Strength.

"He's always been a damn endurance freak. He still looks smaller, but he could out-bench and out-squat the hell out of me," Rugrat complained but then smiled as he created a solid flame of mana in his hand. "Never thought of being a wizard. Archer mage is much more badass than a sword mage." Rugrat grinned and scanned the tunnel.

He switched through his sensing spells keeping watch.

An hour or so had passed when he frowned, feeling something was wrong. He scanned again through his scope and didn't see anything.

Wait, I can't see it, but— He tilted his head, filtering out other noises.

"George! Do you hear something!" Rugrat's voice cut through the area. Everyone stilled and glanced over to George, whose ears perked up, and he turned toward the tunnel.

His ears twitched as he lowered himself.

Gilly hissed, and George growled.

Rugrat used the communications channel. "I can hear footsteps, a lot of them, walking toward us."

"Finish up what you're doing. Get to your positions," Storbon said.

Unless things came to hand-to-hand fighting, Storbon would be in charge. Followed by Rugrat, Yuli, and Erik.

It took an hour for them to hear the footsteps clearly; another hour, and Rugrat caught sight of what was making the noise.

There was a tide of orcs. They were larger. All of them were at least commander level, and they'd all reached at least level sixty. Their bodies had a rough appearance. Most of them had reached Body Like Iron. Some released a stronger aura as they were half-step Body Like Sky Iron.

Their weapons were better maintained, and their armor showed some similarities. There were fifty of them altogether, including the group of ten shamans behind the big brutes.

"Wait till they hit four hundred meters. Rugrat, pin them down. Gilly, Erik, Yuli, see what you can do to slow them if they charge. Everyone be ready to fire on my command. If they get to two hundred meters, Yao Meng, Tian Cui, I want you to engage with grenade launchers." Storbon rattled off orders, getting everyone's head in the game.

Rugrat shifted so he was kneeling into the pile of rubble so he could traverse, select, and shoot on multiple targets faster.

Rocks shifted under him as they dug into his legs and knees.

He breathed out, forcing the dust away from him. He shifted his shoulders to perfectly secure the rifle, pinching it between his shoulder and his collar.

With a breath out, he regripped his foregrip. He allowed his gun to float, scanning the enemy line and watching the ugly damn bastards as they continued forward.

Rugrat picked out his target: the largest orc he could see, shuffling forward, wiping his snout on his forearm, right in the middle of it all.

Rugrat picked out three other orcs along the line, looking to get the greatest effect with his combat technique.

Tension racked up as the seconds went by.

"Fire!" Storbon's order was a welcome relief.

Rugrat fired, doing what he was born to do.

The line erupted with fire, everyone shooting into the oncoming orcs. The ground started to shift and change. Rugrat hit two targets; black circles appeared on the ground below them and chains shot out, grabbing onto their main targets and digging into their flesh.

The other chains grabbed at the orcs nearby, pinning down the line so the orcs behind them ran into their backs.

The line was in disarray. The firepower hit them like a hammer, taking out a dozen of their number. With time to aim and Erik sharing the weaknesses of the orcs, they went for knees and legs, which were smaller and compact, having trouble supporting the weight of the orcs' bodies.

The sudden fire surprised the orcs and put them on their back foot. Their surprise turned to anger as a third of their fighters sprawled on the ground, their legs broken.

George roared and sent fireballs into the orcs. Those on the ground could only scream out, trying to pull their bodies out of the flames as the rest of the team focused on cutting down more.

Poison based off the orc plague covered the rounds. Erik had created a concentrated version and combined it with several poisons. It was just a matter of time for the orcs that were hit.

Rugrat had created four more Chains of Darkness and two more Chains of Adverse Effects.

The orcs, although they were strong in body and had a high mana resistance, didn't have a good Affinity to mana; they had to force their way out of the spells with their bodies.

They were being clumped up and captured. George worked with Rugrat, attacking the orcs that were stuck in the chains.

The chains bit in harder, and George's flames drove them to madness.

Orcs collapsed one after the other.

The shamans put down their totems, creating a barrier. The orcs rushed forward, quickly passing the barrier that couldn't extend far due to the low tunnel.

Tian Cui and Erik had been focusing on the shamans. Several had been hit with rounds.

Just half of the orcs were left alive, and half of that were captured in chains.

Their poisons were the variety that fed off mana and were eating the shamans from the inside.

The shamans behind the barrier collapsed, unable to take the wounds. The orcs up front stepped into the traps. The ground collapsed under a group of five, and they disappeared, never to be seen again.

George ignited a barrage of steam spikes. They pierced through several orcs, pinning them to the wall of the tunnel.

The rest were finished off before the grenadiers even had time to pull out their launchers.

"Cease fire!" Storbon said after a few moments.

Everyone eased up. Rugrat felt the adrenaline streaming through his body as he breathed out, forcing himself out of the black, and looked over the line.

He canceled some of his spells; the chains moved around lazily as there were only corpses in their range.

The orcs were dead or dying.

George growled.

Rugrat looked over at him and then back to the tunnel. "Don't get too comfortable. George thinks another group is coming. Looks like wave tactics."

"Yuli, reset the pits. Erik, could you get Gilly to reset the steam spikes?" Storbon said.

"On it!"

Rugrat stuffed the empty magazines into his storage ring and put down fresh ones, checking the magazine in his rifle and tapping it to see where it was or not.

"Half mag." Rugrat thought for a second before tossing it into his storage ring and pulling out a fresh mag. He had the magazines, so he might as well put them to use.

They had just about finished resetting when the next group of orcs appeared.

"I hate it when they're smart," Rugrat muttered.

The shamans created a relay—putting down a totem and creating a barrier, then the group would pass through; another shaman would put their totem down, and the formation would move forward again, constantly remaining under cover.

Rugrat had an odd feeling when he saw the expressions on their faces. He wanted to ask the others about it, but now wasn't the time.

"Rugrat, put a few rounds into the barrier. Yuli, give me your best estimate of how strong it is," Storbon said.

Rugrat cleared up his gear and aimed at the orcs. He gave the barrier a double-tap. The shaman near the rounds jerked back from the two ripples that formed on the barrier.

Rugrat turned and left his position, moving to another.

A shaman's totem cast a blast of green light that hit the position Rugrat had been ten seconds bef. The rubble exploded into a dust cloud.

"Based off the mana used, we could break the barrier. Would take like fifteen minutes to break just one of them. The totems really boost their power, and we can't employ explosives at this distance," Yuli said.

"Rugrat?" Storbon asked.

Although he wasn't a pure mage, he had the greatest sensitivity and control over mana. "We'll waste ammunition shooting at it. Unless they can get out in the open and we drop spell after spell on their heads, I say it would be good to see how our traps work."

Rugrat wanted something to do, but sometimes the best thing was to do nothing. They had a lot of ammunition, but once it was spent, they would need to manufacture more. All of them had the gear to do so themselves, but they couldn't make it in mass quantities like the ammunition factory in Alva or Vuzgal.

They sat there and waited as the orcs kept moving forward.

"Damn, there is another group," Erik said.

Rugrat used his scope to look past the first group of orcs. There was another right behind them and catching up.

"And it went from fifty to a hundred," Rugrat muttered, not transmitting it. Instead of fear, he felt anger; he felt excitement. The stronger the enemy, the greater the challenge. He felt that he could unleash more power.

He was scared, but his mind turned that into nervous excitement and anger. They were the strongest tools one could have. Fear kept you alert. Being afraid made you tactical in your actions; excitement made you move; anger made you think of how every action could have the greatest impact.

But there was no hint of panic, no hint of desperation. He was closer to George than he was to other people—a true hunter, a predator.

"Hey, Erik," Rugrat asked on a private channel.

"What is it?" Erik asked.

"Are you grinning, you battle maniac?" Rugrat could feel every fiber of his being alive, a subconscious grin on his face, hidden under his helmet.

"As wide as you are," Erik said.

That's my brother; he understands me down to my core. He felt a deeper attachment to Erik and those with him. He would do anything for them, and they would do the same for him. It filled him with energy!

Rugrat breathed deeply. The motion calmed him down; the pain from his body from lying in awkward positions, for leaning on rubble and holding his rifle faded to the back of his mind.

The orcs were reinforced and started to progress faster, using twenty shamans to advance.

Massive pits opened, and holes opened in the formations.

Twenty or so orcs tumbled down into the massive pits. Others behind them were knocked forward accidentally. They fell nearly ten meters to meet the three-meter-long spikes and sharpened pyramids.

They cried out as the other orcs forced their way back.

"Fire in the hole!" Storbon said.

The tunnel shook as explosives behind the pits went off. Poison-covered shrapnel and rusted weapons from the previous castle owners that Rugrat had cut apart with his mana blades stabbed into the orcs. They let out screams as the poison took root.

The formations fell into chaos once again. The orcs wanted to charge forward, but unlike the common orcs, these commanders had some control.

Rugrat watched, forcing himself to breathe and drinking from the tube inside his helmet that was connected to his water bladder.

Take your time, reorganize yourselves. Rugrat's eyes fell to the orc bodies on the ground from the last group. They were showing pustules, and their bodies were turning black and gray. Most wouldn't see the green or red mist coming off them.

The poison created from the orc plague was transforming the bodies, incubating in them and spreading at a rapid rate.

The orcs that had been hit with the shrapnel looked bad as the poison spread through their bodies. They were pushed forward and skirted around the spike pits.

A trap formation went off, creating blades of stone. They cut out like a blender, slicing through the orc's legs. Other orcs shuffled around them, avoiding where they fell. As orcs moved around, steam spikes shot out and speared the orcs, some passing through two orcs before they lost their momentum.

More shrapnel bombs went off, and the shaman controlling the forward totem was killed.

"Fire!" Storbon said.

Erik fired so fast it was as if his rifle were automatic while he cast Unhallowed Ground; the red-and-black circle lashed out at the orcs in its area of effect, draining their life force and leaving deep wounds on their bodies. Yuli and Gilly shot spears out of the tunnel walls, floor, and ceiling. Yao Meng, Tian Cui, Storbon, and Rugrat targeted the shamans with their poisoned rounds.

Lucinda joined Erik, and the two of them shot as many orcs in the legs as they could.

George glowed with blue flames as he unleashed a ray of fire.

Rugrat was shooting without feeling the recoil, following a shaman to the ground till a tombstone appeared. He cast Increased Impact, leading his next target and firing.

Green mist colored the air, and another shaman dropped.

Rugrat switched again—aim, double-tap, tombstone, new target, aim, double-tap, adjust, fire, tombstone, new target.

He switched targets. Seeing them drop, he altered his aim and fired.

Another shaman's barrier snapped into place as Rugrat's round struck the barrier.

Rugrat cast Chains of Adverse Effects, and he shot around the barrier, feeling the drain of mana. Mana chains lashed out at the barrier, trying to reach the shaman inside.

Rugrat moved from his position, identifying targets and engaging them.

"Reloading!" Rugrat yelled, ducking into cover. He stripped the mag, slapping in a new one and striking the bolt catch.

Rugrat forced a breath out and stood up, locating a new target and firing.

"Back in!" Rugrat yelled, feeling the recoil in his shoulder as an orc collapsed.

The spells that were inside the barrier wreaked havoc. Even the orc commanders that were more coordinated than their common orcs were unable to take it. Some started to rush forward, and others joined them, quickly leaving the mana barrier.

Yuli activated the buffing effect of the formation, increasing everyone's power. Trap formations were activated. The attack spells killed those in their area of effect. Sometimes it killed a couple of orcs; other times it took out nearly a dozen, sowing destruction among the orcs.

Rugrat was moving and shooting at the same time; cartridge cases spat out the side of his rifle. His rifle was like a snake—he would switch from target to target, firing as fast as he could, the dust around him thrown up in excitement as his bolt slammed to the rear.

"Reloading!" He smacked the old magazine out, grabbing one near at hand, slapped it in, and hit the bolt release. He fired on the orcs again. "Back in!"

Tracers cut into the orc ranks as they ran through hell. The altered terrain slowed them, and the traps reduced their numbers.

The orcs reached the first obstacles like mid-calf-tall stone walls and holes perfectly sized for someone to put their foot in accidentally. They yelled out when they got caught up in the obstacle.

It turned into Yao Meng's killing field as he fired his grenade launcher. The round landed among the stuck orcs, clearing the barbed wire patches.

Storbon controlled the explosives and the traps, using them to the most effect and targeting the shamans.

The orcs weren't advancing in any way, and some threw their weapons in frustration but were unable to hit the enemy.

A group of shamans sent out attacks, hitting the trench where Lucinda was.

"Motherfucker!" she yelled as she ducked and ran.

"You good?" Erik yelled.

"Fine!"

Everyone's hearts calmed as they kept focused.

The shamans were hitting back.

Yao Meng yelled as he was struck and tossed backward.

"Mana barrier! Erik!" Storbon yelled.

Yuli activated the mana barrier, covering the defenders.

"On it!" Erik stopped firing. He turned and ran. The trench he was in turned, but he jumped, clearing the trench and the obstacles between it and the next trench; he hit the ground rolling.

He got back up to his feet and leaped between trenches. He slammed into the wall of a trench with a grunt. The stone cracked as he got up and moved to where Yao Meng was.

"Hey, Yao, you hear me?" Erik yelled, inspecting Yao. "Nothing broken, but there's shrapnel and head trauma." Erik opened the command channel. "I'm moving him back to the aid station!"

"All right, everyone lay down covering fire on my mark!" Storbon ordered.

The trenches seemed to quiet as they all rapidly reloaded.

"Covering fire!"

Everyone stood out of their positions. A wall of fire greeted the orcs.

Erik stood up with Yao Meng. He barely felt his weight as he ran through the trenches. "I'm out of the trenches." Erik moved among the broken buildings.

They had set up an aid station. Now, Erik's efforts would be focused there.

"Tian Cui, move up to support Lucinda. I'll assist," Storbon said.

They moved up to the front lines. Rugrat and Gilly were the Mid ground support with Yuli, and George as their rear support.

Rugrat dropped another empty magazine. He turned and ran from his position as he slapped in a fresh mag and hit the bolt catch once again and tossed it into his storage ring, pulling out two grenade launchers.

He fired the grenade launchers, sowing a line rounds in front of the shamans, blocking their vision, and picked out the biggest groupings of orcs.

Explosions bloomed among the orc groups, sending them flying.

He dropped down, tossing one grenade launcher into his storage ring. He unloaded the other. He took out the entire cylinder, throwing it in his storage ring and pulling out a loaded one.

He dropped it into place and smacked it shut. Rugrat stood, taking in the scene around him, and fired again.

Orcs were being cut down in rifle fire through spells and grenades, their lines collapsing as all sense of control disappeared.

"Reloading!" Erik called out.

"Dropping Fireball spell on the group hiding behind that pillar-looking rock!" Yuli yelled.

"Tian Cui, two hundred meters, under that bush, hit that fucker for me, will you?" Storbon asked.

The team coordinated fire and communicated, shifting as they needed, gaining the upper hand and holding the momentum of the fight.

Rugrat reloaded and fired his single grenade launcher as fast as possible now. With the shamans' vision covered in explosions, their spells wouldn't be as accurate.

Traps were still going off. Gilly and Yuli altered the terrain at will, turning it into a hellish obstacle.

Lucinda and Storbon took out kneecaps and legs, while George sent out Fireballs that exploded upon impact.

The weight on the battlefield changed. The orcs had reached a wall, and there were forty or so remaining. The tide turned, and they started to run away.

Rugrat stopped firing as they got too far away. The grenade launcher's parabolic arc was too high, and the tunnel's ceiling was too low for him to hit the orcs anymore. Yuli and Gilly slowed their attacks, then finally, the front-liners slowed down.

"How is everyone?" Storbon asked.

A series of goods came back from the others.

"Reset. I have a feeling we haven't seen the last of them." Storbon fired his rifle, killing an orc that had been stabbed into a wall by a steam-spike.

Dead and dying orcs lay across the battlefield. What was once orderly was now a mess. The floors started to regrow, and stone covered the different pits; spikes were reformed, and water collected at their bases.

The charges and trap formations couldn't be added to unless someone ran out into the battlefield, and none of them would even think of that when the enemy could show up at any minute.

"Erik, how's Yao Meng?" Storbon asked.

"He's a tough bastard. He was hit with three shaman attacks—blood magic, it looks like. He passed out. Feeding him healing potions and the like. The damn guy is a bullet magnet. He should be fine, just needs time. Should be good in a few hours," Erik said. "I'll stay with him. Once he wakes up, I'll feel better about leaving him."

"Got it," Storbon said.

"More coming," Rugrat said after George had informed him through their connection.

He kicked some shells out of his way and moved to a new position, putting his grenade launchers away and grabbing his rifle.

"Get set! Yuli, have that barrier up the entire time. I don't care about the mana stones," Storbon said.

"I need a bigger gun." Rugrat stared at his rifle. "Be cool if I had a rail gun. Something that could just punch through these bastards."

Rugrat paused in preparing his next position. In his mind, images and half-baked thoughts formed—in his smithy, back on Earth working on firearms, sitting at the top of Vuzgal with Matt, seeing the flow of power in everything. An image reel appeared in his head.

"It would be science-fiction on Earth, but I've been thinking too small. I still think of firearms as an external tool and device. They are, but if complementing their user, a weapon can be altered to the situation—sniper, rifle, grenade launcher. Flowing with the power of the Ten Realms, built with the knowledge of Earth." Rugrat spewed out words, his mind working faster than he could speak.

His mind focused on seeing Vuzgal, taking the raw, unaltered landscape and then bringing it to order. Watching the flow of people, he saw the flow of power through his body, through people, through the Ten Realms.

It all slammed into the back of his head, and his body shook.

Rugrat closed his eyes for a second, reviewing the information. He opened his eyes after a few moments. "Once I get out of this shit show, I have to find myself a forge."

He focused on preparing his position.

Erik's attention was on Yao Meng. His armor had taken the impact, but the orcs were used to fighting one another with bodies that were at least as strong as Body Like Iron. Yao Meng had a crushed rib, broken shoulder, and deep wound running up his neck. Erik had patched him up. With his stronger body, Erik was able to heal faster, and Yao Meng's own body was leading the fight to recover.

"Shit, they're making it into the second line!" Lucinda said.

"Pull back to the buildings!" Storbon ordered.

"Dammit, they're bringing up shamans and their totems!" Rugrat yelled.

Erik kept watching and checking Yao Meng's vitals.

"Watch out, they're casting a ritual!" Yuli said.

"Shit, it's one of those green whirlwinds. Tian Cui, you're in its path!" Rugrat yelled.

Erik heard the howling winds overtaking the explosions and rumblings of the weapons fire and spells mixed in with the orc war cries.

"Fuck!" Tian Cui yelled.

There was a muffled explosion.

"Shit. Tian Cui's hit!" Lucinda yelled.

"Doc!" Rugrat yelled.

Erik checked Yao Meng's vitals once again, sending a surge of healing into the man's body as he grabbed his slung rifle. He turned from Yao Meng and grabbed his rifle in both hands. "I'll get her," he said.

"She was cut up bad and hit a green building, eight o'clock from the front line," Storbon said.

"Got it." Erik altered where he was going. His speed lifted dust behind him as his feet slammed into the ground. He swung around a building and stretched out his domain.

He turned down a street and saw the unfolding battle. Flashes of tracers covered the trenches that were boiling over with orcs; shamans were grouped together at the edge of the barrier, casting their spells. Grenades hit the shamans, killing some and wounding others. Three more grenades dropped on them, leaving nothing. Grenades appeared among the orcs that were jumping into the shelled front-line trenches.

Beams of Fire and Water struck the orcs.

Erik didn't waste time to stop and shoot. He cast Unhallowed Ground on the front lines and bolstered its effects. Orcs cried out in pain as they collapsed, their vitality being sapped from them.

Erik's domain picked up something. He ran through a doorway. Scanning the room, he saw the collapsed wall that Tian Cui had smashed through.

At some point, her helmet had been ripped off, and her face and head were a mess of deep lacerations.

Erik used his domain to monitor the area and assess Tian Cui. He moved to her, putting his rifle to the side and pulled out his medical kit.

She was making noises and sobbing as she started to get her energy back. She coughed and bucked.

Damn, most of her tongue is gone.

She tried to put her hands on her face, but Erik swiped them away.

"Tian Cui, it's Erik. I have you, all right? You're fine, just a few scrapes. I'll have you fixed up in no time." Erik put a hand to her chest and applied pressure on the breastplate to reassure her; his other hand moved through his medical gear. Tian Cui's armor was torn up. The armored plates showed deep scars and grooves. Blood covered her, and any exposed skin had been torn apart.

He got to work. Finding a vein on her neck, he got an IV in. He crouched and put the IV bag under his knee. The pressure forced it into her body faster.

She had cuts right down to the bone in places. It was as if she had been through a blender.

Erik used an adhesive wrap filled with painkiller; he didn't want to put her out.

She started coughing and convulsing.

Erik shifted her; she writhed in pain and spat out blood.

He used his Clean spell, and the blood and liquid in her lungs were forced out, making her gag and shiver.

Erik watched with one corner of his eye as he took out a needle filled with Stamina potion. He added it into the IV feed and squeezed harder.

She had broken bones, blood loss, and was cut up to hell, but the plates had saved her. She had lost her eyes, her hearing might have been fucked, but she had tucked her neck in and there was nothing wrong there. Internally, there weren't many issues.

"Tian Cui, you're fine. You'll be on your feet in no time, all right!" Erik yelled, as he pulled out scissors, dressings, and gauze. He used his Clean spell on her again, this time on her entire body. He released her breastplate, and Tian Cui started to panic.

He tapped her breastplate again to reassure her. Using his domain, he focused a healing spell on her ears.

"I'm here, all right. Don't worry. I'm not leaving you," he yelled as he prepared his gear with one hand.

She seemed to half nod, trying to talk.

"Don't worry about it. I have you." Erik tried to sound as reassuring as possible.

"They're just—ah, shit! There's another group coming right behind them!" Rugrat yelled.

"If they make it past the second line, we blow the tunnel ceiling," Storbon said.

"Agreed," Rugrat said.

Erik used his scissors to cut Tian Cui's clothes to get access to the wounds.

He held the boot of one leg, shifting it under his armpit as he started to cover her wounds. The dressings and gauze had been treated by the Alchemy department to assist with healing. They would fuse with the patient, turning into new skin and assisting in healing areas directly touching them. They had their own organic compounds, so it didn't require as much Stamina from the patient, becoming a low energy-cost healing item.

He worked diligently as the sounds of battle continued outside. Once he was done with the legs, he moved to Tian Cui's face. He wanted to do her legs first to comfort her as that was where most of her skin had been opened.

"Shit, I hate shamans!" Rugrat said.

"You hit?" Storbon asked.

"Just a scratch. I'll be fine," Rugrat said.

Erik worked quickly, turning Tian Cui into a mummy. She was strong, and her body was starting to recover already. Erik supported those changes. He had dumped copious Stamina potion into her body to give her the energy reserves she'd need to recover.

Yuli yelled, and there was a change in the air.

"Shit, they created a spell above Yuli and dropped it on her. It hit her and the formation. Mana barrier is down, and our buffs are gone," Storbon said.

Erik took out another large syringe and put it into the IV feed. The red healing potion was like blood. It entered Tian Cui's body, making her gasp. Her skin started to shift, her body working on reversing the damage. Her bloodstained bandages became tight as they created the framework for her body to grow within, like a butterfly in a cocoon.

"I'm the closest; I can go," Rugrat said.

"Drop a second formation. We need those buffs and support. Throw down one for George and Gilly. Have them use them to amplify their attacks," Storbon yelled.

"On it!"

"I'll be at the aid station." Erik sent a command to Gilly through their bond. He hooked the IV bag to his vest and picked up Tian Cui. She hissed as her clothing and armor pressed against her wounds.

Erik didn't have time to care about her discomfort as he held her like a pizza box in one arm and grabbed his rifle in the other, easily supporting the weight.

He went out the door he entered and took off at a jog toward the aid station.

He barged in and put his rifle to the side, placing Tian Cui into a prepared stretcher. He checked on Yao Meng with his domain, using healing spells on him.

Yao Meng breathed out, reaching around as he got up off the stretcher.

"You're all good there, Corporal! How you feeling?" Erik said as he put Tian Cui down.

"Shit, uh, I'm okay," Yao Meng said. It was distorting going from fighting and in pain to not being in pain and somewhere unfamiliar.

Erik hung up Tian Cui's IV bag to a line he had running across the ceiling at head height.

"They need help out on the front. You're pretty much good to go. Bruising and cuts now, just some reminders." Erik turned and stared at him.

Yao was shaken up, that was clear, but he got off the stretcher. "Where's my rifle?"

Erik nodded, grabbed Yao Meng's rifle, and tossed it to him before he pulled out his grenade launcher. "Your launcher's fucked. Use this one." Erik handed it over.

Yao Meng put it into his storage ring. He slung his rifle and shifted his armor around, grabbing his helmet beside him.

The door burst open. Yao raised his rifle to see Rugrat burst in with Yuli on his shoulder.

"Here!" Erik waved to a stretcher, and Rugrat laid her down. "I have her."

Erik started checking her as Rugrat slapped Yao Meng on the shoulder.

"Good to go?"

"Yeah." Yao nodded.

"All right, you're with me." Rugrat was covered in dust and blood, but he paid it no attention. He grabbed his slung rifle and headed out the door with Yao behind him.

Erik could hear the fighting. It was like a raging storm just beyond the door, growing in intensity.

"If you have Wind magic, use it to hurl as much of the plague into the tunnel as you can!" Storbon yelled.

"Fire in the hole! Get your heads down!"

Erik threw himself forward to protect as much of Yuli and Tian Cui as he could. A rolling explosion resounded through the tunnel and the area the castle covered.

Dust rained down, and the building he was in shook. But nothing fell.

He felt the shuddering of the tunnel collapsing.

There were broken sounds of weapons fire and fighting.

Erik used his Clean spells on his patients. Yuli twitched and hissed, waking up. Her side looked as though she had been struck with lightning.

She looked up and saw Erik.

"You're in the aid station. What happened?" he asked as he continued to cover her in gauze.

"Formation got hit, overloaded. I jumped out of the way, got hit by the rampaging power." She groaned, glaring at Erik as he worked.

"Suck it up, buttercup." He worked efficiently, not caring about her pain.

"Your bedside manner sucks," she said through gritted teeth.

Erik smiled. Being a leader of Alva made him and Rugrat feel lonely; having people still treat them like normal people was refreshing. "Ah, that's not bad. I had one guy on my medic's course who had the nastiest breath. Called him Doctor Death because anyone who woke up around him would probably pass out from his breath."

Yuli laughed and winced in pain. "Not funny," she said.

"Erik, how are we looking?" Storbon asked.

"Yuli has some nasty burns on her side, walking wounded at this point. Tian Cui needs time to heal, nasty cuts on her body. She'll take more time to recover, and she's going to be weak to start."

Tian Cui made some noise from her bandages.

"All right, keep me updated. I'm sending Rugrat your way to help."

Yuli and Tian Cui were head to head, so Yuli hadn't noticed her.

"Hey, sister," Yuli said, staring at Tian Cui and not knowing where to touch.

Erik tapped his chest; Yuli pressed on Tian Cui's breastplate.

"Got it," Erik said.

"Storbon out."

Tian Cui made a noise.

"Yeah, it does suck." Yuli coughed. The two of them had lived and worked together so much that they could figure out what the other meant.

The two of them talked, one muffled and unable to form words, the other hissing as Erik put balms on her wounds and then bandaged her up.

Rugrat appeared sometime later. He looked like hell. He put his rifle to the side, staring at Erik.

"Tian Cui needs Stamina and healing. Start from the head down. I'll work on Yuli's leg."

The big man nodded in his faceless helmet, and the two of them got to work. They didn't speak.

Yuli and Tian Cui talked to each other. Tian Cui's words started to make more sense and were less muffled.

In ten minutes, Rugrat removed the bandages around her face. "Well, you've got a new haircut." Rugrat tapped her breastplate. "You're a righty shooter, right?"

"Yeah." Tian Cui's tongue fell over the word. It was half-regenerated and would take time to get used to.

Rugrat repaired her hand first so she could use a firearm, and then he worked on her legs so she could run.

By the time Rugrat was finished on her legs, Erik had finished with Yuli.

"You'll need to get some new clothes, but you'll be fine. There is a privacy screen back there." Erik pointed to a curtained-off section.

"Thanks," Yuli said.

Erik nodded and turned to help Rugrat with Tian Cui.

Storbon came in later, checking up on everyone and taking off his helmet to reveal a sweat-stained face.

As Tian Cui was finished, she headed to the privacy screen to take off the bandages with Yuli's help.

Erik and Rugrat took off their helmets as well.

"Shit, that feels nice." Rugrat scratched his head.

"So, what is the plan?" Erik asked.

"We take everything that we have and move back to the rear; we circle around and see if we can get entry to whatever is on the other side of the tunnel through discreet means. I'm worried that the enemy might be looking to flank us right now," Storbon said.

"The caves and tunnels here are a damn maze. If there is a way around them, we wouldn't know about them until it was too late." Rugrat looked at Erik.

"Makes sense to me," Erik said.

"I have Lucinda sending out her scouts," Storbon said. "We'll head out in ten."

They broke apart. The newly healed Yuli and Tian Cui wore new clothes and their armor showed signs of the battle; there was still blood in some places.

Erik cleared up his aid station and headed out. He saw the battlefield; it was a mess. The tunnel had collapsed completely, and there was barbed wire, orc remains, weapons, and armor all over the place.

Erik stood and stretched. It had taken hours to loot all the tombstones. He was hoping some of it could be used in Alva or sold by the traders.

He checked his notifications, the only good part about the whole fight.

You now control the Stronghold

Do you wish to:
  Take command of the Stronghold
  Destroy the Stronghold

Erik put his finger on "Destroy the Stronghold," and a new screen appeared.

Destroy Stronghold: Dherrurd
You will receive:
  27 x Clay Tankard
  4x Cold Weather Outfit
  Courtier's Outfit
  3 x Grindstone
  3 x Large Iron Box
  3 x Light Catapult
  14 x Manacles
  14 x Miner's Pick
  43 x Riding Saddle
  7 x Small Cask of Dried Figs
  8x Salted Boars
  1x Full-Plate Mortal Iron Armor (Apprentice)
  4x Greatsword (High Apprentice)
  1x Greatsword (Low Journeyman)
  2x Heavy Steel Shield (Low Journeyman)
  6x Heavy Wooden Shield (Mid Apprentice)
  11x Vial of Exotic Ink
  78x Necklace

Do you wish to destroy this Stronghold?
  YES/NO

15,927,204/108,500,000 EXP till you reach Level 61

Truly, a hellish battle had happened here.

The group gathered together, heading out with the scouts out in front, the boars behind them, and everyone else mounted up.

They once again saw the destruction that the plague had brought upon the orcs. Settlements were cleared out as they advanced, trying to circle around and into the orc territory.

"Patrol coming," Lucinda yelled.

They hid the boars in a side tunnel. Gilly and Yuli created a hole in the side of the tunnel and they all jumped in, storing their mounts. They sealed up the tunnel again, leaving a slit they could shoot through and to allow air in, and created a tunnel behind the hole so they could run away from the orcs if a fight broke out.

"They're here," Lucinda said on the communications channel.

Everyone grew silent as footsteps approached.

The ground shook. War boars as big as a bear grunted and snorted, searching for food. On their backs sat proud orc commanders, wearing their well-maintained weapons and armor. They had four ogres with them that wore haphazard armor and wielded large trees wrapped in metal to create weapons. Shamans walked behind them, controlling the massive beasts.

There had to be around a hundred orcs in the patrol.

They didn't sense anything amiss and kept moving.

The group pushed past them.

"We should leave the boars behind. If they keep following us, someone might figure out where we are," Lucinda said.

"Send them off in different directions," Storbon ordered.

Without their boars, they pressed forward, going in the direction the patrol had come from.

Their tunnel came to a door made of wood and metal.

"Damn, that is a strong door. Would take some serious damn Strength to get through," Rugrat said.

"So, what do we do?" Storbon said.

"Oh, well, the door is strong, but are the walls?" Rugrat smirked.

With the power of magic, they carved into the walls. They created a rat tunnel into the area past the doorway. Lucinda let her rat scouts out, and they went through the hole, creating a map.

"Okay, it looks like there are ten or so orcs guarding the gate. There are some eating food right here. Some more are wandering around here. Most of them are watching a fight here." Lucinda pointed to positions on the map.

"We take out the ones wandering, then the ones eating food and the ones watching the fight. Yuli, they're yours," Storbon said.

Everyone got their tasks. Erik and Gilly worked together, moving through the rock and into position.

Yuli did the same with her group, Storbon and Yao Meng.

"Three, two, one!"

On Storbon's command, Erik and Gilly opened the last few feet of stone.

It was still dark past the open rock, but their Night Vision spells helped them greatly, turning the darkness to light.

Erik and Tian Cui moved to the left with Gilly; Rugrat and Lucinda went to the right. George was in his holding crate on Rugrat's hip. His body naturally gave off light, and as dark as it was, having him around would alert the orcs.

All of them used silencing socket formations on their weapons.

Erik moved forward, his body tense as his weapon followed where his eyes were looking. They flowed around the building that they had come out near.

Erik saw his targets and slowed his movements.

Tian Cui moved up beside him, pushing up against his elbow, so even if they turned, they would run into each other, stopping the possibility of friendly fire.

Erik scanned the area, staring at his targets. They were just fifteen meters away, but they didn't notice anything.

An explosion went off in the distance—Storbon and his team making their entrance.

Erik and Tian Cui fired, but they were a half-second too late. Gilly's spears shot through the stools and ground, piercing the orcs and pinning them in place as the rounds struck them.

Erik moved forward; Tian Cui followed him past a building. Erik was just expanding his domain when there was a yell from above. A group of orcs on the roof of one of the buildings jumped off.

Erik didn't have time to yell out as he jumped to the side. One of the orcs hit him, but he was able to roll away and get to his knees.

Tian Cui wasn't as lucky; an orc jumped on top of her and hit her with his sword. Her armor held, but she was laid out on the ground.

Gilly jumped backward from her attacker. She sent out a blast of Water, cutting the orc's arm and tossing them backward.

Erik fired with his rifle, nearly point-blank, into the orc's chest that had jumped him. The orc took the hits and fell back. Gilly condensed water in the air into spears and shot them at the orc that had attacked her and the one readying an attack on Tian Cui.

Gilly rushed the attack, and the first orc was covered in just water as the one over Tian Cui was pushed slightly.

Tian Cui rolled to the side with a grunt. She fired up at the orc, her rifle butt under her arm and in the ground as the rounds made a line up his chest to his head.

The orc's head snapped backward as they stumbled and collapsed.

The orc Erik was firing on collapsed. The one Gilly had covered in Water ran at her with his axe raised high; they slipped on the Water, becoming unstable.

Erik shot them in the back, making them tumble, and Gilly's claws swiped the air where the orc had been.

Tian Cui rolled in the dust and mud, her rifle level with the orc's head as they hit the ground. She lost her point of aim and held her fire; the chance of hitting Gilly was too high.

The orc threw itself forward, striking out at Gilly's leg.

Her stone-like skin deflected the attack as she whipped around to face the orc.

Her roar made the orc shudder. Mana in the area distorted, and her body seemed to expand. Her head darted forward, and her jaws tore through the orc's neck, separating head from body, before she crunched down again and tilted her head back, swallowing.

Erik's domain alerted him to more orcs rushing around the building. He had been counting the rounds he had shot and knew that he was out.

"Orcs coming behind you, Gilly!" He dropped his rifle, letting it hang from his sling.

Tian Cui rose to her knee and aimed while Gilly turned to face the orcs.

They came around the corner and into Gilly's path.

A spell formation appeared on the ground. Spears rose out of the ground as another formation appeared above the orcs. They slammed into the ground, the spears stabbing through their bodies.

Gilly's brown colorings glowed as the blue markings lit up and she leaned forward, a beam of water shooting out from her mouth. It cut through buildings, orcs, and anything else in her way.

Tian Cui snapped off rounds.

Erik punched the air, firing out mana bullets that caused buildings to explode and killing orcs in one blast.

"Other side!" Tian Cui yelled.

Erik turned to see Tian Cui drop three orcs.

An orc came around and threw their axe. The axe missed but made Erik flinch as it sailed past. It gave time for another orc to lash out with a sword.

Erik was hit in the side. Planting his feet, he channeled the power of Earth mana, increasing his defense and recovery, maintaining his stability as the power of Fire mana swelled in his veins, exploding into motion.

A poisonous cloud appeared around him. Like snakes under his command, flames glowed through his mask, and his muscles grew.

His fist howled, turning into two semi-illusionary fists. The orc dodged one, another missed, but the main fist hit the orc.

They grunted, and Erik felt something snap. Another orc using a halberd swung it like a bat, hitting Erik in the leg.

He cried out. His leg buckled, and he felt his knee shift. The halberd's wood snapped, and the blade deformed.

Gilly's Earth-focusing spell activated around Erik and the orcs.

The orcs' attacks were slowed as they fought against the focused Earth mana dragging them to the ground.

Erik smirked under his helmet, leaning to one side as his powerful body started to recover his mangled leg.

They had reached Body Like Iron, but his body was as strong as Body Like Sky Iron. He had bathed in Earth mana for so long that its power accelerated his healing.

An orc used a blade, aiming to stab it into Erik's stomach. He grabbed their hand and slammed his face into theirs with a yell. They stumbled back with a broken nose and tusk.

Erik's leg recovered enough; he slammed it on the ground and released his controls. Mana fluctuated wildly around him as he became drunk on the power in his veins.

He gripped his hands, crushing the orc's wrists.

Using Earth mana, he toughened up his shoulder and braced himself. His clothes were torn apart by a blade that hacked at his arm.

The blade cut Erik's skin but bent; it was maintained, but the orcs were not master smiths and the weapons they had were used and abused. None of them had the original durability they once enjoyed.

Erik kicked the orc with the broken wrists, sending him into the orc that had thrown his axe at Erik. His gloves started to glow with a red light, consuming the blood from his enemies.

Erik turned his attention to the sword-wielding orc. A burst of Fire mana accelerated him as he charged forward, sweeping his leg. The orc collapsed, and Erik fired out a mana bullet, hitting the remaining orc trying to close in on him. It didn't hit the orc, but it slowed them down. Erik, using his domain, didn't waver as he brought up his leg and stomped it down on the orc's neck, driving them into the stone ground, the impact enough to make a dent.

The orc grasped at their neck as Tian Cui fired on the two orcs who were running to get backup.

The axe user stood up into her line of fire. Having time to aim and distance, her rounds struck the orc in the head. They dropped bonelessly to the ground.

A stone spear passed Erik's ear, so close he felt the wind and the chill running down his spine. It struck the wall of the building, causing it to collapse and send out dust. Erik rushed to meet the halberd-wielding orc.

The orc hit Erik in the chest with a fist.

Erik grunted, taking a half-step backward. The orc swung again. Erik braced and drove his head forward; the orc yelled out as Erik's helmet crashed into its hand.

Erik punched the orc, lifting him off the ground and sending him backward.

A tombstone appeared above him. Another orc hacked at Erik with an axe.

Erik grabbed the axe and punched the orc in the face.

The orc dropped to the ground, dead, as the axe bloomed with flames in Erik's hands. He threw it, burying it in an orc's chest. He ran forward, removing the limits he had placed on his body.

He leaped forward, shoulder-checking an orc into its fellows. Erik's foot kicked out, smashing one orc through a wall.

A machete attacked his head. Erik grabbed the blade from the air and punched the orc's chest. He caved it in as he cast Unhallowed Ground. Orcs charged him from some feet away, but he paid them no attention as he fired two mana blasts at orcs advancing down an alleyway.

The alleyway exploded. Dust shot out, covering Erik.

The orcs stopped charging and shuddered before collapsing. Steam came from their bodies, but there were no tombstones.

Erik reached out, and the ground rose to his hand. He grasped it. A hammer appeared in his hand. He swung it, killing the orc husks around him.

Gilly was launching spears of Earth and Water; orcs struggled under spell formations that dramatically increased the Earth mana.

Tian Cui reloaded; she was firing on automatic. Her bursts cut down orcs that were trying to charge through the rubble around her.

Erik turned and looked down the road through the broken buildings.

Orcs yelled and charged.

Erik roared, and the world fluctuated around him.

He raised his hands, struggling as if he were lifting the world. Spears rose from the ground, pointing at the orcs. Power coursed through Erik's body, even as he was yelling. His eyes shone, and the corners of his mouth pulled back in a crazed smile.

Red and black lines traced and cracked along the stone spears, red and green lights appeared in Erik's eyes and traced away from his temples and down his body. He turned his hands and pushed them forward.

The spears shot forward with the sound of rushing wind exploding on impact, releasing powerful poison one after another.

It was like a rocket barrage.

Erik stumbled, coughing. He reached out his hand. A wall collapsed and stone twisted into a hammer.

He walked forward across the rubble and the bodies.

Some orcs made it through the attack and started to get up from the ground, shifting the rubble and bodies over them.

An orc got up and rushed Erik.

Erik threw his hammer. It struck the orc; a needle extended from its handle and had buried deep in their chest.

Erik reached out again. Two new hammers appeared in his hands, and he threw them. They howled through the air as he put his Strength into the attacks.

Orcs dropped from the hammers.

Erik's stopped moving. His eyes glowed. They seemed to see through all of existence.

There was nothing left. He turned to look at Gilly and Tian Cui. They were covered in dirt and sweat, but their fights had come to an end.

Tian Cui stared at the scene of destruction around Erik.

Erik threw a hammer without looking, and it smashed into a wall. The wall exploded, and an orc came out the other side of the half-destroyed building.

"Clear here," Storbon reported in.

"No one wandering around here. Nothing got out," Rugrat said.

"We had more than we anticipated. All good, though," Erik said.

Tian Cui was covered in a healing glow, and Erik's eyes dimmed.

"What was that?" Tian Cui asked.

"That was me using all my power, not holding back, and combining Mana and Body Cultivation. I think hammers might be more useful than just my fists. Come on, let's meet up with the others."

Secret Origins of the Orcs

The group gathered together. Erik could feel it and see it on everyone's expressions. Since they had entered the orc territory, they'd had little in the way of rest. They had been on alert or fighting the entire time.

They were worn out, but they continued to drive forward.

"Everyone good?" Storbon asked.

They all nodded.

"All right, then get ready to move out. The longer we stay here, the greater chance of discovery. Erik, Tian Cui, Yao Meng—up front. Rugrat, Lucinda, and myself in the middle. Yuli, George, and Gilly in the rear."

Erik checked his notifications.

Skill: Marksman

Level: 86 (Expert)

Long-range weapons are familiar in your hands. When aiming, you can

---

zoom in x2.0. 15% increased chance for a critical hit. When aiming, your agility increases by 20%

Blackfire Spear
> *Expert*
> Create a spear of Earth, Fire, and poison
> Cost: 200 Mana

For teaching yourself an Expert-ranked spell, you gain: 5,000,000 EXP

Stone Hammer
> *Journeyman*
> Create a hammer of Fire and Earth.
> Cast: 85

For teaching yourself a Journeyman-level spell, you gain: 500,000 EXP

Skill: Healer
> *Level: 83 (Expert)*
> You are an Expert on the human body and the arts of repairing it. Healing spells now cost 10% less Mana and Stamina. Patient's Stamina is used an additional 15% less.

Skill: Throwables
> *Level: 51 (Journeyman)*
> Your throws gain 5% power
> Stamina used for throwing is decreased by 15%

Upon advancing into the Journeyman level of Throwables, you will be rewarded with one randomly selected item related to this skill.

You have received the Weapon: Iron Darts

+100,000 EXP

Erik checked the darts quickly.

The darts looked decent and were Mid Journeyman level, but he had other rounds that went faster and could use grenades and melee weapons that were stronger already.

Erik stored them. He'd dump them off in Alva for sale.

21,537,204/108,500,000 EXP till you reach Level 61

You have come into contact with a Stronghold

Do you wish to:

Take command of the Stronghold

Destroy the Stronghold

Erik put his finger on "Destroy the Stronghold," and a new screen appeared.

Destroy Stronghold: Ruzgerd

You will receive:

5 x Anvil

Backpack

10 x Barrel of Ale

Bolt of Linen

5 x Bookcase

2 x Bottle of Honey

3x Candles

Chisel

Grindstone

---

24 x Hemp Rope

15 x Hide Tent

1 x Portable Ram

Sack of Animal Feed

Sickle

6 x Tiny Wooden Box

7 x Vial of Exotic Ink

31x Necklace

Do you wish to destroy this Stronghold?

YES/NO

Erik sighed as he opened and closed his fist.

"Orc loot sucks ass and makes no damn sense. What the fuck is it with them all having exotic ink? Makes no damn sense!"

All the orcs' tombstones had been recovered. Their own mana destroyed them from inside. The Ten Realms always won in the end.

Don't bet against the house!

A few minutes later, they were all ready and headed away from the gate and the fading orcs.

Lucinda's scouts revealed the maze of tunnels that continued to run through the rock.

When a group of orcs was headed toward them, they hid in the walls, using Earth magic.

"We can't keep advancing like this. As we get closer to the center, there will be more patrols," Rugrat said.

"Slow and steady," Erik said.

"Well, there is another option," Lucinda said, capturing their attention. "We could get one of my scouts to lead the way. They're small enough, and the orcs don't pay any attention to them. If we get into one of the large beast-holding crates, we would be fine."

"We won't be able to wear our storage rings and items," Erik said.

Storage items could hold other storage items, though there was an upper limit, only one or two storage items inside one another, or else the space inside could collapse. Also, the storage items being stored couldn't have a larger holding space than the storage item they were being stored in. When they took Vuzgal, they had put storage rings on strings or in simple boxes. Beast storage crates were much more fragile than regular storage items. They could take some low powered storage items. Taking tens of high-powered storage items was way past their limits.

"Tie them onto other scouts, spread them out," Rugrat said. "Gilly and George can get small. George should come with us, but Gilly can create holes in the walls. We get out there and grab our gear before we deal with whatever is in here."

The plan went ahead. They broke into two teams of two and one team of three. They put ammunition on their carriers and slung their extra weapons and equipment. The storage rings and storage crates were tied up and strapped to the scouts. The team got into the crates on different scouts. The beast storage crates had been built with a function to allow those inside to leave.

If they were on the run, then a medic and their patients could be inside to work on the wounded, or people could be resting, waiting to jump out and fight or ambush people as needed.

Erik had called them Trojans, to Rugrat's immature chuckling.

One idea had been to use them to transport troops into a city. They had some drawbacks.

They could fit ten people, max, inside. Each crate was as big as a fist or an adult's head. When entering a city, formations would scan the crates to find out whether there were people inside. The more people or creatures inside, the fewer storage rings could go inside.

For large-scale operations, they weren't that useful. For the special teams, they were incredible.

Tactics in the Ten Realms were to have the weakest wear out the enemy and gradually send forward your most powerful people. For the crate trick to work, the strongest people among the attackers needed to go into a crate and attack the enemy.

It was seen as dishonorable, and Experts who lived in a world of treachery and greed had to put their lives in another person's hands.

It was a great custom, but it flew in the face of cultural norms of the Ten Realms.

All aboard, Lucinda controlled their scouts and Erik communicated with the mini-Gilly. At her small size, she was unable to control all her mana, making her much weaker. In less than a second, she could swell to her full size to use her true power.

The scouts took off and dodged past the orcs and patrols, heading deeper into their territory.

"I think we found their base of operations," Lucinda said, using her communication device. "The area is largely barren, but there are well-worn roads that enter a large, walled area. Carriages of people are heading toward the walled place. There is a tower that sticks out of it, looking over the area. Orcs are on the walls. These ones are much stronger than the orcs we've fought previously, Mid-sixties. Scouts are damn well terrified. I can get us inside, though."

"Find us a corner. We'll scout it first, and then we'll think about getting inside," Storbon said.

Rugrat used a peephole in their hidden passage to study the tower and its defenses. "Looks like a mage's tower. Big defenses, and just the single tower in the middle. Carts of people go in; empty carts come out. This has to be where people are disappearing to," Rugrat said.

The gates opened inside the tower.

Orcs with simple furs and low levels stumbled out of the gate, pushed ahead by the orcs behind them.

Rugrat frowned and checked his storage ring, pulling out a simple leather necklace with a gem in the middle of it. "This is the necklace that most of the stronger orcs have been wearing since we got past the stronghold guarding the tunnel entrance. All of the orcs around the castle are wearing it."

He studied it, trying to figure out its abilities.

Necklace???
  Takes up slot: Necklace
  Durability 67/100
  Formation 1:???
  Formation 2:???

Usually, when he studied an object, information would pop into his head, but the formations in this piece remained a mystery to him, unlike any other formation he had worked on in the past.

"That's annoying." Rugrat rubbed the gem, studying the formations closely.

"What's up?" Yuli asked. They were using their communication devices so that no noise left their hidden outpost.

"None of the orcs roaming beyond the defenses were wearing this necklace. I don't know what it means, but I don't have a good feeling about it." Rugrat rubbed the necklace again, as if it would reveal its secrets before he offered it to Yuli.

She took it and looked it over as Rugrat looked through his scope once again. The young and confused-looking orcs were being herded away from the tower. Based on their bodies and their aura, they were weaker than the orcs outside of the defenses.

"Guess they are new trainees to head off to the training camps." Rugrat continued studying them. It was some hours before there was another change, one that made Rugrat completely alert.

"What is it?" Yao Meng, who had replaced Yuli, asked.

"Humans," Rugrat said, confused.

"What?" Yao Meng asked.

"Lucinda, get your scouts to confirm the group entering the cavern," Rugrat asked over the communication's channel.

"Got it."

There was silence as Rugrat watched the group. There were four mounted guards studying the area with their hands on their weapons. One person was driving a carriage that floated above the ground, glowing with defensive and flotation formations.

Rugrat drew in his domain. The guards were a higher level than him. Higher-leveled orcs were a problem, but higher-level humans could have many secrets and trump cards that could defeat the group easily.

Lena Lindenbaum assessed the test results from her latest experiments.

There was still too much deviation, and the control issues were annoying. Recreating orcs from Earth lore was a stroke of genius, but with the reduced mental abilities, they needed simplistic instruction until they were trained again. Removing their old memories was necessary to make them malleable. The orcs that had grown up without the control unit had turned into a rabble, useful for keeping out intruders, but useless for business means. She needed to capture more of them for further study and see if there were deviations from the original batch.

She reached for her tea and hissed as sudden pain assailed her body, running through her being. She grimaced and winced. She took out an inhaler, shaking up the powder contained within before she pressed it to her lips and depressed the button that aerosolized it, breathing it in.

A shiver ran through her body. She relaxed as the pain numbed, and her eyes became sluggish. She sighed as the pain receded, closing her eyes in bliss.

Smacking her lips together, she turned her eyes to the paper notes in her hand. "What I would do for a computer or tablet, even a simple phone," she complained and threw the pile of paper on her desk.

She stood up, the chair creaking as she walked to the top of the tower. The cages below were filled with new material.

The new experiments were being pushed out of the tower and toward the tunnels. There, they would be trained and put to work, expanding the underground empire she was creating and increasing their ability.

She went back to her work. Beyond her paper-covered desk, tables were covered in different lab equipment. Magnifying formations and tools were grouped together, all of them oddly made as she had to create most of them herself or request them from her backer.

She took her time staring at cultures and different samples. All Lord Vinters cared about was results. He didn't care about things like time. At least he was prompt with delivery of the test subjects.

She felt the pain coming back and took another shot from her inhaler.

A knock at her door forced her lidded eyes open.

"Come in," she yelled. Her voice shook the glass equipment and experiments in the room.

A large orc opened the door. She wore a hide-created lab coat. In Lena's eyes, the female orc was like a child.

"What?"

"Thur… be… ba-ackers… uming." The orc stumbled over her words, but she was one of a few who could actually communicate, making her invaluable. The scars on her body revealed that she was one of the most frequent test subjects.

"Backers are coming?" Lena said, her anger growing.

The female orc grunted.

"Just what I wanted. I will meet them in the main hall. Don't harm them," Lena said.

Lena finished with the equipment she was using and then headed out of her office. She took a lift down, controlled by two strong orcs that struggled with their job.

The lift reached the bottom, and she walked out. She reached the main hall, which had a large stone seat and a comfortable plush seat facing it.

"Lord Vinters." Lena took the stone seat, ignoring the looks from his guards. Vinters was a middle-aged man, smartly dressed with a pointed, serious face. He moved in an unhurried way, but his eyes were as sharp as the seemingly decorative blade on his hip.

"Researcher Lindenbaum, I have sent you another four hundred experimental material as you requested. Has there been any progress?" the man asked.

Lena snapped her fingers. One of the statues against the wall moved and walked over. They were actually all orcs and had remained unmoving the entire time.

The orc wore a hide kilt and held a large broadsword.

"Three major lines. The first—laborers. With the orcs at your beck and call, all you need to do is feed them and they will work tirelessly, only requiring a few hours of sleep a week to keep functioning. Their bodies, upon delivery, will reach the Body Like Iron standard. If they are fed monster cores, their levels and power will increase. Unlike humans, they will be able to consume multiple cores and gain power from eating strong beasts. Their mental capacity is low, but their Strength can't be underestimated.

"The second group are fighters. They can act as training dummies, taking and giving attacks. They will recover with time and serve as a great training aid for your students. They can also act as defenses or attacking forces, if you require.

"The third line is shamans. They can work independently to cast magic. Their magic is reliant on materials and items, such as totems. They are harder to produce, but they can buff and assist regular orcs and are smarter. When they work together to cast spells, their power will increase. Linked by the control unit, they can cast group spells easily. Casting speed is slower with mental limitations. With time, if new totems and rituals can be perfected, then their combat power will surge."

Lena's explanations were bland, as if she recited information she had memorized for years.

Vinters's cold eyes showed interest, and a smile spread across his face.

The guards all had expressionless faces as they looked away.

"Good! Good!" Vinters said. "You have some kind of demonstration to show off their abilities?"

"Of course," Lena said.

Everyone was alert as Rugrat told them about the carriage that had reached the tower and gained entrance without being attacked.

He grew silent as the group came back out of the gates. There was a group of orcs with them. One wore armor, another caster's robes and shaman items, and the other just wore a hide kilt and held a pickaxe.

"What in the fuck is that?" Rugrat stared at a hulking beast that walked beside one of the humans. She was nearly twice the height of the orcs. She looked as if an orc, an ogre, and the Hulk had been thrown together and never did leg day.

She had small legs but an overdeveloped upper body. She walked with her legs and her fists, much like a gorilla. Her head had not increased in proportion with her body. Her long hair was pulled back in a bun. She wore a white lab coat and had a pocket filled with items on her chest.

The humans watched her and the orcs; the woman was talking to a man who must've been riding in the carriage.

The orc with the pickaxe attacked a small rise, turning it into rubble as he worked like mad.

The shaman cast magic, and the orc fighter went up against one of the guards. The guards were able to defeat them in five moves. The heavily injured orc's anger stilled as its body started to repair itself.

Once the demonstration was done, the group went back through the walls.

The worker and shaman picked up the fighter and carried them back inside. The doors closed behind them.

"Well, shit. What the hell is going on?" Rugrat said.

"Looks like a dog-and-pony show," Erik said.

"Fuck." Rugrat started to make conclusions he didn't like. "If it is, then this…?"

"It might not be a natural dungeon. Someone is making the orcs," Erik said.

"So, what is the plan?" Storbon asked.

"Save the people, blow this fucking place apart, and get the hell out of here. Tell others so they can clear this out," Rugrat said.

"Sounds like a plan I can get behind," Erik said.

"Lucinda?" Storbon asked.

"I'll scout the tower and inside the walls."

It was sometime later when Tian Cui was on watch that anything changed other than their updated maps.

"The guy in the carriage is leaving," Tian Cui said.

"Good. One less thing to deal with. Those guards would not be easy to deal with." Rugrat leaned against a rock wall. He turned to Erik.

"Storbon is working on the plan." Erik pulled out jerky from his storage ring and offered some to the others.

They passed around the jerky, eating as Lucinda and Storbon talked on a private channel, working out a plan together.

They rotated people on watch. The others tried to relax and get some sleep and eat; they used their Clean spells, but it wasn't the same as a shower.

The glowing crystals embedded into the ceiling and the glowing plants started to dim, removing the little light in the area. It wouldn't affect the orcs much, but they hoped the massive abomination was put to sleep.

"All right, let's go," Storbon said.

Everyone got into the beast crates, and the rat-like scouts ran through a small tunnel they had created out of their hiding spot.

Rugrat gripped his rifle, sitting down, ready to act at a moment's notice.

"We're at the wall, looking for ways in," Lucinda said. The tension seemed to increase four-fold.

"Found a hole in the door. We're moving on. Past the first gate, the second, and we're into the main area. The orcs are on the wall. Others are in their huts against the outer wall. Humans are in several large holding areas. There are orcs moving around the tower entrances wearing lab coats. They're checking and studying the humans. I'm heading to the tower."

The silence was the worst. At any moment, they could be discovered, and Rugrat had no idea what they would be facing.

"We're in the tower, heading to where the mana concentration is the highest. Looks to be at the top of the tower."

Silence continued as Lucinda controlled the rats, hiding from groups of orcs wearing lab coats and then charging forward. She took her time, making sure to not rush.

Everyone else held their breath, not daring to interrupt her.

The rats went up the tower's winding stairs. Thankfully, they were largely unused.

"Looks like there are all kinds of experiments being carried out. The orcs are awkward, but they're recording everything," Lucinda said as they climbed, giving them snippets of information as they went.

"I think the lower ones are gathering raw information, and the orcs on the higher levels are compiling them. Some are even speaking in ways that I can understand—broken words and thought."

Lucinda's heavy voice said, "I'm at where the mana is the highest."

"I'm sending you in, Erik and Yao Meng."

"Okay, looks like a large lab—shit!" Lucinda yelled in a panic, setting everyone on edge. Rugrat was a split second away from jumping out of his cage.

"Shit, all right," Lucinda said, recovering and settling herself. "The abomination is asleep in the office, fell asleep on a desk. Looks like she's out of it."

"Get me close to her. I'll jump out and hit her with a few concoctions that will make sure she'll stay asleep," Erik said.

"Don't kill her—we might need information," Rugrat said.

"Got it," Erik said.

"Okay, just getting you closer," Lucinda said. Storbon didn't countermand their orders. "I'm moving the rest of us into the room, and we're all here. Erik, you're right next to her."

Erik exited his beast cage. His hands held onto a bag of powder. Seeing the sleeping abomination, he tossed it lightly onto the desk. The bag was open, leaving a trail of browns and golds in the low light.

The abomination was snoring. Her nose twitched, and her eyes fluttered as Erik raised his rifle, training it on her face. She snuffled, and he watched the powder being drawn up and into her nose. With each breath, she took in more, and her body completely relaxed.

Erik extended his domain over her.

"All right. She's out." Erik turned and examined the rest of the room. Yao Meng was right behind him the next second, and the others quickly left their storage crates, filling the room.

Erik moved to a door and opened it. Pushing inside, he swept the left of the room and Yao, the right.

"Bedroom." Erik waved to the bed. Yao Meng lifted the sheet, and Erik looked under it. It was just stone.

They moved to the next door, revealing a bathroom.

The others opened the closets and checked the rest of the room. Rugrat watched the door. Lucinda's small scouts ran between his feet as he closed the door.

Yuli enchanted it, reinforcing it. Tian Cui placed a formation that would make sure that no noise left the floor.

Storbon and George stared at the sleeping beast, ready to fight. Gilly used her magic to create a stone seal around her.

Rugrat looped chains around her with formations enchanted in them to weaken the one affected. After the slaver ring he had broken up, he'd created these power-sapping manacles; the police force had taken his designs and created their own versions.

With so many powerful people capable of smashing buildings, they were necessary.

Yuli and Tian Cui stood with Storbon, watching the abomination.

"Yuli, Rugrat, Erik, start gathering notes and figuring out just what the hell is happening to please the quest. Yao Meng, on the door. Lucinda, with him. Tian Cui, you're with me. Mind if I borrow Gilly and George?" Storbon asked.

"All yours," Erik said.

"Don't burn down the tower," Rugrat told George, who rolled his eyes. Rugrat patted his neck with a smirk, appeasing the wolf.

Erik let his rifle hang behind him as he grabbed the notes on the desk and moved back so he wasn't in front of anyone's line of fire.

Rugrat and Yuli searched the other rooms, closets, and desks.

"Look for journals, notes, information on who that prick with his guards is," Erik said, flipping through notes, scanning information and dumping the papers on the floor that weren't useful.

Erik went through the drawers next. He pulled out a cellphone. "Shit." Erik held up the cellphone. "Rugrat!"

"What is it?" Storbon asked.

"Fuck." Rugrat shook his head and returned to searching.

"She's from Earth, or she knows someone who is," Erik said.

"Lena Lindenbaum," Yuli said. "Calls herself a genet-i-sist?"

"Geneticist?" Rugrat asked.

"Could be?" She passed him the book she had picked up.

"Yeah." Rugrat glanced over to Erik. "Fuck. So, what? She made these orcs…for what?"

Erik remembered the demonstration. "Laborers, fighters, and shamans."

He flicked through a book, trying to push his thoughts to the side.

They fell into silence and kept looking through the information, and they soon had a complete idea of what was happening here.

"I thought she was messed up from how she looks, but her mind is worse," Rugrat spat.

"So, the orcs we've been fighting?" Yao Meng said.

"They were all orcs, but orcs are humans' close cousins. I thought something was strange about them. They didn't have monster cores. I thought they might not have formed them yet. I didn't think it was because they were converted. The fact that the poison worked on us to some effect as well as the orcs—while highly effective against orcs but not as strong against us—it is like how we share diseases with monkeys."

Erik sunk into thought and closed his eyes, picturing the orcs and going through their internal structure. "Their bodies are a lot like ours. They have been combined with some other creatures to make them stronger. Their brains were basically destroyed in the process. They clearly have some level of reason, like beasts, but they can't complete complex thoughts. They just don't have that part of their brain. Unlike normal orcs that grow stronger from eating monster cores and their enemies' flesh, these orcs can get stronger through training and cultivation.

"Orcs in the wild are as strong as wild beasts and hide from people. In the higher realms, they can gain understanding and are part of the beast sects. These ones she's created are aggressive instead. She was able to stay here because she controlled the strongest with the beast-taming collars, that necklace with the gem in the middle of it," Erik said.

"She was looking for a way for humans to absorb multiple mana cores in the beginning. She was self-testing, which turned her into this. Then she found someone interested in creating the orcs," Yuli added.

"I think I have our man. Lord Vinters. She kept a schedule. I guess today is a Tuesday."

"Feels like a shitty Monday to me," Rugrat muttered.

A notification went off as information rolled down their screens.

Quest Update: From Orc Jaws

Lena Lindenbaum has been converting humans into orc slaves against their will. Destroy her and her research.

Requirements:

Destroy Lena Lindenbaum's research

Kill Lena Lindenbaum

Save the remaining humans

Return the humans to safety

Rewards:

Wandering Hero Title

EXP (Depends on final result)

"Well, I think it is pretty clear," Rugrat said. The others nodded in agreement.

"Nothing about Vinters though?" Storbon asked.

"Elan will be able to find him. Once we secure the people downstairs, we'll see if they know anything." Erik stored the reports.

Erik pulled out a syringe and a poison bottle. He put the needle into the bottle and drained it. He removed the stone seal around her with just a thought and found a vein on Lena's arm. He pierced her skin, injecting the poison.

Lena Lindenbaum shook. Her veins swelled, and blood trickled from her nose and mouth, foam appearing between her teeth. She collapsed, and a tombstone flashed above her.

Experience flowed into them all, but they didn't seem to care.

Erik looted her tombstone and took off the different restraints.

"Secure any remaining information. Storbon, get this place wired to blow. Any clues as to who the troll was working with, store it and we'll check it—"

Roars rose from the area around the tower.

"That does not sound fucking good!" Rugrat yelled, turning to face the door.

"Lucinda?" Storbon barked.

"Orcs are pissed off. They're losing it and attacking one another. The people in the cages."

"Use your storage rings. Grab the notes. Rugrat, you've been working on that Gliding Step technique, right?" Erik moved to a window, looking down the thirty-story tower to the ground below.

"Fuck me," Rugrat grunted and moved to Erik, staring at the fall. "I fucking love my job. Full of safety harnesses and pillow fights."

Yao Meng and Lucinda covered the door. Everyone else ran around, placing everything in the tower into their storage rings.

"Anyone else got something to get through the air?" Erik's eyes darted over the people in the room.

"I can use spells to slow my descent—maybe two others, four at a stretch," Yuli said.

"Rugrat, you head down in the lead. George can take Yao Meng and Tian Cui; you will provide supporting fire. Yuli, you take Lucinda and Storbon. I will follow down on my own power." Erik said.

"Clear?" Erik barked.

"Clear!" Storbon yelled.

"Rugrat first, George second!"

George appeared from his storage crate.

"I have the door; I'll be the rear guard." Erik pulled his rifle up, covering the door and moving to Yao Meng.

He turned and jumped up on George. Tian Cui was already mounted.

Rugrat ran and jumped out of the window without pausing. "Fuck Airborne!"

Dickhead.

George inhaled and released a Fireball, expanding the window into a wall-sized opening. His claws left gouges in the floor as he ran out. His wings snapped out, catching the air as he banked away from the opening.

"Lucinda!" Yuli yelled.

Lucinda stared at Erik.

"Go!"

She turned and ran. Yuli grabbed onto her and Storbon, and they jumped out of the tower.

Erik heard a noise at the door. He fired through it, hearing pained screams and surprised grunts as he hit those on the other side.

Erik pulled his rifle to the side, securing it with bungee cord, and grabbed a grenade as he moved toward the opening. He pulled the pin on the grenade, tossing it underhand at the door.

He sprinted and jumped out of the opening, trying to not launch himself too far from the tower. "Fuck!" Mana was sucked into his body as he exerted his domain. Reaching out to the tower, stone expanded outward, creating platforms.

He smashed through them, but his speed slowed.

The top of the tower exploded in a gout of flame.

"Heads!" Erik yelled through the comm.

Stone rained down as Erik slammed through stone sheets, taking the impacts with his legs.

The cages were right between the outer wall and the tower in the middle. The orc guards were at least the level of orc commanders in the outer regions.

There had to be between fifty or sixty of them spread out around the tower.

They settled their own grudges between one another, slowing the flow of orcs that were pushing toward the four cages where captives were pushing one another to hide in the middle. As if it would somehow make them safer.

Erik looked at the wall. Rugrat was walking on it; orcs dropped ahead of him without the time to fully react or understand what was happening.

Rugrat casually cast chains among the groups of orcs. George was running, flapping his wings. He'd just dropped off Tian Cui and Yao Meng, who used spell scrolls.

Green blades formed ahead of them, bulldozing into the orcs.

Yuli had barely stepped on the ground when she threw out a formation plate. Lucinda fired a grenade launcher into the orcs. Storbon tore a spell scroll.

A blue mana blast shot out from the spell scroll. It met the orcs with an explosion, leaving a smoking crater and throwing orcs away.

Erik grabbed his rifle, unlimbering it and holding onto his beast storage crate. He hit the ground, releasing Gilly.

Rugrat detonated his chain spells, leaving bloody holes in the orcs. Rugrat had picked a place on the wall and provided deadly accurate fire from there.

Between Erik and the cages, there were no more than ten orcs.

George swept down, releasing flame upon the orcs in his path. The wave of heat hit Erik a moment before the smell and the sound of stone exploded from intense heat.

Erik gripped his rifle and pulled on his trigger. He killed two orcs between him and the cages before they realized the threat behind them.

Erik dropped another and turned. He switched targets; as he pulled the trigger, nothing happened. *Jam!*

Gilly's Water Beam spell killed two more.

Erik pulled the rifle to his side with his left hand. His right hand rose, twisting mana into the shape of a spike. He released it, cutting through several orcs.

The orcs ran toward him with their weapons.

With his left hand, he unclipped his rifle and stored it, making it easier for him to move. "Gilly!"

She picked up on his thoughts. Stomping her foot, the ground cracked and turned into a waist-high wave, striking orcs to Erik's right.

Erik summoned stone spears behind the orcs.

They looked down in shock at the bloody holes through their armor.

Erik released the spell and punched forward. Fire and Earth mana formed fist-sized meteorites that hit two orcs, pushing them back.

Erik was upon them in the next second. He punched the machete-wielding orc to the left in the ribs. Erik felt the bones crack as the orc crumpled to protect his side.

The orc that had been behind them saw his opening and swung his war hammer.

Erik roared and grabbed the shaft of the war hammer. He drove his hip into the orc's side, pulling and turning, hip-tossing the orc.

The orc released his war hammer. His arms flailed, and he hit the ground awkwardly.

Erik raised a sheet of stone behind him.

The orc with the broken ribs couldn't stop, and the wall of stone broke.

Erik turned the head of the war hammer, showing lines of lava.

The orc tried to blink stone dust out of its eyes.

Fuck you. The war hammer exploded from the stresses of Fire mana and the force of Erik's liberated war hammer versus the orc's head.

The orc was thrown to the side, his head at an unnatural angle. Parts of the war hammer head landed around him.

Erik turned to face the last owner of the war hammer. Gilly stared at him, her talons covered in orc blood.

"Erik! Pull back to the cages!" Storbon yelled through the comms.

Erik ran toward the cages.

The special team had cleared from the tower to the wall and fifty meters away along both sides. They were spaced out, each using spell scrolls and their rifles to create interlocking fields of fire.

George dropped from the sky, leaving a trail of flame through the fortress.

Erik and Gilly turned outward. Gilly's Water Beam played across the remaining orcs. Erik ripped up spell scrolls.

Rain started to fall before the wind picked up. The orcs pushed through the rain, but they had to be careful of their steps.

Erik tore another.

A lightning field bloomed. Racing along the water-slick floor, lightning illuminated the orcs.

The orcs started to run. They fought one another as they fled the tower and the walls.

"Cover your arcs!" Storbon yelled. "Rugrat, watch for counterattack. Lucinda, watch those orcs!"

Storbon used Detect Life. The fleeing orcs were quickly leaving the spell's range.

"Doesn't look like anything but the rats and fleas left," Yao Meng reported.

"The orcs wearing lab coats were in among the fighting. The other orcs attacked them first," Rugrat said.

"Erik?" Storbon asked.

He stared at the cages filled with people huddled together. There were no more than forty people.

"Rugrat, get us a route out of here. Looks like that VIP came in a different path. Everyone, check to see if you have something like a map from what we looted. Yao Meng, Storbon, organize the people here. Get them ready to move. We have some of those carts. Let's cut the bars off them, hook them up to the panthers, and we can use them to move our new travel companions," Erik said.

"You sure this route will work?" Erik asked.

"I used the map fragments and the maps we recovered. It looks like the route out. Side tunnel bypasses a lot of the orcs. Not sure where it comes out, though. Checking it against the maps we have, it must come out somewhere near Daskama Outpost." Rugrat pointed to the outpost on his map. "Though, we're not going there. That's probably the VIP's home ground. We'll swing away to the south, skip around the outposts there, and get distance from the orc-held lands. Should take us four days of hard riding. Outpost here, on the smaller size—uninteresting place called Knugrith."

"You think we're going to be able to ride hard?" Erik checked behind at the people mounting the modified cage carts.

There were kids, teenagers, even the elderly. There were some middle-aged people, too, and the group was split half male and female. A perfect testing group.

Their eyes darted from one place to the next, hunched over, as if waiting for the next blow. Scared to let hope in. They didn't stare at the helmeted and armor-covered special teams closely, only sneaking glances. The food they'd been given was gone already.

"Say a week and a half." Rugrat's voice softened slightly.

Erik grunted. He looked at Storbon, waving his hand in a circle and then waving it forward. "Get up there. I'll take the rear." Erik shifted on Gilly's saddle. "Let's get the fuck out of this place."

George carried Rugrat to the front as Tian Cui, riding the first panther, started forward.

The convoy rolled forward, out of the fortress gates and toward the cave the VIP had come from. Yao Meng held out a clacker covered in formations.

"Don't mind if I do." Erik took the detonator, removing the catch. "Fire in the hole!" His voice was projected to everyone as he depressed the lever.

Explosions rippled through the fortress and the tower. The recent prisoners closed their eyes against the sudden wind.

When they opened them again, all that was left was some faint stone lines as rocks rained across the cavern.

Erik tossed the detonator back to Yao Meng. "Seen enough orcs for a lifetime."

"Yes, boss."

The convoy pushed into the darkness, Rugrat leading the way on George.

They marched through the caves. With a complete map, they passed the cave system easily; the bypassing tunnel circumvented the defenses and any remaining orcs.

It took them a day to leave the orc tunnels and caves behind.

Erik took the time to check his notifications and stats

Skill: Marksman

Level: 87 (Expert)

Long-range weapons are familiar in your hands. When aiming, you can zoom in x2.0. 15% increased chance for a critical hit. When aiming, your agility increases by 20%

21,571,860/108,500,000 EXP till you reach Level 61

Name: Erik West

Level: 60   Race: Human

Titles:

From the Grave II

Blessed by Mana

Dungeon Master III

Reverse Alchemist

Poison Body

Fire Body

City Lord

Earth Soul

Mana Reborn

Strength: (Base 54) +51	1050
Agility: (Base 47) +72	654
Stamina: (Base 57) +25	1230
Mana: (Base 27) +79	1166
Mana Regeneration: (Base 30) +61	73.80/s
Stamina Regeneration: (Base 72) +59	27.20/s

They rested once they were outside the caves. The captives were more receptive to them after using Clean spells on them, healing their injuries, and feeding them.

Erik, Rugrat, and Storbon met with an older man who had volunteered to talk on their behalf.

"Where did you come from before this? What happened?" Erik asked.

"I'm just a simple man—a smithing Novice. One night, I was going home and some people captured me, used something to make me sleep. I woke up several times, but then I finally woke up in one of them orc carts." He shivered. "They took people from the carts, but we continued on. I heard their screams."

He took some time to recover before he shook his head. "We arrived at the tower. People were taken. Any who went into the tower didn't come out."

"Are you all from the same place?" Erik asked.

"No, we're from different academy grounds. Most of us are from the surface. We're not strong enough to live in the dungeons."

"Do you know someone called Lord Vinters?"

"Lord Vinters? He is from one of the clans. The Vinters clan are alumni from the Faded Scroll Academy." The man seemed confused at the sudden subject change.

They talked for several minutes more before the old man returned to his group, and the three turned to one another.

Erik pulled off his helmet, shaking his hair out.

They had all been growing field beards. Erik and Rugrat had been growing theirs for a couple of months, extending down further. They looked like been picked off a street corner. The armor and weapons showed another reality.

Rugrat slid off his boulder with a groan, putting his helmet to the side. He pressed his back against the boulder, working his shoulders; he looped his hands into his armholes to get some circulation under the armor.

Storbon looked better than the two hobos with him, but he seemed tired, as if his soul had been dragged out of him. They'd put everything into the operation. It had lasted for nearly three weeks, and it showed.

Erik rubbed his face and took a deep breath, focusing himself. "All right, where the hell are we and where are we going?"

Storbon took a knee and pulled out a map, putting it between them all. "We're here. We have three different outposts in walking distance. The two closest are supply stations. The third has a route up to the surface." Storbon pointed to the map.

"What are you thinking?" Erik asked.

"We take these people to the supply station farthest from here. We drop them off and then we move farther into the dungeon. We miss these three places completely and go to another outpost. We can use that place to rest up and plan our next move."

"You got a route?" Rugrat said.

"Somewhat." Storbon manipulated the map as he spoke. "We hit the supply station Knugrith, then we head for the Ivaris Outpost."

Rugrat and Erik glanced at each other briefly, trusting in Storbon.

"Works," Rugrat said.

"I need a damn bed and out of this armor," Erik agreed.

"What about this Vinters thing?" Storbon said.

"Dude needs to die," Rugrat said.

Erik rubbed the back of his neck. "Yeah, he does, but we can't go off half-cocked. Otherwise, we aren't going to do anything but die. We don't have any power in this realm, and we're a small group. His guards cultivated their mana and bodies. Although they aren't as strong as Rugrat and me, they have at least three-quarters of our power. This is more Elan's thing," Erik said, the words sour in his mouth.

There was a cough from the side. The three looked over and saw Yuli.

"A young girl who wants to talk to you," Yuli said.

Erik and the others pulled on their helmets again, hiding their features.

"She say what she wants?" Erik asked as Storbon put the map away.

"She has a request," Yuli said.

The three masked men finished with their helmets.

"I might need to shave this thing. Gets stuck in the damn clips. Ow!" Rugrat complained.

Yuli turned back, getting the girl and bringing her over to the trio.

She was young, just a teenager. Her eyes were turned to the ground in nervousness.

There was something different about her. Her skin seemed different, and her muscles, although small, were dense. A Body Cultivator? A special constitution?

"Go on," Yuli prompted the girl as she played with her sleeves.

"I need to meet with my teacher. He wanted me to meet with someone, and I snuck out to see an old friend, but I was captured. I, uh, I want to see him again," the girl said.

"Do you know where he is?" Rugrat asked.

"Blue Crystal Inn on the Faded Scroll Campus."

Quest: Mysterious Teacher

Take Melika Nemati to meet with her mysterious teacher.

Requirements:

Lead Melika Nemati to Blue Crystal Palace in the Faded Scroll Campus unharmed.

Give him a copy of information about Lena Lindenbaum's operations.

Rewards:

1,250,000 EXP

Erik shared a look with the other.

What the hell? It felt like the Ten Realms was trying to guide us somewhere.

"We will consider it," Erik said.

Melika nodded and quickly turned to leave, looking downtrodden.

Yuli guided her back to the group.

"Well, looks like we have a new task," Rugrat said.

"Why the hell is the Ten Realms making this a quest?" Storbon asked.

"The Ten Realms is a self-regulating machine. The quests allow it to maintain itself. I don't know if it is sentient, but if something affects its balance, then it self-corrects. It seems to be unable or unwilling to use its own power to do so, but the quests push the pieces together. We put our damn noses into so many things that we get a lot of notifications. Most people don't get many quests in their entire lives. The ones they do are guiding quests that lay out a path for them to help them become stronger," Erik said.

"I have a theory. The Ten Realms, as long as its core systems are unaffected, is just trying to nurse us all to make us as powerful as possible. In its eyes, any and all means to become powerful are fair."

"For what purpose?" Storbon asked.

"That part I'm still figuring out." Erik looped his fingers into his armholes.

"Plenty left to be learned. Maybe we'll get some more answers in the higher realms," Rugrat said. "When we get somewhere that's less risky, I have a date with a forge."

"You had a breakthrough?" Storbon asked.

"Maybe. Have to wait and see." Rugrat leaned back against his rock and rested his helmet against it, adjusting where his rifle was. George padded in from where he had been hunting with some of the panthers and Gilly; they were still wandering the area, eating their fill and acting as scouts.

George laid down next to Rugrat.

"Wake me up when we're ready to move," he said.

"I'll take first watch," Erik said.

Storbon nodded and laid down on the stone ground.

Erik checked his rifle and scanned the area from where he was sitting.

"Erik…" Storbon started, halting his words.

"What's up, champ?" Erik asked.

"How can you still be excited by the Ten Realms? Everything we've seen, people killing one another over resources, even the smallest treasure…"

Erik sat there in thought. "The Ten Realms isn't a paradise by any means. People can be monsters, much worse than the beasts we encounter. Death and loss are constant. We have stepped upon six different planets, six different realms. Among all that darkness, we can be consumed by it or we can acknowledge it, understand it, and fight against it. Look at Alva— people from all walks of life, from various realms, working and living together. The Ten Realms is filled with wonders, a place where things that were impossible in the last realm are commonplace in the next. Dungeons are treasures in the Fourth Realm. In the Sixth Realm, they are training grounds for academy students. They use them to gather resources and train their students. There is so much to see, so much to learn and explore. Never ignore the darkness, but aspire for the light," Erik said.

"You say that as we prepare for war," Storbon said.

"Seek peace, but do not be afraid to use war to defend it," Erik said. "Sometimes everything else fails, and we must fight. If the Willful Institute were in the Fifth and higher realms, we would only be able to compete in a bloodless battle. In the lower realms, war, not competitions, decides the fate of people and sects. There are too many interests in the higher realms that no one wants to deal with a war."

Storbon was quiet as he took it all in, coming to his own conclusions. "See you in the morning."

"Sounds good," Erik said.

Author's Note

T hank you for your support and taking the time to read **The Sixth Realm, Part One**.

The Ten Realms will continue in Part Two of the **Sixth Realm**

As a self-published author I live for reviews! If you've enjoyed The Sixth Realm, please leave a **review**! (https://readerlinks.com/l/1445052)

Do you want to join a community of fans that love talking about Michael's books?

We've created this Facebook group for you to discuss the books, hear from Michael, participate in contests and enjoy the worlds that Michael has created. You can join using the QR code below.

Thank you for your continued support. You can check out my other books, what I'm working on, and upcoming releases with the QR code below.

Don't forget to leave a review if you enjoyed the book.

Thanks again for reading ☺